THE COURTESAN'S AVENGER

THE COURTESAN'S AVENGER

DESERTERA BOOK TWO

KATE M. COLBY

BOXTHORN
PRESS

Published by Boxthorn Press

New Haven, CT

ISBN-10: 0-9967825-4-0

ISBN-13: 978-0-9967825-4-8

Library of Congress Control Number: 2016953154

Cover design by Damonza.com

Editing by Red Adept Editing

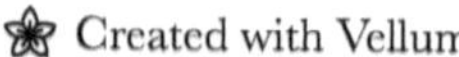 Created with Vellum

To Jess,

Thank you for being my alpha reader,
my best friend, and my sister in spirit.

1

Dellwyn Rutt listened, slack-jawed and wide-eyed, to the palace bishop as he issued King Lionel's latest decree. Ever since King Lionel's coronation the month before, His Majesty had made several amendments and redactions to Desertera's laws—laws that had not changed since the *Queen Hildegard* anchored and their ancestors settled around it—but none of them had been this drastic. Aya had told Dellwyn that King Lionel was nothing like his late father, King Archon. Dellwyn finally believed her.

The bishop, no doubt seeing the blank looks on the brothel workers' faces, squared his shoulders and repeated the newest change to Desertera. "By decree of His Royal Majesty, King Lionel Willem Monashe, adultery is no longer punishable by death, nor is it a crime in any respect. While King Lionel encourages the strict upholding of Desertera's morality, His Majesty recognizes that the criminalization of adultery can lead to more heinous acts. He believes the salvation rains will not come through a poorly enforced law, but by the actual fidelity, in body and spirit, of the royal family."

As the last word echoed against the Rudder's iron walls, Dellwyn scanned the room, observing the reactions of her fellow courtesans. Most of the women stood with their hands clasped and lips pressed together as Madam Huxley had instructed before the bishop's arrival. Kalinda and Jasmine huddled together and whispered to one another behind their curtains of black hair. Alisa leaned against the wall, arms crossed, and shook her head. Augustus, who stood next to Dellwyn, tapped his fingertips on the tops of his thighs and bounced like an excited child. On Dellwyn's other side, Sybil covered her mouth with her hand and looked up at Dellwyn with watery hazel eyes.

Dellwyn placed a hand on Sybil's shoulder. "Shh. Everything is going to be fine."

"What does this mean for us?" Sybil whispered, tucking a lock of copper hair behind her ear. Sybil had only worked at the Rudder for a few weeks. Madam Huxley had taken her on as a cleaning girl, and in a couple years, she would start Sybil with priming appointments, teaching her to be an appetizer before becoming the main course. The moment Sybil had walked into the Rudder, with her gangly legs and glassy, naïve eyes, all Dellwyn had seen was a young Aya.

Thinking of Aya made Dellwyn's chest hurt. Even though Aya was finally back in her true home, Dellwyn couldn't help but worry about her. The night Aya had come back to the hovel, she had rushed to her room, snatched up her mechanical frog Charlie, and cradled him in her arms as she explained all that had happened. Dellwyn had needed to sit down to process everything—King Archon's demise, Aya's reclaiming of her father's cogsmith shop, the fact that Dellwyn's favorite client, Lord Collingwood, was uncle to the new king, and that the new king was Aya's lover.

Once Aya had taken a moment to breathe, Dellwyn had hugged her and told her how happy she was for her. And she had meant it. Aya had despised working at the Rudder—and only two days after King Archon's trial, she had moved back into her father's shop. Despite Aya's insistence that Dellwyn come with her, Dellwyn had chosen to stay behind in Sternville. Aya Cogsmith, with her doll-like figure and old-world craft, belonged in Portside, if not Starboardshire. Dellwyn had been born into this life, branded for rutting from the moment she took her first breath, and luckily, it suited her fine.

"Dellwyn?" Sybil tugged at her sleeve.

"I don't know yet." Dellwyn squeezed Sybil's shoulder. "But Madam Huxley will tell us once she does."

As if hearing Dellwyn's words, Madam Huxley cleared her throat. Dellwyn did not have to see the madam to know that she stood behind her workers at her tall, wooden podium, her totem of power, as Augustus called it. "Bishop, does this mean that King Lionel shall forgive the trespasses of those who committed adultery before its legalization?"

"King Lionel forgives all past indiscretions, Madam." The bishop held out both hands in a gesture Dellwyn assumed signaled his goodwill. It looked more as if he intended to receive a loaf of bread.

The first time the bishop had come to the Rudder, a chorus of giggles had spread through the courtesans. How could a man so tiny be so powerful? While his bejeweled rings and crisp white robes had only incited more whispers, his booming voice had quieted all teasing. Dellwyn had literally jumped at its force. After all five of his visits to the Rudder, it still surprised her to hear such a sound come out of the little man.

"I'm relieved to hear that," Madam Huxley replied. Dellwyn heard the madam's long fingernails tapping against the wood. "And what about this establishment? There is no use in pretending that King Lionel does not know what goes on here. Does the king intend to allow my business to run as usual?"

"Is that even a question?" Sybil whispered. "Every other king let this place run unchecked, even when adultery was a crime."

Augustus leaned over in front of Dellwyn, his pale skin cast yellow by the lantern light—the moon to Dellwyn's night sky. "You bet they did. If they hadn't, the people would have found more sinister ways to satisfy their needs."

Dellwyn scoffed. "You make it sound like we're the unsung saviors of Desertera."

"You're damn right we are." Augustus winked. "Though I have made quite a few men sing in my day."

Sybil stifled a laugh. Dellwyn rolled her eyes and swatted Augustus's arm. He grabbed his bicep in mock pain, and Dellwyn replied by baring her teeth playfully. If anyone could lighten the mood on the day one of the three capital crimes was legalized, it was Augustus.

"The better question is, why is King Lionel really legalizing adultery?" Augustus asked.

Sybil shrugged. "Maybe he knows the rains are never coming, and he's sick of seeing his people executed over a lie."

Dellwyn shook her head. "He's trying to prove that he's not like his father. He wants to atone for King Archon's sins."

Augustus ran his fingers through his blond hair. "Who cares?"

"He does," Dellwyn said. *And so does Aya.*

The bishop glared at the three friends before craning his neck to meet Madam Huxley's eyes. Dellwyn wondered if they should have found him a box to stand on. "As you have never had a patron, Madam, King Lionel considers you a private business owner. You are to run your establishment as you see fit, so long as it does not violate any of Desertera's other laws."

Madam Huxley inclined her head. "I understand. That should no longer be an issue."

Wrinkling his nose, the bishop returned her nod. Every time he had come to the Rudder, the bishop had shown distaste. After his first visit, Dellwyn had asked Aya what she knew about him. Aya had told Dellwyn that the bishop presided over all the official palace proceedings, that he was the keeper of the ceremonies and holy salt water. That statement had sent Dellwyn's drink through her nose. She knew the farmers over in Bowtown still clung to the faith—but the nobles? In that, she found the definition of hypocrisy.

"Do you have any other questions, Madam?" The bishop glanced toward the courtesans' hallway. At the end stood the exit door, which led into the main areas of the palace. Dellwyn wondered if he were merely disgusted by the brothel or anxious to spread the news to the rest of the kingdom.

"Not at the moment." Dellwyn heard Madam Huxley's smile in the lilting of her voice. "I'll send word if I think of anything."

The bishop bowed and scurried toward the exit. Once he had disappeared down the corridor, Madam Huxley clapped once, and the courtesans turned to face her. Dellwyn noticed the madam's skin was flushed—something that only happened when she was filled with rage or joy.

"This is splendid news, isn't it, everyone?" Madam Huxley beamed, not waiting for anyone to answer. "Once the people start to trust King Lionel's word, I expect our clientele will begin to grow rather nicely."

Alisa guffawed. "That's an understatement. We're going to be flooded."

Madam Huxley's grin fell into a smirk. "I hope you're right, Alisa, dear. I think more business would do wonders for all of our purses."

"Especially hers," Augustus muttered. Dellwyn elbowed him.

Madam Huxley continued. "Given this expectation, I think it's best for us to begin preparing now. Therefore, starting tonight, all priming girls will take turns receiving training from our veterans." A few of the younger women squeaked, and Madam Huxley quieted them with a wave of her hand. "Alisa, Augustus, as our top courtesans, may I count on you for this?"

Dellwyn breathed a sigh of relief, happy that she remained in Room G, sixth in ranking, for the time being. On the few occasions she'd been called to assist with training, she had hated it. With the right clients, her job could be fun, but having the younger women watch from the corner, or try to get involved, had made her skin crawl. As nerve-wracking as it could be, Dellwyn thought the budding courtesans should just be given a few hours alone with a gentle client—let intuition do the work and save everyone the embarrassment.

"Does this mean I'll have to help with priming?" Sybil's

voice wavered, and Dellwyn did not have the heart to meet her gaze. The thought of her, a girl of just fourteen, having to touch an adult in that way…

Dellwyn shook her head. "Not yet. Madam Huxley knows you're too young. Besides, the clients are only interested in grown women." She inclined her head toward Augustus. "Or him."

"I heard that." Augustus smirked, his green eyes sparkling. "And trust me, they're *all* interested in me."

Sybil's brow smoothed, and she giggled. Dellwyn allowed herself to smile.

"It appears it's nearly time to open." Madam Huxley gestured behind the group of courtesans to the pink light seeping through between the palace's propellers. Dellwyn shivered, imagining what this part of the ship must have been like when it sailed—dark, cold, engulfed in the churning of the blades and water. Only a few inches of steel and iron separating the inhabitants from endless nothing.

Madam Huxley wiped a bead of sweat from her brow. "Before I send you all to your rooms, does anyone have any questions?"

Kalinda stepped forward, her long black locks swaying across the top of her hips. "What do we say to our clients? Do we tell them about the new law?"

Dellwyn rolled her eyes. Leave it to Kalinda to worry about talking to customers. That was the last thing they wanted from her full, red lips.

"I daresay the rest of the kingdom already knows, or will before night's end." Madam Huxley wrapped her hands around the side of her podium. "However, in case we are the first to hear of it, let's not broach the subject with our clients unless they open the discussion."

A murmur of approval rippled through the group. Alisa pushed herself off the wall and walked toward the madam. "And what about our wages?" Alisa squinted, her blue eyes sizing up Madam Huxley. "If business improves, shouldn't our pay?"

The madam pursed her lips. "As always, your wages shall depend on your room assignment, seniority, and the quality of your work."

Alisa snorted. "So nothing will change, then."

Madam Huxley's knuckles turned white as she gripped the edges of her podium tighter. Before she could retort, Augustus raised his hand. "Madam, what I believe Alisa is trying to ask is, if our workload increases, will our pay rise alongside our labor?"

As Madam Huxley's grip relaxed, Dellwyn bit her lip to hide her grin. Augustus had a way with most people, hence his popularity with clients, but he had an incredible knack for defusing Madam Huxley. Over her years at the Rudder, Dellwyn had used Augustus to calm or distract the madam many times. Dellwyn even thought some of his charm might have worn off on her.

"If each courtesan's number of clients and nightly visits increase drastically, then I suppose I will have no choice but to increase pay." Madam Huxley stared out over the group, her dark-green eyes flitting from one anxious face to another. "In fact, if demand for our services rises, I suspect prices may as well." She smirked. "You all better make it worth their while."

A few of the women chuckled nervously. Dellwyn put her hands on her hips. She admired Madam Huxley's business sense; the madam was always a step ahead of her clients. With adultery's legalization, the business would be changing in unthinkable ways, at least to Dellwyn, but she knew Madam Huxley would foresee and adapt as necessary.

Dellwyn tilted her head to the side, watching the madam as a hawk would watch a snake. She noticed the lines around the madam's eyes and the sagging skin in her cheeks and jowls. Madam Huxley was not getting any younger—surely she would be searching for a successor soon, someone to pass the Rudder to when she became too old to stand sentry behind her podium. Maybe, if Dellwyn worked hard enough and put on more Augustus-style charm, she could climb her way to Room A and win the madam's full trust.

Alisa had been crabby lately, and Augustus was a man. Though in high demand, he did not understand the madam and her position as a woman could. Besides, Dellwyn had been there almost as long as Alisa and Augustus, and the other courtesans respected her, sought her counsel. She would be the perfect heir. She just had to make Madam Huxley see it.

"Are there any other questions?" The impatient tapping of Madam Huxley's toe sent pulses through the room. Before anyone else could respond, she gave the group a dismissive wave. "Off to your rooms, then. Alisa, please be sure to take one of the priming girls with you."

Alisa's jaw clenched, and Dellwyn smirked. It served her right for giving the madam lip. This was not the time, nor place, to be worried about pay raises, not until they saw how the new law truly affected the business.

"Have a nice evening, ladies," Augustus crooned, swiping a blond curl off of his forehead. "I know I will."

Dellwyn wiggled her fingers in a playful farewell before turning to Sybil. "When you finish your chores this evening, will you do me a favor?"

Sybil's hazel eyes darted between Dellwyn's brown ones. "What is it?"

"Gather your things from the storage room and take them to my hovel." Dellwyn placed her hand on Sybil's cheek. "I want you to come live with me."

Sybil beamed. "Really?"

Dellwyn's hand fell to Sybil's shoulder, and she squeezed reassuringly. "Really."

Sybil's eyebrows knitted together. "You don't think Madam Huxley will mind?"

"I think she would be happy with one less mouth to feed." Dellwyn smiled to soften the truth. Nodding, Sybil glanced at the madam out of the corner of her eye. Dellwyn followed her gaze, watching as Madam Huxley spoke to one of the priming girls. A lump swelled in Dellwyn's chest. She couldn't protect Sybil from what went on behind the Rudder's doors forever, but Dellwyn could give Sybil somewhere to lay her head at night that belonged to only her, with no scent or memory of clients lingering on the pillows.

"Now then, I need to prepare for Lord Collingwood. I'll see you at home before sunrise."

Sybil's grin returned. "See you at home."

With her chest lightened, Dellwyn headed toward Room G. After the bishop's announcement, she was even more pleased that Lord Collingwood had booked her for the entire night. She didn't have the energy to fake enjoyment with one of her other clients or puzzle over the desires of a new one. Besides, if she acted like the distressed damsel, Lord Collingwood might divulge King Lionel's reasoning for legalizing adultery, or more of his future plans.

As Dellwyn reached the hallway, Madam Huxley called out to her. "Come here for a moment, would you?"

Dellwyn walked to the madam's podium, holding her breath for fear that Madam Huxley would ask her to take on a girl to train at the last moment. "What is it, Madam?"

"Lord Collingwood's valet came by with a message this afternoon." The madam's eyes scrutinized Dellwyn's features. "It seems Lord Collingwood is unable to make his appointment tonight."

Dellwyn kept her face neutral, but inside, her stomach sank. Hopefully, he was just wrapped up in business with the king. As much as she'd been looking forward to a comfortable evening, she could forgive Lord Collingwood's absence if it meant more information for her to source from him the next time. "Do you want me to handle walk-ins, then?"

"No, no." The madam waved her hand. "There are plenty of other girls to serve anyone without an appointment. I sent word to Lord Derringher, and he's delighted to see you this evening."

"Lovely." Dellwyn bit the inside of her cheek to avoid groaning—of all the nights to have to deal with Lord Derringher's sausage fingers. "If that's all, I'm going to get ready."

Madam Huxley nodded. "That's all."

Dellwyn turned on her heel and huffed. She didn't realize she was practically stomping away until she heard the madam chuckle.

"Now, now, Dellwyn." Madam Huxley *tsked*. "Play nice with Lord Derringher. I have a feeling you'll be seeing a lot of him over the coming weeks."

The madam's words cut through Dellwyn's annoyance, and she smirked, finally seeing the opportunity before her. She would play nice, all right—so nice that Lord Derringher would be spent and out of her hair within fifteen minutes.

Maybe the evening wouldn't be so tiresome after all.

2

———————

When Lord Derringher closed the door to Room G behind him, Dellwyn heard the doorknob rattle in his shaking hand. Sweat beaded across his brow and upper lip, which he licked as his eyes landed on Dellwyn's curves.

She smiled. Even after several years of coming to visit her, Lord Derringher still acted like a boy first experiencing a woman, as though his mother would walk in and catch them at any moment. His shyness was charming. Too bad his love-making techniques were equally underdeveloped.

"Good evening, my lord." Dellwyn curtsied, pulling back her skirt at the slit to reveal her bare thigh.

Lord Derringher swallowed and stepped toward her. "Have you heard the news?"

Dellwyn straightened and frowned. So the whole kingdom did know, then. "Yes. The bishop came to tell us right before we opened."

Lord Derringher wiped his hands across the front of his white dress shirt, leaving dark spots where his sweat met the fabric. He stood before her as impenetrable as a wall—not only in frame, which was blocky and tall, but also in face. She couldn't tell what he was thinking, and it made her nervous. She didn't want him to be thinking at all.

"Are you all right, my lord?" Dellwyn closed the distance

between them, slid her hands to his shoulders, between his smoking jacket and shirt, and shrugged it down his arms.

"Yes." Lord Derringher allowed her to remove his jacket and toss it across the room onto the velvet fainting couch opposite the bed. He glanced between the bed and Dellwyn before grinning. "Yes."

Dellwyn saw relief flicker in his blue eyes. Hoping to prevent further conversation, she reached up and untied his gold cravat. Before she could fling it on top of his jacket, Lord Derringher grabbed her hands and brought them to his lips. "I don't have to hide anymore." His breath was hot on her fingertips. "My family won't be pleased, and my wife will give me quite a row, but that's all they can do. They can't hurt me for doing what I want."

Dellwyn pulled her hands away and cupped his face, his stubble pricking her fingertips. "You're right. And you won't be the only nobleman, that's for sure."

Lord Derringher rested his forehead against hers. "Don't talk about anyone else." He lowered his hands to her sides, and the ends of his fingers fiddled with her corset's strings. "You're mine, Dellwyn. You alone understand me, all of me."

Dellwyn wanted to say that she knew, that she had over a decade of studying lonely, unloved, and power-hungry people, that she could tell him things about himself he couldn't even fathom. But she knew better than to spoil the illusion. She feigned a blush, pulled Lord Derringher's face to hers, and kissed him.

He responded instantly, one hand entwining in her dark hair, pulling it a little too hard, and the other fumbling with the buckles on the front of her corset. Dellwyn let him struggle for a minute, but when his breathing began to quicken, she pulled away. Sure enough, his face burned crimson with embarrassment and frustration.

Smiling, Dellwyn gently pushed him back toward the bed. Lord Derringher sank into the plush, jewel-toned comforter. It had been a gift from Lord Collingwood—and a pointed response to the silk sheets Lord Derringher had given her.

As Dellwyn ran her fingers over Lord Derringher's smooth head to soothe him, she noticed his gaze wander to the gold-framed mirror that stood next to her armoire. His hungry eyes drank in Dellwyn's round behind before falling to the ornately patterned violet-and-indigo rug under her feet. The rug was another gift from Lord Collingwood, in retaliation for the scenic wildflower tapestry from Lord Derringher that hung over the bed.

Sliding her fingers down to the nape of Lord Derringher's neck, Dellwyn rubbed the knot at the top of his spine. She knew she needed to bring him back to her. If he became too jealous or anxious, he would add a little roughness to his clumsiness, and with the possibility of an increased workload looming, she didn't need sore wrists or love bites marring her skin.

"You've had such a trying day," Dellwyn cooed. "Why don't you let me serve you?"

Lord Derringher frowned, and the wrinkles on his nose hinted at his internal conflict. To be served like a king, or to control like one? It had always been his hang-up. He wanted power, or at least, to feel powerful, and he never knew how to express it. Luckily for his desire, and for her impatience, Dellwyn usually managed to make the decision for him.

She stepped back from the bed and slowly unfastened the first buckle of her corset. "Why so cross, Your Majesty?"

Lord Derringher's face smoothed, and Dellwyn could see his excitement stirring. Playing king was his favorite game—a good standby to bring out whenever he acted particularly difficult.

"It's my duty to serve my king, is it not?" The top three buckles now undone, Dellwyn tugged her corset down just enough to allow her ample bosom to spill over the top. "Don't you want me to serve you?"

Lord Derringher licked his lips again, holding out his meaty hands like an infant begging for its mother's milk. Dellwyn made him wait a moment longer as she undid the last two buckles and let the corset fall to the floor. When she finally allowed him to touch her, Lord Derringher's fingers trembled as he clenched her sides, and his hot breath came out shaky as he nestled his face in her breast. He may have been the one craving the power, but his reaction told Dellwyn that she held every speck of it.

"Now then, Your Majesty." Dellwyn lowered herself onto her knees in front of him. "Why don't you tell me precisely what you want?"

⌇

It took longer than fifteen minutes, but Dellwyn had Lord Derringher satisfied and out of Room G within the hour. As he shut the door behind himself, Dellwyn stretched on the bed, feeling her muscles groan in protest. He had been hesitant at first, but once his instinct had taken over, he had gripped her tighter than usual, and she could still feel his fingers digging into her ribs. It seemed the new law had made him bolder now that he didn't have to fear execution, and Dellwyn wondered whether this had been but a glimpse into the new Lord Derringher. She hoped he wouldn't become much more forceful—at least, not without learning to better control his movements. She didn't know whether her body could take it.

After a little rest, Dellwyn slipped into a clean dress and went to find Madam Huxley to ask whether there were any other clients on her schedule for the evening. If not, maybe she could sneak home before Sybil arrived and fix up Aya's old room or scrape together a welcome meal. Dellwyn grinned, imagining how Sybil would squeal with delight when she realized she had her own room, one without cleaning supplies and soiled sheets piled inside.

When Dellwyn reached the lobby, she stopped short. The room was empty—entirely. Even Madam Huxley was not perched behind her podium. Normally, a few clients lingered about with hats or hoods pulled down to cover their eyes as they waited to be served. But tonight, as Dellwyn left the courtesans' hallway and headed to the other corridor that ran parallel to it—the one with empty, unneeded rooms and the madam's private chambers—her soft footsteps echoed throughout the lobby.

Had something happened, some kind of accident that had closed down the Rudder for the evening? Was the new law a lie? King Lionel didn't seem the kind to play tricks, but maybe he had issued some test to the people, and the courtesans at the Rudder had been left out of it on purpose. Or, most nerve-wracking possibility of all, maybe there were no clients tonight.

As Dellwyn rounded the corner into the other corridor, she saw a strip of light shining beneath Madam Huxley's door, and she sighed with relief. At least the madam was still there. That meant no accident. Before Dellwyn could raise her hand to knock, the door opened in front of her, and Alisa came barreling out, her bony shoulder knocking into Dellwyn's as she hurried past without an apology.

Dellwyn rubbed her shoulder and peered into the office. Madam Huxley sat behind her desk, hands folded on top, as if she had been expecting Dellwyn. Dellwyn raised her eyebrows. "Was Alisa crying?"

Madam Huxley pursed her lips. "I believe so."

Dellwyn shook her head. "I don't think I've ever seen her cry." Before she could stop herself, she added, "I didn't think she had it in her."

Madam Huxley smirked. "Tears?"

"No." Dellwyn snickered. "An emotion other than anger."

"Trust me when I say, those *were* tears of anger." Madam Huxley unfolded her hands and patted her red hair. "Now, I assume you had a reason for coming to my office?"

"Oh, yes." Dellwyn leaned against the doorframe. "Do I have any more clients this evening? I'm through with Lord Derringher."

Madam Huxley inclined her head. "Are you through with him, or is he through with you?"

"Both." Dellwyn widened her eyes and inhaled sharply. "He exhausts me, and not in the way I exhaust him."

"I see." Madam Huxley leaned back in her chair. "You do not have any other scheduled clients. Lord Collingwood had booked your entire evening, and Lord Derringher was the only other of your regulars who could come on short notice."

Dellwyn nodded. She thought about turning to leave. If she hurried, she could still make it home before Sybil. But as she studied the madam's office, she realized the madam had nothing to do. The coins were stacked in neat, counted rows along the edge of her desk, and the guest book sat closed on a table, with the ring of keys to the courtesans' rooms resting on top. If Dellwyn wanted a time to talk to Madam Huxley in private, this was it.

She pointed to the single chair in front of the madam's desk. "May I?"

Madam Huxley motioned for Dellwyn to sit, and she did. She waited for the madam to speak, but the older woman only stared at Dellwyn expectantly.

"Busy night, isn't it?" Dellwyn offered.

Madam Huxley snorted. "Is there a statement of significance hiding behind that idiotic question?"

Dellwyn bit her lip. "I just mean, is something wrong? Or do you think it's about the new law?"

"It will take time." Madam Huxley shifted to cross her ankles. "There will be distrust at first. But once the people realize that King Lionel is a man of his word, they'll return. We might lose some, perhaps those who only came here for the thrill of getting caught, or those seeking to satisfy whims they couldn't with the ones they desire in their social circles. However, I daresay we'll see more new clients than we'll lose."

Dellwyn considered the madam's words. It hadn't occurred to her that they might lose clients. Like Augustus, she had assumed the worst in people, that they would be swarming the propellers in a sandstorm of lust.

"Do you trust King Lionel's word?" Dellwyn whispered the question, as if Aya might be nearby to overhear and become upset.

Madam Huxley cocked her head to one side. "I do. Don't you?"

Dellwyn licked her lips. "I want to. I mean, after everything he's done for Aya..." She let the sentence trail off. Dellwyn didn't need to explain anything about Aya to Madam Huxley. The madam knew the details of Aya's involvement in over-throwing King Archon and her subsequent romance with the then Prince Lionel, probably better than Dellwyn did. "I guess part of me fears that he will end up like his father, or that all his changes are coming too quickly, that something will go wrong."

Madam Huxley crossed her arms. "Are you concerned for yourself or for Aya?"

"Both." Feeling her opportunity to turn the conversation, Dellwyn looked the madam straight in the eyes. "And for the Rudder."

Something akin to recognition glinted across Madam Huxley's face, and the wrinkles on her forehead smoothed out. "Don't worry about your wages, Dellwyn. The Rudder has been doing steady business for decades, as it did under Madam Bovan before me."

Dellwyn scooted to the edge of the chair. "And what about after you?"

"Well, I intend to be around for a long while, and I suppose what comes after isn't much your concern. Besides, if the Rudder does fail, I'm sure you could find a generous cogsmith to shopkeep for."

Dellwyn's cheeks burned. "And what if I don't want to move on from here? What if I want the Rudder's future to be my concern?"

Madam Huxley smiled. Dellwyn imagined the look was similar to how King Archon used to grin when he trapped witnesses into damning themselves during his trials. "I didn't realize you felt that way. I thought you would go in one of the typical ways."

Dellwyn shook her head, her straight, ebony locks whipping her neck as she did so. She wasn't about to lie around, waiting for a potential husband to come along and rescue her. And she certainly wasn't going to stay in bed until old age, sliding back down to Room Z, passing more and more nights alone until the new madam deemed her unprofitable and kicked her out to starve.

"I don't think I'm made for either of those options, Madam."

Madam Huxley shrugged. "Very well, then. What do you have in mind?"

Dellwyn swallowed. She wasn't quite sure how to phrase what she wanted to say, and subtlety had never been her strong suit. *Screw it.* "You're getting older, Madam. I'm sorry, but it's true. You don't have any children or family, and I doubt you want the Rudder to go up for auction to the highest-bidding nobleman when you die."

Madam Huxley scrunched her nose. "Go on."

"And me, I'm not getting any younger, either. I'm closer to thirty than twenty. In a decade, if I'm lucky, my clients are going to start trading me in for younger women. It's inevitable, and I'd like not to get thrown out on the street when it happens."

Madam Huxley tapped her fingers on her desk. The clacking of her nails made Dellwyn's heart race. She hoped she hadn't been too blunt. "As much as it pains me to admit it, you make a fair point—for both our futures."

Dellwyn let out a long breath. "I'm not asking to be handed anything. I'm just asking you to think about it."

"I shall." Madam Huxley glanced over Dellwyn's shoulder. "In fact, I can think of a couple of your coworkers who may appreciate the same consideration."

Dellwyn clenched her skirts in her fist, silently cursing the madam's manipulative nature. Of course she had to turn this into a contest. Why couldn't Madam Huxley just keep quiet and let Dellwyn think she had no competition, even if it weren't true?

Madam Huxley patted her dress, as if they had been discussing the ever-unchanging weather. "Is that all?"

Dellwyn closed her eyes, rolling them behind the safety of her lids, and let out another breath. "That's all." She stood to leave.

"Are you heading home for the evening?" Madam Huxley smirked. "Or would you like to stay so you don't lose any wages?"

Dellwyn's stomach churned. "Um, I can stay." The wicked gleam in the madam's eyes never meant anything good, and Dellwyn knew that after the conversation they'd just had, she was being tested. "What can I help you with?"

"Apparently, Alisa did not feel able to handle her training duties tonight." At the madam's words, Dellwyn's stomach went from churning to completely overturned. "I hope that I was able to convince her of the importance of the task, but as you saw, she left in such a fuss."

"And what would you like me to do?" Dellwyn couldn't keep the defensive edge out of her voice, not that she'd tried particularly hard.

"Could you go check on Room A? If Alisa is there, as I hope she is, you can go." The madam had equipped her high, feminine lilt, the one she loved to use to lord her authority over others. "If not, could you see how Elsie and Captain Ferris are getting along?"

Dellwyn moved to put her hands on her hips, but thought better of it and deflected by feigning to straighten her corset. "And if they aren't getting along?"

Madam Huxley grinned. "Why, then help the poor girl. She shouldn't be abandoned by all her mentors."

Another tug on the corset. "And if they're getting along well just the two of them?"

Madam Huxley tucked a stray curl back into her bun. "You know what they say, Dellwyn. The more the merrier."

Dellwyn paused long enough to force a thin smile to her lips and present the madam with a terse nod. Then, for the second time that evening, she turned on her heel and marched away from Madam Huxley. In all her years at the Rudder, Dellwyn had never once longed to see Alisa's cross face, but at that moment, she wished with every step she took toward Room A that Alisa would be there.

3

————

The sound from Room A followed Dellwyn out of the Rudder the next morning, and even as she seated herself at the hovel's common room table, she still couldn't shake it from her memory. *Eee! Hee! Eekee!*

When Dellwyn had cracked open the door to Room A and saw that Alisa hadn't returned, she invited herself in and joined Elsie and Captain Ferris, as Madam Huxley had directed. When the time came for Elsie to pretend to reach her peak, she squeaked the noise, sounding every bit like a rusty door hinge. Captain Ferris was too caught up in his own enjoyment to notice the sound, but Dellwyn heard it in painful detail as she faked her own shakes and moans. As if the entire "training" situation itself wasn't humiliating enough, Dellwyn knew that sound would haunt her for days.

After Captain Ferris had left, Elsie asked Dellwyn if she had done a good job. Dellwyn replied that she had done fine, making a mental note to tell Madam Huxley the exact opposite. As much as Dellwyn didn't want the poor girl tossed out onto the street, she didn't want to hear Elsie's squeals ever again—even as dull shrieks through the Rudder's thick, metal walls.

Pink light filtered through the common room window, and Dellwyn heard rustling coming from Aya's—Sybil's—room. A few moments later, Sybil emerged. Her copper hair was wild and dimples dented her freckled cheeks. She pointed behind her. "Is this whole room mine?"

Dellwyn chuckled, a yawn slipping out at the end. "You bet."

"Oh, thank you." Sybil clapped her hands. "I've been so excited, I couldn't sleep. I just keep tossing in my blankets and stretching out as far as I can reach." She demonstrated, her legs and arms spreading out until her body formed an X.

Dellwyn grinned, remembering the too-short bed that she once had slept in as the Rudder's maid. "Much better than that little closet, huh?"

Sybil pulled her door shut behind her, and the hinges whined. "Infinitely."

Dellwyn shuddered. "What time did you get in?"

Sybil glanced at the window. "A few hours ago." She shuffled over to the trunk where they kept the kitchen utensils and a few other useful items. "I did some exploring. I hope you don't mind."

"Of course not. It's your home, too." Dellwyn winced as the hinges on the trunk creaked. Elsie's puckered lips flashed before her eyes, and Dellwyn pressed her fingers against her temples.

"Are you okay?" Sybil retrieved two tin cups and closed the trunk's lid.

Dellwyn had another flash, this time of Captain Ferris's round belly bouncing in front of her. For a guard, he certainly hadn't looked fit for fighting. She swallowed, doing her best to ignore the bitter taste in her mouth. "Just tired. Alisa went home early, so I had to stay late to cover for her."

Sybil uncorked the glass water jug and filled the tin cups. Some of the water splashed onto the hard-packed dirt floor, creating a thin layer of mud that Dellwyn knew would dry within minutes. Dellwyn opened her mouth to offer Sybil help with the jug, but upon seeing Sybil's forehead scrunched in determination, she closed it. A few drops of water were a small price to pay for Sybil's self-respect.

"That doesn't seem fair." Sybil inserted the cork into the jug and picked up the cups. She slid one over to Dellwyn, and the tin bottom scraped across the tabletop, making Dellwyn's eye twitch.

"It wasn't." Dellwyn drained her cup in three long gulps. As she set it down on the table, she noticed a blond hair from Elsie lingering on her cloak. She grimaced and brushed it off.

Sybil's brow furrowed. "Did Lord Collingwood show up?"

"No. I served Lord Derringher instead." Dellwyn closed her eyes, searching for a pleasant image to meditate on—what her next encounter with Lord Collingwood would entail, or even her slightly rough encounter with Lord Derringher—but her mind only found the beads of sweat rolling down the captain's back and Elsie's thighs. "Then, a guard that was meant to see Alisa."

"That sounds so intimidating." Sybil giggled and spun her tin cup by its base. "Lords and soldiers. So powerful."

"They're just people." Dellwyn rubbed her temples again. "Remember that. No matter what titles they hold, when they disrobe, they're the same as you and me."

Sybil shrugged. "I wouldn't know how to talk to people so important, let alone…" She shifted her weight in her chair, and the wooden rods of the back creaked.

Dellwyn turned her head away, and a lock of hair fell across her face. As she breathed, she smelled the sour mixture of exerted flesh and Elsie's cheap perfume. It was the last straw. She bolted upright and pulled her cloak tighter around her. "Well, you're going to have to figure it out."

Sybil stood. "Why? What's going on?"

"I can't stand myself right now. Get your cloak on. We're going visiting."

"To see who?" Sybil called, already rushing to fetch her cloak.

"The future queen."

"ARE you really going to be queen?" Sybil's voice faltered on the last word, and her wide eyes shone with a mixture of fear and wonder. Dellwyn stifled a chuckle and glanced around the cogsmith shop in a futile attempt at appearing innocent.

Aya's green eyes narrowed into slits, but a telltale flush spread across her neck. "Did Dellwyn tell you that?"

Dellwyn raised an eyebrow and gestured to the cluttered room. "Don't act like I lied. Look at this place! King Lionel is practically begging for your hand." Not only had King Lionel given Aya her father's shop and tools back, but he had sent over every dormant machine and cogsmithing book he could find in the palace's rooms and libraries. The modest workshop overflowed with mechanical gadgets, and as Aya gazed at the splendor around her, Dellwyn saw nothing but love reflected in her eyes.

"She's exaggerating, Sybil." Aya crossed her arms. "The king is merely sending me as many relics of my craft as he can because having a working cogsmith is in the best interest of all Desertera's people, himself included."

Sybil nodded, a frown crossing her face.

Dellwyn leaned over and whispered conspiratorially to Sybil. "If I exaggerate, Aya is too modest. Some men send pastries or wildflowers; the king sends cogs. He knows it's the fastest way to Aya's heart."

"Is this what you do?" Aya huffed, a smile playing on her lips. "You come here and bathe in my basin then harass me about my nonexistent love life when I should be working?"

Dellwyn smirked and ran her fingers through her wet hair. When she and Sybil had shown up at Aya's door at sunrise, Dellwyn hadn't even needed to ask. Aya had noticed the way Dellwyn scratched at her skin and had pulled her inside, saying, "Keep as much water in the basin as possible. It can be dirty, but I need it for the machines."

"I'm sorry." Dellwyn touched Aya's hand to show she meant it. "Perhaps I got ahead of myself. I just want you to be happy, and the king seems to make you happy."

Aya gathered her brown curls in her hand and draped them over one shoulder. "You can call him Lionel, you know."

Dellwyn laughed. "No, *you* can call him Lionel. And whatever else you like, I'm sure."

Sybil giggled. She turned away from the two older women and scanned the shelves in the workshop. As she began to squirm in her seat, Aya laughed. "Go have a look around. Everything on the shelves is functioning or fragile, but you can tinker with anything on the floor."

Sybil was already leaning out of her chair. "Are you sure?"

"Absolutely." Aya waved her hand. "Let me know if you figure out how to fix anything. I'm at my wit's end with some of them."

Sybil nodded and wandered into the back room. When she was out of earshot, Dellwyn leaned forward. "So how is business?"

Aya shrugged. "It's good. I had forgotten what it's like in the merchant world, though. They're just as gossipy and manipulative as everyone else." She lifted her chin. "But no matter what stories they fabricate, I'm the only one who can fix their broken machines. That's satisfying in its own right."

"I'd imagine so." Dellwyn grabbed a loose gear from the table and spun it between her fingers. "What about your personal projects? Any luck with repairing Charlie?"

Aya's face fell. "Not yet. Will—Lionel has sent me a few molds, but none of them are for a vortric cog, and without one, Charlie won't work again." She picked at a loose thread on her sleeve. "I finally figured out how to melt the metals in the forge, but I'm not precise enough to make anything from scratch yet."

Dellwyn raised an eyebrow. "Still Willem?" When Aya shrugged, her green eyes downcast, Dellwyn continued. "Can't you ask to borrow King Lionel's bird? You can make a mold from the vortric cog."

Aya shook her head. "Lionel doesn't know what he has. He knows I fixed Penelope, but I didn't tell him that I used the vortric cog. He thinks I figured out how to fix her on my own."

Dellwyn inclined her head. "Which you did."

"Yes." Aya sighed. "But Lionel doesn't know I used the cog, and he believed my father when he claimed they were all gone. Penelope's wings hide her core. Lionel couldn't see the cog without taking her apart." Her brow furrowed. "And even if he did, I'm not certain he would remember its significance. He remembers that day differently than I do. He was focused on his fear of King Archon. That day was a repeat of Queen Lisandra's death to him, not the day the last cogsmith died to protect a cog."

Dellwyn pursed her lips, unsure how to phrase what she needed to say. "Are you positive it was all about the vortric cog? I mean, it could have been—"

"It was." Aya's entire body stiffened. "King Archon had the butler search my father's toolbox for it. He had his guards scour this workshop. I don't know why the blasted thing is so important, but it is."

"Are the books helping at all?"

Aya rubbed her forehead. "Not with that. I've learned a million other useful aspects of the craft, but there's no mention of the vortric cog anywhere."

Dellwyn frowned. "Did your father leave anything behind? Notes or something?"

"Not that I can remember." Aya's eyes flitted across the room. "I know he kept account records, and I think he used to scribble notes in his ledger from time to time, but he didn't like to waste the paper. Most of the craft was in his head, but we can't find the ledger anyway. We think King Archon must have burned it."

Dellwyn forced her face into an encouraging smile. "If anyone can figure this out, it's you. You're the most brilliant cogsmith I've ever known."

Aya grinned and shook her head. Despite looking at Dellwyn, her eyes appeared distant, as if she were remembering some private joke. "Dellwyn, I'm the only cogsmith you've ever known."

Dellwyn winked, gathering her damp hair over her shoulder. "Still the best."

"Enough of my problems." Aya straightened. "Now that you're clean, I have to ask. What happened last night?"

Dellwyn frowned. "I had to help train one of the priming girls."

Aya's lip curled into something between a grimace and a snarl. "I thought you were still in Room G? Doesn't Madam Huxley usually make her top two courtesans do the training?"

"Normally." Dellwyn scoffed. "Alisa decided she didn't want to help and stormed out. Madam Huxley asked me to fill in."

"That was… generous of you." Aya squinted, and Dellwyn imagined the gears spinning in the cogsmith's head. She considered telling Aya why she had volunteered, but a knot in her gut held her back. While Aya would understand why Dellwyn wanted to get out of the courtesans' corridor, she wouldn't understand why Dellwyn wanted to stay at the Rudder permanently. Dellwyn didn't have the energy to explain herself.

"If things continue like last night, I'll need all the extra wages I can get." Dellwyn let out a long whoosh. "The lobby was entirely empty."

Aya's eyes bulged. "Really?"

Dellwyn nodded, placing the gear back on the table. "I don't think it will last. Give everyone a few nights to realize that your king's law isn't a trick, and they'll be out in greater numbers than ever."

Aya narrowed her eyes, and Dellwyn grinned, expecting a jab about Lionel and a playful change of subject. Instead, Aya shook her head. "Unfortunately, I'm sure you're right. I don't know how you stand it."

Dellwyn bit her tongue. Aya had never hidden her incredulity at Dellwyn's enjoyment of the work, and her disgusted tone grated on Dellwyn's nerves every time it appeared. "It is what it is. I'll get through it, same as always."

Aya smiled softly. "I know you will. I've always admired that about you."

Dellwyn's indignation still burned in her chest, so she glanced in Sybil's direction to avoid responding. Sybil sat on the floor, legs crossed, examining a metal box with a glass bulb protruding from the top. Wires were wrapped around the machine, and Sybil traced them with her finger before turning the crank on the side. The box made a humming sound, but nothing else happened.

"That is the key to electricity," Aya said, inclining her head toward the box. "Power has to be generated either by physical energy or by a system of steam and turbines. Obviously, with the water shortage, I can't create much steam."

Dellwyn let out a breath, relieved for the change of subject. "So, if you can get it working, that glass bulb will light up?"

Aya beamed. "Exactly."

Dellwyn's eyes widened. As she watched Sybil turn the crank, the smooth motion and its possibilities hypnotized her. "Wow. Imagine being able to see at night without lighting a fire."

"I know." Aya sighed. "The palace is still set up for power like this, but I doubt we have enough materials to bring it out to the villages. I could probably create a few generators like that one for nighttime emergencies, for the doctors and midwives and whoever else to use, but that would be about it."

Dellwyn shrugged. "It would still be better than candlelight."

"So it would." Aya looked out the window toward the palace, and Dellwyn followed her gaze. The sun had climbed to the middle of the sky. Already midday.

The realization sent Dellwyn's stomach rumbling, and she stood. "Sybil and I should head out. I haven't eaten since yesterday, and I need to get some sleep before work tonight in case the situation improves."

Aya rose. "Are you sure you don't want to eat here? I'm planning on making a stew, and there will be plenty extra."

Dellwyn raised her eyebrows. Since when did Aya use so much water in her cooking?

Aya must have guessed Dellwyn's thoughts because her eyes widened. "You don't have to make it with water. One of the farmer's wives told me to use animal stock or blood." Aya wrinkled her nose. "As long as you don't put too much in, you can't taste it. It's really more of a mash than a stew."

Sybil came to stand at Dellwyn's side. "Are we leaving already?"

"Already?" Dellwyn chuckled. "We've been here all morning."

"Really?" Sybil glanced out the window to check the position of the sun. "I didn't realize."

Aya smiled. "Are you sure you won't stay for lunch?"

Sybil's face brightened, and she opened her mouth to speak, but Dellwyn put a hand on her shoulder. "We're sure. We've got some cactus pulp, and a farmer is scheduled to drop off two pork chops this afternoon."

Aya nodded and moved to open the door for them. "Well, if you ever do want to get out of Sternville for a meal, you're always welcome here. Benevolent Queen knows I'm tired of eating alone."

So Aya still believed in the divine goddess, even after all she'd been through. A lump rose in Dellwyn's throat, but she swallowed it down. She turned and stared pointedly at the great moored ship that served as the palace, only a few streets in front of them. "You don't *have* to eat alone."

Aya followed Dellwyn's line of sight, and her face flushed. "For the last time, Lionel and I aren't together right now."

"Fine, fine." Dellwyn pretended to button her lip. "I won't bring it up again."

Aya reached out her hand to Sybil. "It was nice meeting you, Sybil." She frowned. "I meant to ask earlier, are you related to Emil Tanner?"

Sybil shook Aya's hand. "Mr. Otis Tanner is—was—my stepfather. My mother married him when I was a baby. My father was a butcher."

"Oh, good." The crinkles around Aya's eyes softened. "I hope to see you again soon."

"You, too"—Sybil smiled and gave Dellwyn a conspiratorial wink—"Your Highness."

Aya laughed. "Dellwyn Rutt, you are a terrible influence."

"What?" Dellwyn snickered. "You turned out fine."

Aya playfully rolled her eyes. They said their goodbyes, and Dellwyn and Sybil began the trek back to Sternville.

As Dellwyn walked away from Aya's shop, she noticed a tightness in her chest. Now that Aya was back in the merchant class, she didn't treat Dellwyn any differently. However, Dellwyn felt differently about Aya. Whenever they talked, Dellwyn could picture the anchor chain that divided Sternville from Portside. The chain was one of four that secured the ship, and it marked an invisible line she always felt it necessary to toe. They were the same women, but they were now separated by circumstance, no longer fighting the same battles. Aya had bettered herself, moved up the proverbial anchor chain, and if King Lionel had his way, she would only get further and further away from Dellwyn.

That was why Dellwyn kept pushing Aya toward the king. It was inevitable, really, that Aya would succumb to his romantic intentions and become his queen. What woman wouldn't? Dellwyn wished it would happen quickly, like pulling a cactus splinter from her finger—a little discomfort, a minute of sting, then forgotten in a day when the prick faded. But this long, drawn-out process—Aya insisting on holding her independence and acting as if nothing had changed—hurt Dellwyn.

Everything had changed. And it would all change again soon. She just wanted it to hurry up so she could feel justified, not guilty, about her bitterness at being left behind.

4

_____

Dellwyn glanced out the window of the hovel and checked the position of the sun. It still hovered above the horizon, but night would come within the hour. She had killed all the time she could spare. With a sigh, Dellwyn placed the utensils she had been dusting back into the trunk and tossed the dust rag under the window to be beaten out in the morning. If her evening was anything like the previous seven had been, she would need something to hit when she returned home.

Alisa still refused to help with training, and Madam Huxley had begun sending one of the priming girls and some mid-rank client to Dellwyn's room at least once a night. The madam had been kind enough to inflict Elsie the Squealer on Augustus, but after a few nights with the Screamer and the Mute, Dellwyn almost wanted Elsie back. Almost.

With her cloak tied loosely around her shoulders, Dellwyn stepped into the dry evening heat. A gust of wind smattered dirt across her exposed legs, but she didn't bother to pull the cloak tighter around her. She didn't have anyone important to stay clean for.

Lord Collingwood still had not visited, nor had he sent any further messages about when Dellwyn could expect him to return. Every night when her door opened to reveal a client other than her favorite nobleman, Dellwyn's heart sank a little deeper into her stomach. As much as she hated to admit it, Dellwyn would be disappointed if Lord Collingwood had decided to give up their relationship, or whatever it could be called, in favor of King Lionel's vision of fidelity.

Another fierce breeze whipped at her cloak, and Dellwyn gritted her teeth. At least Lord Derringher wouldn't mind the dirt—given his new proclivities, he would probably welcome it. He had visited Dellwyn every night for the past week, and each time, he grew bolder. In his most recent visit, he had grabbed Dellwyn right as he'd walked in the door and threw her on the bed. He had become fond of holding her hands together over her head and had started to insist on finishing in her from behind. His pace and enthusiasm only seemed to increase as she winced and gripped the pillow for support. As much as it astonished Dellwyn to admit, especially as she rubbed her sore wrists and back every night, she actually missed his clumsiness.

As Dellwyn approached the Rudder, she noticed something shuffling across the ground in front of the propellers. Squinting against the darkness, she tried to make out the figure. It was short, round, and waddled. A pig, perhaps? Loose from Bowtown?

When she moved closer, Dellwyn realized that it wasn't an animal at all, but a man. He crouched low in the dirt, his boot-clad feet sidestepping, and his tan, freckled arm outstretched toward the ground. Dellwyn walked up to him carefully, hoping he wasn't heat-scrambled. "Sir? Are you all right?"

The man whipped around, still crouched low, a farmer's scythe in his callused hand. Dellwyn jumped back and put up her hands. "I don't want any trouble."

The man looked from the tool to Dellwyn. With his other hand, he tipped his flat, black cap in greeting. The goggles wrapped around the base of his cap glinted in the fading sunlight. "I'm not who'll bring you trouble, miss."

Dellwyn took another step back, her eyes locked on the raised scythe. Its handle was shorter than most used in the Bowtown crop fields. It barely extended past the man's wrist, and it appeared to be engraved with some kind of metal filigree. The blade was also shorter than a normal scythe's—not nearly long enough to hack down grain stalks. However, it seemed curved at just the right angle to pierce an animal's gut and hook under its rib cage.

"Good." Dellwyn kept her hands up anyway, emphasizing that she was not a threat, either. "But you know, playing in the dirt with a dangerous weapon might bring *you* trouble."

The man smiled and stood, revealing himself to be a few inches shorter than Dellwyn. He wiped the scythe's blade on his loose black shirt before sliding it back into place in his tool belt, between a canteen and a leather seed pouch. Definitely a farmer, then.

With his scythe put away, the man looked straight at Dellwyn for the first time. She gasped. From under his shaggy brown hair peeked the strangest pair of eyes Dellwyn had ever seen. One shone green in color, the other as gray as a cloud, both bulging as if they would pop out of their sockets at any moment. They seemed to look right at Dellwyn and yet through her all at once, as if one of them saw the waves at her surface and the other dove deep into her soul. They were beautiful and frightening, and they wouldn't stop staring at her.

"What are you doing out here?" Dellwyn crossed her arms, as if they could block the farmer's internal sight. "In the dirt, I mean."

"The same as you." The farmer motioned to her ensemble, and Dellwyn suddenly felt naked with her stocking-clad legs peeking out from her cloak. "I'm offering the people a choice."

Dellwyn raised her eyes to the sky and glared. Of course. He was a farmer. They were all religious fanatics. "And what choice is that?"

The farmer pointed to the ground. Dellwyn stepped forward and saw the message he had been scratching into the dirt. *FIDELITY*. Gracious. Why couldn't he have been a typical wellman, drawing a design with his piss?

She scoffed. "You certainly picked a tough audience."

"There's no point in speaking to the faithful." The farmer

tugged at his shirt sleeve. "They're already doing their part to bring the rains."

Dellwyn rolled her eyes. "You're not speaking to anyone. All you've done is scribble a cryptic message in the dirt. It'll blow away before half the clients see it, and most of the wellmen won't even be able to read it."

The farmer looked down at his feet. Dellwyn noticed he was blushing, and pride bloomed in her chest from ruining his game.

"It was supposed to be a mystery," he said. "They were supposed to see it, without me, and know it was a sign from the Benevolent Queen."

Dellwyn laughed. "That seems a little dishonest, Mister Moral Superiority."

The farmer's bicolored eyes met Dellwyn's, and she stopped chuckling. "It's not a lie. The Benevolent Queen wants us to be faithful. She merely needs help in reaching us, and I choose to deliver Her message."

"So, are you a prophet?" Dellwyn knew her tone sounded sarcastic, but a lifetime of cynicism overpowered her will to be polite.

"No. She speaks to all of us." The farmer smiled and leaned toward Dellwyn, as if sharing a secret. "I'm just the only one who listens to Her."

A lump swelled in Dellwyn's throat. He made it sound so easy, so beautifully simple, to be connected to the goddess. A part of her wished he were right, but she dismissed the thought with a shake of her head.

The farmer reached into a deep pocket on his tool belt and pulled out a bronze-and-silver device. It was circular and flat, albeit a half inch or so thick, and had several markings on it. Little lines around the rim and a network of interconnected, curved lines peeked out from behind more metal circles and engravings. On top of all the circles was a metal bar that seemed to divide the device in half.

Dellwyn remembered Aya's description of a certain piece

of technology, and her fingers twitched with the desire to touch the legendary object. "Is that a clock?"

The farmer held the device up in front of his face and moved the bar until one end aligned with his green eye and the other pointed at a particular spot in the sky, a star, Dellwyn guessed. He pulled away from the circle and checked the bar's position against one of the markings. "You should go. The Rudder opens for business in about eleven minutes."

"How do you know that?" Dellwyn moved closer to get a better view of the device. "Did the clock tell you? They tell time, right?"

"It's not a clock." The farmer tucked the device back into his pocket. "I know when the Rudder opens because I have used this device to time its operations for weeks." He pointed at the message in the dirt. "You weren't supposed to be here to see this. No one was."

Dellwyn chose to ignore his disturbing confession and grinned. "Your fancy circle may tell time, but it can never tell you what people will do."

The farmer studied her before nodding solemnly. His crest-fallen face made Dellwyn's stomach churn with guilt. If he'd been stalking the Rudder in service of his religious delusions, he must be going through a rough time... or he was heat-scrambled after all. The least she could do was show him the kindness others probably wouldn't.

"I won't tell anyone." Dellwyn put her hand on his shoul-der. "I don't think your message truly comes from the Benevo-lent Queen, but that is only my opinion. We should let the Rudder's clients decide for themselves."

The farmer smiled and removed her hand from his shoulder to shake it. "Thank you. You have Her gratitude as well."

Dellwyn nodded. She didn't know what else to say, and she expected the farmer to leave. He didn't. Instead, he gazed back up at the stars, ear cocked up as if he were listening. After a moment, he turned back to her. "She says tonight, the test will begin."

"Test?" Goosebumps erupted on Dellwyn's flesh. "What test?"

"Enough time has passed since His Majesty's decree. They will come to the Rudder tonight to be tested. She will be watching."

"Who will come?" Dellwyn pulled her cloak tighter around her shoulders.

The farmer's gaze drifted over Sternville. "They will. More than have ever come before."

Dellwyn tried to stare out at the village, but her eyes couldn't help wandering back to *FIDELITY*. She wondered whether the farmer was right. Would the Rudder receive a record client count tonight? Madam Huxley and Alisa had predicted as much when adultery was legalized, and business had been picking up over the last night or two. Of the clients who did come, no matter how many, would any of them notice the farmer's message? And if so, would it incite obedience or defiance?

Dellwyn guessed the latter. If she knew anything about her clients, it was that they didn't like being told what to do. All the men, and the occasional women, she served were looking for a sense of control of or an escape from their lives. A message in the sand didn't seem likely to make a difference, but then again, if some sophisticated, time-telling device couldn't predict human behavior, why did she think she could?

$\sim$

THE RUDDER'S lobby was empty. Dellwyn cursed under her breath. She had missed the nightly workers' meeting, so if there had been any important news from Madam Huxley, or any other royal decrees announced by the bishop, she would have missed them, too. Instead of heading straight to Room G, Dellwyn went to the communal changing room to see if anyone was still dressing. If so, they could tell her anything she might have missed. Dellwyn knocked softly on the changing room door.

"Come in," someone within called out.

Dellwyn opened the door and stepped inside. Alisa and Kalinda, both already clothed in corsets and stockings, stood in front of the mirror, bobbing and weaving around each other while fixing their hair. Augustus sat on the fainting couch, wearing only tight brown pants and a cream scarf around his neck. For not the first time, Dellwyn let her eyes travel down his sculpted chest, thinking what a shame it was that he would never be interested in a little recreational diversion with her.

"Come to pretty up with the girls, Delly?" Augustus patted the blue velvet cushion. Dellwyn sat next to him, and he slung his arm around her shoulders.

She raised her eyebrows. "Aren't I already pretty enough, Auggie?"

Alisa snorted, and Dellwyn wished the teasing comb would snag in the woman's silky blond hair.

"You're always gorgeous." Augustus gave Dellwyn a squeeze. "Though not always punctual."

Dellwyn poked Augustus's side, and he let out a playful yowl. "I admit, at first, I was dawdling." She glared at Alisa. "It's just so exhausting to do the job of two women."

Alisa turned, and her eyes narrowed into slits. "Don't you mean the job of half a woman? It can't be too tiring when you've got a pretty young flower there to help."

"You almost sound jealous, Alisa." Dellwyn folded her arms over her chest. "If you want your priming girls back to train, all you have to do is ask."

Alisa laughed and put her hands on her hips. "Don't get cross with me. It's not my fault you're so keen to be Madam Huxley's pet. Some of us have enough self-respect to draw lines in the sand."

"The sand." Dellwyn snapped her fingers and turned back to Augustus. "That's the second reason I was late." Alisa stomped her foot to regain Dellwyn's attention. Without looking back at her, Dellwyn replied, "I just drew my line with you, Alisa. You can go now."

Alisa let out an exasperated growl, but she stormed out of the room.

Augustus shook his head. "Well, now I know what to say the next time I want to get rid of her. I wonder why training sets her off like that?"

Kalinda giggled, and Dellwyn's head snapped up. She had forgotten the other woman was there.

"It's gross." Dellwyn wrinkled her nose. "And awkward."

Augustus wiggled his eyebrows. "I kind of like it."

"Of course you do." Dellwyn rolled her eyes. "Can we get back to my story now?"

Augustus chuckled. "Sorry. Something about sand?"

"Yes. When I arrived at the Rudder, there was a farmer outside. He was using a scythe, a strange, short one, to write a message in the sand in front of the propellers."

Augustus leaned forward and placed his elbows on his knees. Kalinda pulled up an ottoman to sit in front of Dellwyn and Augustus, and her dark eyes widened.

"What did it say?" Kalinda asked.

Dellwyn sighed. "Fidelity."

"Fidelity?" Augustus snickered. "I'm guessing he wasn't a client, then?"

Dellwyn shook her head. "He thinks the Benevolent Queen talks to him, that She wants him to help the people be faithful to each other so She can bring the salvation rains."

"Maybe he can." Kalinda looked down at her hands. "Maybe he's the key to saving us."

"We don't need saving." Dellwyn threw her hands up. "Why does everyone think that? Our people have lived here for over two hundred years. Maybe there was a world before, and maybe there was more water there. But I'm sure they had their own problems. Rain won't make us happy. We'll always find something to be miserable about."

Augustus raised his eyebrows. "And you say *I'm* the one with the astounding faith in humanity."

Dellwyn crossed her arms and shrugged. "Tell me I'm wrong."

"Did he say anything else?" Kalinda bit her lip. "The farmer."

Dellwyn frowned. "He said we will be busy. Apparently, the Benevolent Queen informed him that more people than ever will come to the Rudder tonight." She considered telling them about his weird clock-like device, but she held her tongue. If she had learned anything from Aya, it was that technology wasn't safe in all hands. Dellwyn wouldn't say anything about it until she spoke to the cogsmith first.

"This farmer might be right." Augustus tapped his chin. "Not for the reasons he thinks, of course. But he might fulfill his own prophecy. If he starts causing trouble, it could attract a lot of attention for us."

"I thought the Rudder didn't like attention," Kalinda said.

"That was before. When we had to hide our services to married individuals." Augustus smiled. "Now that we're a fully legal business, attention can be positive. It can bring more clients."

"Unless they believe the farmer." Kalinda twirled the end of her braid. "Some might, anyway."

"Maybe." Dellwyn pursed her lips. "But I think more will delight in defying him. The louder and less powerful the authority, the more people like to rebel."

"I suppose we'll have to wait and see if his prophecies come true." Kalinda stood and tugged up her stockings. "My first client will be here soon." When she reached the door, she turned around and grinned. "Augustus, remember every detail of Dellwyn's face when you tell her the news. I want to be able to picture it exactly." With that, she left.

Dellwyn could hear her heart pounding in her ears. "What news?"

"You don't have to train anymore." August squeezed her knee. "Madam Huxley is forcing Alisa to take the duty back."

Dellwyn wanted to smile, but suspicion kept her lips straight. "Why didn't Alisa say anything?"

Augustus scoffed. "You and I both know she wanted to

hold that over you for as long as she could. Not that you gave her the satisfaction."

"Fair enough. But why would Madam Huxley give the girls back to Alisa?" Dellwyn chewed the inside of her cheek. "Did I do something wrong?"

"What has gotten into you?" Augustus shook Dellwyn's shoulder. "You're entirely over-thinking this."

Dellwyn noticed her face beginning to break out in a sweat. "Then what is it?"

"He wants you all to himself." Augustus adjusted his scarf. "That's all."

"He?" Dellwyn wiped her forehead with the back of her hand. What new games would Lord Derringher try now? "He who?"

"Calm down, Delly. For goodness sake." Augustus rolled his eyes. "Lord Collingwood is coming tonight."

Dellwyn let out a sigh of relief that ended in a hearty laugh. *It's about damn time.* She didn't know why Lord Collingwood had been absent for so long, but she knew one thing. He had a lot of explaining to do.

5

Dellwyn spent the next hour pacing. Every time a set of footsteps neared her door, she paused and listened, only to resume pacing as they passed. Madam Huxley had told Augustus that Lord Collingwood would return tonight, but Dellwyn refused to believe it until she saw him with her own eyes. In all the years she had served the nobleman, he had never stayed away from her bed for more than a few nights. This week without him had been torture—rough, embarrassing, unsatisfying torture.

And Dellwyn still wanted to know what in Desertera was going on in the palace. Maybe a few tidbits of the right information could earn her even more of Madam Huxley's favor. The training had been a decent start, but now that it had ended, she would need another way to stay in the madam's exceptionally good graces.

The door's hinges creaked. Dellwyn whirled around to face the entrance, praying that it was not another client or one of the other courtesans checking up on her. A familiar head of gray hair peeked around the corner, and Dellwyn rushed to embrace Lord Collingwood at last.

"You have no idea how wonderful it is to see you, Dell." Lord Collingwood burrowed into Dellwyn's ebony locks. His hot breath tickled her neck and sent a tingle down her spine.

She inhaled the familiar scent of his cologne—musky and subtle—and wrapped her arms around him. Her fingertips traced the smooth fabric of his emerald smoking jacket. "Where have you been, Stanton? I was worried sick."

Lord Collingwood pulled away, a smile playing on his lips. He loved it when Dellwyn used his given name. Being so casual with a client, even one she liked as much as Lord Collingwood, made a lump rise in Dellwyn's throat, but she swallowed it down. He needed emotional intimacy, and she needed answers.

Dellwyn sat down on her bed and patted the space next to her. Lord Collingwood seated himself and stared across the room.

Dellwyn rubbed Lord Collingwood's back, and she felt the muscles relax against her touch. "Tell me what's bothering you."

"My nephew, Benevolent Queen bless him." Lord Collingwood leaned forward, his spine rounding under Dellwyn's palm. "He's so eager to prove himself. He's already restructuring the government."

"More than just the laws?" Dellwyn tried to keep her voice level, but Lord Collingwood still straightened and looked at her with his gray eyebrows raised.

"I assume they already told you about the adultery repeal?"

Dellwyn held the lord's gaze, soaking in his handsome face. If she didn't know better, she would have sworn he had more wrinkles than the last time she'd seen him. "Yes. The bishop came by last week."

Lord Collingwood stroked his goatee. "Damn it, Lionel. That's precisely what I mean. He's changing everything, issuing all these decrees and sending them out to the people before he's thought them through."

"The law has definitely changed things here." Dellwyn sighed. "Business is starting to pick up, and some of my clients are acting… well, different."

Lord Collingwood's brow furrowed. "What do you mean?"

Dellwyn shook her head. "You don't want to know."

"Of course I do." He took her hand, and his hazel eyes bore into hers. "Please tell me. Are you all right?"

"I'm fine." Dellwyn bit her lip. "Lord Derringher has just been a bit… forceful lately." Her hand wandered to her neck, which was still sore from the way Lord Derringher had tugged her hair to lift her body to his. "He's been coming every night. I don't know how much longer my body can take it." She tried to brush it off with a chuckle, but Lord Collingwood didn't let her.

"That bastard." Lord Collingwood gritted his teeth. "I hate that you have to serve him. His whole lineage is scum. The only reason they're nobility is because his ancestors were willing to steal and cheat their way to wealth."

Dellwyn frowned. So the rivalry between Lord Collingwood and Lord Derringher extended beyond the walls of the Rudder. She opened her mouth to ask about Lord Derringher's family, then thought better of it. Instead, she scooted closer to Lord Collingwood until their legs touched. "Let's not waste any more breath on him." She let her fingers trail across her exposed décolletage to distract Lord Collingwood, and his eyes followed. "How else is His Majesty troubling you?"

"He's implemented a new council." Lord Collingwood licked his lips, and Dellwyn knew she only had a few more minutes of conversation left for the evening. Not that she blamed the nobleman—she was hungry for him as well. "Instead of making all judicial decisions himself as king, he's created a board to advise him."

"Who's on the council?" Dellwyn cocked her head, hoping her wide eyes made her question appear innocent enough.

"Lionel appointed the bishop, the queen dowager, and myself."

Dellwyn wrinkled her nose. "What do you all call the bishop? He has a name, doesn't he?"

Lord Collingwood shrugged. "I'm sure he did at birth, but he gave it up when he went into the Benevolent Queen's service."

Dellwyn struggled not to roll her eyes. "Hmm." She wondered if the farmer had a name, or if he simply called himself Prophet. "That's an interesting trio His Majesty has pulled together."

"It won't be just us." Lord Collingwood failed to disguise the disgust in his voice. "My nephew is also allowing the different villages to *elect* a representative to be on the council. Have you ever heard of such a thing?"

Lord Collingwood brushed a strand of hair behind Dellwyn's ear, but she tilted her head away, staving off his advances. "What do you mean?"

He huffed. "The council will be nine in total. Lionel and his three appointed members, but also a merchant from Portside, a farmer from Bowtown, a wellman from Sternville, a nobleperson from Starboardshire, and a palace worker. Lionel insists it will—oh, what does he say?—'represent all of Desertera's interests equally.'" Lord Collingwood clenched his jaw. "All it's done so far is give me a damn headache."

Dellwyn lifted her arm and rubbed the nape of Lord Collingwood's neck. Once again, he relaxed into her touch, and it took all her strength not to take him right then. But with how forthcoming he'd been with his information, she thought she would press her luck one last time. "His Majesty's work doesn't seem all that bad," she cooed. "After all, now that adultery is no longer criminalized, we don't have that big, dark cloud hanging over our visits anymore."

Lord Collingwood grimaced. "I fear we will have even more clouds, Dell. With the last barrier removed, even more men will be clambering to nab my time with you. Lord Derringher is obviously taking advantage."

Maybe you should have been here, then. Dellwyn sighed. "Don't talk like that. You know that no matter how many clients I have, you will always be special to me."

Dellwyn placed her hand on Lord Collingwood's cheek, drawing him in for a gentle kiss. His arms wrapped around her waist, and her heart beat faster. She pulled him closer, willing the conversation to close before he ended up too gloomy or too angry. After the past week of discomfort and training, every inch of her body screamed for release—she craved mindless self-indulgence, just the two of them, alone.

Lord Collingwood melted into her embrace, and Dellwyn breathed a sigh of relief into their kiss. While Lord Collingwood's attentions and gifts made her pride swell, his overprotectiveness deflated it just as quickly. Whenever he commented on her other clients, Dellwyn couldn't help but remember that, no matter how sweetly Lord Collingwood talked or touched, he still viewed her as property—something for his enjoyment that could be bought, a possession he did not want to share with others.

As Lord Collingwood pushed Dellwyn back onto the bed, the tightness in her chest loosened. His hands and mouth fell into the usual pattern of exploring her ample curves, starting at her breasts, moving across her soft stomach, then sliding over her hips. After so many years together, Dellwyn could recite each motion in turn—she knew exactly where his lips would connect with her skin and exactly when his hands would slide up to her corset. She smiled as he undid the first buckle, right on time. A part of her wondered if this was what it felt like to be married.

Predictable, still enjoyable, but most importantly, safe.

LORD COLLINGWOOD LEFT a few hours later, but not before giving Dellwyn his customary kiss on the crown of her head. As he shut the door behind him, the air seemed colder, the room emptier. Dellwyn doubted she should expect another client at this late hour, so she decided to find Madam Huxley so she could apologize for being tardy and share the information Lord Collingwood had divulged.

The moment she stepped into the hallway, Dellwyn noticed the change in the Rudder. Every single doorway was shut— even the one belonging to Room Z, where the lowest-ranking courtesan entertained the poorest clients. Moans and giggles erupted from behind the closed doors. From the end of the corridor, the boisterous chatter of men reverberated off the metal walls, reminding Dellwyn of the machines that hummed in Aya's shop.

When Dellwyn entered the Rudder's lobby, her jaw dropped. Whether he had truly been told by the Benevolent Queen or was simply an astute guesser, the farmer had been right. People filled the entire room. A cluster of noblemen stood against the far wall, their faces hidden behind a cloud of pipe smoke. A group of merchants gathered near the nobles, discussing their businesses and occasionally breaking into the noblemen's conversations with comments on prices or trade opportunities. Wellmen littered the back of the room, staining the floor with red mud where they trekked.

Most surprisingly, a handful of women stood outside the corridor. Some of them gossiped about the infamous Augustus, while others gabbed about Alisa. Still, a few of the women wore sleeveless dresses with slits up the skirts and stood quietly, pushing out their breasts and sizing up the clients in the room.

One of these women perked up when she saw Dellwyn and strode forward. "Is it my turn?" Her voice carried through the room, and she flung her brown curls over her shoulder and smiled at the crowd. The men didn't stop talking, but their attention turned toward the woman and Dellwyn, and they shuffled their feet like anxious horses getting ready to run the moment the reins relaxed.

Dellwyn looked the woman up and down. "Excuse me?" She was skinny—too skinny. Her corset was laced so tightly that the strings fell near her knees, yet it still sat loosely around her stomach. And her legs, well, they were about as big around as Dellwyn's arm. Even Aya, with her naturally petite physique, would have looked plump next to the woman.

"Am I next?" she repeated. Her eyes were bright and hopeful, though inset deeply into her face, as if her body had sucked them in farther in its hunger. "To be interviewed?"

Dellwyn glanced behind the woman to the group she had

been standing with. "Interviewed?" So this was why they had come into the Rudder dressed as if they belonged in the back hallway. Dellwyn had assumed they were merely prepared for a night of fun or perhaps trying to steal clients who were too impatient to wait their turns. But who had told them to come? Madam Huxley hadn't put out word about hiring new courtesans, had she? Surely she wasn't thinking about expansion, not after only a night or two of increased business.

Dellwyn straightened, affecting an air of authority. "How did you hear that we were conducting interviews?"

The woman raised an eyebrow. "A girl came around Sternville to announce it. She said that the Rudder was overwhelmed. That anyone who wanted work for the night, or to be considered for a permanent position, should come to the Rudder and be interviewed."

Dellwyn put her hands on her hips. "I see." So Madam Huxley had gotten a little too excited. The rush had kicked in, and instead of raising prices or forcing customers to return the next night, she had sent out one of the priming girls to drum up more workers. And probably even more clients, too, with the way news spread between those thin tents and hovel walls.

The woman crossed her arms and huffed. "Is it my turn or not?"

"Not yet." Dellwyn turned and hurried over to Madam Huxley's podium. She could hear the woman complaining behind her, loudly of course, about the incompetence of the current workers and how she would be much politer and more efficient. Dellwyn rolled her eyes. *Yes, because whining speaks to your professionalism.*

When the madam saw Dellwyn, she smirked and patted her frazzled red hair. "Oh, Dellwyn, I'm glad you decided to join us." Her mocking didn't last, and her face broke into a grin. "Can you believe this?"

"No." Dellwyn's eyes widened. "How many are there?"

"Seventy." Madam Huxley beamed, taking a handful of coins from a carpenter. "Plus another twenty-five or so in line."

Dellwyn stared at the stacks of coins lining the madam's podium. She realized the madam hadn't even retrieved the guest book from her office, no longer needing mutually assured discretion. "Do we even have enough time slots for them all?"

"Of course. I'm keeping the maximum at sixty minutes and allowing them to linger for a second round if there is time before dawn." Madam Huxley rose up on her toes and looked past Dellwyn's shoulder. "Tilly, come here!"

Tilly, one of the priming girls, scurried over to the podium. Dellwyn noticed that the back of her hair was matted and her neck had purple splotches on one side. Apparently, calling for interviews was not the only way the madam had found enough slots for all the clients. Dellwyn hoped her training had prepared the young women enough.

"Could you handle taking these payments for me? The price is four gold coins per half hour." Madam Huxley shoved Tilly behind the podium, and the girl winced. "Dellwyn, let's speak in my office."

Once inside, Madam Huxley shut her office door behind them, and the sounds from the crowd died away. Dellwyn found herself breathing deeply, as if she had been holding her breath while among the throng. After the boisterous lobby, Madam Huxley's small, near-empty office seemed confining and sterile. Dellwyn wondered if the madam's quarters were as barren, but she supposed it would be fitting. The madam had always relied on herself alone. She didn't seem the type to surround herself with frivolous possessions.

As they seated themselves in their respective chairs, the faint lantern light cast shadows across Madam Huxley's face, making her pleased grin appear sinister. "I know I said it before, but can you believe it? The people have finally decided to trust King Lionel's word."

Dellwyn pulled her skirt over legs and smoothed down the fabric. "Are you sure that's it? It seems unlikely that a hundred people decided to trust His Majesty all at once."

Madam Huxley's smile morphed into a smirk. "Clever girl.

Maybe you do have a knack for business after all." She pulled a loose coin from her pocket and bounced it in her hand. "When business started to decline, I reached out to the clients who were still coming in, as well as those I had not seen for a few days. I told them that if they came tonight, I would only charge them half the normal rate. And for each friend they referred, I would give them a free hour with the courtesan of their choice."

Dellwyn nodded, and her heart sank. What if Lord Collingwood had only returned tonight to take advantage of the discount? What if he hadn't really missed her and hadn't intended to return? *No, Dellwyn. Not now. You can wallow in your doubt later.*

Dellwyn straightened in her chair and focused on the matter at hand. She knew fate had nothing to do with business picking back up. Luck didn't exist in Desertera, or at least, not in the Rudder. She wondered whether the farmer had heard about the madam's little promotion. Who was she kidding? Of course he had. It wasn't like the Benevolent Queen could have *actually* told him people were coming to the Rudder tonight.

"And what about the women who are here for interviews?" Dellwyn folded her hands in her lap, the way she had seen many merchants and noblemen do when discussing business. "Was that another part of your plan?"

Madam Huxley dropped the coin on the table. The clinking sound made Dellwyn shiver. "I admit; the interviews were an impromptu decision. However, when more and more clients kept coming in, I knew we needed the help. So, I sent Sybil to ask around and see if there was any interest. She brought back about a dozen women and more clients still."

Dellwyn fixed the madam with a hard stare. "The priming girls weren't enough?" Most of the girls were still only sixteen or seventeen. Legally, they shouldn't be *fully* serving clients yet, even with the training Dellwyn had given them.

"Oh, don't think I blame you." Madam Huxley smiled. It was almost motherly. "You trained them well. They were skilled enough. There just weren't enough of them."

Dellwyn wanted to correct the madam, but instead held her tongue. Best to stay on Madam Huxley's good side for now. "And where are you putting all these extra girls and clients for the evening?"

Madam Huxley gestured to the corridor beyond the door. "I've opened up the empty hallway. The accommodations aren't as nice, but they'll do. Plus, some of the lower-ranked girls are doubling up, two couples in each room."

If Dellwyn believed in the Benevolent Queen, she would have thanked Her for keeping her in Room G, high enough to avoid such embarrassment.

"And I daresay you're hoping to retain some of the interviewees." Dellwyn arched an eyebrow. "Fill the empty hallway for good."

Madam Huxley nodded. "Precisely."

"Forgive me, Madam." Dellwyn swallowed. "But do you think it's wise to make such plans after one busy night? After all, if most of the clients are only here for the promotion, what makes you think they'll return?"

The madam's jaw tightened. "They'll return. I've made sure their every desire is met. I'm making our services impossible to refuse."

Dellwyn thought back to the bruises on Tilly's neck. Had they been love marks or remnants of something else? "And what does that mean for us? What are we going to be put through for the sake of business?"

"Whatever must be done." Madam Huxley's nostrils flared. "Without the Rudder, you all are nothing. Each one of you came to me with your sob story, and I took you in. I gave you jobs, shelter, fed and clothed you. You all owe me."

"We certainly owe you gratitude." Dellwyn's hands balled into fists. "And perhaps we owe you our labor and loyalty, too. But none of us, no matter how dire our previous circumstances, deserve to be put through whatever bruised Tilly's neck tonight."

"It's not a question of what you deserve." Madam Huxley stood, placed her palms on her desk, and leaned over to stare down at Dellwyn. "It's a question of what must be done. Speaking of which, I seem to recall several women in the lobby waiting to be interviewed. I think that's something *you* must do, Dellwyn."

Dellwyn stood as well. She was far shorter than Madam Huxley, but she held herself with dignity. "I trained *all* the priming girls because Alisa couldn't stomach it. And now you want me to do this, too?"

"It's your job." Madam Huxley patted her skirts. "And as you say, Alisa won't help."

"You punish me whenever I speak too boldly." Dellwyn shook her head. "And yet you let Alisa blatantly disobey you without so much as a scolding."

"I am giving you more responsibility. Isn't that what you wanted?"

"This isn't responsibility." Dellwyn's lips curled back over her teeth. "This is disgusting."

Madam Huxley clicked her tongue. "*Tsk tsk.* The first step in running a successful business is hiring the right people. If the Rudder is to be yours one day, don't you want a say in who works for you?"

Dellwyn's clenched fists trembled at her side. Leave it to Madam Huxley to frame something so revolting as a privilege of entrepreneurship. "Not like this. I've humiliated myself for you enough this week. Get someone else to do your dirty work."

"Very well. I'm sure Augustus will oblige." Madam Huxley gave a nonchalant wave of her hand. "Take the rest of the evening off."

Dellwyn gave an involuntary jerk, and her eyes widened. "You're not firing me?"

"Of course not." Madam Huxley chuckled. "But trust me, clever girl, you'll need all of the energy you can muster for tomorrow night."

As much as she wanted to bolt from the room, Dellwyn's body had gone stiff. Her insatiable curiosity held her in place, forcing the question through her lips even though she had already guessed the answer. "What's happening tomorrow night?"

Madam Huxley grinned, looking as satisfied as a snake that had swallowed a whole chicken egg. "Room reassignments."

6

*D*ellwyn didn't sleep that night, or at all throughout the day. The more she thought about her encounter with Madam Huxley, the more her skin burned. Dellwyn should have realized room reassignments would be coming, and she should have helped with the interviews, no matter how revolting she found them.

Normally, Dellwyn wouldn't worry. She would feel safe in the knowledge that Lord Collingwood would pay whatever it took to keep her at the Rudder. But his week of absence still had her second-guessing his affections. The fact that he had returned on the night of Madam Huxley's promotion only made the tightness in Dellwyn's chest squeeze harder.

The moment the sun set, Dellwyn hurried out the door and to the Rudder. As she passed under the propellers, she felt her stomach turn over. Most of the workers were already gathered in the lobby, which made Dellwyn look late, even though she had arrived early. She spied Augustus's head of blond curls and Sybil's messy red locks and wound through the crowd to where they stood.

When Dellwyn reached her friends, Sybil pointed to Madam Huxley's podium. On the floor in front of it sat the twenty-six brass letters that ordinarily marked the workers' doors. And as Dellwyn had expected, in front of them rested eight brass numbers from the previously empty corridor. Dellwyn pursed her lips. Madam Huxley was going full steam ahead with her plans after only one night. Had she truly concocted some master scheme, or was this pure arrogance?

Augustus rubbed Dellwyn's back. "It's going to be all right, Delly. You're finally going to move up again."

Dellwyn shook her head. "I pissed her off last night. She wanted me to help with the interviews, and I refused."

"That doesn't mean anything." Augustus said the words confidently, but Dellwyn saw the cloud pass through his green eyes.

"Augustus is right." Sybil smiled up at Dellwyn, her expression confident. "You're great at what you do. The madam won't punish you over a quarrel. She needs you too much."

Dellwyn returned Sybil's grin, hoping her smile appeared more genuine than it felt. "I'm sure you're right."

At that moment, Madam Huxley emerged from her office and moved to stand behind her podium. She beamed out over the workers, like a queen preparing to address her kingdom. "Good evening, everyone. You have probably noticed a few new faces in the room." She gestured toward the group. "I am happy to say that eight women and two men have joined our establishment."

A few of the new employees waved, only to have their hands shoved down by veterans near them. Another few started to clap, and the stunted sound echoed awkwardly throughout the lobby. Dellwyn closed her eyes and placed her hand over her forehead. If they were truly pleased to be there, then they were more idiotic than the farmer.

Madam Huxley waved her hands to dismiss the odd actions of the newcomers. "As the experienced courtesans will have surmised, with the new workers moving into rotation, we will need to hold room reassignments. It's the only way to ensure that everyone is fairly placed in the room best suited to her or his skill level."

Mumbles and groans chorused through the group. Dellwyn didn't emit any of her own for fear of irritating Madam

Huxley worse than she already had. Room reassignments always brought out the worst in the courtesans. Each clamored to shag their way up a few rungs on the ladder to the merchants or nobles, who tipped better and had less odorous bodies. Dellwyn smiled at the memory of her first visit with a nobleman. After all the sweat and dirt she'd tasted on wellmen, she could have devoured his flesh all night. Maybe that was why Lord Collingwood had favored her all these years— Dellwyn had certainly made a positive first impression. Hopefully, it remained.

"I'll explain the room reassignment process in depth. However, I want to begin by saying that, despite the disgruntlement of your coworkers, you should not fret." Madam Huxley's lips curled up in what Dellwyn knew the woman considered a motherly smile. "All you need to do is be yourselves and perform your job as usual. In that way, you will all place yourselves."

Dellwyn squinted. Madam Huxley had neglected to mention what happened in the lobby. While the workers treated their customers like kings and queens, Madam Huxley made the clients pay like royalty to keep their favorite whores around. Room reassignments were an auction. The most valuable courtesans moved up, and the least valuable moved down —or out. The only way an unwanted courtesan stayed around was if she had some other, non-bodily value. Dellwyn had only seen Madam Huxley let two untalented seductresses stay at the Rudder—a girl who had a knack for crafting herbal remedies for venereal diseases, and Aya, the last living descendant of the cogsmiths.

Madam Huxley stepped out from behind her podium and motioned to the brass figures. "As you can see, the letters from the workers' corridor have been removed from the doors. Likewise, the numbers from my private hallway have been removed, except for numbers one and two, which are my office and private chambers."

Dellwyn didn't need to figure the math in her head. She already knew there wouldn't be enough rooms.

"For those of you who are not skilled in mathematics, this means that we have two more workers than rooms." Madam Huxley licked her lips. "Now, unless two of you would like to volunteer to be a—shall we say—an exhibition here in the lobby, cuts will have to be made."

Sybil prodded Dellwyn's side. "Why would she hire more people than she has room for?"

"To give herself the largest pool from which to choose the talent." Dellwyn waited for Madam Huxley to turn toward the other side of the room. "And to start a bidding war between clients to keep their preferred courtesans here."

Madam Huxley cleared her throat. "Now then, the room reassignment process is rather simple and will only take one night. All of you will go to your current rooms for the evening. New employees, you will have to take turns using the rooms in the smaller corridor. I highly suggest you use your idle time to cozy up to waiting clients."

Dellwyn scanned the crowd for reactions. The old employees looked either bored or nervous, while the new employees looked either too terrified or too excited. As she completed her appraisal, Dellwyn's eyes locked with Augustus's, and he raised his to the ceiling in exasperation at the madam's theatrics. Dellwyn repeated the gesture and returned her gaze to Madam Huxley.

"During the evening, you will be assigned random clients. The rates for all clients are the same tonight and only tonight, no matter which of you they see. After you serve them, they will provide me with a brief report of their experience. For your sake, I hope it is good." Madam Huxley tapped her fingers together. "Of course, if one of your regular clients insists on seeing you, I will allow it for an extra charge. If that happens, I hope you prove worth the fee."

Dellwyn remembered the last round of room reassignments and repressed a shudder. She had spent the entire night bouncing between crude wellmen, rough merchants, and noblemen who didn't realize they weren't the king. While she felt bad for the lower-priced courtesans, who had to deal with those clients on a regular basis, she felt grateful that she had grown to be as valuable a commodity as she had. Maybe Lord Collingwood would come in and book her for the entire night —that was, if he still cared for her the way he used to. More than anything, Dellwyn wanted to see him again, to reaffirm his affection and silence the doubts Madam Huxley's promotion had placed in her mind.

Madam Huxley returned to stand behind her podium. "Are there any questions?"

One of the new women, the one whom Dellwyn had spoken to last night, raised her hand. "What happens if we are not assigned a room?"

Dellwyn shook her head. The poor woman didn't even realize what she had gotten herself into—none of them did. They thought they could waltz into the Rudder, get their brains shagged out for fun, and get paid all the while. They didn't realize the madam would actually make them *work* for it.

Madam Huxley raised her eyebrows. "What do you mean?"

"Will there be another interview?" The woman spoke with her hands, moving them around as if she could grasp her words from the air. "Are there second chances? What if we aren't compatible with a client?"

"I don't see how that's my problem." Madam Huxley shrugged. "If you're not good enough, you're not good enough. Go work elsewhere."

The woman nodded and squared her shoulders to show that it wouldn't be an issue. Dellwyn sighed. The woman didn't yet understand that sex out there and sex in here were two very different experiences. But she would by the night's end.

Another woman raised her hand, and Madam Huxley motioned to her. "But what if we have no elsewhere to go? What if this is all we can do?"

Dellwyn lowered her eyes. Nearly every person in that room had been there before. Until the law changed, until last night at that, no one had come to the Rudder willingly. Even Dellwyn—who had taken to pleasing others like a cactus to the desert, and who had grown to enjoy the work when handed the right clients—hadn't entered the profession out of interest, skill, or passion. The Rudder was a place of necessity, and for all her bluntness and faults, Madam Huxley had always been compassionate to that truth. As a businesswoman, she had to keep the best workers on hand. She couldn't afford to feed and lodge every wayward soul, but she always sent them out the door with a pat on the back, a loaf of bread, and a full canteen. It wasn't the kindest system, but it wasn't cruel—one of the reasons Dellwyn and the other courtesans, even Aya during her time there, respected the madam so much.

But after what the madam had said the previous evening, Dellwyn knew that compassion wouldn't be the policy any more. With adultery legalized, people could screw each other as they pleased, and competition, whether from another brothel or individuals working alone, was inevitable. Madam Huxley hadn't been so forthcoming in their conversation, but Dellwyn had figured it out for herself. Business was good now, and it needed to be capitalized on before anyone else could rise up and threaten it. And the madam would do whatever she could to prevent that from happening, whatever *must be done.*

"Well?" The woman's voice cracked. "What if we have nowhere else to go?"

Madam Huxley stared at the girl, deadpan. "You can die of thirst in the dirt for all I care. It won't be my fault."

Dellwyn's hand latched onto her throat, and her eyes narrowed into slits as she watched the madam soak in the crowd's reactions. How dare Madam Huxley use *those* words. It couldn't have been a mistake—not after the way Dellwyn had defied the madam last night.

As Madam Huxley turned to walk to her chambers, she glanced back over her shoulder, and her eyes lingered on Dellwyn for a moment too long. So that was it, then. The madam had forsaken both compassion and respect in favor of authority. She had sent a clear message to Dellwyn—a reminder of Dellwyn's place and a warning to stop questioning the madam's strategies and start complying with her requests—however repulsive Dellwyn found them.

Sybil placed her hand on Dellwyn's elbow. "You've gone pale. What is it?"

Dellwyn's hand slid up to her mouth, and she fought back the tears that threatened to fall from her eyes.

Augustus wrapped an arm around her shoulders. "It's all right, Delly. Madam Huxley is simply using fear to motivate the girls."

"It's more than that. It was a message." Dellwyn inhaled deeply, and her breath came out shaky. "Those were the last words my mother ever spoke to me."

Dellwyn watched as her two little brothers hovered over the Sternville well, throwing pebbles into it, racing to see whose would splash into the water first.

"Yes!" Mikel thrust his fist into the air. "I win."

"Nuh uh." Harl stomped his foot. "Mine was the brown one."

Mikel pushed Harl. "No. Yours was the gray one."

Harl shoved him back. "No!"

"Stop it, you two." Dellwyn ordered. She turned back to her three younger sisters, who sat in front of her, the four of them forming a circle. Dellwyn had been trying to teach them a game, one where they sang a song and slapped hands around the circle. The girls kept yanking their hands away from each other, no one wanting to have her palm touched as the song ended for fear of being the loser.

Between the girls' skittishness and the boys' orneriness, Dellwyn didn't know how much longer she could keep them out of the tent. Their mother had come home, as she did almost every night, with a drunken wellman hanging off her, red splotches already forming along her collarbone where she had allowed him to sample her. Mother had stormed into the tent, grabbed up the little ones by the arms, and shooed them out. To Dellwyn, she had said, "Keep them out of here until the moon passes over the palace." Upon seeing the wellman's eyes linger on Dellwyn's hips, her mother had added, "And don't get into any trouble, you little whore."

Dellwyn shook her head and restarted the song, hoping it would push any bad thoughts from her mind. It wasn't her fault she had received her womanhood at twelve. She would have gladly stayed bloodless, breastless, and hipless for many more years. As her body had changed over the last several months, she noticed the people around her changing, too. Younger girls excluded her from their games, while older girls treated her coldly, as if they were all in some kind of competition. Dellwyn didn't know what exactly they were competing for, but she had a feeling it had to do with the men, who had begun staring at her with a mixture of desire and disgust in their glazed eyes.

The boys started roughhousing again, and Dellwyn stopped the song. She snapped her fingers to get their attention. "Come here." When the boys ignored her, she whistled sharply. They froze. "Don't make me drag you over here."

Bowing their heads, the boys waddled over and crammed themselves between their sisters. The girls groaned, but they moved to allow the boys room to sit.

"Go home," Mari whined, rubbing her tired eyes. She was only three, and Dellwyn hadn't been able to convince her to nap earlier in the day. She wouldn't last much longer.

Dellwyn glanced over at the palace. The moon was just beginning its arc over the ship. "Just a little longer, Mari."

"No." Phyla crossed her arms. "We want go home."

Dellwyn rolled her eyes, waiting for Dien to complain next, only to see her slumped over. Her sleeping head dangled, and drool pooled on her dress.

"Okay." Dellwyn sighed. "Let's go home." She scooped Dien up and held her against her hip with one arm, reaching her free hand out to her other siblings. They all linked hands, forming a dusty chain, and Dellwyn led them home.

When they arrived back at the tent, Dellwyn heard the familiar sound of connecting flesh coming from behind the tent flaps. Her siblings stared up at her expectantly, waiting for her to pull back the flaps and let them in. Dellwyn corralled them to the side of the tent. "Let's sit out here for a bit," she whispered. "Mother still has company."

Phyla and Mari began to cry, and Dellwyn used her free hand to stroke each of their heads in turn. "Shh. It's okay. Just a few more minutes."

Once her sisters calmed down, Dellwyn turned to thank the boys for being so quiet, but they were gone. Before Dellwyn could run to find them, she heard the entrance to the tent open. Seconds later, she heard Mikel's shrill voice. "His peepee's so much bigger than mine!" Then Harl cackled.

Her mother screamed in surprise, and the wellman let out a disgruntled shout. There was a commotion inside the tent; Dellwyn wasn't sure whether things were being shoved about or whether her mother was being hit. Her sisters wailed, and Dellwyn clutched them to her, doing everything she could to keep from crying herself. A few neighbors peeked their heads out of their hovels, but when they saw it was Dellwyn's family, the cause of ruckus yet again, they muttered to themselves and shut their doors or windows. Dellwyn's face grew hot, and she wished she were anyone but herself in that moment.

The wellman stomped out of the tent, knocking down Mikel in the process. Dellwyn untangled herself from her sisters and ran to the front of the tent. She knelt down beside Mikel and moved to hug him, but he pushed her away. Dellwyn inspected him anyway. Other than a few scrapes where he'd caught himself with the heels of his hands, he was unharmed.

As Dellwyn stood, her mother slapped her hard across the face. Dellwyn gasped and grabbed her cheek, barely able to see her mother through her watering eyes.

"You idiot," her mother hissed. "I told you to keep them out of here."

"I'm sorry." Dellwyn wiped at her eyes. "But Dien fell asleep, and the others were exhausted. I thought—"

"You ruined everything." Her mother glared down at Dellwyn, then at the younger children. She pointed to the tent. "Get in there. And you better be asleep when I'm done with your sister."

The little ones scurried inside, and Dellwyn heard whimpers through the thin fabric walls. "I'm sorry, Mother."

"No, you're not." Her mother grabbed her by the collar of her dress. "You've done nothing but destroy my life since before you came into this world."

Dellwyn had heard this speech several times, and if it were not for fear of the beating she knew would follow, she would have rolled her eyes.

"I used to work at the Rudder. I used to be someone." Her mother spat on the ground. "And then you came along and got me fired. The midwife couldn't even get rid of you, you'd latched yourself onto me so tight."

Dellwyn didn't speak. It took all of her strength to meet her mother's furious dark eyes. Looking at the ground would only get her in worse trouble.

"And now, thanks to you, I have to peddle myself on the streets. No more rich clients. No more tonic to keep me empty. That whole litter is your fault."

Dellwyn clenched her fists, trying to keep the anger and hurt out of her face.

"You think it's easy supporting all of you? How am I supposed to feed you when you scare away the men?"

Dellwyn straightened, holding her head high. "I can help, Mother. I'm a woman now. I can get a trade, maybe work with—"

Her mother laughed, and the sound grated down Dellwyn's spine. "Oh, we can all see that you're a woman now." She swatted Dellwyn's breast. "But you're a fatherless bitch, Dellwyn Rutt. You were made during a rutting, and that's all you'll ever be good for. Just like me."

Dellwyn bit her lip, willing the tears not to fall, but they slipped down her cheeks anyway. "That's not true. I can help. Please let me try."

"Fine. I'm done arguing with you." Mother shook her head, releasing Dellwyn's collar.

Dellwyn breathed a sigh of relief. "Thank you, Mother. I promise I'll— "

Mother held up a hand to silence her. "Get out of here, and don't you come back."

"What?" Dellwyn's blood ran cold. "You... you can't do that."

Her mother turned away and stalked into the tent. She reemerged with Dellwyn's cloak and her only childhood toy, a doll woven from tumbleweed fibers, and shoved them into Dellwyn's arms. "Leave. You're a woman now. Take care of yourself."

"Mother, please!" Dellwyn clutched her belongings to her chest and dropped to her knees, ready to beg the vile woman to let her stay, if only to look after her younger siblings. "Please, you can't send me out. I'll help you take care of the little ones. I'll help make money."

"You did this to yourself, Dellwyn Rutt. This is no one's fault but yours." As Mother turned to stride back into the tent, Dellwyn latched onto the hem of her dress. Mother stopped and glared down at her.

"What will I do?" Dellwyn hiccuped through her tears. "Where will I go? I have nothing!"

"You can die of thirst in the dirt for all I care." Mother kicked Dellwyn's hand away. "It won't be my fault."

~

DELLWYN'S VISION BLURRED, and she realized her whole body was shaking. For years, she had pushed memories of that day out of her mind and avoided her family at all costs. Even when her mother, and then Phyla, had succumbed to venereal disease, Dellwyn hadn't attended their funerals.

Her remaining siblings had been young enough that they either had forgotten Dellwyn or had accepted their mother's story that Dellwyn had run away from home. And on the rare occasions Dellwyn caught a glimpse of one of them in Sternville, she turned and scurried away in the opposite direction. Mikel and Harl had each taken a trade, and Mari and Dien had married young and added a few new wellmen to Desertera. They had never sought Dellwyn out, and she knew it was best. They didn't need another whore in their lives. Their mother had been enough.

"Dellwyn?" Augustus stood in front of her, his hands clasped around her upper arms. As Dellwyn's eyes focused, Augustus's wrinkled forehead smoothed out and his grip relaxed. "Are you okay?"

Dellwyn rubbed her temples. "I'm all right."

"Are you sure?" Sybil bit her lip. "Do you need to go home?"

"No!" Dellwyn's protest echoed off the walls, and she blushed under her coworkers' curious glances. When they looked away, she whispered, "I got caught up in my thoughts, in memories, that's all. I'm fine."

"Madam Huxley knew what she said, didn't she?" Augustus nearly growled the words.

Dellwyn nodded. "I told her on the night I came here."

Augustus frowned and glanced over his shoulder. "You

weren't joking about pissing her off." Madam Huxley had retreated to her office to prepare for the evening, and the other courtesans had begun to disperse. "Do you want me to talk to her for you? I might be able to charm her into some mercy."

"Please don't. It would only make things worse." Dellwyn straightened and gently pushed Augustus back a step. "Madam Huxley made her point, reminded me of my place. Like you said, she adores her theatrics, but I'm sure it's over now."

Augustus wiped his face with his shirt sleeve. "If not, it will be soon enough."

"What do you mean?" Dellwyn's eyes flitted between him and Sybil, but Sybil merely shrugged.

"You know how it is with Madam Huxley. She likes to hold a grudge." Augustus put his hands on his hips and gazed out toward the propellers. "But she won't be able to, not for long." He sighed. "She's about to be hit with more than she can handle. We all are."

7

———————

When she left Room G at dawn, Dellwyn knew there wasn't enough water in all of Desertera to make her feel clean again. Her first client during room reassignments hadn't been that bad. In fact, she'd rather enjoyed his company. A guard of the palace, he had been muscular and attractive, straddling the line between rough and playful in a delicious way.

Unfortunately, the night had only become disappointing from there. She'd served ten clients over the eight-hour period, and she still couldn't decide which had been the worst. She settled on a tie between the wellman who insisted on twisting her like a knot and the cobbler who demanded she only touch him—all of him—with her feet.

As she walked to the lobby, Dellwyn did her best not to wince. Her hip bones had already started creaking, and no doubt would be screaming tomorrow. The burning sensation emanating from between them suggested she'd called for ointment two clients too late. At least she would be back to a more routine schedule the next day. Tiny-peckered noblemen with king complexes had never seemed so appealing.

"Dell?" A voice called to her from the other side of the room.

Dellwyn's head snapped up, and her eyes landed on Lord

64

Collingwood. His hair appeared ruffled, as if he had been running his fingers through it all night. His eyes had dark circles underneath, and his cravat lay untied around his neck. He held a velvet bag in one hand, and he reached out the other hand to her as he approached.

"Lord Collingwood." Dellwyn placed her hand in his, and he kissed her knuckles. His lips felt rough, chapped. "Not that I'm unhappy to see you, but what are you doing here? The Rudder is closed for the day."

"I know." Lord Collingwood released her hand and ran his fingers through her straight hair, extending his impatient, nervous tick to her body. "I came to see you tonight. I wanted to surprise you. But it seems I was the one to get the surprise instead."

Dellwyn nodded. "Room reassignments." Her heart panged. Was she not worth the cost? Even for an hour? "I apologize. The madam insists on the extra fee. Everything should be back to normal tomorrow night."

"I hope so." Lord Collingwood wrapped his arms around her, and Dellwyn's stomach twisted as she realized that moment was more intimate than anything she had experienced that night. "I told Madam Huxley that I would pay whatever it took to see you, but she informed me it was too late in the evening to fit me in."

Dellwyn's heart fluttered. He did still care. "Why did you wait? You could have sent a message like you usually do."

Lord Collingwood shook his head. "I didn't think that would be right, not after the week we spent apart. I wanted to assure you of my affections in person and prove that Lionel's new law hasn't changed anything for me."

Dellwyn didn't know how to respond. She stared up at him, admiring his strong jaw, the soft lines of his face, and his warm hazel eyes. For a moment, with nothing but the gentle light of sunrise and the scent of his cologne surrounding her, she felt as though he were hers. But the clanging of a door startled her back to reality. He could never be hers. She could only be his.

A smile spread across her face, an involuntary protective mechanism. "Nothing has changed for me either, my lord."

Lord Collingwood grinned. "I am pleased to hear that, Dell." He unwound his arms from her waist and held up the velvet bag. "I brought you something. An apology."

"Oh, my lord, you didn't have to—"

"Nonsense." His grin widened. "I wanted to. I enjoy making you happy."

Dellwyn untied the golden strings and pulled open the bag. Inside lay a metal flower, crafted from all manner of trinkets. Smooth, bronze plates made the petals, while various cogs and bolts clustered together to form the center. To represent the stem, the flower had a cylindrical base with a winder on the side. Lord Collingwood turned the winder, and it clicked. When he released his hand, a soft melody played from within the flower.

Dellwyn gasped. "It's lovely. Thank you." She placed her hand underneath the flower and scooped it out of the bag.

"You're most welcome." Lord Collingwood didn't even attempt to hide the pride in his glowing eyes. "This music box has been in my family for generations. I've been waiting to find the perfect woman to give it to. It shouldn't have taken me so long to realize you are her."

Tears stung Dellwyn's eyes, and her fingers trembled around the flower. "Stanton, this is too much. I can't—"

Lord Collingwood placed his palm against her cheek. "Of course you can. It's a gift, Dellwyn. A way to reach me whenever you need."

"You've already given me so much." Dellwyn's voice cracked, and she stared down at the metal flower, which seemed to be mocking her with its melody. How could she have doubted him? "I wonder what I've done to deserve your affection."

Lord Collingwood cupped her cheek. "You have been you." His thumb brushed across her bottom lip, and Dellwyn saw the flame ignite in his eyes. And of course, she had done *that.*

"Did you want to go back to my room?" Dellwyn shuffled her feet, cringing as her womanhood protested the small movement. But she had to ask, didn't she? It was the whole reason he was there, bringing her a gift, the whole reason he'd brought her gifts in the past—to stay in her good graces, in her bed, in *her*.

Lord Collingwood glanced toward the corridor, as if he were considering her offer, but when his eyes returned to her, she saw that he looked stung. "Do you really think that's all I want from you? Dell, darling, this isn't payment. It's just a gift." He smiled, and Dellwyn thought for a moment that he might say the forbidden words. "Something to show you how much I care."

A weight lifted from Dellwyn's chest, and she clutched the flower tighter in her hands. "Thank you, Stanton. You know I care a great deal for you as well."

"Of course." Lord Collingwood leaned down to kiss her, but Dellwyn turned her head, and his lips landed on her cheek.

"We can't," she whispered. "Not here. It's not allowed."

Lord Collingwood closed his eyes and huffed. "Of course. It all has to stay in that room, doesn't it?"

Dellwyn bit her lip. "I'm afraid that's all there can be for us."

"Only if you declare it so." His lips hovered above hers, inviting her to close the distance, to damn the rules of the Rudder and take their relationship to a new level. But she couldn't bring herself to do it. She didn't know how to be anything other than a fun night or an unobtainable dream, and her heart ached at the idea of risking what they did share.

"You should go home." Dellwyn took a step back. "I should, too."

Lord Collingwood straightened and tugged his jacket into place. "If that's what you think is best. I'll see you tomorrow night, Dell."

Dellwyn nodded. "Until then, my lord."

Lord Collingwood placed a kiss on the crown of her head then sauntered down the workers' corridor to the exit that led into the palace. Dellwyn stood in the lobby until she heard the echo of the door shutting behind him. When the sound reached her, she went back to Room G and placed the flower on top of her bedside table. She stood and stared at the flower for a long moment.

Whether he had realized it or not, Lord Collingwood had offered her a way out of the Rudder. If she were to give herself to him, in body and heart, she wouldn't have to stay there. She would no longer be his courtesan. She would be his *mistress*, tucked away in a glamorous apartment high above the Rudder, never again to bed anyone dirty, unskilled, or rough.

As much as Dellwyn's chest ached for Lord Collingwood, being his kept woman wasn't what she wanted. No, Dellwyn belonged at the Rudder despite all its faults. She wanted to make something of herself there, to rise to the position of madam and help as many girls like herself as she could. Maybe one day, when she had achieved that goal, she could see Lord Collingwood as a lover and not as a client. But for the moment, she had to keep their boundaries firmly in place.

As Dellwyn reentered the Rudder's lobby, she heard shouting outside. With gritted teeth, she jogged toward the propellers and emerged into the pink light of morning. The rising sun blinded her, and she held her hand over her brow to shade her view. Three figures took shape in front of her, standing about twenty feet away from the propellers. Two of them had their backs to Dellwyn, but she would recognize Madam Huxley's fiery hair and Alisa's skinny frame anywhere. The other person faced her and the Rudder. The farmer.

Dellwyn stepped forward, debating whether to listen to the argument or make a wide berth around them and head for home. Before she could decide, the farmer's bicolored eyes pierced her, and he pointed at her. "She'll tell you! She knows I speak the truth!"

Madam Huxley and Alisa whipped around and glared at

Dellwyn. For a second, her heart skipped as she found herself under the madam's cruel stare once again. Madam Huxley's words from the previous evening still stung, and the sickly sweet acid of anger and fear bubbled at the base of Dellwyn's throat. Dellwyn considered backing away, but Madam Huxley crooked a finger and beckoned her over.

Not wanting to anger the madam further or appear weak, Dellwyn pushed her shoulders back, marched over to the trio, and feigned an air of annoyance. "What's the matter?"

Madam Huxley scowled at her. "Apparently, you're acquainted with this delinquent."

"I met him the other night." Dellwyn fought the urge to swallow by clenching her jaw. "What of it?"

"This farmer intends to set up a camp outside of *my* business." Madam Huxley's voice dripped with venom. "He claims he will not leave until the people of Desertera see the error of their ways and become faithful again." Madam Huxley grabbed Alisa by the arm, and the girl winced. "And *she* is defending him! Do *you* defend him, too?"

"Let me go." Alisa jerked her arm, but Madam Huxley held it firmly in her grasp.

The farmer balled his hands into fists. "Release her."

Dellwyn wondered what the Benevolent Queen's stance on violence was. She nodded toward Alisa's arm, which the madam had begun to twist without realizing it. "Madam Huxley, you're hurting her."

A look of shock crossed Madam Huxley's face, but nonchalance quickly replaced it as she released Alisa's reddened bicep.

Dellwyn crossed her arms. "For goodness sake." She turned to the farmer. "What are you planning to do exactly?"

The farmer straightened, but Dellwyn noticed he did not unclench his fists. "I will live outside the Rudder until the people of Desertera decide to follow the Benevolent Queen's divine commands."

Dellwyn glared up at the sky and jutted out her hip in the same way defiant teenagers mock their mothers. "Did She tell you to do this?"

"Yes." The farmer answered in such a matter-of-fact tone that Madam Huxley and Alisa both gaped at him.

"And why does She want you to squat outside the Rudder?" Dellwyn rolled her eyes. "Does She really think you can make a difference by yourself?"

"She says I must have faith." The farmer placed a hand over his heart. "She says that if I do as She asks, She will help me save the rest of Her children."

"I see." Dellwyn turned to the two women. "And Madam, I presume you're worried that his presence will negatively affect *your* business."

"A bit." Madam Huxley's lips curled into a smirk. "Though, I'm more concerned about what the... rougher clients will do to him. Not to mention the resulting publicity."

Dellwyn grimaced and turned to Alisa. "You're fine with him stationing himself outside of the Rudder?"

"I never said that." Alisa rubbed her arm. "Madam Huxley was going to report him to the guards. They might throw him in the dungeon and torture him. He's *obviously* crazy, harmless. I say let him sit out here. Who cares what happens after that?"

Dellwyn repressed a smile. This may have been the first time she and Alisa had ever agreed on anything. It was a perfect opportunity to defy Madam Huxley, and Dellwyn practically salivated at her chance for revenge.

Taking a deep breath, Dellwyn allowed her face to go blank. "Alisa makes a fair point, Madam. After all, the farmer can sit out here and die in the dirt. It won't be your fault."

Madam Huxley opened her mouth, most likely to protest Dellwyn's twisting of the phrase, but she closed it again when Dellwyn raised an eyebrow.

"That being said," Dellwyn continued, "why did you need me to play mediator?"

Again, Madam Huxley made to speak, but the farmer piped up before she could offer a snide remark. "You saw me two nights ago at sunset. You know I truly speak for the Benevolent Queen."

"I know no such thing." Dellwyn scoffed. "All I know is that you admitted to lurking around the Rudder, tracking the workers' movements, and trying to scare away clients."

The revelation earned the farmer scowls from the madam and Alisa. He smiled, unperturbed. "Yes, but I told you something else. The Benevolent Queen foresaw that the Rudder would be busy that night. And She was right, was She not?"

"Are you sure the Benevolent Queen told you that?" It was the farmer's turn to be on the receiving end of Dellwyn's condescending raised eyebrow. "Or did you overhear news about Madam Huxley's promotion?"

The farmer blushed. "I do not follow gossip."

"*Mhmm.*" Dellwyn shook her head. "Well, frankly, I have no idea why I'm standing here at all. Madam, clearly you have the right to do whatever you think is best for your business, but honestly, I don't see the point in turning him in to the guards. King Lionel is as likely to feed him as imprison him."

"Exactly!" Alisa stomped her foot. "His Majesty is soft. He opened the floodgates on the Rudder with his new law. It's his own religiosity—wanting people to be faithful for piety and not fear. He would release the farmer anyway"—Alisa glared between the farmer and Madam Huxley—"without wasting my time."

"Forgive me for thinking you might like to help safeguard your wages." Madam Huxley pursed her lips. "Fine, Farmer. I won't call the guards, but I won't be held responsible for what happens to you out here."

The farmer clasped his hands behind his back and smiled. "As I will not be held accountable for what happens to you in *there*, Madam."

A flicker of concern crossed Madam Huxley's face, but before Dellwyn could be sure she had truly seen it, the madam turned and stormed back into the Rudder.

Dellwyn chuckled. "Lovely. As if I needed her to be even angrier with me."

Alisa rolled her eyes. "Whatever could you have done wrong, oh precious one?"

The blonde was trying to pick a fight, but Dellwyn

shrugged it off. It would be nice for her and Alisa to get along for more than a few minutes. "I refused to help interview candidates the other night."

Alisa spat in the dirt. "Lowering yourself to my level, eh?"

"We all have our limits." Dellwyn offered a small smile. "Mine are just further down the line than yours, apparently."

Alisa nodded. "I'm glad to know you have them."

Before Dellwyn could allow herself to get offended, the farmer broke in. "As am I, ladies. Your growing intolerance for depravity is promising. She is speaking to you. You will hear Her if you listen."

"I don't know…" Dellwyn winked at Alisa. "It's difficult to hear Her over all the moaning."

Alisa threw her head back and laughed. The farmer lowered his eyes to the ground, his lips moving as if he was praying for their souls. He probably was.

"I'm going to head home." Alisa yawned. "Long night. Good luck with your protest, Mr. Farmer. I hope you scare a few of them away. I'm not sure how much more my hips can take."

As Alisa walked away, the farmer raised his eyes to Dellwyn. She shivered under their scrutiny. "You two defend me then mock me. Why?"

"We defend you because you do not deserve Madam Huxley's wrath." Now Dellwyn blushed and ran her fingers through her hair. "I can't speak for Alisa, but I mock you because you make me uncomfortable. I don't believe in your goddess. I think you're wrong for having faith in people to change."

The farmer stroked his stubbled chin. "I see. You fear what you do not understand."

"Oh, I understand you perfectly." Dellwyn put her hands on her hips. "You cling to the Benevolent Queen because you want to be saved from this desert wasteland, to go back to the utopia of our ancestors. Well, guess what? *If* that world ever existed, it is long gone, and it's not coming back."

"No, you don't understand." The farmer sighed. "The

Benevolent Queen is terrifying. She allowed the world to be flooded with Her sorrow, and She didn't even realize that Her children were drowning. And Her anger is what shriveled the land without a thought to what we would drink. She could save us if She wanted to, but She doesn't. She refuses aid until we fulfill Her demands. She is cruelty incarnate."

"Then why do you serve Her?" Dellwyn widened her eyes in frustration. "If She is so evil, why don't you turn away from Her like everyone else?"

"Because She is my mother, our mother. She is alone out there, forsaken by Her Almighty King and scorned, perhaps justifiably, by Her children." The farmer's brow furrowed. "But She is right. Whether it brings us water again or not, we need to be kinder to one another."

Dellwyn took in his words. She had no sympathy for the Benevolent Queen. If the hypothetical goddess did refuse to restore the world's water, then She deserved to be neglected and unloved. As for kindness, well, Dellwyn couldn't argue there. She could use more kindness in her own life.

"Maybe we should be kinder to each other." Dellwyn shrugged. "But you can be kind without serving Her. You don't need Her to be a good person."

"True." The farmer frowned. "But I'm not afraid like you."

"I'm not afraid of Her." Dellwyn scoffed. "I don't even believe in Her."

"You're afraid *to* believe in Her." The farmer gestured toward Sternville. "Without Her, your suffering means nothing. It is just your lot in life. But with Her, your suffering means everything. It means She is punishing you for your wickedness. With Her morality as divine law, you fear She will judge you as wicked, and you can't face that."

Dellwyn grabbed her skirts and let her tone deliver the slap her hand longed to give. "Don't pretend to know a thing about me. You know nothing about my life."

The farmer shook his head. "If I am wrong, then why are you upset?"

"Don't ever speak to me again," Dellwyn hissed. "Next

time, I'll call the palace guards myself. I have connections to His Majesty. I can make sure you never see the sun again."

The corner of the farmer's mouth lifted. "You won't do that."

"What did I say about your assumptions?" Dellwyn's fingernails dug into her palm through the fabric. Real or false, the farmer's connection to his goddess gave him no right to insult Dellwyn.

The farmer's grin fell away, replaced by a smooth serenity. "I said you *fear* that you are wicked, not that you *are*." He turned his face to the sky and closed his eyes, as if listening to the goddess's distant whispers. "You're a good person, Dellwyn Rutt. She believes in you, even if you won't believe in Her."

He had known her name. It didn't occur to Dellwyn until she had already walked halfway back to her and Sybil's hovel. When the thought hit her, she stopped mid-step, one foot hovering above the ground. Her arms instinctively tugged the edges of her cloak tighter around her torso.

The farmer had known her name. How? Why?

"Calm down, Dellwyn." She kept her voice low and glanced around to make sure no one lurked nearby to hear her paranoid self-admonishing. "There has to be an explanation."

Yes, there had to be a simple reason. She thought back to the confrontation—surely Madam Huxley or Alisa had said her name. She shook her head—she couldn't remember, but even if one of them had called her by her first name, neither of them would have used her surname. Granted, Rutt was a reasonable guess. Nearly all children born to women of the night were called Rutt, and several of them ended up back at the Rudder eighteen or so years later.

So, maybe the farmer hadn't heard her name in that particular conversation. But he'd been lurking outside of the Rudder for days, weeks probably, gathering his information. The other night, he had known Dellwyn was late to work and should not have been walking to the Rudder at that time. If he had studied her movements, he could have overheard her name.

Then again, maybe the Benevolent Queen had told him. At this thought, Dellwyn laughed out loud. Yes, *that* was it. She had spoken to him in divine provenance and told him to watch out for the nonbeliever, to save the wayward courtesan. And now that Dellwyn had figured it out, the Benevolent Queen would whisper into her ear and divulge the secrets of salvation.

Dellwyn stopped laughing. She hugged her body tighter. The last thing she needed was to start hearing voices.

"Are ya gonna stand there all day laughin' to yerself?"

Dellwyn snapped her head around to see Mrs. Pattie Wellman's withered face sticking out of her tent. Dellwyn rolled her eyes. "And what if I am?"

Mrs. Wellman grimaced. "I'll be callin' the guards. I don't want no sun-sick whore outside my home."

"I'm not sun-sick," Dellwyn muttered. She turned away and continued walking. Without even thinking about it, she headed in the direction of Portside. She needed help figuring out how the farmer had known her name, not to mention why he'd taken the care to learn it, and that meant talking to someone from outside the situation, someone whose judgment was unmarred by paranoia and fear.

Dellwyn realized she was heading to see Aya, and for the second time, her shock made her halt. The anchor chain loomed ahead in the distance, stretching from the corner of the palace's deck to the far edge of the villages, and it felt as if a steel wall had gone up between them.

No. She wouldn't run to Aya. Whenever Aya had encountered someone strange at the Rudder, she had always been the one who had gone to Dellwyn. Aya wouldn't know what to do any better than Dellwyn would—and on top of that, she would probably want to get the king involved. That would make Dellwyn look like a fool, especially when it turned out that the farmer had simply overheard her name at some point in time. Besides, Aya had left the Rudder behind for good. She didn't need, or want, to deal with its problems.

With a sigh, Dellwyn almost turned back toward her hovel. However, even with the bitterness building up inside her gut, she couldn't shake the nagging feeling that something was wrong, that the farmer had more sinister intentions than his holy exterior let on. Therefore, Dellwyn kept walking and turned before reaching the Portside-Sternville border. She followed the anchor chain to the end and stopped outside the last house in Sternville. She hoped its resident had made it home already.

The house was better-constructed than most of the dwellings in Sternville, complete with a front step—alluding to a wooden floor inside—and shuttered windows. Dellwyn had never been inside the house before; she had only seen her intended host enter it once as she walked to Portside, and she hoped he actually lived there.

With her shoulders squared, she knocked on the door. Inside, someone groaned, and Dellwyn heard shuffling and a chair scraping against the floor. After a few moments, the door opened, and Dellwyn faced a bleary-eyed Augustus.

"Dellwyn?" Augustus rubbed a line of dried drool from his chin. "What are you doing here?"

She glanced around, suddenly concerned that someone— the farmer—might have followed her. "I need a friend."

At this, Augustus's eyebrows perked up, and he placed his hand up high against the doorframe, leaning into it until his body formed a seductive curve. "Delly, honey, you know we can't be *friends*."

"What?" Dellwyn wrinkled her nose. "Is my pecker too small for you?"

Augustus smirked.

"This is serious, Augustus." Dellwyn crossed her arms. "I need someone to talk to, and I can't bring this to Sybil. I don't want to worry her."

He straightened and scanned the neighboring hovels, much as she had done. "Is everything all right?"

Dellwyn tapped her foot. "Can we talk inside?"

"Of course." Augustus placed his hand on her arm and

ushered her into his house. He motioned for her to sit at the kitchen table. "Would you like something to drink?"

Dellwyn chuckled and seated herself. "Does that mean you have something besides water?"

"Indeed." Augustus opened the cabinet above the stove and retrieved a dark bottle. He waggled it—and his eyebrows—at her. "Wine."

Dellwyn raised her own eyebrows. "A little early for wine, isn't it?"

"We've been up all night." Augustus retrieved a corkscrew from the trunk next to the stove. "This is late for us."

"Oh, really?" Dellwyn tapped her chin. "So I didn't catch you sleeping, then?"

"A pre-slumber nap." Augustus tapped the bottle. "Do you want the wine or not?"

"Please." Dellwyn bit her lip to contain her smile. If nothing else, at least his jovial attitude had cheered her. "May I ask how you came by such a luxury?"

Augustus placed two tin cups on the table and bowed, mocking Dellwyn's formality. "Why, a generous nobleman gifted it to my humble personage last night."

"On room reassignment night?" Dellwyn let out a low whistle. "You must have put on some show."

Augustus winked. "Never doubt it." As he uncorked the bottle, his playfulness subsided, and his brow furrowed. "Actually, it was odd. He requested to see me despite the fee, but I'd never served him before. I guess my reputation precedes me."

"Some reputation." Dellwyn held the base of her cup while Augustus poured, and eyed the liquid as it flowed into her cup. She opened her mouth to ask Augustus if he was sure this man and his gift were trustworthy, but decided to swallow down her paranoia. "I wish Lord Collingwood would give me wine. I have much more use for it than for all the dust-collecting trinkets he showers upon me."

Augustus laughed. "But you do have the most nicely furnished room in the Rudder."

"True, true." Dellwyn raised her cup and gave it a swirl.

Scents of fruit wafted from it, and she nearly laughed at herself. How would she tell if the wine had been tampered with? She knew hardly anything about wine.

Augustus drank from his cup, and Dellwyn waited with bated breath. When he showed no sign of alarm, Dellwyn inwardly rolled her eyes at her foolishness and took a sip. She relished the heat as the wine burned down her throat— suggesting it wasn't too expensive, yet still young and searing with alcohol. With a shake of her head, she dismissed the last of her concerns. "So, do you want to tell me what you had to do to earn this?"

Augustus smiled and held a finger to his lips. "As with a lady, a gentleman does not kiss and tell."

"Fine." Dellwyn stuck out her bottom lip. "Can we talk about my night, then?"

Augustus took another drink. "I've been waiting."

Dellwyn sighed. "The evening went relatively well… I mean as well as room reassignments ever go."

Augustus nodded.

"But at the end of night, when I left, Madam Huxley and Alisa were standing outside the propellers, arguing with that farmer. You remember, the one I told you about the other night?"

"The one writing in the sand?" Augustus frowned. "What was he doing now?"

"Apparently, he has resolved to station himself outside the Rudder. He's going to live up against the propellers until every single client listens to the Benevolent Queen's word and practices fidelity."

"Doesn't he know that all of our clients aren't adulterers? Some are unattached."

Dellwyn cursed under her breath. She should have thought of that. How would the farmer rationalize that with the Benevolent Queen's message? "I don't know if that matters to him. He seems determined to shut down the Rudder completely."

Augustus rubbed his forehead. "I assume Madam Huxley and Alisa weren't pleased?"

"Madam Huxley was angry, as you'd expect. She threatened to call the guards." Dellwyn licked her lips. Her tongue felt fuzzy from the wine. "But Alisa didn't want to. She thinks the farmer's harmless."

Augustus tilted his head. "Do *you* think he's harmless?"

"I don't know. He carries that scythe…" Dellwyn shuddered, suddenly aware of the open window and the cool morning breeze blowing into the room. "But I don't think he would hurt anyone. I mean, that goes against the Benevolent Queen's teachings, right?"

Augustus shrugged. "I never learned much about Her rules, to be honest. Other than 'don't shag those who don't belong to you,' of course."

Dellwyn chuckled. "Fair enough. Well, I'm not sure whether he would be violent, but he still makes me nervous. The other night, he told me that he observed the Rudder before going to write his message. He knew our schedules and that we would be swamped that night."

Augustus nodded. "I remember."

"Right." Dellwyn shook her head. "And this morning, after Alisa left, he got all prophet-like on me. He was so superior, acted like he knew everything about me just because I don't believe in his goddess."

Augustus shrugged. "They always do."

"But the strangest part is, he knew my name." Dellwyn fiddled with the fabric of her cloak. "My full name. He spoke it as if he had always known me, as if we were old friends."

Augustus raised his eyebrows. "Is that what has you so unnerved? Delly, dear, I daresay *your* reputation precedes *you* as well."

"That can't be it." Dellwyn rubbed her temples. "If he knew it before, why wouldn't he have addressed me by my name sooner? Wouldn't it have increased his credibility as a prophet if he had come right out with it?"

"Maybe he didn't take an interest in learning it until after your first conversation." Augustus waved his hand, as if they were merely analyzing an unsatisfied client. "Or maybe he *didn't* want to scare you. Maybe he said it now out of some sort of companionship. After all, you did defend him against Madam Huxley."

Dellwyn traced her fingers across her chest, hoping to calm the erratic beating of her heart. "But what does he mean by using my name?"

Augustus sighed and blew out a long breath. "Well, typically, it means that the person wants to address you."

Dellwyn stomped her foot under the table. "I'm serious, Auggie."

Augustus's lips twisted into an arrogant smile at her childish outburst. "So am I. Why must you assume the farmer has a sinister purpose? He probably learned your name through his spying, or someone revealed it in conversation—either when you were present or not. Honestly, Dellwyn, he probably just slipped up when he used it. He's probably huddled under whatever tent he's constructing outside the Rudder, cursing himself for the crack in his prophet facade."

Dellwyn nodded. Augustus had to be right. After all, she had thought of those same explanations before coming to his house. Yet, she couldn't shake the trembling in her gut, and she had learned long ago never to ignore what her body tried to tell her. "What if the Benevolent Queen told him?"

Augustus froze mid-drink, narrowed his eyes to slits, then swallowed his wine with an exaggerated gulp. "I'm not going to dignify that with a response."

"But he knows things." Dellwyn widened her eyes. "He has gadgets. What if—"

"No. We both know that's not possible." Augustus *tutted*. "Since when is your non-belief so easily shaken?"

Dellwyn bit her lip. "It's not. I don't believe in Her. But that doesn't mean She's not real."

"Yes, it does." Augustus crossed his arms. "She is a legend from that fundamentalist, shit-shoveling village, a figment of his heat-scrambled imagination, that's all."

Dellwyn looked down at her chest, noticing that she had begun to scratch at her skin. She rested her hand on the table, and Augustus reached across and placed his over it. "Look, I know you've been having a difficult time since Aya left."

"Aya has nothing to do—"

"Yes, she does." Augustus squeezed her hand. "You've been searching for something to fill the gap Aya left when she moved back to Portside. At first, it was taking in Sybil. Then it was trying to be Madam Huxley's prodigy. Now it's religion."

Dellwyn pulled her hand away. "How did you know I was interested in running the Rudder?"

Augustus smirked. "Delly, you know Madam Huxley can't resist my charm. I like to stay aware of everything that happens behind closed doors. It's not only my unique services that raised me to Room B."

"Do I have any competition?" Dellwyn interlaced her fingers. "I mean, it will be years until Madam Huxley is ready to retire. Things could change, but I'd like to know, just in case."

"Of course you have competition." Augustus chuckled. "Do you really think everyone else is content to be bedded for the rest of their lives?"

Dellwyn shrugged. "Until recently, I was."

Augustus pointed at her with his cup. "Well, not everyone gets to open up for the dashing Lord Collingwood and his parade of presents."

Dellwyn started to protest but instead pressed her lips together. She had been fortunate. From the first time she'd served him, Lord Collingwood had picked Dellwyn out as his favorite. Once she'd received her own room, Lord Collingwood had never let another courtesan touch him. She had always been his.

"You need sleep." Augustus yawned. "And so do I."

Dellwyn grimaced. "I don't know if I can."

"You will." Augustus stood. "Go home, have a bite to eat, then curl up in your blankets. The mean old farmer can't get you there."

Dellwyn wanted to glare at Augustus, but the teasing smile

on his face stopped her. She rose. "Fine. But only because I want to."

"Yes, yes, independent woman." Augustus put his hands up. "Seriously, though, do you feel better? Do you feel safe?"

"I do." Dellwyn touched his arm. "Thank you for listening. And for the wine."

"I'd say any time, but I don't like to share."

Dellwyn smiled. "Your problems or wine?"

Augustus's face was solemn. "Both."

They said their goodbyes, and Dellwyn stepped out of the house into the sunshine. Now that she was out of the safety of Augustus's home, goosebumps pricked her forearms. Her eyes searched the nearby homes again.

"It's just your nerves," she whispered. Her footsteps were small but quick, in time with her racing heart. "Everything is as it's always been."

She winced. That sentiment didn't make her feel any better. She turned to look back at Augustus's house, hoping the feeling of comfort would reach out to her from within and fill her with enough security to get home and into bed.

And that was when she saw him. Nestled flat against the side of Augustus's house, shimmied up right under the window. A man dressed in all black.

9

———

"Hey!" Dellwyn called out.

The man's head snapped in her direction, but she was too far away to see his face. She pulled up her skirt and jogged back toward the house. When he realized she meant to chase him, the man stumbled backward against the wall. He caught himself then reeled around and dashed behind the structure.

"Shit." Dellwyn ran faster, gathering her skirt up higher with one hand and holding her bobbing breasts down with the other.

When she reached Augustus's house, she banged her fist against the wall. "Augustus! Come out here!"

He didn't answer her. Either he had already fallen back to sleep or did not care for more of her drama. Muttering another curse, Dellwyn rounded his house. The black-clothed man had made it to the Portside-Sternville anchor line and stopped. He shaded his eyes and looked back toward the house, no doubt checking to see whether she would follow him.

"It's going to take… more than that… to lose me!" Dellwyn shouted at him between breaths. "Maybe just a minute more…" she whispered to herself. She was not accustomed to this sort of exertion, and between her corset, her aching hips, and her carefully kept voluptuous shape, she didn't know how far she could chase after the man. But she wanted to at least get close enough to see who he was. It had to be the farmer—or perhaps one of his farmer friends doing his spying for him. Who else in Desertera would be self-loathing enough to wear all black in the sun? But she wasn't about to take her paranoia's word for it.

When she kept advancing on him, the man turned and bolted into Portside. As Dellwyn passed under the anchor chain, she saw him dart down Cobbler Street. She nearly laughed at the irony, given that this running would probably be the final blow to her old leather shoes.

People filled the lane—delivering the morning's goods, fetching their daily ration of water, visiting with neighbors—and the bustle slowed the man down. He weaved through the crowd, quiet and slick, like sand slipping through crevices. Dellwyn didn't have his need for stealth. She hollered at the people in front of her to make way, and upon seeing an unkempt courtesan barreling down the street, most of them leaped backward, some shielding the eyes of their children. The clear path allowed her to return to a jog and save some of her breath while still gaining ground on the man.

By the end of Cobbler Street, only about twenty feet separated Dellwyn and the man. From the glimpses she got of his short, slender frame as it appeared between people, she became ever more confident that he was the farmer. He was not wearing his tool belt—a smart move, given that the clanging of his tools would have alerted Dellwyn to his presence sooner—but he still had a flat cap atop his head, and he held it in place with one hand as he ran. Dellwyn begged the wind to blow it off so she could spy the man's hair color, or so he would turn and reveal his face.

The farmer rounded a corner and broke free from the crowd. His gait changed to a sprint, and Dellwyn watched his figure shrink in the distance. She tried to increase her pace, but a sharp pain stabbed into her side, and she realized she could run no further. She halted in the middle of Blacksmith Lane and hunched over to gulp in as much air as her lungs would allow.

Before she could catch her breath, someone grabbed her elbow and jerked her upright. Fearing that the farmer had come back for her, Dellwyn yelped and yanked her arm away. She looked up into the face of a palace guard. His eyebrows were knitted together, and his mouth pressed into a hard line.

"Damn it," Dellwyn muttered. She returned her hands to her sides because clenching her abdomen seemed to be the only way to ease the stabbing pain.

The guard glared at her. "What did you say, whore?"

"I said 'Damn it.'" Dellwyn sucked in a long breath, taking a moment to scan his uniform. She didn't recognize the patch on chest. *Damn it, indeed.* "That was exhausting."

The guard's steely eyes appraised her. "You mean that little show you put on back there?"

"It wasn't a show." Dellwyn crossed her arms, her indignation outweighing her physical discomfort. "I was chasing someone. A man. He's been stalking me. If you want to interrogate someone, go find him."

"Right now, I'm concerned with you." The guard gestured to Dellwyn's clothing. "You're barely dressed. You aren't decent to be seen."

Dellwyn looked down at her outfit. Yes, her cloak had billowed behind her in her running, but her breasts hadn't fallen out of her corset, and her skirt covered her legs. A little cleavage never hurt anyone.

She lifted her gaze to retort, only to realize that the disrupted crowd of villagers had gathered around them to watch the spectacle. She felt herself blush under their scrutiny, but the heat in her cheeks quickly turned to rage.

"I'm not decent to be seen?" Dellwyn laughed and pointed out to the crowd. "As if you and half of Portside haven't seen women like me before. In fact, I see a few familiar faces." Dellwyn wheeled on the villagers, and many averted their eyes. She didn't actually see anyone she recognized, not for certain, but she knew there had to be clients in the crowd. She wanted them, and everyone else, to know that she wasn't the only one who should be ashamed.

"That's another matter." The guard's voice was calm, condescending. "How one dresses in private and in polite society are two different issues. You cannot run through the streets unclothed with your..." The guard gestured to her chest. A mumble of consent and a few chuckles chorused through the crowd.

"Ah, yes, they're nearly popping out, aren't they?" Dellwyn made no move to reposition her corset. "Well, I apologize for interrupting everyone's morning, but I will not apologize for my attire or for trying to catch the man who has been stalking me."

The guard held out his hand. "I understand that you were distressed, Madam, but I still must detain you."

Madam. Dellwyn smiled. *Doesn't that sound lovely?* Pleased as she was with the title, it took her a moment to register what the guard had said.

"Detain me?" She swatted his extended hand. "Whatever for? The last time I checked, His Majesty had no laws about what women wear in *polite society*."

A few women in the crowd stated their agreement, and a few others snickered at Dellwyn's mocking of the guard.

"That may be so, but His Majesty has requested that we bring any behavior we judge inappropriate or dangerous before him and his council." The guard straightened. "They are using these situations to craft new laws, and I daresay"—his eyes fell to Dellwyn's chest once again, and his mouth curved into a devious smile—"your attire will be deemed far too dangerous for public viewing."

Someone stepped forward from the crowd. "I must object, sir." Dellwyn craned her neck around the guard to see Aya's tiny frame squared in defiance. "I seem to recall His Majesty has a soft spot for dangerous women, especially when unclothed."

The guard's face turned bright red and—to Dellwyn's

immense satisfaction and slight horror—he knelt before Aya. "Miss Cogsmith, my deepest apologies."

Aya, too, seemed unnerved at the guard's show of respect. Her face turned a matching shade of crimson, and she frantically waved her hands, beckoning the guard to stand. As he did, Aya shook her head. "What in Desertera was that about?"

The guard glanced between Aya and Dellwyn, his face a muddle of confusion. "His Majesty has instructed the guards to treat you as our queen."

Dellwyn barely contained her shocked guffaw by clasping her hand over her mouth. Aya did the same, but her face had turned pale, and fear shone in her wide green eyes. "Please remind His Majesty that I am not your queen."

The guard tugged on his leather armor. "Miss Cogsmith, it is not my place to—"

Aya marched up to him and stared up into his eyes. The top of her head barely reached the guard's shoulder, and if Dellwyn hadn't been so furious and embarrassed by the whole exhibition, she might have laughed.

"So, you insist on treating me as your queen?" Aya waited for the guard to nod. "Fine. Then I *order* you to deliver a message to His Majesty. Can you remember it?"

The guard swallowed hard before nodding again.

"Deliver this message to him in these exact words." Aya poked the guard's chest. "Willem, you consummate asshole, you command your guards to treat me exactly like every other citizen."

"I can't." The guard stepped away from Aya. "That would be—"

"He won't punish you for it. He's not like Archon." Aya's face twisted into something between fury and pain, and Dellwyn thought her friend might spit in the dirt. "He'll know it's from me. He'll probably *reward* you even, knowing his sense of humor."

"I... I..." The guard kept backing away, and Aya matched him step for step.

"*I* gave you an order." She pointed toward the ship. "Follow it."

The guard seemed to recover his senses, and he bowed low before turning and scurrying toward the palace. A section of the crowd separated to let him through, and Dellwyn put her head down. In the midst of watching Aya and the guard, she had forgotten about the onlookers. But there they stood, gawking as Dellwyn was chastised by a guard then rescued by the king's lover. Indignation bubbled up in Dellwyn's throat. She had been standing up to the guard. She would have talked her way out of it, sooner or later.

"What are you all looking at?" Aya pivoted in a circle, staring down the nosy villagers. "Go back to your lives. The spectacle's over."

Dellwyn walked up to her friend, and Aya reached out and placed a hand on her arm. "I'm sorry about barging in like that." She led Dellwyn away from the villagers. "You were giving that guard a good verbal thrashing, but I just couldn't let you fight him alone. You saved me so many times in Sternville; I thought it was only right I come to your aid in Portside."

Though Dellwyn's skin still burned, her anger simmered down. It was a fair trade. She offered a smile. "I would have worn him down eventually."

"While I have no doubt in your powers of wit, trust me when I say, that guard would have matched your cleverness with stubbornness." Aya's brow furrowed. "I've seen him around before. He rarely lets up once he sets his mind on berating someone. I thought if I jumped in, I could get the crowd to turn on him."

Dellwyn smirked. "I understand." She could have allowed the subject to drop there, but a little teasing seemed a fitting penance for Aya embarrassing her. "So, when is the wedding?"

They had reached Aya's shop, and Aya glared at Dellwyn over her shoulder as she unlocked the door. "Oh, there's that wit again."

"What?" Dellwyn widened her eyes. "I'm simply asking... Your Highness."

Aya grabbed Dellwyn's elbow and pulled her into the shop. She slammed the door behind them and whirled around to face Dellwyn. Her face had turned bright red again, and Dellwyn found herself giggling openly now that the danger had passed.

Aya stomped over to her dining table and collapsed into a chair. "It's not funny, Dellwyn."

Dellwyn sat down across from her. "It's a little funny."

"No, it's not. Besides the fact that it is entirely disrespectful to me and my wishes, it creates such a horrible impression on the people. Will—Lionel can't give me special treatment like that. Do you know how it makes us look?"

"Do you think it could have been a joke?" Dellwyn smoothed down her hair, finally realizing how frazzled her appearance had become in her chase. "Surely, His Majesty would have known how you would react."

"I don't know." Aya huffed and crossed her arms, retreating into herself the way she always did when she felt vulnerable. "Either way, it's a careless thing to do as a leader and cruel to me. Do you know how much people in Portside loathe me?"

Dellwyn froze while retying her cloak. "Why would they hate you? Aren't you like some kind of savior returning to the people?" She gestured to the machines cluttering the shop.

"Hardly. First, they spurned me because they thought my father was a traitor. Then, they despised me for whoring myself to survive." Aya flinched at the sentiment and looked at Dellwyn with guilty eyes. Dellwyn waved it away with her hand. "Now, they hate me for how I returned to my shop. They have no idea that I helped get rid of Archon. They think I screwed Lionel until he gave me my shop back. They think I'm a *great* whore."

At that, they both chuckled. Dellwyn went quiet and stroked her hair, averting her gaze from Aya's. "I'm sorry. I didn't realize it had been difficult for you here."

Aya shrugged. "I didn't want you to worry."

Dellwyn reached out and patted Aya's hand. "I always worry about you." As bad as she felt that Aya had to put up with the judgmental villagers, her chest loosened at the knowledge that she wouldn't lose Aya to them. "But it's nice to know that I've been worrying about the wrong things."

A loud knock thudded against the door, and Dellwyn jumped up, tipping over her chair. "He found me!" she gasped.

Aya held a finger to her lips and tiptoed to the door. She peeked through the peephole, groaned, and wrenched open the door. "Can I help you?"

Dellwyn peered around Aya to see another palace guard. This one bore a badge depicting a golden bird perched atop a golden cog. With a sigh of relief, Dellwyn picked up her chair and sat back down.

"His Majesty sends his apologies, Miss Cogsmith," the guard said.

Dellwyn shook her head. King Lionel certainly worked fast; she had to give him that.

"This is unnecessary." Aya's voice sounded firm, but her eyes sparkled.

"His Majesty insists."

Dellwyn's eyebrows rose. Did King Lionel send Aya another gift? She looked around the front room. It overflowed with books and mechanical devices. Anyone else would have thought they were simply tools of the cogsmith's craft, but Dellwyn knew they all came from the king—partly out of necessity for Aya to perform her trade, but mostly out of devotion.

"Of course he does." Aya sighed. "Tell him that I accept his apology, but that sending me gifts is in direct opposition to my request."

"Yes, Miss Cogsmith. Anything else?"

"No. That's all." Aya closed the door and walked back to the table. Despite her protests, she carried a large, rectangular object. She turned it around for Dellwyn to see. It was a painting of a body of water surrounded by tall, green plants. A creature sat on a green circle in the middle of the water, and Dellwyn realized it was a frog—a real one.

Aya laid the painting on the table and returned to her seat.

Dellwyn reached out and touched the intricately carved frame, finding the wood smooth under her fingertips. The gift wasn't even for her, and her heart swelled in her chest. She could only imagine how it must make Aya feel.

Dellwyn wanted to ask Aya how long she intended to snub the king, but as she opened her mouth, Aya held up her hand. "Don't. I'm not repeating everything I've already said."

Dellwyn pressed her lips together. Her fingers hovered over the canvas, but she dared not touch it for fear the paint would chip. Even still, it was as if they were connected—her and the artist. The painting was a bridge through time and space, allowing them to share something intangible, if only for a moment.

"Who were you chasing?" Aya's voice brought Dellwyn back to the present. "And why are you worried that he would have followed you here?"

Dellwyn shook her head. She had purposefully gone to Augustus instead of Aya to help her figure out what was going on with the farmer, yet there she sat in Aya's shop, about to tell her friend everything anyway. It made Dellwyn wonder if there was such a thing as fate and whether there was any use in trying to escape it.

Without meeting Aya's concerned gaze, Dellwyn recounted her experiences with the farmer. While she spoke, Aya remained quiet, the creases on her forehead growing deeper with each encounter Dellwyn recalled. When she finished, Aya let out a long sigh, as if she hadn't breathed through Dellwyn's entire tale. "Does he have strange eyes? Each one a different color?"

A jolt of fear pierced Dellwyn's chest. "How did you know that? Is he harassing you, too?"

"No, but I've seen him before." Aya brushed her hands on her skirt, and specks of dust flew into the air. "Do you remember, during my mission, the day Lord Varick sent me to the bathing house?"

"Of course." Dellwyn grinned. "I don't think I've ever seen you so excited, or so clean."

Aya narrowed her eyes at the jest. "Indeed. Well, if it is the same man, he was outside the bathing house that day. He was preaching about water, how we shouldn't waste it on our flesh. And of course, he worked fidelity in as well."

"That sounds like him."

Aya nodded. "The messages in the sand, even the camping outside of the Rudder, I understand. They both follow in line with the farmer's past activities. But lurking outside Augustus's home? Spying on you? That doesn't seem like something a prophet would concern himself with. Not that you're not fascinating, but why would he care about you when he thinks he needs to save the entire kingdom?"

"I don't know." Dellwyn wrapped her arms around herself to prevent the shiver that threatened to course through her body. "You're right, it's strange behavior for a street prophet. But it had to be him. The farmer had to learn my name somehow, and the man I chased wore all black, exactly like a farmer."

"But you didn't see his face." Aya gave Dellwyn a hard look. "You can't assume it was him because of his clothing."

"I know it was. I can't explain; I just know." Dellwyn bit her lip. "Can you please believe me?"

Aya's mouth curved into a soft smile. "Of course I can. Is there any way I can help? Do you want me to ask around the villages or see if any of the nobles acted as his landlord?"

"No. I don't want word getting out about him. He's already going to cause enough trouble for the Rudder with his camping stunt." Dellwyn's gaze drifted around the room, and as her eyes scanned the gadgets, she nearly slapped her forehead. "There is something! I was so wrapped up in everything that happened today, I forgot about his device."

Aya sat straight up in her chair, her eyes bright with curiosity. "His device?"

"Yes. I think he had a clock, but I'm not sure." Dellwyn motioned with her hands. "It was a circular object, all metal, and there was a bar bisecting it that spun around the face."

Aya stood and walked to the back of the shop. She called out over her shoulder. "Did it have numbers on the face?"

"Numbers, symbols, all kinds of lines." Dellwyn squinted. "It was about the size of both my hands put together."

Aya emerged from the back room with a circular object. It was white with black numbers around the edges and two bars that seemed able to move independently of one another. "This is a clock. Did it look like this?"

Dellwyn shook her head. "No. Like I said, it was made of metal. The markings were all engraved and much smaller than that. Some were around the edges, like those numbers and notches, but some of the lines wove through the middle of the circle as well. Plus, there was only one bar that spun around the center, not two."

Aya nodded and placed the clock down next to the painting. "Did the farmer do anything with the device, or did he just glance at it?"

"He held it up in front of his face." Dellwyn demonstrated, lifting her hand as if something dangled in front of her. "He looked up at the stars and aligned the bar with one of them. Then, he saw where it matched up with the markings, and he told me the Rudder would open in about eleven minutes."

"I think you were on the right track. It must be some kind of time-telling device. I'd say it measures time against the sun and stars like we do, only in a more precise manner." Aya tapped her fingers on the table. "The other markings must have a different purpose. Navigational, perhaps. In the books I'm reading, it talks about devices that the sailors used to map their way across the ocean, before the flood, of course. It might be related to that."

Dellwyn didn't understand what use a device like that would be to the farmer, and she frowned. "Will you look into it?"

Aya beamed. "Try and stop me."

Dellwyn returned her smile. "Thank you. I know I sound insane, but the farmer's obsession with the Rudder, and now with me, has me on edge."

"You'll be fine." Aya squeezed Dellwyn's hand. "Even if he comes after you, he's a sickly little fellow. You can take him."

Dellwyn scoffed. "I might be nervous, but I know I can handle him. It's not me I'm worried about; it's the other girls. Some of them are young and fragile. If he did anything to Sybil—Sybil!" Dellwyn bolted upright. "I have to go. What if he went to our hovel after I lost him in the crowd?"

Aya followed Dellwyn to the door. "He was running from you. He's not about to go back to your home. I'm sure she's fine."

Dellwyn took a deep breath, hoping Aya's logic was right. "But still, I didn't come home after work. She's probably worried."

"I'm sure she is." Aya opened the door. "You take care of Sybil. And yourself. I'll see what I can find out about this device."

"Thanks." Dellwyn rushed out the door and made for Sternville. As she hurried through the streets of Portside, she realized two things.

First, Aya would always be her friend. Even though Aya had her father's shop back and was being pursued by King Lionel, she was still Aya, and she still loved Dellwyn. Neither of them fit perfectly in their so-called homes, but they fit perfectly together.

Second, she shouldn't run. Ever. Her leg muscles burned, and her feet ached from her stiff, pinching shoes. Running, even for such a short time, had left her sorer than any rough client she had ever served. Then again, her aching hips from room reassignments hadn't helped either. She slowed to a walk and smiled to herself, thinking how relaxing it would be to lie back and let Lord Collingwood exhaust her tonight.

10

———

"And for that matter, you could have been kidnapped." Sybil hung on Dellwyn's arm as they walked to the Rudder. The kidnapping line was the latest in a string of reasons why Dellwyn could never again leave the Rudder, or the hovel, without informing Sybil of her destination first.

Dellwyn had arrived home mid-morning to find Sybil pacing across the floor, her copper hair a frizzy mess from running her fingers through it. At first, Dellwyn feared that Sybil was upset with someone else, that the farmer had found her and scared her somehow. But Dellwyn's worry hadn't lasted long. Sybil had run straight to her, hugged her, then immediately started in with a lecture: "Where have you been all morning? I was worried sick about you. I thought a client had harmed you. What would I have done if you didn't come back?"

The reprimanding had continued through the afternoon—though Sybil had paused to allow Dellwyn a long nap—and had resumed the moment Dellwyn emerged for dinner. Underneath her lengthy groans and dramatic eye rolls, Dellwyn had to admit, Sybil's concern touched her. It was comforting to know how much Sybil cared.

Though, she was regretting telling Sybil about the farmer.

"Seriously, this farmer sounds dangerous." Sybil squeezed

Dellwyn's arm on the last word. "What if he hadn't run away from you and had snatched you up instead? Or what if Aya hadn't been there to shelp? You could have been arrested—and I would have had no idea where you went. I would have had to go back to live at the Rudder. And with how busy it is—"

Dellwyn stopped walking and placed her hands on Sybil's shoulders. "Breathe." Sybil did, deeply. "Nothing happened to me. We're both fine. And you never have to worry. If anything ever *does* happen to me, Augustus or Aya will take care of you. You won't have to take a position like mine at the Rudder—not for many years, and not unless you want to."

"How do you know?" Sybil pushed the dirt around with her foot. "How do you know they wouldn't turn me away? It's happened before."

"Don't talk like that." Dellwyn tucked a curl behind Sybil's ear. "Augustus loves you, and Aya would never abandon you, especially not after what happened to her when she was young. You're worth protecting."

Sybil lifted her chin, and her lips twitched at the corners. "Really?"

Dellwyn pretended not to notice the tears that welled in the girl's eyes. "Absolutely."

Sybil feigned a yawn and wiped at her eyes with the sleeve of her cloak. "All this worrying about you is exhausting."

Dellwyn playfully jabbed Sybil's side. "Now you know how I feel."

Sybil smiled, and they continued walking to the Rudder in silence. As they neared Mrs. Pattie Wellman's hovel, Dellwyn heard a chorus of voices drifting through the desert air. The sound grew louder with each step she and Sybil took, though the words were indistinguishable. Sybil grabbed Dellwyn's arm again and looked up at her with wide eyes.

"I'm sure everything is fine." The lie felt sour in her mouth. She could guess what was happening ahead, and everything was not fine. Still, Sybil had worried enough for one day. If Dellwyn held her composure, maybe she could keep Sybil calm long enough to get inside where it would be safe.

As they emerged from behind the last row of tents, Dellwyn's eyes scanned the scene. Her suspicions had been right. An angry crowd gathered around the entrance to the Rudder, and although Dellwyn could not see past the throng of sweaty bodies, she could hear the farmer shouting above the dull roar of the mob. "You must control your carnal desires! This institution of unfaithfulness must fall!"

Dellwyn turned to Sybil and held her by the shoulders. "We've got to go through them." Sybil's face paled at her words, and Dellwyn gave her a reassuring smile. "Remember, the crowd is on our side. They want the farmer to leave and let them enjoy the Rudder's services. They won't hurt us."

Sybil bit her lip and stared at the barricade of backs—nearly as wide as the palace's stern and six bodies deep—all jostling and bumping into one another like tumbleweeds trapped in a canyon. "Are you sure?"

Dellwyn swallowed. She didn't know. But she hoped the villagers were thinking clearly enough to allow them to pass.

The farmer's voice rang out again. "The Benevolent Queen demands fidelity!"

Dellwyn sighed. "We don't have a choice. Stay close to me and don't let go of my hand."

Sybil nodded, her knuckles turning white as her fingers laced through Dellwyn's. Dellwyn fought the urge to cringe at Sybil's tight grip and instead squeezed back. She led Sybil toward the edge of the crowd, where it was thinner. The side of the palace offered a direct line to the Rudder's entrance. If they could shimmy their way to the front row, they could slip through the propellers without going near the rowdiest individuals—or the farmer himself.

Dellwyn stepped up to the back of the crowd and reached her arm in between two women. "Excuse us. We need to get through." The women went to stand closer together, but when they saw Dellwyn's stockings peeking out from under her cloak, they nodded and allowed her and Sybil to pass. Dellwyn muttered her thanks, aware that, first and foremost, she was in a mob of clients and needed to be polite.

"Deny your lust, and Her waters will cleanse you!"

They made it by the next row of people just as easily, but as they reached the center of the crowd, the bodies packed in tighter and the noise grew louder. Dellwyn stopped, watching for an opening to naturally emerge as the onlookers shuffled from foot to foot or leaned over to holler at the person next to them.

The man in front of her bent down to talk to the woman beside him and allowed Dellwyn her first glimpse of the farmer. She expected her heart to start racing but found herself breathing calmly as she observed the farmer from her concealed position in the crowd—perhaps the only safe part about the mob. Sure enough, the farmer appeared as short and slender as the man who had chased her, and the proof plastered a smug smile onto her face. He still wore his black clothing, though he had retrieved his tool belt from wherever he had stashed it while he spied on her and Augustus.

A poorly erected tent squatted in the sand beside the propellers. The farmer had fashioned it out of copper pipes and a length of tarp, tied together with leather straps. Dellwyn wondered if he had gone to Bowtown after he'd escaped her pursuit to gather supplies for his tent. She assumed that was where he lived, or at least had at one time.

The farmer's mismatched eyes bulged bigger than Dellwyn had seen them do before, and a shiver slipped down her spine. "The Benevolent Queen is always watching. She sees everything Her children do. You must cease your wickedness, or She will never save us!"

Something flew out of the crowd—a piece of rotten meat —and hit the farmer in the chest. Sybil shrieked and scooted closer to Dellwyn, while the bodies around them jostled with hearty laughter. With one hand, Dellwyn covered her nose, and with the other, she gripped Sybil's hand tighter. But her eyes never left the self-proclaimed prophet.

The farmer kept preaching, but his face reddened, and his voice stuttered. At this show of weakness, the crowd crushed in tighter around him. The first row of people stood only an arm's length away from the farmer. The movement sent Dellwyn lurching forward, and she found herself wedged between two burly men, her body pressed flat against the back of another. A pain in her arm told her that she still had a grip on Sybil, though the girl was further back in the crowd, and both of their limbs strained to stay connected.

For the first time, the noise of the crowd overpowered the farmer's speech. Dellwyn began to sweat, and not just from the heat of the bodies.

"Get away from the Rudder, you fool!"

"What an ass!"

"We'll do whatever we damn please!"

"Your queen ain't watchin' nothin'!"

A tug wrenched Dellwyn's arm, and a scream followed. The mob had pulled Sybil away. Dellwyn couldn't move, but she craned her neck, trying to see where Sybil had gone. Surely, Sybil stood nearby—she was probably shoved to one side, enough to make her hand slip out of Dellwyn's grasp. Dellwyn tried calling Sybil's name, but the mob's shouts and cackles drowned out her voice.

Suddenly, the crowd—and the farmer—fell quiet. Dellwyn turned back to the farmer, expecting him to have regained their attention somehow, and her stomach nearly dropped to her feet.

A man had emerged from the crowd, and he held Sybil in front of him. One hand gripped the back of her neck, and the other slid around her waist, pinning her backside against him. Sybil stood stiff, clearly too scared to struggle against the man. Not that it would have done any good. He was tall, muscular, and—judging from his mud-covered boots and the sharp trowel that hung from his belt—a digger, a wellman in charge of widening and deepening the wells by hand. Dellwyn's lungs begged to cry for help, but she swallowed down the urge. What would this man do to Sybil if he felt challenged?

"Look what I found, Farmer." The digger nestled his nose into Sybil's hair and breathed in deeply. "A fresh little Rudderling."

The farmer squared his stance. "Let her go."

"I don't think I will." The digger's hand traveled up Sybil's side. He gripped her small breast, and Sybil's quivering lip stilled long enough for her teeth to clench. "I think I'll take her on inside. I think I'll do all kinds of nasty things to her while your Benevolent Queen watches."

"You will not." One of the farmer's hands balled into a fist, and Dellwyn watched the other twitch toward his scythe.

No, he couldn't do that. It would start a fight, and Sybil would be the first casualty. Dellwyn pushed her way through the crowd. The digger was so caught up in himself that he either didn't notice the grunts and exclamations of the people Dellwyn shoved, or he didn't care.

"Oh, I will. I bet I can moisten this little girl and your queen right up." The digger goaded the farmer, his hand sliding back down Sybil's body. Too low. But Dellwyn was almost there. Only a few people stood between her and Sybil. She reached her arm out, grabbing for the digger's shoulder, but before her hand connected with him, he dropped to the ground.

Dellwyn broke through the crowd and grabbed Sybil in her arms. The contact seemed to jar Sybil from her trance, and she collapsed into sobs against Dellwyn's body. "Shh. It's all right now. You're safe."

The farmer stood with the scythe in his hand, blunt side extended. His eyes were lifted to the Benevolent Queen in silent prayer. The digger lay unconscious on the ground, a purple bump already forming on his temple. Part of the crowd dispersed—the excitement and energy of the heckling ruined by the digger's crude display. The other part stayed to gape— the farmer's sudden, violent outburst inspiring fear and respect.

"Go now." The farmer's voice was deep, quiet, and he did not move his eyes from the sky. The lingering individuals shared uncertain glances. "The Benevolent Queen wants no more of your scorn this evening."

Dellwyn watched over the crest of Sybil's head as the rest of the villagers trickled away. When the last person had finally turned his back, Dellwyn glanced between the farmer and the digger, who still lay motionless on the ground. "Will he be all right?" she asked, nodding toward the unconscious man.

The farmer started, as if she had awoken him from a deep sleep. "I don't know. He is at Her mercy now."

Dellwyn leaned over Sybil's shuddering frame and spat on the digger's back. "You used the wrong end."

"He did not deserve death." The farmer tucked the scythe into his tool belt. "But the Benevolent Queen allows violence in the defense of the innocent."

Dellwyn thought that seemed fair. After all, if the stories were to be believed, the Benevolent Queen banished the Almighty King and stripped Him of all His power. It would be hypocritical of Her not to allow Her children a good beating from time to time.

"And what does She say about stalking the innocent?"

The farmer blushed. "What do you mean?"

Dellwyn glared at him and raised her chin. "We both know what I mean." She didn't want to say what needed to be said next, but she had her own sense of morality to obey. "I appreciate what you did—saving Sybil from that madman."

The farmer smiled, and Dellwyn nearly growled the rest of her warning. "But if you come near me, or her, or Augustus again, I will alert the guards, and I will see you thrown in the dungeon. Need I remind you, I have *very* close connections to His Majesty—the *real* monarch in charge—and I'm not afraid to have him arrest you."

"I don't understand." The farmer shook his head, once again staring up to the sky. The orange glow of the setting sun seemed to reflect in his glassy eyes. "I'm trying to save you. All of you."

"Well, stop." Dellwyn gently pushed Sybil away and wiped the remaining tears from the girl's eyes. "Let's get you inside."

Sybil nodded and allowed Dellwyn to lead her through the propellers. Without looking back at the farmer, Dellwyn said, "We don't need your saving."

THE REST of the Rudder's workers huddled around Madam Huxley's podium. Although Dellwyn could not determine the words, she could hear the low, authoritative tone of the madam's voice, met every few seconds by murmurs or sighs. When the sound of Dellwyn and Sybil's footsteps echoed through the lobby, several heads whipped around—some faces showed relief, some fear, others disgust.

Augustus rushed over and embraced them both. He pulled away, but Sybil didn't let go. Her fists fastened her arms around his muscular torso like a belt.

"Are you okay?" His blue eyes shone with concern, and he stroked Sybil's hair. "What happened?"

"We're both fine." Dellwyn glanced over her shoulder, as if the mob were still surrounding the entrance. "A man in the crowd grabbed her and used her to taunt the farmer."

Augustus's eyebrows knitted together. "Used her?"

"He didn't hurt me." Sybil's voice was muffled against his shirt, but it did not waver. This time, Augustus's eyebrows rose with a silent question, and Dellwyn nodded.

Sybil pulled away and stared up at Augustus with a stony resolve. "He wouldn't have done anything. He just scared me."

At Sybil's bravery, Dellwyn felt as if her heart had swollen and risen up into her throat. This was merely the first of a thousand thoughtless cruelties Sybil would undergo if she stayed at the Rudder—and at fourteen, she was already being forced to harden herself against them.

"Are you happy, Dellwyn?" Madam Huxley's tone cut through Dellwyn's thoughts like a knife through goat butter.

"Pardon, Madam?" Dellwyn stepped forward to join the group. Kalinda and Jasmine parted, allowing her a place directly across from Madam Huxley. A rare sheen of sweat glistened across her décolletage. Alisa, who stood on Madam Huxley's left, looked even worse—her entire front, from forehead to shoulders, had flushed crimson, and her nails left half-moon indentations on her skin where she gripped her crossed arms.

"This is all your doing." Madam Huxley's eyes narrowed. "I wanted to call the guards on the farmer. You and Alisa insisted that he be allowed to camp outside our entrance. And now look what's happened."

Dellwyn scanned the faces of her coworkers. Their features revealed varying degrees of upset, but none of them appeared to be harmed. "Is everyone all right?"

"Apparently, poor Sybil was violated in the street." Madam Huxley's lips twisted into something between a concerned grimace and a smile, then ended up in a snarl. "Thanks to you."

Sybil stomped her foot. "I was not!"

Dellwyn's fists clenched, and she felt heat flushing her face, partly out of indignation and partly out of shame. Madam Huxley might not have been exaggerating the truth too far. "You heard Sybil. Besides, *the farmer* is the one who stopped the man."

Madam Huxley smirked. "And yet, if he hadn't been there in the first place—"

"It doesn't matter," Dellwyn snapped. "It's over now. The crowd left."

"See?" Alisa spoke through clenched teeth. "I told you it would break up before nightfall."

"Yes." Madam Huxley tapped her fingernails on the podium. "You also predicted that we would be busy tonight on account of the farmer's dramatics."

Alisa glanced at Dellwyn. "I did."

She could practically read the fuming blonde's thoughts: *Shit. Now what?*

"Well then, if there are extra customers to attend to, I suppose you're the one to serve them." Madam Huxley looked Alisa up and down, narrowed eyes begging her to refuse. "After all, I'm sure your brilliant foresight will tell you exactly what they want."

One of the new girls huffed. "And what if the rest of us want to earn the extra wages?"

"*You* should consider yourself fortunate that I'm not doling out room assignments tonight. Given Alisa's prediction, I'm going to keep you all on for another evening." Madam Huxley reached out and patted the young woman's hand. "Besides, my dear, who said anything about extra wages?"

The girl froze under the madam's touch. Alisa gritted her teeth so tightly that Dellwyn could hear them scraping together. She didn't blame Alisa. The recent influx of clients had already pushed the workers to their limits each night. To take on even more customers without more pay—Dellwyn's knees squeezed together at the thought.

"Madam, I hate to be a killjoy"—Augustus slipped in on the madam's right, his charming smile already gleaming—"but there are very strict regulations on labor and wages. Given His Majesty's current obsession with the laws, I don't think now is a wise time to break any."

Madam Huxley glared at Dellwyn and Alisa. "And who would tell?" She didn't bother to threaten any of the other workers, and Dellwyn wondered if the action showed trust or arrogance.

"That's the thing about gossip." Augustus placed his chin on his fist and leaned his elbow against the podium. Even Dellwyn found herself amused by his boyish grin. "In the end, it doesn't matter who starts it or how it spreads—only that it does."

Madam Huxley pursed her lips. Dellwyn imagined the calculations swarming in the madam's head, along with whispered words and royal decrees stacking themselves on top of one another.

"Fine." Madam Huxley smiled. It seemed genuine, and Dellwyn nearly gasped. "Alisa will receive *something* in recompense for her additional labor this evening."

The madam turned to Alisa. Augustus widened his eyes at Alisa, another silent statement. After a haughty sigh, Alisa raised her chin. "Thank you, Madam."

"You're welcome, dear." Madam Huxley clapped her hands together. "Now then, current workers, off to your rooms. Prospective workers, I'll assign shifts momentarily. The sun has set, and we've dallied in the lobby too long."

Dellwyn glanced at the entrance and noticed the soft evening light filtering through the propellers. Her shoulders shook—a shiver of instinct more than actual cold.

The workers hurried away, many sharing nervous glances or frustrated whispers. No doubt they'd had enough of Madam Huxley and Alisa's drama for the evening. Dellwyn had had enough for a lifetime.

"Dellwyn?" Madam Huxley's voice had shifted to the lilt she used with clients.

She swallowed. "Yes, Madam?"

"I would have asked you to help Alisa this evening, but your night has been reserved."

Dellwyn fought the urge to grin. In her preoccupation with the farmer, she had forgotten Lord Collingwood would be coming that night—but she would thank him in every way she knew how.

Madam Huxley placed a hand over her chest. "My, my, Lord Derringher will be delighted to know you are so thrilled to serve him."

Dellwyn opened her mouth to correct the madam but quickly shut it. Another rush of heat flushed her. *Thank goodness I'm not fair-skinned.* As long as Dellwyn held her features steady, she could cling to the frail satisfaction that Madam Huxley couldn't read the embarrassment on her flesh.

Only pride kept Dellwyn from asking about Lord Collingwood. Had Madam Huxley purposefully rescheduled Dellwyn's evening? Or had Lord Collingwood failed to make his appointment early enough, thus leaving Dellwyn open to Lord Derringher, to the madam's delight?

"Of course, Lord Collingwood will be disappointed." Madam Huxley stuck out her lip in an exaggerated pout. "But I'm sure I can find another girl to entertain him. It's about time he moved on to something younger, anyway."

Dellwyn thought back to the flower he had given her the night before, how he'd offered, in not so many words, to make her his mistress. She had Lord Collingwood securely wrapped around her finger, but she didn't know whether Madam Huxley realized how tightly he was wound. She did know she shouldn't let the madam figure it out.

"You can't do that!" Dellwyn's eyes widened at the volume of her own voice, and she nearly laughed. Her acting hadn't improved one bit since her and Aya's roleplaying practice.

Regardless, Madam Huxley seemed to believe her outburst. "Don't cause a scene. Goodness knows we've had enough of them for one evening."

"He won't leave me." Dellwyn made a show of stomping her foot. "And he won't take another girl, either. I won't let him."

"*Ha!* As if either of you have a choice in the matter." Madam Huxley patted down her skirt. "But I wouldn't overestimate your seductive skill, nor would I underestimate a man's lust."

Dellwyn almost said that it was more than lust, that she suspected Lord Collingwood had fallen in love with her—but she didn't. That would be too suspicious, too confident for a nervous courtesan clinging desperately to her best client.

"Very well, Madam." Dellwyn unfastened her cloak and flung it over her arm. "Take Lord Collingwood if it will satisfy your petty need to punish me. I don't need him. There are a dozen more noblemen where he came from."

"I don't think you'll be seeing many more noblemen, Dellwyn." Madam Huxley's brow creased in sincerity, but her lips formed a mischievous smile.

"Fine." Dellwyn shook her head, ready to call the madam's bluff. "I can make a living from merchants and wellmen. I'm worth the extra coins."

Madam Huxley chuckled. "Oh, my dear, you don't understand. You won't be seeing them, either."

Dellwyn's heart skipped a beat. Madam Huxley couldn't be firing her—she brought in too much profit. Besides, Madam

Huxley would never pass up the opportunity to let the entire Rudder witness Dellwyn's shame.

"Then what?" Dellwyn hated herself for the waver in her voice.

"Don't you see? You'll only have one client from here on out." Madam Huxley winked. "Your nights now belong exclusively to Lord Derringher."

11

Dellwyn didn't have a chance to react. Before her tongue could catch up with her racing mind, the first clients of the evening strolled in under the propellers. She glanced between them and Madam Huxley, trying to decide whether it was worth risking her livelihood to cause a scene in front of the small group of merchants—but in the end, her years of training won out. Dellwyn glared at Madam Huxley before heading to the safety of her room.

Once the door closed behind her, Dellwyn leaned back against the cool metal and shut her eyes. She inhaled deeply, hoping a few large breaths would clear her head. A memory of Lord Derringher ripping her stockings off—then proceeding to wear them like a cravat—crossed her mind, and she grimaced. Of all the clients to be shackled to, it had to be her most destructive.

Dellwyn opened her eyes, and her gaze fell on the metal flower Lord Collingwood had given her, resting on her bedside table where she had left it. Would it be wiser to follow in Aya's footsteps and leave the Rudder altogether? Would it be better to be tied to Lord Derringher by force or to Lord Collingwood by choice? Sure, Lord Collingwood had always pleased her more than her other clients. He knew exactly how to caress her, how to make her feel safe and desired. But he didn't want to possess her at the Rudder, where she belonged to Madam Huxley and could control the rules. He wanted her in *his* world, as his secret concubine, and that was even more terrifying.

Whether at the Rudder or in the palace, the last thing Dellwyn wanted was to exist for the pleasure of one man. Her occupation, of course, necessitated servitude, but the dignity in it was that she didn't serve a person—she served a *need*. A visceral, human need. A need for touch, for connection, for a sense of empowerment. A need so powerful, thousands of people had been willing to risk decapitation to have it filled, if only for an hour at a time.

No, Dellwyn couldn't serve just one person, no matter the situation. Her purpose was greater than that, and it was the one thing she refused to have stripped from her.

She opened her eyes and paced along the edge of her rug. All right, so Madam Huxley had promised Lord Derringher that he would be Dellwyn's only client. While that seemed like a perfectly sinister punishment for Dellwyn's recent defiance, she knew there was no way Madam Huxley would have secured such an arrangement without Lord Derringher's prompting. After all, Lord Collingwood alone made up nearly half of Dellwyn's wages. Lord Derringher must have devised the offer himself, and it must have been enormous.

If Madam Huxley had not planned the arrangement on her own, then she would likely be receptive to an alternate proposition. If Dellwyn could come up with an even more profitable arrangement, surely Madam Huxley would break the deal with Lord Derringher. But how? Dellwyn didn't see any way to increase the madam's profits without selling her time to a higher bidder. She could try to reach out to her other clients and talk them all into paying a higher price to have her available—a collective outbidding, so to speak. But she had no idea how to contact all of them without Madam Huxley finding out.

Before King Lionel had legalized adultery, Dellwyn would have considered asking her coworkers to band together with her. After all, finding workers for the Rudder had always been difficult—only the most desperate people sought Madam Huxley's shelter—and the madam would have been forced to compromise to keep the business afloat. Dellwyn nearly laughed at the thought of staging some kind of workers' protest now. With how many people showed up to interview for positions after the law changed, Madam Huxley would have no problem replacing anyone who became more hassle than they were worth.

Dellwyn sighed and collapsed onto her bed. No, she couldn't figure this out at the moment. All she could do was wait for Lord Derringher to arrive, try to please him as quickly as possible, then hope he left so she could think some more. Besides, she still didn't know how honest Madam Huxley had been. Maybe this arrangement was just for one night or a few days. Maybe the madam had been unnecessarily dramatic to give Dellwyn a good scare and remind her of her place.

Yes, that sounded more like the madam. She wouldn't be careless enough to permanently shackle one of her best workers to a single client. She'd always had better business sense than that. And she still did, even with the stresses of the farmer's squatting—right?

"You look troubled, Dellwyn. Is everything okay?"

Dellwyn rolled onto her side to find Lord Derringher standing in the doorway, his wide frame filling the entire space. She feigned a stretch, using the motion to slide her stocking-clad leg out from under her cloak and arch her back to better accentuate her curves. "Now that you're here, my lord, all is well."

Lord Derringher grinned, and Dellwyn returned it. At least he seemed to be in a good mood. That would help her get rid of him quicker. He closed the door behind himself and locked the handle with a deafening click. A wave of exhaustion washed over Dellwyn, and she gave herself a little pinch on her side to wake herself up. No matter how tiresome the evening—and any subsequent evenings—would be, she had to put on her best face. If this oaf of a man was to be her only source of income, she might as well milk him for every piece of gold he carried.

Dellwyn traced her fingers down her side to her bum and back up. "So, what game shall we play tonight, my lord?" A smug smile overtook her lips as she watched Lord Derringher's hungry eyes follow the motion of her fingers.

"I don't want to play a game." He sat on the edge of the bed, and Dellwyn felt the sensation of falling as the mattress angled toward him.

She straightened and scooted closer to him, her hand finding its way to his thigh. "But I thought you liked it when we played games. Don't you, Your Majesty?"

Lord Derringher reached up to the leather strings that fastened Dellwyn's cloak around her shoulders. He untied the first half of the bow, his fingers not fumbling once, then held the still-crossed strings by their ends.

Dellwyn swallowed. Why did he stop? Why was he staring at her like that?

After a moment, Lord Derringher pulled on the strings, slowly, the way one would tighten shoestrings, until the place where they crossed connected with Dellwyn's throat. In another situation, Dellwyn wouldn't have minded the pressure there. She would have welcomed a little roughness to spice up the evening. But with Lord Derringher's dark eyes boring into her, she felt beads of sweat break out along her chest. She realized, for the first time in her entire career, that if she screamed, no one would be alarmed. They would smile, thinking of how much fun she was having or how fine an actress she was.

"I want to be myself today." Lord Derringher licked his lips. "Is that all right?"

She nodded, and he released the strings, finally uncrossing them and sliding Dellwyn's cloak off her shoulders. He leaned over and placed a kiss on her exposed collarbone, causing her skin to erupt into goosebumps. Dellwyn couldn't decide what he was playing at. As much as it pained her to think, she almost missed the way he had been before the new law had been passed.

"I kept my promise, you know." He untied his cravat and tossed it onto the rug. "I told my family that I've been coming here for years. I told my wife that every time I bed her, I'm thinking of you."

Dellwyn grimaced. She knew some of her clients must do as much, but assuming and knowing were two different things. The idea of her face or her breasts imagined onto some noble-woman made her stomach twist. And she felt bad for Lady Derringher, guilty even. Lord Derringher could be no more than forty, perhaps only thirty-five, and Lady Derringher was surely younger, probably not past her childbearing years yet. To know your youth had been wasted on a man like that, it had to be heartbreaking. Dellwyn hoped Lady Derringher would take a lover or two of her own, or that King Lionel would be gracious in allowing divorces to clean up the domestic devasta-tion of his law.

Lord Derringher stared at Dellwyn expectantly, and she cleared her throat. "What did they say?"

"My father said he would never recover from the shame." Lord Derringher chuckled. "My mother was suspiciously quiet."

In spite of her discomfort, or maybe because of it, Dellwyn giggled. She wondered which of Augustus's gray-haired, overly made-up clients had given birth to the man before her. "And your wife?"

Lord Derringher sighed. "When she finally stopped crying, she told me that she would have divorced me, only she didn't want to embarrass our family. She said she doesn't want my lechery to lessen the children's chances of obtaining respectable marriages."

Dellwyn raised her eyebrows. "Why should it matter?"

"Divorce is as connected to the religion as marriage. When we marry, we are, in theory, honoring the Benevolent Queen with our intentions of fidelity. When we divorce, we are breaking that promise to Her and thus continuing our mortal punishment." Lord Derringher scoffed. "Even though few in the noble class believe that rubbish, the association has remained. If my wife and I divorce, neither of us will ever obtain a proper marriage again and neither will our children. They'd be forced to marry merchants."

Dellwyn pretended not to notice the way Lord Derringher scowled on the word 'merchants.' Remembering her duty, Dellwyn placed her hand on the nape of his neck. He'd always loved to be touched tenderly, to be comforted. It seemed like the right thing to do now, especially with what she was about to say. "Perhaps it will all work out. You can play the happy family in social gatherings. Then, when night falls, you can be with me—and anyone else you like—and your wife can do the same."

Lord Derringher reached back and grabbed Dellwyn's hand. "I must say, I'm rather surprised to hear you say that. Would you believe my wife made the same suggestion?"

Once again, Dellwyn found herself marveling at the surety of his movements and the calmness in his voice. The law had taken away Lord Derringher's fear. It had given him freedom to be his true self. And not for the first time, Dellwyn found herself hating it and him.

Her nostrils flared. "And what did you say?"

Lord Derringer placed her hand in his lap, forcing her to rub her palm against his growing excitement. "I told her that she would do no such thing. That she belonged to me alone."

He released Dellwyn's hand. She tried to pull away from him, but when her hand slid too far toward his leg, Lord Derringher bared his teeth. Dellwyn returned to her work, using more force, and he groaned under her touch. "Do you want to know what I did next?"

"Yes." Her reply came out quiet, breathy. She bit her lip to keep it from quivering.

Lord Derringher's eyes lit up at her tone, no doubt mistaking it for desire. He slid his hand up her leg, occasionally stopping to give the strings of her fishnets a little snap against her skin. Dellwyn's body froze, an instinct that rarely consumed her, and it took all of her concentration to keep her palm moving for him.

"I touched her, just like this…" His fingers connected with Dellwyn's womanhood, and she whimpered. She hadn't had time to prepare herself, and his touch burned, as if his fingers had connected with an open wound. She looked away and found herself staring down at the flower. Another stab, this time, in her heart.

Lord Derringher laughed. "She made that same noise."

Dellwyn flinched and sucked in a deep breath. She closed her eyes and let her mind wander, sorting through her hundreds of memories, trying to find one that would inspire her. She landed on one from her first year at the Rudder—a handsome young baker, flour in his hair, the scent of fresh bread on his tanned skin. It had been his first time, and the way he'd surrendered to Dellwyn had made her feel more powerful than she had ever felt before.

With new resolve, Dellwyn grabbed Lord Derringher by the collar of his shirt and pulled him on top of her. She kissed him feverishly, starting with his lips, then moving down his neck, unbuttoning his shirt to expose his shoulders. Her skin crawled as she touched him, but she would be damned if she was going to lie there like a scared society lady and allow him to relive the sick, forceful torment of his wife. If they had to do this, then *she* would bed *him*.

Despite his size, Dellwyn rolled Lord Derringher onto his back and straddled him. She pinned down his chest with her palms and leaned over him, her dark hair falling around them like a curtain. Lord Derringher's face showed surprise, but also delight and hunger. He craned his neck upward and captured Dellwyn's lips with his own, his teeth grazing her bottom lip in a playful bite.

Dellwyn pulled away—his forwardness had startled her— then disguised the motion by reaching up to unbuckle her corset. Lord Derringher grabbed her hands, and Dellwyn yelped.

He shook his head. "Keep it on."

Dellwyn lowered her hands, and Lord Derringher wriggled underneath her. She realized he was trying to get out of the bed, so she rose up on her knees to allow him room to move. Her thighs cramped under her weight, and she cursed herself for chasing after the farmer that morning.

Once freed, Lord Derringher walked to the center of the room and picked up his discarded cravat. Dellwyn's heart pounded in her chest from both fear that she had displeased him and from hope that he would leave. Perhaps he had an appointment to keep, and they had wasted too much time talking at the beginning of his visit. Or perhaps he was simply returning to his old ways, his shyness finally catching up with his eagerness.

When Lord Derringher didn't tie the cravat around his neck, Dellwyn felt her stomach sink. When he skulked toward her, the cravat held wide in front of him, her stomach nearly dropped to her feet.

"Hold out your hands." Lord Derringher's bright grin was the only thing that made Dellwyn obey. So he was returning to his new standby and planning to wring her wrists out a bit. That was all. Fine. She could handle a little soreness there to distract from her aching legs.

The smooth fabric of the cravat cut into Dellwyn's wrists, and she winced. He hadn't tied it that tightly before. She stared down at the knot—a small, intricately woven ball—and she wondered if Lord Derringher had been reading up on the nautical arts.

"You'd make a fine sailor." Dellwyn chuckled, dipping her chin toward her bound hands.

Lord Derringher winked. "I know more. I'll show you." He turned to Dellwyn's armoire and flung open the doors. He rifled through the upper section, shoving aside her dresses, before combing through the drawers and flinging undergarments on the floor.

"Hey!" Dellwyn stood and stomped toward him. Her bound hands trembled with fury as they tried to yank the clothing out of his grasp. "How dare you. Those are my private belongings."

Lord Derringher grabbed her by the arm and shoved her

back onto the bed. Dellwyn couldn't catch herself. She slipped off the edge and fell to the floor.

"Nothing is private in here," Lord Derringher said. "Not even you. Besides, noblemen like me bought all of this. There's no reason I can't make good on our investments."

"What are you talking about?" Dellwyn pushed herself upright with her elbow and winced. Her side ached where it had hit the edge of the mattress. "Gifts or not, they're mine. You have no right to—"

"Ah, here we are." Lord Derringher had reached the bottom drawer, where Dellwyn kept her stockings. He pulled out a fistful, decided on two, and tossed the others back inside. "I think these will do nicely."

Lord Derringher stalked back over to Dellwyn and knelt down before her. He took one pair of her stockings, a beautiful silk set from Lord Collingwood, and wrapped them around her ankles. Dellwyn realized what he intended to do, and she kicked him square in the chest. He stumbled backward but caught himself before she could scramble to her feet.

"Hold still," he growled. This time, he held both of Dellwyn's legs in the crook of one arm while using the other to wrap the stockings around her ankles. Dellwyn struggled against him, but his grip was too strong. In less than a minute, he had her feet securely tied together.

Lord Derringher smiled and patted her legs. "There we go. Is that tight enough?"

"Help!" Dellwyn banged her tied feet on the metal floor, hoping her earlier thoughts had been wrong, and that one of her coworkers would hear her cries and investigate.

Lord Derringher chuckled and grabbed the second pair of stockings. "I wanted to keep your mouth free, but once again, you understand me better than I understand myself."

Dellwyn felt her face pale. She whipped her head back and forth, still screaming as loudly as she could. All she managed to do was fall over, and her temple smacked against the floor.

"Are you all right?" Lord Derringher's eyes showed genuine concern, and his hands were gentle as he pulled her up. He leaned over to examine her head, his lips soft as he kissed the injured area. How could he act so kind when he was in the middle of tying her up like an animal?

"Let me go," Dellwyn hissed. "You can't do things like this. It's against the Rudder's policy. You can't tie me up, can't force me."

Lord Derringher smirked. He wrapped the stockings around Dellwyn's head and tied them in the back, careful not to pull any of her hair in the knot. Dellwyn bit the fabric and tried to speak through it, to beg him to stop.

"You're so thoughtful. Don't worry about me. I won't get in trouble." Lord Derringher caressed her cheek. "Madam Huxley explicitly said that I could do whatever I like with you. She said that I had more than earned my freedom with how much I paid to have you to myself."

Dellwyn screamed through her stockings and thrashed her body as best she could. How could he think she was worried about him? Did he really believe she cared for him? How could Madam Huxley have agreed to this?

Lord Derringher kissed her forehead, still stroking her cheek. "You know I wouldn't hurt you, Dellwyn. Trust me. You'll like this. It's just another game. And it's easy. All you have to do is be your beautiful self and let me take care of the rest."

Dellwyn felt tears prick her eyes. Lord Derringher actually cared about her. He actually thought she would enjoy this, that they were just playing. What kind of sick delusion was he under? And how long would she have to endure this? How many nights had he and Madam Huxley agreed to? Dellwyn bit down on the stocking to keep herself from crying. It didn't matter what arrangement they had made. Dellwyn would see it broken. She wouldn't spend another night humiliated and bound. It didn't matter whether Lord Derringher thought he was pleasing her, and it didn't matter what she might lose. She would never be in this situation again.

As Lord Derringher tugged down her fishnets, Dellwyn heard a loud click, and her door flew open. Alisa burst in, clad only in her undergarments. In her hands, she held the master key ring from Madam Huxley's office. Dellwyn glanced back and forth between Alisa and Lord Derringher. She didn't think she could handle it if Alisa were joining them for the evening.

Lord Derringher must have had the same thought, because he puckered his lips. "Two for the price of one?"

"I'm terribly sorry to interrupt, my lord." Alisa performed a curtsy, and if the situation had been any different, Dellwyn might have laughed. "There was a message for you. It's urgent. The guard wouldn't give me any details, only that you are to return home straight away."

Lord Derringher's jaw clenched, and a vein pulsed in his neck. "Are you certain it cannot wait?"

"Oh, yes, my lord." Alisa widened her eyes. "The guard insisted. A family emergency."

Lord Derringher cursed and turned to Dellwyn. He reached out to touch her cheek, and she recoiled from his hand. "Don't be cross, Dellwyn. I know we were having fun, but I'll see you tomorrow. I promise."

Dellwyn told him that it would rain before she would see him again, but her stockings muffled her words. Lord Derringher smiled and shook his head. With a practiced, fluid motion, he untied her hands. Dellwyn rubbed her sore wrists, cringing at the marks in her flesh. Lord Derringher tied his cravat, bid both women good evening, and left.

Once he was far enough down the hallway, Alisa locked the door behind her and rushed over to Dellwyn. She helped Dellwyn unfasten the stockings. "Are you all right?"

Dellwyn nodded, unable to find the right words.

Alisa bit her lip and glared down at the floor. "I'm sorry to barge in. I hope it was the right thing to do."

How could Alisa be so uncertain? She had saved Dellwyn from a miserable night, from a crime Dellwyn couldn't have defended in public. Dellwyn had never felt affection for Alisa— only competitiveness and the occasional bout of professional admiration—but in that moment, Dellwyn loved Alisa like a sister. She wrapped her arms around Alisa, and after a moment of hesitation, Alisa squeezed back.

"Thank you." Dellwyn realized the tears she had been withholding had escaped. "I didn't think anyone would hear me scream, or if they did…" She took a shaky breath, and a thought occurred to her. "Wait, aren't you supposed to be tending the extra customers? How did you even…"

Alisa pushed Dellwyn away, gently but firmly, and held her at arm's length. "It seems a lot of families are having emergencies tonight."

Dellwyn smiled—and the action, brought about purely by human instinct, reminded her that she was strong, that she could recover from anything.

Alisa didn't return Dellwyn's grin. Instead, she snarled and something under her breath.

Dellwyn leaned in closer. "Pardon?"

"I said, she's gone too far." Alisa stood and started pacing the room. "Madam Huxley. She has to be stopped. It's one thing to deduct wages or demand extra work. But to allow a client to do *that* to you… it's wrong."

"Yes, it is." Dellwyn pushed herself up onto her bed. "But how can we stop her?"

Alisa massaged her scalp with her fingers. "I don't know. But the second I figure it out, she better watch her back."

"Alisa!" Madam Huxley's shrill voice echoed down the workers' hallway.

"Shit." Alisa adjusted her undergarments to look askew and mussed her hair. "Are you sure you're all right?"

"I'm fine." Dellwyn relaxed back onto the bed, hoping the lazy position would help convince at least one of them. "Go before you get into trouble."

Alisa nodded and tossed Dellwyn the key ring. "Hide it under your mattress. I'll sneak it back into her office in the morning."

Dellwyn fingered the keys. "Thank you."

"Don't mention it." Alisa stalled, her hand on the doorknob. "Again. Ever."

After Alisa had shut the door behind her, Dellwyn got up and locked it. With the keys in her room, no one could disturb her. She was, for the moment, entirely safe. She returned to the bed, pulled the blanket off, and dragged it over to the fainting couch. Curled up between the velvet cushion and the feather comforter, Dellwyn finally felt her heartbeat slow to a normal rhythm. Her sore muscles relaxed into the warmth of her nest, and she closed her eyes. She didn't know when her thoughts became dreams, but when she awoke hours later to Sybil's soft knocking on the door, she realized they had all been peaceful.

12

———

$\mathcal{D}$ellwyn lay awake on her thin mattress. She stared down at the hovel's dirt floor, where she had drawn a picture with her finger. A stick-figure girl looked back up at her —or she would have, if Dellwyn had poked dots for her eyes— with a flower clasped in her hand. Dellwyn had given the girl a smile, but it was too big for her small, round face and made her head appear as if it had been divided in two.

With a groan, Dellwyn threw her own head back onto the pillows then cursed herself as her still-aching muscles screamed against the movement. Her legs and hips had grown even sorer from her running stint, but thanks to Lord Derringher, she now counted her arms, ankles, and cheeks among the injured.

Before that morning, Dellwyn had never had difficulty sleeping after work—even with the slivers of sunlight that peeked through the slats of her wall. She tried to tell herself that her inability to sleep came from her nap, but she knew it was more than that. Her body felt exhausted beyond her muscles—she hurt down to the bone. And her mind felt even worse, as if someone had dug out her brain and replaced it with a boulder. It had taken all of her focus to lift her head and draw, and she feared that simple action might add her neck to the list of broken parts.

What had even happened to her? Over the last few days,

she had been stalked by an insane religious zealot, then nearly rap—no, she wouldn't think it—then forcibly *mishandled* by a client who had meek and clumsy. What in Desertera was going on? Could a law—words spoken by the lips of her best friend's lover and recorded in some ancient, unfathomable tome—really change the world? People's nature? Her?

No, the law hadn't changed her. But the world it had created might. The law had already corrupted the Rudder, the one place in Desertera where Dellwyn had felt a sense of belonging, where she had thrived. Perhaps she had been naïve, but she had always viewed the Rudder as the place where she could express her own desires and grow her talents, her life, even. She thought Madam Huxley had respected her—if not as an equal, then as a valuable worker. But Dellwyn's night with Lord Derringher had shown her the truth. Madam Huxley didn't respect her or value her. Madam Huxley only cared about how many coins Dellwyn could rake into her purse.

She leaned back over the picture she had drawn. Tears fell from her eyes, smudging the image. Disgusted, Dellwyn wiped at the dirt until nothing remained but the smooth swipes of her palm.

She understood now. Madam Huxley's betrayal had hurt her even worse than Lord Derringher's depraved, misguided behavior. Dellwyn could overcome the disrespect of her body, but the disrespect of her person… it was intolerable.

Alisa was right. Not only did Dellwyn need to escape the arrangement with Lord Derringher, but something needed to be done about Madam Huxley. If the woman continued to run her business at this rate, all of the Rudder's workers would end up little better than slaves, and Madam Huxley would end up with half the wealth of the kingdom.

Dellwyn didn't know how to stop any of it, not yet. But she knew she wouldn't be sleeping, and lying in bed all day wouldn't help anything.

With a huff, she threw her covers off and stood. She went to her dressing trunk and opened the lid. Folds of expensive, jewel-toned fabric greeted her, each one practically singing the name of its buyer. Frowning, Dellwyn pulled out a plain blue dress, one of the few garments she had purchased herself. As she slipped into it, her frown deepened. The worn fabric strained over her breasts and hips, tugging tightly on her skin in a way she didn't remember it doing before. Once, it had made her appear modest, like the baggy, lifeless frocks Aya used to wear, but now it pulled against her shape, yet another reminder of the physical domination of her curves.

Dellwyn tiptoed into the main room, relieved to see Sybil's door shut. She sighed. At least she didn't have to figure out what to say to Sybil just yet. Last night, Dellwyn had blamed her quietness on a stomachache. It hadn't been a complete lie, but her mouth tasted sour at the thought of adding to it.

The sound of laughing children chimed through the streets, and Dellwyn realized that she couldn't remember the last time she had genuinely had fun. Sure, she had enjoyed her romps with clients and time spent with Sybil and Aya, but when was the last time she had done something purely for pleasure, for herself and no one else?

She went to the window and watched the children as they chased each other in circles, their bare, brown feet kicking up dust, and their ragged clothing flapping in the wind they created. Their smiles shone in their dirt-smudged faces, and they giggled and squealed whenever an adult shot them a disapproving look.

The children didn't realize what their lives would be— toiling under the hot sun, marriages of necessity, raising their own restless brood—they were still too young to fear the future. Dellwyn moved away from the window, retrieved a gold coin from its hiding place in the bottom of the kitchen trunk, then stuck it between her breasts. Her dress didn't have any pockets, but even so, the children would hunt anywhere they could reach. They knew enough about life to understand hunger.

Dellwyn picked up the glass jug by the leather strap wrapped around it and slung it over her shoulder. Aya had come up with that idea, one of her less-technical innovations, and it had made carrying water easier. Of course, when Aya had lived there, they'd walked much farther to quench their thirst. Her friend couldn't stand to drink the mucky water from Sternville and had always insisted on trekking to Bowtown.

Dellwyn had to admit, Bowtown's water was cleaner—less sediment and less risk of bodily fluids—but she didn't feel the need to gather from the Bowtown well now that Aya was gone. Dellwyn had been born and raised in Sternville—who was she to think herself above her home village? She was no better than any of those children, all of whom would gulp down at least two cups of that murky liquid when they got home, to the irritation of their parents, no doubt.

The sunlight stung Dellwyn's eyes. As she shielded them, the children swarmed her, tugging on her dress and patting at her feet.

"Go on." Dellwyn waved them away. "I don't have anything for you."

A few of them skittered away, but a few stayed and stared up at her with tearful eyes and trembling lips.

"Oh, no you don't." Dellwyn chuckled. "I know that act. Go on."

The children's faces hardened. One stuck his tongue out at her. But they ran back to their games. Dellwyn shook her head and set off for the well.

They had dug the well on the very edge of Sternville, one of the farthest possible points from the palace. Dellwyn realized she didn't know who 'they' were. The first generation, the people who had sailed on the ocean… or maybe their children or grandchildren were the first to return to the ground, the first stuck in this wasteland. She sighed. No, she didn't believe the flood story. For all she knew, the wells had always been there, perfectly cylindrical, natural holes.

And why did anyone think the palace would float? Dellwyn had seen coins accidentally dropped in the wells. They may not be the same metal as the palace, but they were still metal. And they sank. Straight down, out of sight. The palace was even bigger, even heavier. There was no way it ever would have floated on water. It was probably built right there in the sand, the anchors used to steady it, not to keep it from floating away.

The floods were stories for thirsty children, a distraction from the bleak truth. This was their world—their dry, desolate world—and they needed to learn to deal with it.

Dellwyn wondered what King Lionel believed. If he didn't believe in the adultery law, maybe he didn't believe in the stories of the Benevolent Queen and the flood. Maybe he would be the first king brave enough to speak up for the truth. Of course, Aya still believed in the flood, if not the scorned goddess, too. That didn't mean King Lionel believed, but Dellwyn figured it meant he wouldn't try to disprove it all, not if it would hurt Aya.

When she reached the well, the wellman looked her up and down, and Dellwyn hugged the jug closer to her chest. He grinned at her with his yellow, dirt-stained teeth. "Yer early, darlin'."

She tried to force herself to smile, but her lips wouldn't go up. "Am I?"

"For you." The wellman nodded at the gaping hole in the ground. "Still, evr'body else has already been. Done stirred 'er all up."

"Good." Dellwyn's face still felt stuck. "I don't know if I could stand to drink clean water."

Either the wellman didn't understand her humor, or he didn't find it funny. He simply extended his hands, motioning with his fingers for her to pass him the jug. With a sinking feeling, she pulled the strap over her head and handed it over. As the wellman took the jug from her, the strap caught on Dellwyn's wrist—and she was back to the night before, limbs tied, mouth gagged. She shrieked.

The wellman jumped back, jug in hand, and the strap slid off of her wrist. "What's wrong with ya? What are you hollerin' for?"

Dellwyn clasped her wrist, glaring between it and the wellman as if they had conspired to send her thoughts back to last night. Rubbing her sore tendons brought a sense of calm, and she breathed in a long, slow breath. "It startled me. Just fill it, will you?"

"Don't get snappy." The wellman strapped the jug to the chain and started to crank. Metal groaned against metal, gray marred with rust from years of dipping into the water. The sound vibrated in Dellwyn's chest and relaxed her. It was the sound of work, of a recurring system, of mindlessness. She could have listened to it all day.

"Miss? Hey!" The wellman leaned forward with his hand out. "I said, that'll be one gold coin."

"Oh, of course." Dellwyn fished into her cleavage for the coin, ashamed to feel her cheeks burning under the wellman's hungry gaze. *It's the money he wants,* she reminded herself. *No one out here has any use for me.*

By the time Dellwyn returned to the hovel, her sore muscles ached even more than they had that morning. She'd once overheard a midwife say that walking helped stiffness. The woman must have been a liar, or delusional.

Dellwyn leaned her weight against the door, cradling the heavy jug in one hand and twisting the doorknob in the other. As she pushed the door open, it swung back all the way, and she stumbled, nearly falling into the common room.

Sybil stood next to the door, hand clasping the other side of the knob, and gasped. "I'm so sorry! I meant to help you."

"It's all right." Dellwyn set the jug down next to the table. "I'm almost used to getting startled."

Sybil smiled and dragged the jug by its strap to its rightful place next to the storage trunk. Then, she stood and dusted off her hands. "Have you eaten yet?"

Eaten? Dellwyn wrinkled her forehead. It hadn't occurred to her that she should be hungry. "No. I'm not feeling too well."

"Still?" Sybil tucked a strand of hair behind her ear. "Is it the same thing as last night? The stomachache?"

"Yes." Guilt simmered in Dellwyn's chest. "It's the same thing as last night."

Sybil nodded. "You should still eat. Why don't you sit down and let me fix you something?"

Acid welled in Dellwyn's throat. Sybil shouldn't have to take care of her, but she didn't have the energy to do it herself. She sank into her chair and rested her chin in her hands. As Dellwyn's gaze dropped to the wood, she noticed a folded letter on the table. What in Desertera was paper doing in their hovel?

Before Dellwyn could ask about it, Sybil glanced back over her shoulder. "One of Lord Collingwood's guards dropped that off for you."

Dellwyn recoiled from the letter as if it were a snake.

Sybil continued. "He didn't say he served Lord Collingwood, but I remembered the badge. A red square with a black-and-white cross. Just like you taught me."

"Good." Dellwyn wasn't really listening. Why would Lord Collingwood write to her? He always passed messages verbally, often leaving Dellwyn to unravel a riddle or ponder his vague language. What would be worth wasting such a precious resource? Worth hiding, even from one of his trusted servants?

"Are you going to open it?" Sybil placed a plate in front of Dellwyn. It held a slab of cactus meat and a hunk of bread lathered with goat butter.

Dellwyn raised her eyebrows at the creamy luxury.

Sybil blushed. "One of the young farmers gave me a sample of the butter. You know, so if I like it, I can buy it from his farm in the future. I didn't tell him I don't normally eat it."

For the first time since before the incident with Lord Derringher, Dellwyn's lips curved into a smile. "And so it begins."

Sybil tried to disguise her embarrassment by taking a bite of her bread. "If oo don't ohen it, I wull," she mumbled as she chewed.

Dellwyn sighed and picked up the letter. It was lighter than she'd expected, the paper smooth and crisp under her fingertips. A stamp sealed the back—a square of red candle wax with a cross pressed into it. With a tug, the stamp gave way. Dellwyn unfolded the paper and read the message: *She won't let me see you, and I must. Come to my chambers tonight. Your flower holds the key. Yours, S.*

Dellwyn set the paper down, folded her arms, and laid her head on them. Lord Collingwood had never summoned her before. He must be desperate to see her. As much as Dellwyn hated to admit it, her heart panged for him, too.

But how could she give Lord Collingwood what he wanted when every bone and muscle in her body revolted at the thought of being touched? When all she wanted was to sleep for days? And how could she face him after what had almost happened last night? After what might happen when Lord Derringher returned tonight?

Dellwyn groaned and rolled her forehead against her fore-arms. She couldn't think about Lord Derringher. Not now. Instead, she focused her mental energy on the less certain part of Lord Collingwood's message. Her flower held the key? What did that mean? The metal object he'd given her was a trinket, an ornament to sit on her bedside table and remind the other lords that someone else held her favor—or at least, that was what it would have done if Dellwyn had been allowed to see her regular clientele.

"Well, what did it say?" Sybil's voice chirped through the veil of Dellwyn's hair.

She didn't have to see Sybil's face to know that it was bright and curious. She hoped it would stay that way, that innocent flirtations with young farmers would be all the masculine interest Sybil had to bear, at least until she wanted more.

Dellwyn raised her head and smirked. "I shouldn't say." Her words were the truth, but her expression was meant to soften it.

Sybil stuck out her lower lip. "Oh, come on. Who am I going to tell?"

"That's not the issue. You know I trust you." Dellwyn nibbled on her own piece of bread, if only to prevent Sybil from chastising her again.

"What, then?" Sybil's eyes widened, and she threw her hands to her cheeks in a dramatic gesture of scandal and delight. "Is it dangerous? Oh, Dellwyn, if something's wrong, then you have to tell me. Remember the farmer chasing you?"

"Of course I remember." Dellwyn swallowed her bite of bread, waiting for the inevitable sensation of dread to creep up through her gut. It didn't. And she realized, with a prickling feeling not unlike being dipped in cold well water, that she now had something worse to fear. The farmer may have followed her, may have harassed the Rudder's clients and had his brain scrambled by the heat, but he had never harmed anyone—other than the man who had attacked Sybil at the protest.

The events of the last few days finally became real to Dellwyn in a way they hadn't before that moment. She had been stupid to fear the farmer. Lord Derringher could do far worse to her, and no one could stop him.

Before she knew what was happening, Dellwyn was bent over in her chair, spewing bread mush and bile onto the dirt floor. Sybil jumped up and ran to her side, valiantly scooping her hair out of the way. "Shit! Are you okay?"

"Don't say 'shit.'" Dellwyn coughed and wiped her mouth with the back of her hand. "You're too young. Even if you do hear worse at the Rudder."

Sybil crouched down next to Dellwyn and placed her hand on Dellwyn's forehead. "You don't feel hot." Sybil's face paled. "You're not—"

"No!" Her stomach nearly upturned again at the thought.

"Are you sure?" Sybil pushed her toe around the pile of vomit, slowly shoving dust over Dellwyn's mess. "You remembered your tonic every night? When's the last time you had your red rains?"

"I'm not pregnant. I just…" She couldn't tell Sybil the truth, not without alarming her, and she was too distracted to think up a plausible lie. "Would you stop that?"

Sybil froze, foot pointed.

"Leave it." Dellwyn stood. "I'll clean it up later."

Sybil stared down at the hardly touched bread and full slice of cactus meat. "What about your food?"

"I'm not hungry." Dellwyn shrugged. "You eat it."

Sybil didn't refuse. Not many who lived in Sternville would have. "What are you going to do? We've only got a few hours of daylight left, and we've got to go in early for room reassignments."

"I'm going to lie down." Dellwyn headed toward her room, wondering if she still had any of her presents from the brewer tucked away in her dressing trunk. He always brought her a bottle as a tip.

"Are you sure you're okay?" Sybil was already chewing Dellwyn's cactus slice.

"I'm fine." Dellwyn closed the door between them, then pressed herself against it and closed her eyes. "It's the rest of the world that isn't."

13

For once, when Dellwyn and Sybil arrived at the Rudder, Madam Huxley was not at her podium. The farmer hadn't been outside, either, but his tent stood dutifully next to the propellers. Dellwyn figured he was sleeping or perhaps off stalking someone else until the clients arrived.

She glanced around the lobby. Everyone seemed accounted for—hopeful employees and all. She hadn't paid attention to the position of the sun, only to Sybil's insistence that it was time to head to work. So she turned around to discern the color of light filtering in through the propellers. Dark orange.

"We're not *that* early, are we?" Dellwyn whispered.

"Not particularly." Sybil shrugged. "We got here just when I'd planned."

Despite herself, Dellwyn smiled. Sybil had taken nicely to being in charge of their little household, if only for the afternoon while Dellwyn tried, unsuccessfully, to escape her fears. Maybe she shouldn't coddle Sybil anymore. At least, not as much.

As the two approached the crowd, Dellwyn's hands started to sweat. She couldn't decide what made her more anxious: seeing Madam Huxley again or the long, drawn-out wait for room reassignments. Either way, when the meeting was over, Dellwyn would be out of Room G and into whatever hole

Madam Huxley demoted her. Changing rooms wouldn't erase the memory, but it would make her feel better. She didn't know whether she could prevent Lord Derringher from trying his— what did they call it in Bowtown?—hogtying again, but she was going to try, and a fresh room was as good of a clean slate as she would get. Who knew, maybe she could push Lord Derringher from his unhealthy obsession with her into some kind of gentle puppy love like Lord Collingwood held for her. The two were closer than one might expect.

Dellwyn spotted Augustus toward the side of the group and went to stand next to him. Sybil stood on his other side. He wrapped his arms around them both and took a deep breath through his nose, as if inhaling the scent of a fresh rain. "Ah, beautiful night, isn't it, girls?"

Sybil smiled up at Augustus with starstruck eyes. Dellwyn shook her head. Yes, the young farmer would only be the beginning. She wondered if she needed to explain to Sybil why, beyond her age and inexperience, Augustus would never be interested in her.

"Why so glum, Delly?" Augustus squeezed Dellwyn's shoulder and grinned even wider. "I bet you're in for a promotion tonight."

Dellwyn snorted. "How do you figure?"

"You've just become the Rudder's steadiest source of income, and I daresay secured yourself years of handsome presents. That is, if the rumors about you and Lord Derringher are true." Augustus waggled his eyebrows.

"What rumors?" Dellwyn shrugged his arm off. "You make it sound like we're to be wed."

"No, preposterous." Augustus laughed. If it hadn't been at her expense, the melodious sound might have lifted Dellwyn's mood. "Now, of course, if I'd heard that Lord Collingwood meant to marry you, that wouldn't surprise me. I hear the men in that family have a weakness for whores."

Anger flared inside Dellwyn, and Lord Collingwood's note, tucked into her corset, seemed to burn against her skin. She swatted Augustus's arm. How dare he imply that she would seize such an opportunity. And even worse, how dare he use that word for Aya.

"What?" Augustus rubbed his bicep, all joking gone. "I don't blame Aya. Or you. If King Lionel or a member of his family had chosen me, I'd be climbing my way up the royal ladder, too."

Dellwyn didn't dignify Augustus's implication with a response. If she denied interest in establishing a more permanent relationship with Lord Collingwood, Augustus would either think her a liar or stupid or both. Instead, she offered a smirk as a truce. "Unfortunately, I think King Archon executed all of his wives long before they bore him any more children."

Augustus snickered and returned his arm to Dellwyn's shoulder. "So selfish."

Sybil laughed. "Surely he had Rutts, though. Would they be good enough for you, Augustus?"

He put his hand to his chin as if considering a business proposal. "In a pinch, I suppose an illegitimate royal would do. As long as the money was there."

"Not a chance." Dellwyn knew she was spoiling the fun, but doing so filled her chest with a pleasant warmth. She wasn't ready to forgive Augustus for his barbs, however complimentary they had been meant. "King Archon was too smart for that. He never committed adultery, only bedded his legal wives."

"Well, at least his son had the sense to end that for all of us." Augustus looked down at Dellwyn, but when he saw she wasn't smiling, he winked at Sybil instead.

Dellwyn turned away and looked toward the front of the crowd. A bang issued from the secondary corridor, followed by tempered footsteps.

Sybil's breath hitched. "Here she comes."

"Finally." Dellwyn and Augustus spoke the word in unison —her with a groan, him with a chuckle.

Despite how anxious she was to leave Room G behind, Dellwyn felt the chill of dread creep down her spine and settle in her stomach. When Madam Huxley walked into view, her stomach leaped into her throat. There was the woman who had bound her to Lord Derringher. Madam Huxley had better hope that Dellwyn stayed miserable, because if she figured out how to turn Lord Derringher into her puppet, the madam would have a whole lot of pain in store.

Madam Huxley positioned herself behind her podium, spine straight, fingers wrapped menacingly around the edges. She seemed to tower over the room, even though Dellwyn had to stand on tiptoe to see her.

"Good. You all decided to be punctual this evening." Madam Huxley smirked. "If only that would become a habit."

A few employees snickered, as if earning the madam's favor at the last moment would have an effect on their rooms. It took Dellwyn a moment to remember that there were some who still cared about being in the madam's good graces. She rolled her eyes. How foolish she had been, only a week or so ago, to think she had a chance to gain Madam Huxley's respect. How long would it take for the rest of the workers to learn the same lesson for themselves?

"As you all know, there are not enough rooms for everyone who has applied for a position." Madam Huxley stuck out her bottom lip in a faux pout. "However, those of you who I'm not able to employ at this moment, I encourage you to stay close by." Her eyes narrowed. Dellwyn followed her line of sight and found Alisa on the receiving end. "I am sure vacancies will arise throughout the coming months."

Dellwyn swallowed. She wondered if things were really bad enough between Madam Huxley and Alisa that the madam would consider firing her.

"Now then, for the good news." Madam Huxley clasped her hands together. "All of you who have been in my employ will be staying at the Rudder."

A collectively held breath whooshed through the lobby. Dellwyn didn't allow herself to be relieved. There would be a catch; there always was.

Madam Huxley grinned. "And as a little 'thank you' for all of your hard work over the last few days, I've hired guards to move your belongings into your new rooms. This way, when our meeting here is through, you all can settle right in."

Some of the newer employees smiled. Dellwyn shook her head. What Madam Huxley failed to mention was that she had snooped through their belongings. Any kept secrets would now be in her possession, and any stray coins would have disappeared from their hiding spots—and the workers couldn't even accuse Madam Huxley of stealing without the risk of being accused of the same. It was why Dellwyn and Aya had always taken their tips back to their hovel.

"When I announce your room assignment, please go to your respective corridor and stand in front of your door." Madam Huxley's eyes lit up as the workers shuffled their feet and glanced between the two hallways. "As is custom, the lettered rooms will have higher status, with A as the top. For the numbered rooms, three shall be highest, and ten shall be lowest ranking."

Madam Huxley paused to make sure the courtesans understood. When she saw enough nods, she cleared her throat. "Room A."

Dellwyn's gaze drifted back to Alisa, who stepped forward and weaved her way toward the front of the group.

Madam Huxley smirked. "Augustus."

Dellwyn's joints locked in shock, and she nearly stumbled when Augustus's side brushed hers as he moved toward the corridor. With a quick glance, Dellwyn saw that Alisa had stopped in the middle of the crowd. Her skin was flushed, and her jaw had clenched. Alisa had been in Room A for nearly her entire tenure at the Rudder—just shy of a decade. No one had ever come close to usurping her before.

"Room B." Madam Huxley's face turned to stone. "Dellwyn."

A gasp flew from Dellwyn's lips before she could prevent it. One of the other girls sneered and uttered a remark, but Dellwyn couldn't hear it over the rush of blood in her ears. If it hadn't been for Sybil grabbing her elbow and edging her forward, Dellwyn might have stood there all night. Apparently,

Augustus had been right—Lord Derringher must have paid a very good price to have her to himself.

Somehow, Dellwyn's feet carried her through the crowd, which parted for her. Her coworkers' faces had become blurry, and the corridor seemed to grow narrower as she entered it. She stood across the hallway from Augustus.

"I told you so." Augustus leaned back against his door, crossing his arms and grinning smugly. "I bet you bring in more money than me. I bet Madam Huxley only put me here over you because I can still serve the other high-profile clients."

Dellwyn didn't say anything. Alisa strode past and kicked the door to Room C, which sent a loud clang reverberating through the corridor.

Augustus chuckled. "Don't be so sour. Won't it be nice to have fewer clients? Your hips must be nearly worn out."

Alisa glared at Augustus.

Dellwyn narrowed her eyes, too. "You're older than her, you ass. Besides, aren't your knees about ground to nubs?"

Augustus made a *tsk*. "Now, now, Delly. No need to be crass. I'm only joking."

"Gloating, you mean." Alisa spat on the floor, the glob barely missing Augustus's shoes.

Augustus scrubbed the spit away with his toe. "Maybe the clients want someone with better manners."

Kalinda skipped down the corridor, nearly tripping on his outstretched leg, and stopped next to Dellwyn in front of Room D. Still bouncing, she let out a triumphant giggle. "I can't believe I got D! I hope Jasmine is in E. Won't it be so much fun, the five of us at the top?"

No one answered her, but it didn't matter. Jasmine came down the hallway next, and she and Kalinda grabbed onto each other's arms and squealed.

"At least someone's happy." Augustus scoffed, then pasted on his trademark smile again. "Good for you girls! I'm so glad we're neighbors."

Kalinda and Jasmine crushed him in a hug. Dellwyn leaned to look around them and shared an empathetic eye roll with Alisa. When another girl came down the corridor, the merry threesome separated and returned to their respective doors.

More girls—and the two male applicants—filed down the hallway one by one. Eventually, Room Z received its new resident, and Dellwyn heard the footsteps echo through the lobby and fade away in the parallel corridor. When the footsteps ended, Dellwyn heard muffled, but clearly heated, words followed by soft sobs. After a few moments, Madam Huxley's voice rose over the sounds, and whoever had not gained employment left.

Madam Huxley emerged in the corridor's entrance. "Hello, my stars." She craned her neck to peer all the way to the end of the hallway. Her gaze paused on Alisa. "Ah, yes, good. Looks like everyone is in their proper place."

Dellwyn bit her cheek and looked down, willing herself not to look at Alisa.

"You may enter your rooms now." She placed a hand over her heart. "Let me know if any of your personal items have been misplaced. I instructed the guards to reassemble each of your rooms precisely the way you had them before, so you should feel right at home."

Dellwyn's nostrils flared. She didn't know if she could handle opening the door and seeing a replica of Room G staring back at her. She'd hoped her belongings would be heaped in a pile, as much a mess as she felt.

"If you have any questions about your assignment, come find me between clients." Madam Huxley glanced up, as if checking the position of the sun. "The first appointments of the evening should be arriving in a few moments. I'm going to speak with the other courtesans, then we will be open for business as usual." With that, she left.

Her coworkers rushed into their rooms, and Dellwyn found herself alone with Alisa in the corridor. As the last door slammed shut, Alisa crossed her arms. "I can't believe her."

Dellwyn shook her head, embarrassed to find her eyes watering. "Neither can I."

Alisa reached out her hand to Dellwyn, then frowned and withdrew it. "Are you going to be okay tonight?"

Dellwyn shrugged. "I don't have a choice, do I? But I think so. Even when he was..." She shivered. "Lord Derringher acted like he genuinely cared about me last night. I think there's opportunity in that."

Alisa nodded. "Make him love you."

"That's the plan." Dellwyn sighed. "I'd rather fight off cuddling than..."

Alisa squared her shoulders. "If anything happens, you scream, all right?" She wrinkled her nose. "I'm only *one* room away."

Dellwyn offered a small smile. "Thank you. And trust me, if he tries anything, every person in this palace, from the Rudder all the way up to King Lionel's private chambers, will hear."

~

NOTHING HAPPENED. Dellwyn spent the beginning of the evening pacing the floor of Room B, trying to keep her legs from shaking and repeating her strategy for keeping Lord Derringher in line. If he truly cared about her, one glimpse of the purple rings around her wrists and ankles should be enough to prevent him from tying her up again—at least for a few days. And by the time the bruises faded, he would be well on his way to falling in love with her.

When Dellwyn heard doors opening and shutting around her, along with footsteps coursing through the corridor, she knew the first round of clients were leaving for the night. That meant at least an hour, maybe two, had passed. There wasn't a set schedule, but the nights tended to follow a predictable pattern. How long of a bedding could one client take, after all?

After another hour went by without Lord Derringher's arrival, Dellwyn took it upon herself to reorganize her room. Room B was slightly bigger than Room G, and while it was enough to keep her skin from crawling, it wasn't enough to put her entirely at ease. One futile push told her she couldn't move her armoire, but she managed to switch the position of her bed and nightstand with her fainting couch. She thought about changing out her comforter with one of her spares, but when she remembered that it had been a gift from Lord Collingwood, she allowed it to stay.

Another succession of creaking doors and slow footsteps told Dellwyn that two more hours had passed. Lord Derringher still hadn't showed. Half of her was filled with relief, while the other simmered with dread. Dellwyn wondered if she would still be paid on the nights when he didn't come. She didn't think she and Sybil could afford to live on only part of her salary and Sybil's meager income.

To distract herself, Dellwyn pulled Lord Collingwood's note from her corset and read it again. He wanted to see her; that much was clear. Her eyes flitted over the second part of the message: *Your flower holds the key*.

Dellwyn set the note on the nightstand and picked up the metal flower. *Let's hope this key comes with a map.* A few twists of the winder only produced music, and the winder itself couldn't be removed. She wiggled the petals and found that they did wag back and forth, albeit not much. Looking closer at the petals on the outer ring of the flower, Dellwyn realized that their bases were hinges, like those on a door, which allowed them to pivot. However, something seemed to be locking them into place. Cursing under her breath, Dellwyn wished she could walk down to Room V and have Aya look at the device. She would know how to examine it.

But Aya wasn't there, and Dellwyn couldn't wait until morning to get her help. Carefully, Dellwyn turned the flower upside down to look at its base. At first, it appeared solid, merely a cylindrical stand. However, when she inspected it closer, she noticed a seam about a quarter inch up the stem. Maybe it was a lid of some sort—the base could be a canister, a jar in which to hide this "key."

Holding her breath, Dellwyn twisted the bottom of the base. It did twist, but to her surprise, it didn't come off. Instead, it elicited a series of clicks. Dellwyn stopped and looked the flower over. Sure enough, some of the petals had bent backward. Keeping the object upright, she turned the base again, eyes widening in awe as each row of petals lay flat before her.

From the center of the flower extended the handle of a key. Dellwyn slid it out and held it up in front of her. The blade was small, its teeth short and thin. Dellwyn worried they would snap off the second she tried to use the key—but her worry was quickly replaced with joy. Along the middle of the key, words revealed her destination. They weren't as helpful as a map, but they would be enough.

Level 6. Eastern corridor. Ram portrait.

Dellwyn couldn't fathom why Lord Collingwood would want to meet her by a painting of a sheep, but she resolved to find it, even if it took her the rest of the night. Before leaving, she sifted through her armoire and put on the most respectable dress she owned. If she were going to traipse around the palace —especially at such a late hour—she should at least look as though she belonged there.

Once dressed, Dellwyn stuffed Lord Collingwood's note and key down the front of her dress. She rewound the flower until all the petals stood upright once again, then placed it back on her bedside table. Before leaving the room, she spared a final look at her new quarters. Everything seemed in order. No clues to her mission had been left behind. Dellwyn didn't know what she would say if someone came looking for her, but she trusted herself to think of something. She'd had years to perfect the art of fooling the wealthy.

An ear pressed against the door told her that no one walked in the corridor or near the exit to the lobby. Dellwyn left her room, careful to shut the door behind her without a sound. Her footsteps padded lightly in the hallway, making only dull thuds on the metal floor.

Halfway down the corridor, a door opened. A man—a tradesman of some sort, judging by his tool belt—came stumbling out. The busty brunette behind him gave Dellwyn a quizzical glance before closing the door. Dellwyn let out a relieved sigh, grateful for Madam Huxley's insistence on discretion. The tradesman weaved his way to the lobby, and Dellwyn moved faster until she reached the back exit.

Dellwyn had never actually used the stairway before, but Aya had told her about the route to Lord Varick's quarters. Dellwyn climbed all the way to the top, the level where Aya had said the nobleman lived. It seemed as good a place as any to begin her search.

As she reached the top of the stairwell, Dellwyn leaned in close to the door. She couldn't hear any noise coming from the other side, but the metal did appear quite thick. With a deep breath, she squared her shoulders, raised her chin, and strode into the palace.

After all of two steps, the grandeur stunned her to a halt. Iron beams stretched across the ceiling, and ornate lanterns hung from the walls, with squat, white candles glowing behind their glass panes. The marble floors flowed the length of the corridor, an aisle of clouds to carry her through this steamship heaven. Statues stood sentry every twenty feet with tapestries blanketing the walls between them. Even the few doorways Dellwyn could see were works of art. All were metal, but some had intricate carvings etched into them, and others featured painted emblems. Dellwyn recognized one as the insignia of Count Meeran. Apparently, the nobles marked their dwellings in the same fashion as their soldiers.

Before Dellwyn could decide which way to head, a door creaked open to her left. She scanned the corridor. The nearest turn appeared too far away to reach without being seen—definitely not without being heard—and none of the statues were large enough for her to hide behind. Her only choices were to duck back into the stairwell and hope the other person did not enter behind her, or to choose a direction and hope she could feign belonging in the palace as well as she feigned pleasure.

As the person stepped into the hallway, Dellwyn turned on her heel and strode away from the stairwell. Her back was to the approaching palace dweller, and she hoped its straightness along with her quick steps would be enough to make her look as if she belonged, and better yet, unapproachable.

All she had to do was round the next corridor and dash out of sight. Aya had told her the palace hallways were like a maze, but it didn't matter to Dellwyn if she lost herself within them as long as she lost the stranger behind her. She didn't know where she was going anyway, and the Rudder would be easy enough to find again. All she had to do was head down and south until she reached one of the many doors she had passed while ascending the stairs. Assuming, of course, that she didn't lose sense of which way was south.

With the corridor in sight, Dellwyn picked up her pace. The footsteps still followed her, and from the way their sound had grown louder, she knew the person was gaining ground. Her heartbeat quickened, and she felt sweat trickle down her spine. Blood rushed in her head until she couldn't differentiate the sound of her thumping heart from her own footsteps, much less those of the stranger.

Leave me alone. Oh, please, leave me alone. Just a few more feet. That's it. Just a few more—

She reached the corner and rounded it quickly, realizing a moment too late that she had almost broken into a jog. Her shoe caught the hem of her dress, then her foot slipped out from underneath her. With a shriek, Dellwyn fell backward. She closed her eyes and braced herself for impact.

It never came. The stranger had caught her under the arms.

14

"*E*asy there, miss." The stranger helped Dellwyn to her feet. "No need to be in such a hurry."

Once steadied, she whirled around to face the stranger. He was an older man with gray hair and a friendly, but crooked, yellow smile. His plain clothing told Dellwyn that he was not a nobleman, and his tan, weathered skin revealed a lifetime of working beneath the sun. She wondered why a commoner would be roaming the palace at this time of night—though she figured the man had every right to wonder the same about her.

Dellwyn took a step back. "Thank you."

"Sorry if I startled yeh." The man's eyes searched her face for a moment, but then he shook himself and shuffled his feet. "I wanted to ask yeh a question."

"Oh?" Dellwyn crossed her arms. "Go ahead."

"Did you come from the Rudder?" The man put his hands up, probably assuming Dellwyn's eyes had widened from offense and not fear. "I mean no disrespect, miss. Yer private business is yers, no doubt. My lord is sendin' me there on an errand, and I don't want to walk down all them steps unless it's still open, you see."

Dellwyn let out a long breath. "Yes, it's still open. For another three hours or so."

"*Humph*." The man frowned and patted his knee. "I s'pose I better get a move on then. Thank yeh, miss."

"Have a nice night." Dellwyn turned to walk away but stopped herself. The servant seemed kind enough, definitely not nosy. Maybe he could help her. "Actually, sir?"

The man spun back around. "Yes, miss?"

"This is level six, right?" She tried to force a blush. "I'm afraid the climb up the stairwell left me a bit disoriented."

"Close, miss. We're on seven." The man inclined his head toward the corridor. "Keep headin' the way yeh were. About halfway down the corridor, you'll see a real frightenin' paintin' of a sea monster. The door next to it goes to a staircase. It'll take yeh down to six."

"Thank you."

The man scratched the back of his head. "They sure do keep us up all hours o' the night, huh?"

"Excuse me?" she asked.

The man tapped his chest, as if a badge were stamped over his heart. "Our lords."

"Yes." Dellwyn couldn't help but smirk. "Mine rarely let me sleep."

The servant's directions proved helpful. Farther down the hallway, Dellwyn spied the painting—a huge canvas depicting a tentacled beast devouring the palace—frightening indeed. When she emerged on the next level down, Dellwyn knew she had to be in the right place. Portraits lined the corridor as far as she could see. And to her inexplicable luck, a placard hung across from the stairwell door, indicating she go left for Port and right for Starboard. East.

As she moved down the corridor, Dellwyn noticed a few doors interspersed between the portraits. She assumed they led to the quarters of the higher nobility and wondered if the ram portrait was not her destination in itself, but rather the most identifiable way to mark the entrance to Lord Collingwood's estate.

All manner of paintings adorned the walls, and Dellwyn took care to glance at each one. Some of them made sense to her—they depicted the palace when it had sailed as the *Queen Hildegard*. Some displayed endless landscapes dotted with colorful wildflowers, and some showed a faceless woman, the Benevolent Queen, crying tears into a vast ocean.

Other paintings Dellwyn didn't understand, and she wondered if they were meant to symbolize the mythical 'world from before.' They showed tall structures, streets made out of flat stones, and large oval objects floating in the sky like metal clouds. Dellwyn shook her head. She didn't know how anyone could believe in a world with such ridiculous villages, where metal could fly like a bird and float like a feather. It couldn't be possible.

After a few minutes, Dellwyn came to the end of the hallway. She assumed she had reached the eastern corridor. A glance in both directions told her that if she turned left, she would come to the end of the corridor quickly, but if she turned right, she could walk much farther. With a deep breath, she put the odds in her favor and turned right.

When Dellwyn had walked another fifty feet or so, she found the ram portrait. It was easy to spot. Like many of the other paintings, it stretched from floor to ceiling. The ram perched atop a boulder, on the side of a mountain covered in white sand. Translucent steam leaked from its flared nostrils, and its thick horns curled in a complete circle, the points sticking out near its ears. The creature looked much more ferocious than the rams of Bowtown, and Dellwyn silently thanked the generations of farmers who had bred the wild out of them.

For as far as Dellwyn could see in either direction, no one stood in the hallway. A sinking feeling tugged at her gut, and she couldn't help but feel foolish. What had she expected to happen? Did she truly think she would show up at the exact same time as Lord Collingwood, or more ludicrously, that he would wait for her in this corridor all night, his misplaced love exposed for every passerby to see? And what if he had? Would he have taken her in his arms and divulged the perfect plan to help her escape Lord Derringher's service? Would he have pushed her up against the wall and taken what he thought he deserved more than his rival?

Dellwyn's cheeks burned. She didn't know why she had come or what she had possibly hoped to gain. With a frustrated sigh, she kicked the corner of the portrait. It moved.

She hurried backward, expecting the painting to clatter to the ground, waking anyone who lived nearby. Instead, a crack of light peeked out from behind the frame, and Dellwyn cringed in embarrassment. A hidden entrance. Of course Lord Collingwood would never meet her out in the open. Why hadn't she thought of it before?

With a shove, she slid the portrait open the rest of the way to reveal a regular door. With a shaky hand, Dellwyn fished the key out of her corset and unlocked the door. It opened. Her heart pounded in her ears again, and she stepped inside. Once she had closed the painting and door behind her, she turned to see an ornate sitting room, twice the size of her room at the Rudder. A large rug covered the floor, its intricate pattern matching the painstakingly painted walls. As for furniture, the room contained only a low wooden table, two puffy navy armchairs, and a matching sofa. Lord Collingwood was perched on the sofa.

He waited for Dellwyn to come to him. Before she could control herself, her feet swept her forward, and he leapt up to wrap his arms around her. Tears flowed from her eyes, and she let her full weight sink into his embrace. She had been strong after her ordeal—to keep Alicia's respect, to prevent Madam Huxley from gloating, to protect Sybil from the possibility of her own future—but now, she didn't have to be strong anymore.

"Shh. It's all right, my Dell." Lord Collingwood rubbed her back in small circles as he sometimes did after they'd shared a night together. "Come, sit down. We need to talk."

Dellwyn seated herself next to him. Unsure where to begin,

she wiped the remaining wetness from her eyes and took a deep breath.

Lord Collingwood must have sensed her reluctance. He took her hands in his and rubbed his thumbs over them. "Are you doing well? Are you happy?"

"What do you mean?" Dellwyn didn't know how to answer, let alone how to act around him. They were in his territory now, their roles undefined. She bit her lip. "Why did you ask me here, Stanton?"

Lord Collingwood smiled at her use of his name, but it faded just as quickly. "When I requested an appointment with you last night, Madam Huxley said you were unavailable. I thought maybe you were ill or had the night off until I met Lord Derringher in the shops, and he decided to brag."

Dellwyn closed her eyes. Of course Lord Derringher would hold this over Lord Collingwood. She opened her eyes, and her gaze landed on the concerned creases around Lord Collingwood's lips. The acid of guilt welled up in her throat—she wasn't the only one pained by the arrangement with Lord Derringher.

"I'm sorry he did that." Dellwyn squeezed Lord Collingwood's hands to show that she meant it. "I would have told you myself if I could have."

"I know." Lord Collingwood looked down at their hands, and again, Dellwyn noticed how pronounced the lines in his face had grown. "At least tell me you're happy with him. Tell me it's what you wanted."

Dellwyn stiffened. After all these years, did he know nothing about her? He had to be fishing for affection. "Of course it's not what I want. You know I enjoy my work. You know I would never want to be shackled to one client. The moment he abandons me, I'm out of a job."

Lord Collingwood's hazel eyes lifted to hers, glistening like the surface of the wells in the sunshine. "You don't love him?"

"Why would you think that?" Dellwyn would have scoffed if she didn't think it would wound him further. "I've never loved him. I've rarely even enjoyed serving him. He *bought* my time. All of it. And I wasn't consulted."

Lord Collingwood let out a long breath. When he finished, his jaw clenched. "I thought you—oh, never mind. Dell, I could have stood it if you loved him. I never imagined... I can't believe Madam Huxley would do this to you."

"Me either." Dellwyn chuckled, but there was no humor in it. She considered telling Lord Collingwood about the previous night, then decided she didn't need any more of his pity. Plus, her heart couldn't stand to hurt him further. "But I don't have a choice. I'm making the best of it."

"You have a choice." Lord Collingwood cupped her cheek, and his thumb found one last tear to wipe away. "Let me speak to my nephew on your behalf. Lionel may not condemn adultery, but he certainly won't stand for slavery."

"I *am* being paid."

Lord Collingwood looked at her, his expression deadpan. "We both know it's not fair compensation."

"Honestly, I don't know what the fair wage for this would be." Dellwyn sighed and wrapped her arms around her stomach, as if the action would hold her together. "But please, don't involve His Majesty. It would only cause more problems for me."

Unable to return his hands to hers, Lord Collingwood placed them on her knee. "What do you mean, darling?"

"Madam Huxley and I are—well, things have been rough." Dellwyn shook her head. "I had the nerve to show some ambition and to stand up to her. That, and this crazy farmer has taken up residence outside of the Rudder, and we don't agree on what should be done with him."

"A farmer?" Lord Collingwood's brow furrowed. "What in Desertera is he doing there?"

"Enforcing the will of the Benevolent Queen." Dellwyn pursed her lips. "Or so he says. I think he's heat-scrambled."

Lord Collingwood nodded. "Probably so. I lost one of my farmers to sun-sickness, maybe four months ago now. He fancied himself a prophet."

Dellwyn swallowed. *Could it be?* "Did he have strange eyes? One gray and one green?"

"Yes." Lord Collingwood raised an eyebrow. "So this is what Rykart chose to do with himself."

Dellwyn sucked in a sharp breath. Rykart. The farmer had a name. Somehow, it made him seem simultaneously more formidable and less otherworldly—he wasn't some specter controlled by the Benevolent Queen or some divine prophet sent to warn them all of their imminent damnation. He was just a man. A sick, unhinged man. And that, to Dellwyn, made him all the more pitiable—and intimidating. If that could happen to him, who else could he infect with his delusions?

When Dellwyn didn't speak, Lord Collingwood squeezed her knee. "I don't know Rykart well, obviously. He merely worked my land. All I know is that he became heat-scrambled and neglected his plots until the crops nearly died from drought. The man who oversees my farms reported him. When I went to investigate, it was clear Rykart could no longer stay in my employ, so I gave his farm to someone else to work."

Dellwyn had to bite her tongue to avoid chastising Lord Collingwood for his inattention. After all, Dellwyn worked for him, in a manner, and he knew her very well. It was different, of course, but Dellwyn thought he should at least take some interest in the people he employed.

An idea struck her. Maybe that was it. Maybe the farmer—Rykart—had targeted Dellwyn because she was Lord Collingwood's courtesan. Lord Collingwood belonged to the noble class, was connected to the royal line. And he was the embodiment of infidelity, of all the farmer wished to stop. Rykart must have found out that Lord Collingwood had a favorite courtesan at the Rudder then decided to find and save her. Dellwyn knew her relationship with Lord Collingwood wasn't a great secret, even before the law had been changed. And if the farmer could convince her to turn to the righteous path, the blow would be dealt just a step away from the crown. That had to be it. Dellwyn resolved herself to confront the farmer when she passed his tent at dawn.

"I'm so sorry, my darling. I feel like your troubles are all my fault." Lord Collingwood shifted in his seat. The rise and fall of the cushion was the only sound in the room. "Say something, Dell." Lord Collingwood's eyes begged her in a way his voice couldn't. She cursed them.

Dellwyn placed her hands over his. "Nothing is your fault, Stanton." She decided not to mention her theory. It would take too much explanation, and she couldn't risk Lord Collingwood having Rykart arrested before she spoke with him again. "And please, don't involve the king. In the mess with Lord Derringher or with Madam Huxley and Rykart. I'll figure this out. There's a reason I've survived at the Rudder this long."

Lord Collingwood frowned at her smirk. "I can't sit idly by and watch you suffer from afar. I will help you, but it will be indirect, I promise."

Dellwyn tried to refuse, but Lord Collingwood placed a finger over her lips. "I'm doing this, Dell. You can protest all you want, but it won't stop me."

Dellwyn sighed. She didn't know whether to thank him for being such a good friend or remind him that he was not her husband, nor really her lover, and should mind his own business. "I appreciate how much you care for me, Stanton, but I wish you would remember that I'm not your problem. You should remove yourself from this before you get hurt."

Lord Collingwood leaned forward and kissed her forehead. His breath tickled the crown of her head as he murmured, "It's far too late, Dell. I think we both know that."

Pulling back, she stared up at him. A soft smile played on his lips and carried through his face to the crinkles in his eyes. He really did love her. Despite her station, despite the fact that she could never fully love him back, he loved her. Dellwyn reached up and placed a hand on the nape of his neck, guiding him to her. As their lips met, the tension in her chest released, and she melted into his embrace. It might not have been true love like Aya and Lionel shared, but it was exactly what Dellwyn wanted: passion and security.

As Dellwyn moved to unbutton his jacket, Lord Collingwood broke the kiss. His face hovered next to hers, the white stubble of his cheek grazing her smooth, dark skin. "You're never going to love me, are you?"

"I don't know." Dellwyn swallowed. "But does it have to be love? Can't affection and desire be enough?"

Lord Collingwood's eyes searched hers, and Dellwyn saw the conflict within them. After a moment, he closed them and sighed. "Down there, but not up here." Lord Collingwood stood, giving his jacket a firm tug to straighten it. "I think you should go."

"You're dismissing me?" Dellwyn winced at his rejection and the whine in her voice. "Please, Stanton. After all we've been through together, what could it hurt? Really?"

"I'm sorry, Dell, but I can't have you here, not if you don't feel the same way." He fidgeted with his cravat. "I'll send you a message soon to let you know what plans are underway."

Dellwyn opened her mouth to protest, but her pride forced it shut. With a curt nod, she stalked to the door. Anger and embarrassment boiled under her skin, threatening to spill out of her eyes in hot tears. She wanted everything to go back to the way it was before. Even if it meant undoing the king's decree and repositioning herself as a criminal, she would rather be back in Room G, with Aya just down the hallway, with her regular stream of clients—no complicated emotional ties, no fighting with Madam Huxley, no farmer.

Hearing Lord Collingwood take a step toward her, Dellwyn hastily opened the door, moved the portrait aside, and entered the corridor. Despite her frustration, she shut both the door and portrait quietly. Alone amongst the paintings, she stared down the hallway at the faces of forgotten nobles, herds of legendary animals, and a world of half water. With each step, she passed another myth, another truth twisted and warped into an unobtainable utopia.

Because that was what all the portraits were: imagination. Even if the artists had painted what was once real life, the paintings would never be real. In them, Dellwyn could only see the world before through the small window of the artist's eyes.

What had lain beyond the edges of the landscape? What finer details had been obscured in a patch of color?

Dellwyn thought about Desertera—its dust-covered houses, its crowds of sun-kissed people, the *Queen Hildegard* towering over them all. She wondered how these artists would have painted it. Would they have shown it from the Starboardshire side—all pretty homes and elegant horses—with Sternville kept out of sight? And where did the poor fit in? There were none in the paintings Dellwyn had seen. What would the artist have done with her?

Spreading her fingers, Dellwyn looked down at her hands, turning them over to inspect them from all sides. The things they had done, touched, caressed. She knew where she would be. The artist would paint her, sure, but like everyone else at the Rudder, she would be obscured—there, but not really there—smudged into the gaping black hole at the rear of the ship.

15

"**W**here in this damn desert have you been?"

Dellwyn froze, one hand still on the doorknob of the Rudder's back exit. She turned around to face a glowering Alisa. With her arms crossed tightly across her chest and her foot tapping hard on the metal floor, Alisa looked like a smaller, younger version of Madam Huxley. Dellwyn opened her mouth to tell Alisa as much but stopped when she noticed the blonde's puffy, red-rimmed eyes.

Dellwyn rushed over to Alisa and instinctively touched her shoulder. "What's happened? Is everything all right?"

Alisa pulled away. "Does it *look* fine?"

Dellwyn glanced down the hallway past Alisa. The workers' doors were shut, and the faint glow of sunrise filtered in from the lobby. If it weren't for Alisa, Dellwyn wouldn't have noticed a thing out of place.

"Other than you, yes." She scanned the corridor again. Nothing amiss. "Why don't you tell me what's happened."

"Where do I even start?" Alisa rolled her eyes, and Dellwyn had to resist the urge to shake her for the dramatic stalling. "Oh, yes. Lord Derringher came for you in the wee hours of the morning. Of course, you weren't here."

"Shit." Dellwyn chewed her thumbnail, her eyes once again scouring the hallway, as if the nobleman might lurk behind one of the doors, waiting to punish her. What in Desertera would possess him to come to the Rudder so late? He'd never arrived at such an hour, never. It must have been an unplanned visit. He must have really felt he needed her. Dellwyn swallowed. "Was he angry?"

"Damn right he was angry." Alisa stamped her foot. "He came out of your room, hollering for Madam Huxley, demanding to know where you were. She tried to play it off like you had gone home sick, but then he got mad that he hadn't been notified the moment you left."

Dellwyn's mouth went dry. "What did Madam Huxley do to placate him?"

The fire went out of Alisa's eyes, and her body sagged. "I can't say it."

Dellwyn's skin prickled across the back of her neck. "What do you mean?" This couldn't be good. In all her years at the Rudder, Dellwyn had never seen Alisa look so defeated. Madam Huxley hadn't… "Did she make you serve him, Alisa? He didn't… did he try to…"

Alisa shook her head. "Worse." She motioned for Dellwyn to follow her down the corridor.

With every step, Dellwyn's heart pounded louder in her ears, until she swore the rushing of her blood was echoing against the metal walls. What could possibly be worse than Lord Derringher finishing what he had started on Alisa? Madam Huxley wouldn't have let him… no, Dellwyn couldn't think it. Sybil was too young. It would be illegal.

They stopped in front of Room B. Dellwyn's heart panged against her rib cage. "Did Lord Derringher leave me a message?"

Alisa inclined her head toward the door. "In a manner of speaking."

With a deep breath, Dellwyn pushed the door open. *No. For the love of Desertera, no.* When her brain caught up with what her eyes saw, she stumbled forward into the room and collapsed next to the bed. Sybil lay at the foot, curled up in a tight ball.

Dellwyn reached forward and brushed Sybil's hair from her

forehead. Her fingers trembled as they connected with Sybil's skin, but Dellwyn knew Sybil wouldn't notice or care—her entire body shook. A damp pool spread across the comforter under Sybil's cheek, but she no longer cried. Her eyes were clamped shut, and she refused to open them.

"Sybil, sweetheart. It's Dellwyn." She ran her fingers through Sybil's hair. "It's all right. You're safe now. You can open your eyes."

Sybil groaned and covered her mouth with her hands.

"What did he do?" Dellwyn took Sybil's hands in hers, slowly peeling them away from the girl's mouth. "I know you don't want to relive it, but I need you to tell me."

Alisa shut the door behind them and sat on the floor next to Dellwyn. "Do you want me to do it?"

Sybil shook her head, and to Dellwyn's immense relief, she pushed herself up to a sitting position. As Sybil hugged her knees against her chest, Dellwyn spared a glance at her back-side and at the bedsheets. No blood. That was a good sign.

"Madam… she…" Sybil sucked in a shaky breath. "Sh… she came to the maid's closet." Sybil's breath caught in her throat, and she held it before releasing it in a sputter. "She asked me… wanted to know if I'd seen you, if you'd gone home for the night."

Alisa glared at Dellwyn, but Dellwyn ignored her, keeping her eyes on Sybil's reddened face. Reaching up, Dellwyn patted Sybil's leg. "What did you tell Madam Huxley?"

"The truth." Sybil snugged her legs closer to her chest. "That I hadn't seen you."

Dellwyn closed her eyes and took a tremulous breath of her own. Why had she left? Why had she thought she could run to Lord Collingwood and get away with it? Hadn't she learned that the world would never give her a break?

Opening her eyes, Dellwyn let out another sigh. "Then what?"

"Madam Huxley told me to come here." Sybil bit her lip. "She didn't say why. I thought… I thought she wanted me to fetch you."

Dellwyn could hear Alisa's teeth grinding. "But Lord Derringher was here, not me."

Sybil nodded.

Dellwyn swallowed down the acid mix of guilt and rage that threatened to choke her. "And he…"

"No," Alisa supplied, her voice flat. "He could tell she was too young for *that*. But it didn't stop him from getting off."

"He made me watch." Sybil ground the heels of her hands into her eyes. "And then he put… in my mouth…" Her hands slipped down to her throat.

The bile that threatened to overtake Dellwyn rose even higher. "I'm so sorry, Sybil." She tipped her face up to hold back the tears. "I should have been here. This is all my fault."

"You're fucking right you should have been here." Alisa's voice came out hoarse. "And it is your fault. But it's that old bitch's, too."

Sybil hiccupped. "Where were you?"

Dellwyn looked down at the floor, heat rising in her chest. "Lord Collingwood summoned me. He wanted to help me escape the arrangement with… *him*."

"Oh," Sybil whispered.

Dellwyn held back another round of tears. "I'm so sorry, Sybil." She had to be strong for Sybil, for herself, so that she could do what needed to be done. "I'm sorry that I left tonight and that this happened to you because of it. I'm sorry that I never taught you, never prepared you for… I thought we had more time."

"I know." Sybil buried her face in her hands, but she peeked through her fingers at Dellwyn. Her eyes were red and puffy, but sincere. "Alisa's right. It's *her* fault, too. It's *his*."

"Still, I shouldn't have—"

"Dellwyn." Alisa's tone had hardened, and she tilted her head toward the door.

Kalinda peeked in, her face pale. "There you two are! You need to come to the lobby right now."

Alisa bared her teeth. "We're busy."

"Shh, Alisa." Dellwyn cocked her head and listened. The

noise was distant, but unmistakable—two people were locked in a heated argument, probably not far from the Rudder's entrance. With a snarl, Dellwyn leapt to her feet. "It's the farmer, isn't it?"

"Yes." Kalinda's head disappeared while she glanced down the corridor. "Him and Madam Huxley."

"Good." Dellwyn looked down at Alisa. "Stay with Sybil. I'll be back."

"Where are you going?" The question came from Sybil, and the quaver in her voice nearly tore Dellwyn's heart in two. She couldn't change what had happened to Sybil, couldn't erase the taste and shock and memories from her mind—no, Sybil would have to do that for herself in time. But Dellwyn could confront the two people who had been making her miserable, who seemed to be at the center of everything that was wrong in all of their lives.

She clenched her fists until her nails dug into her palms. The pain would distract from her grief and keep her from giving in to it. "I'm going to end this feud between the two of them once and for all."

Without another glance, Dellwyn stormed into the lobby. Madam Huxley and the farmer stood facing each other. The madam had her back to Dellwyn, but Dellwyn could see the farmer's face—his features were as calm as ever, but his complexion grew redder and redder by the second. Their words bounced off the metal walls—still quiet, but fierce—and tumbled over one another in an unintelligible mess of frustration and arrogance.

"You must release these people from your den of lust—"

"Remove yourself from my premises at once—"

"—the Benevolent Queen will no longer stand for your ways—"

"—take your religion and shove it down that dumb mouth of yours—"

"—you are drowning all of them with you—"

"—how dare you speak to me that way—"

Inserting herself in between the two of them, Dellwyn held

out her arms. When they acted as if they did not see her, she shook her fists and shouted, "Enough!"

Silence. Dellwyn took a deep breath, relishing her moment of authority. She allowed her face to smooth to demureness before turning to the madam. "Madam Huxley, you should know by now that the more you entertain the farmer, the more you encourage him to harass you."

Madam Huxley pursed her lips. "If you would have been here, you would—"

Dellwyn snapped her fingers, and to her surprise, the madam fell quiet again. She turned to the farmer with a straight face, barely managing to suppress her shock when she saw the bruise around his one gray eye and the swollen cut on his lower lip. "And you, *Rykart*, should know that, for all your good intentions, you're never going to save a single soul in the hull of this ship."

Rykart's jaw trembled. "How did you…"

Dellwyn scoffed. "The Benevolent Queen told me."

Rykart's mismatched eyes brightened. "She spoke to you?"

"No, you dolt." Dellwyn rolled hers. "You're not the only one who knows how to stalk people."

The farmer looked down to the floor.

Madam Huxley sneered at them both. "Dellwyn, I appreciate your attempt at assistance, but you need to leave now. Or should I say, *again*?" The madam's eyes narrowed into slits. "I'll deal with you later."

A lump rose in Dellwyn's throat. "I'm sorry, Madam, but I'm not going anywhere. In fact, when we're through here, *I* intend to be the one dealing with *you*." She straightened. "And I think I speak for everyone when I say that we are sick of your feud with the farmer." She motioned to the main workers' corridor, where Kalinda, Alisa, Sybil, and Augustus now stood. At the sight of Sybil, Dellwyn had to push down another wave of guilt. However, at seeing Augustus, relief washed through her. If he was still there, he could help placate Madam Huxley.

The madam looked over her shoulder and scowled at her remaining workers. "Why haven't you all left yet?"

Before they could answer, Rykart jumped in. "They have nowhere else to go, Madam Huxley. You've chained them to *your* sins, and they'll sink right along with you."

"That's not helping, Rykart." Dellwyn didn't know why, but she felt the childish urge to pull his black cap off his head and stomp it into the floor.

"I don't want to fight." Rykart placed a hand over his heart. "She doesn't either."

Madam Huxley smirked. "Oh, yes I do."

"Not you," Dellwyn and Rykart said in unison. If his proud grin had been any wider, Dellwyn *would* have ripped his hat off.

"The Benevolent Queen wants peace," Rykart continued. "For all of Her children. You are Her child, Madam. You only need to embrace Her to feel Her love."

Madam Huxley lunged at Rykart, but Dellwyn grabbed her by the shoulders and held her in place. Dellwyn didn't know how long her sore muscles could stand the madam's struggling, but luckily, Augustus rushed over to pull Madam Huxley back. In spite of her belief in Rykart's nonviolent methods, Dellwyn hazarded a glance at his tool belt. The short scythe remained sheathed.

"Think about this, Madam," Augustus cooed, his strong hands kneading her shoulders. "He isn't worth rumpling your dress, let alone a stint in the dungeon."

"I wasn't going to hurt him… much." Madam Huxley unclenched her fists, but it did nothing to ease the knot in Dellwyn's stomach.

Rykart smiled, wincing as the gash on his lip stretched. "You may hurt my body, Madam, but you will never hurt my spirit. Not while I am in Her hands."

Dellwyn groaned. "Would you give it a rest? Seriously, can't you understand how you annoy people? This holier-than-thou shit makes you sound insane."

"But I'm not better than anyone else." Rykart's eyebrows knitted together, as if he had never considered that interpretation. "Is that what you think I believe?"

"I think you're out to destroy my business." Madam Huxley

shook off Augustus's hands, but she remained in place. "After the stunt you pulled tonight, I should have you arrested. I *would*, but I don't want anyone else hearing about it. I already had to offer dozens of free nights to keep the witnesses quiet. That is, if they even return after what you've done."

Dellwyn gritted her teeth. So this wasn't just another argument. Rykart had done something even more troublesome than lurking outside the Rudder or gathering a mob to listen to his preaching. Up to this point, Madam Huxley had admitted, however begrudgingly, that his presence near the Rudder hadn't actually harmed business. What could he have done to ward customers off? Dellwyn couldn't imagine the lustful masses scared away by another word etched in the sand or more impassioned warnings from 'the Benevolent Queen.'

"For the love of your mythical queen, Rykart!" Dellwyn rubbed her forehead. "What in Desertera have you done to piss everyone off this time?"

"He made it rain," Augustus answered with a grimace. "My last client came in with it all over his face."

Rykart lifted his chin in defiance. "He should have been honored to bathe in the glory of the Benevolent Queen!"

"Really?" Forget the hat. Dellwyn wanted to throttle the farmer for his selfishness. "You wasted well water?"

"Not well water." Madam Huxley's hand slid to her throat. "Tell Dellwyn what you used, *Rykart*."

The farmer shrugged. "The holiest water of all. Blood."

Dellwyn's veins went cold, and her eyes flitted to his scythe once again. Why hadn't Madam Huxley called the guards? Even King Lionel wasn't liberal enough to allow murder, especially not in the name of this ridiculous religion.

Before Dellwyn could muster up a response, Alisa's voice supplied one from across the lobby. "Are you shitting me?"

"How…" Dellwyn couldn't finish. She backed away from the farmer, unthinkingly putting herself shoulder-to-shoulder with Madam Huxley.

"Pig's blood. From the butcher." Rykart held up his hands to show they were clean. They weren't. Red stains Dellwyn hadn't noticed before lined his fingers, peeking out from his fingerless gloves. "Blood is the water of life. It runs through all of us, tinged red by Her anger. It is the ultimate reminder of what She has done for us and how our ancestors betrayed Her."

Dellwyn bit her lip and forced herself to look at the ground. Out of the corner of her eyes, she spied dots of blood scattered across the floor, no doubt where brave clients like Augustus's had walked. Anyone not blinded by rage and self-loathing wouldn't have missed it—it would take Sybil hours to scrub the floor clean.

Sybil. Dellwyn needed to end this argument so she could confront Madam Huxley herself.

"Rykart, we've all had enough of your stunts." Dellwyn smoothed down her dress, the universal noblewoman's signal for *I'm finished with this nasty business.* "You need to realize that your extremism is only driving the Benevolent Queen's 'children' further away from Her. If you don't change your methods, I will take this matter straight to the king."

To her astonishment, Rykart nodded. "I must search all streets. If this one is empty, I shall take another."

Dellwyn had been preparing for another argument, and his easy acquiescence left her feeling empty-handed. "Well... good." She patted her dress again. "You may leave. I suggest you move your tent."

Without another word, Rykart turned and ambled away. The moment his slumped shoulders disappeared through the propellers, Dellwyn reeled on Madam Huxley. "How. Dare. You."

The madam laughed and waved her hand, as if Dellwyn were a fly she could swat away. "I'm not having this conversation."

"Oh, yes you are!" Dellwyn grabbed the madam by the collar of her dress. She stretched up on her tiptoes and stared Madam Huxley directly in the eyes. "How dare you let him do that to Sybil!"

Augustus swooped in and pulled them apart. "Delly..."

"Stay out of it, Augustus." Dellwyn reached her arm around him and pointed her finger at Madam Huxley. "You could have done *anything* else. You could have waited for one of the priming girls to finish with another client. You could have locked me in my room with him for an entire week when I got back. You could have handled him *yourself*."

"I don't see what's the matter." Madam Huxley lifted a limp wrist to point at Sybil. "The girl is unharmed. Lord Derringher seemed pleased. *You* still have your job, despite disappearing without explanation in the middle of your shift."

Dellwyn pushed away the image of Lord Derringher's smug, post-intimacy smile. "She's only fourteen! You know the law. Sixteen for priming. She's too young!"

"What are you going to do?" Madam Huxley stuck out her bottom lip. "Have Aya tell King Lionel on me?"

Dellwyn's cheeks burned. Madam Huxley had hit the right nerve. Dellwyn was useless, but she had friends in high places, and like any self-respecting noble would have done, she would use the connections to her advantage. "You're damn right I am."

For a moment, Madam Huxley's eyes flashed with something akin to fear, but she quickly replaced it with her steely gaze. "Go right ahead. But if you think demands from the king will change anything, you're more foolish than the farmer."

A thought slipped across Dellwyn's mind—a dangerous shiver of an idea—but before she could think it through, her defiance snapped it up and shot it out of her mouth. "Maybe it won't change anything." Dellwyn leaned over Augustus's outstretched arm, letting her words drip into the space between her and the madam. "But Sybil and I won't be here to find out. We quit."

To Dellwyn's immense satisfaction, Madam Huxley's jaw fell open—then flapped up and down in a wordless stupor. Finally, a squeak escaped her lips. "You can't—"

"I can, and I did." Dellwyn grinned and looked over her shoulder at Sybil, who stood huddled in between Alisa and Kalinda, her green eyes alert. "What do you say, Sybil?"

Sybil stepped forward cautiously. "Can we?"

"Say the word." Dellwyn hitched her thumb toward the exit. "And we're out of here."

Sybil took a deep breath. "Let's go."

Madam Huxley sneered. "You're going to regret this."

Dellwyn didn't spare a glance at the madam; she just watched Sybil walk toward her, one slow step at a time. "I don't think so." Her words quavered ever so slightly, but she told herself it was from emotion, conviction. "In fact, I think you'll regret putting us in this position. Especially when Lord Derringher's regular payments disappear from your account ledger."

Madam Huxley huffed.

Sybil reached Dellwyn, and Dellwyn slid her arm around the girl's shoulders as they headed for the propellers.

"If you walk out that exit, Dellwyn Rutt, there is no coming back." Madam Huxley's voice shook, making its loud echo raspy and sharp. "I won't ever help you or the girl again. You can die of thirst in the dirt for all I care. It won't be my fault."

Dellwyn paused, but only long enough to allow the madam one moment of smugness. Without turning back, she replied, "Same to you."

Madam Huxley grunted, but Dellwyn kept the last word. As she and Sybil emerged from the ship, the morning sun bathed them in light. Clanking noises floated through the cool air as the farmer gathered his belongings, but Dellwyn refused to acknowledge him. She looked down at Sybil, pleased to see a small smile on her friend's lips.

As for herself, Dellwyn shielded her eyes from the sun— pretending that it was the direct light hurting her head—then steered Sybil toward the hovel. All the way home, Dellwyn mentally listed the ways she and Sybil could make money, the people whom they could rely on for help, and the benefits of leaving the Rudder and Madam Huxley's corruption behind.

But her litany of reasons wasn't enough. The moment the hovel door closed behind her and Sybil and the sunlight was dimmed by the kitchen's gauzy, makeshift curtains, the reasons fell silent, and the voice that had been humming quietly beneath them grew louder.

At first, it sounded like Madam Huxley's shrill warning, then it took on the low growl of Dellwyn's mother, then it became her own. But each time, it said the same thing.

You've doomed yourself to ruin. And Sybil along with you.

16

———————

*D*ellwyn awoke to a pounding on the door of the hovel. As her body slowly dragged her mind out of her dreams, her heart mirrored the visitor's fist. *What have I done?*

Whoever and whatever had come to the door needed to leave—Dellwyn had enough problems without them. She had no occupation, no ways in sight to earn money—short of starting her own brothel in the hovel—and about fifty gold coins hidden throughout her tiny room and kitchen. It would last her and Sybil a month if they stopped eating breakfast.

Sybil's footsteps pattered across the common area, and the hinges to the front door squeaked. The visitor kept his voice low and quiet, but the tone was distinctly male. Sybil replied in an equally hushed tone, and Dellwyn sighed. With so much secrecy, it must be a guard. No doubt Lord Collingwood had already caught wind of the news that she'd left the Rudder, and he had sent one of his soldiers to pester her into working privately for him. Dellwyn shuddered and hoped he had sent along a gift to tempt her. She could use something valuable to hawk at the markets in Portside.

A soft tap fell upon Dellwyn's door. "Dellwyn, are you awake? There's, um, there's someone here to see us."

Us? Lord Collingwood wouldn't have any interest in Sybil. It must have been…

Dellwyn threw the blanket off herself and leaped up. How dare Lord Derringher send a guard there the night after he… she couldn't even think the words. It had to be him. Why else would the guard want to speak to Sybil as well? It had to be a business proposition. He would want them as a set—fire and earth, day and night. Well, Dellwyn wouldn't have it.

Dellwyn wrenched the door open, and Sybil nearly fell forward into her. She recovered and followed Dellwyn to the front door.

"It's a guard," Sybil whispered.

"I know." Dellwyn yanked open the door, surprised to see the sun hovering near the horizon. She must have slept through the entire day.

The guard started, and when his eyes took in Dellwyn's thin nightdress, his cheeks flushed red. "Forgive me, miss."

"Tell him no." Dellwyn squared her shoulders and straightened her back, trying to look more formidable than she felt. "Whatever he wants, whatever he offers, I'll—we'll—never work for him. We never want to see him again."

The guard shifted his feet. "I think there's a misunderstanding."

Dellwyn was about to launch into another tirade, but the creases on his forehead stopped her. He hadn't been sent by some pompous lord. Dellwyn put her hand on her hip. "Why are you here, then?"

"I'm not at liberty to say. But I must request that you and the young lady dress and accompany me to the palace." The guard motioned to the patch sewn over his heart.

Dellwyn stared at the insignia, and her breath hitched. A golden bird, sitting atop a golden cog. King Lionel.

Dellwyn glanced behind her shoulder to Sybil, who had her arms wrapped around her torso. "And what could His Majesty possibly want with us?"

"I cannot say." The guard leaned in, his voice dropping to

a whisper. "This is a delicate matter and concerns your former employment."

Dellwyn took a step back. Had Alisa gone to King Lionel on her behalf? Had Lord Collingwood sought help from his nephew after all? And even if one of her friends had turned to the king, what could he actually do for her? Her stomach twisted at the whole proposition, but if accepting charity meant keeping Sybil safe and away from the Rudder, Dellwyn would do it.

Dellwyn motioned toward the common room. "Would you like to wait inside?"

The guard gave a small bow, and when he smiled at her, Dellwyn realized she might have thought him handsome if everything else in her life weren't such a disaster. "Thank you, miss, but I'm fine out here. Please hurry."

Dellwyn nodded and shut the door.

"What's going on?" Sybil's voice trembled. "What could the king want with us?"

"Nothing bad." Dellwyn rubbed Sybil's shoulders. "Remember our visit to Aya? Do you think Aya would be foolish enough to love a man that would hurt us?"

Sybil shook her head.

"Exactly. My guess is that he found out about our situation and wants to help." Dellwyn grinned, a bit bigger than her true confidence reflected. "He might even be looking to prosecute… for justice."

Sybil's eyes brightened a touch. "What should I wear?"

"Your finest dress. I don't think King Lionel will care, but others will."

Sybil nodded and went to her room. Dellwyn sighed and did the same, hoping she hadn't just lied to Sybil.

～

DELLWYN COULDN'T LOOK AWAY. Madam Huxley lay slumped over her desk, the curved blade of the farmer's scythe stuck into her back. Its intricately designed handle glinted in the lamp light, and a single smear of red blood slashed across the bronze filigree. A dark-red stain marred the bodice of the madam's gold dress—a large pool at the top and thin trails where it dripped down to flood her desk. Her mouth hung open, as if frozen in mid-scream. The puddle of blood had stopped inches before her lips. Her neck was twisted, not broken, as if she had turned her head to watch her attacker leave through the office doorway.

And watch she did. Her green eyes were wide and unblinking. Her gaze, even in death, penetrated anyone who dared step in the doorframe to stare back.

The guard had been silent for their entire walk to the palace. Dellwyn had assumed he would take her and Sybil up the Portside gangway, and the tiny hairs on her arm had bristled when he had directed them to the stern and through the propellers. As they walked inside the Rudder, Dellwyn figured she would see Madam Huxley standing at her podium, arms crossed in a huff, accompanied by either an arrested Lord Derringher, a smug Lord Collingwood, a captive farmer, or all of the above.

What she hadn't expected was a crowd of courtesans, guards, and clients. Half stood huddled near the right corridor, where Madam Huxley's office was located. The other half were spread throughout the lobby, conspicuously as far away from the office as possible. The first person Dellwyn locked eyes with was Augustus. He had positioned himself behind the podium, and his eyes were red-rimmed and splotchy, as if he had rubbed them too hard. He looked through Dellwyn, as if she were any other person in the crowd. Next, Alisa caught Dellwyn's eye from where she stood with Jasmine and a few of the priming girls. She gave Dellwyn a slow, deep nod, but Dellwyn didn't know what that meant.

Now she stood staring at the madam's body. How could the farmer have done this? Dellwyn understood *why* he would want to harm Madam Huxley. And she would be a liar if she said the fantasy of the madam dropping dead from heart failure or falling in a well hadn't crossed her own mind once or twice—

but she had never thought to murder her. Besides, the farmer had always been peaceful. When he'd followed Dellwyn to Augustus's house, he had not harmed either of them. He had saved Sybil from the man at the rally without drawing blood. Even his 'rain' stint had left patrons unharmed, though perhaps disgusted. Dellwyn couldn't believe he would succumb to violence now. And yet, there she stood, unable to tear her eyes from the proof.

Someone touched Dellwyn's arm, and she turned to see Aya standing next to her. A wave of relief washed over her. How could she ever have thought that she would lose Aya? They might grow apart, but they would always be there for each other when it mattered—as Aya was in that moment. Dellwyn wrapped Aya into a hug, only a little embarrassed when she began to cry into the cogsmith's shoulder.

Aya pulled Dellwyn closer and pressed their cheeks together. "You're a suspect." Dellwyn nearly pushed Aya away, but Aya held her firm. "Is there somewhere we can talk?"

Without saying a word, Dellwyn led Aya through the lobby to Room B. As they passed Sybil and Alisa in the crowd, Dellwyn jerked her head to indicate that they should follow. They did, and a few moments later, the four women were securely locked inside Room B.

"You've moved up." Aya's gaze drifted over the room, and Dellwyn noticed her pause to admire the metal flower from Lord Collingwood.

"It's a long story." Dellwyn's jaw tightened, and she shook her head. Aya nodded, her eyes crinkled in concern. They stood in silence for a moment, then Dellwyn motioned for everyone to sit.

Alisa sprawled herself across the bed, and Dellwyn sat at its end. Aya perched on the fainting couch. Sybil seated herself next to Aya, her eyes purposefully avoiding the bed, her body turned to the side to shield herself from it.

Dellwyn cursed herself. She should have asked Alisa to let them use Room C instead. But this wasn't the time to spare feelings. A woman was dead, and if Dellwyn and Sybil weren't careful, they could be next. Dellwyn stared at Aya, waiting for her to explain.

"I don't know exactly what has happened." Aya bit her lip, glancing again toward the mechanical flower. "The gossip has already spread to Portside. Everyone I ran into on the street was dying to tell me about my former employer or trying to coerce information out of me. I came as soon as I heard."

Dellwyn rubbed her legs, suddenly feeling cold. "Who thinks I did it?"

"The guards." Aya's neck flushed. "I demanded to know what had happened, and they said Madam Huxley was murdered by one or more of her enemies. One of the workers —they didn't say who—found her a few hours ago. The guards' main suspect is the farmer, given that his scythe, or one like it, is the murder weapon. But you and Sybil are numbers two and three, thanks to the argument you had with the madam last night."

Alisa's forehead wrinkled. "And they just told you all of this?" Then her eyes rolled, and she scoffed. "Oh, yes, of course they did, Your Highness."

"Stop it." Sybil's harsh tone startled Dellwyn, and she saw the other women jump. "Alisa, Aya is here to help. Could you try not to be a bitch for once?"

Even though she had spoken to Alisa, Sybil's eyes remained on Aya, as if she were an anchor, keeping Sybil from sinking back into the bed. A stunned silence followed, and Dellwyn had to resist the urge to admonish Sybil for her language. Now was not the time for mothering, either.

"It's fine, Sybil. I'm used to her." Aya waved her hand. "Anyway, they already have the farmer in custody. You two are in their custody now, whether they've told you or not. You're to be brought before King Lionel later today."

Dellwyn swallowed down the lump in her throat. "Is it a trial?"

"They don't have enough evidence." Aya fiddled with the ends of her long curls. "I think Lionel wants to hear from all perspectives. Though, I'm not sure whether you'll be allowed to go home or if you'll have to stay in the palace until this is all sorted."

Dellwyn closed her eyes. The image of Madam Huxley's body flooded her mind, but more than the blood, she saw the farmer's scythe, its handle shining like the sun against the back of her eyelids. What had he been thinking? Had his goddess told him to do it?

"I need to ask a question." Aya's voice hitched, and Dellwyn opened her eyes to find her friend's face flushed. "Of all three of you, for good measure."

Dellwyn felt her spine stiffen, and even Alisa sat up at attention.

"Did any of you kill her?"

Dellwyn laughed, but when Aya's face stayed still, she stopped. "You're not joking."

Alisa crossed her arms. "Do *you* think we're murderers, Aya?"

"That doesn't answer my question." Aya pursed her lips, but held up her hands in a gesture of peace. "Look, I know a little something about hatred and a little something more about revenge. I will be the last person to judge you if you killed Madam Huxley." She sent Alisa a pointed glare. "Any of you."

Sybil shifted in her seat. "What do you mean?"

Aya let out a long breath. "King Archon had my father executed. I helped get King Archon executed."

"So the rumors *are* true?" Alisa clapped her hands together. "And here I thought the only truth was you screwing your way into the monarchy."

Aya's eyes narrowed, but she didn't respond to Alisa's comment. "I don't care how Madam Huxley died. She was good to me; she was bad to me; and my life will not be particularly impacted by her death. But I do care about justice. The way she had been running this place, the stories the courtesans in the lobby tell—she must have turned into a monster. None of you deserve to die for saving everyone here from a life of abuse."

Dellwyn bit her lip. She didn't know what to think of Aya's

speech. King Archon had been different—he had arranged the execution of countless innocent people. But Madam Huxley hadn't killed anyone. Yes, the madam was the reason Dellwyn had to endure Lord Derringher's sick fantasy, and the madam had allowed Lord Derringher to entertain himself with Sybil. And who knew how many other abuses Madam Huxley had turned her back to. But did she deserve to be murdered? Dellwyn didn't think the question had an easy answer, and definitely not as confident a one as Aya proclaimed.

"I didn't do it," Dellwyn whispered.

Sybil shook her head. "Me either."

The two of them, and Aya, looked to Alisa. The blonde huffed. "I don't owe you anything."

Aya must have been satisfied enough with that answer, for she nodded at Alisa. Dellwyn wondered whether it held the same mysterious meaning as the one Alisa gave her earlier, or if Aya were simply agreeing to let Alisa be.

Sybil picked at a loose thread on her skirt. "When do you think the guards will take us to the king?"

"Soon. Once Lionel has finished questioning the farmer." Aya ran her fingers through her hair. "I'm sure you two won't be the end of it. Alisa, he'll likely want to speak with you and the other workers as well. It may be wise to prepare them, so they can think ahead about what they might say."

Alisa raised an eyebrow. "What does it matter if they're innocent?"

"You'd be surprised what people's minds come up with when they feel threatened." Aya's lip lifted in a snarl. "Or when they have the opportunity to influence the fates of others. For better or worse."

Dellwyn felt her heart skip a beat. No one at the Rudder wished her ill, did they? Surely no one would lie to get rid of her. Not now that she wasn't competition.

Alisa sighed. "Fine. I'll talk to them, feel them out."

Aya offered a small smile. "Thank you." Her hand fished into her pocket and emerged with a flat, circular object, which was fastened to a long, silver chain. Aya looked down at the circle, frowned, then replaced it. "You all should go back to the lobby. We've been gone a while, and the last thing you need is for the guards to think you're hiding."

Dellwyn stood. "Was that a clock?"

"A pocket watch, yes." Aya beamed as widely as a child who had built her first sand ship. "One of the books Lionel sent me finally proved useful. It doesn't quite keep proper time, but I'm getting it closer every day."

"That's great, Aya." Dellwyn reached over and placed her hand on Aya's arm. "I'm so proud of you."

To Dellwyn's surprise, Aya's eyes watered. "Thank you." She took a deep breath to compose herself. "Now, hurry along. You don't want to be late for your audience with the king."

Alisa and Sybil stood as well, and the four of them lingered before the door, each reluctant to end the moment.

"Do you want us to give him a message for you?" Sybil asked. Dellwyn noticed Sybil's body was still tense, but her eyes had taken on the enchanted gleam they always did when she talked about love. A weight lifted from Dellwyn's chest.

"Actually, I do." Aya tapped her finger against her lips, and Dellwyn knew she was choosing her words carefully. "Tell him that when the trial of Madam Huxley's murder is over, I think enough time will have passed. But also warn him not to be an imbecile and rush the verdict because of it."

Alisa snickered, and Sybil gasped. "I can't call the king an imbecile!"

Dellwyn chuckled. "Will he know what it means?"

"Perhaps not exactly." Aya blushed. "But I know he'll take it as I want him to."

Dellwyn nodded and looked at Sybil. "Ready?"

"I suppose," she replied, smoothing down the front of her dress.

They stepped out into the hallway, only to be greeted by the guard who had led them to the Rudder. He bowed and motioned toward the back exit, the one Dellwyn had taken the night before to visit Lord Collingwood.

Lord Collingwood. The gravity of Dellwyn's next thought

smacked her square in the chest, nearly knocking the air out of her lungs.

He wouldn't have. He could have, of course, but he wouldn't have. After Dellwyn had confessed that she didn't love him, after he had spurned her advances, surely he wouldn't have done this for her. She wasn't worth the risk. And yet, Dellwyn couldn't stop repeating the question over and over again in her mind.

Would Lord Collingwood have murdered Madam Huxley for me?

17

———

Dellwyn would have recognized King Lionel immediately, even if he had not worn the customary cog-embroidered top hat. He had his uncle's creamy hazel eyes, and when they washed over Dellwyn, she had to fight the urge to blush. He was everything Aya had described—and everything his former womanizing reputation indicated—tall and lean, with a devilish grin and a boyish swoop to the front of his dark-brown hair.

Although Dellwyn had never met King Archon, she decided that if he had exuded half the charm of his son, she couldn't blame some of the foolish young women for falling into his marriage trap. A weaker woman, a woman without Dellwyn's training and years of experience with suave men, would have been easily captured by someone like King Lionel, or Lord Collingwood, for that matter. She wondered how long Aya had resisted before giving in to those eyes.

As Dellwyn, Sybil, and the guard approached, King Lionel inclined his head to them. He stood outside a set of double doors, no doubt the room in which the interrogation would take place. "It's good to finally meet you, Dellwyn. I've heard so much about you."

"Likewise, Your Majesty." Dellwyn curtsied. "Of course, I had hoped we would meet under happier circumstances."

"As did I." King Lionel turned to her companion. "And you must be Sybil."

Sybil startled, as if awoken from a trance, and gave a deep curtsy.

King Lionel rubbed the back of his neck. "I apologize for having you brought here. It's a necessary formality." He glanced at the doors. "Hopefully, this won't take long. We've been questioning people since late afternoon, and I know they won't want to keep at it long into the night."

"Who?" Sybil's breath hitched when King Lionel's gaze shifted to her.

"The council. All hearings are now presided over by a group, not just the king. It seems a little fairer, don't you think?"

Sybil nodded.

King Lionel smiled. "Are you ready to go inside, or would you like a few minutes to compose yourselves?"

Dellwyn let out a long breath. "I think we're ready to get this over with."

King Lionel turned to open the doors, but Sybil stopped him by touching his arm. "Wait. We have a message for you. From Aya."

When Sybil said Aya's name, something in King Lionel's face changed. His eyes softened, almost glinting with sadness, and his jaw visibly relaxed. "Yes?"

Sybil removed her hand from his sleeve and held it in her other palm. "She says that, when this trial is over, enough time will have passed."

A grin spread across King Lionel's face. "Sybil, may I hug you?"

The girl nodded, and King Lionel scooped her into an embrace and spun her around in a circle. Dellwyn covered her mouth to conceal her shock—and her concern for how Sybil would react to the contact.

"Thank you, Sybil." King Lionel set her down. "I think that's the best news I've ever received."

Released from the king's arms, Sybil wobbled a bit where she stood, but she smiled and said, "You're welcome."

Dellwyn let out a sigh of relief. "Aya said not to rush the verdict, though," she added, smirking. "I think her exact words were 'tell him not be an imbecile,' Your Majesty."

King Lionel chuckled and rubbed his forehead. "That's my Aya. Ruining the romance with practicality."

The guard cleared his throat. Sybil jumped, and Dellwyn nearly did, too. She had forgotten he stood behind them.

"Yes, yes, I know." King Lionel waved his hand at the guard. "Pleasant as he may seem, Sir Laurel is all business when it comes down to it."

"Someone has to be," Sir Laurel quipped before stepping in front of the king to open the doors.

Dellwyn's astonishment must have been evident on her face, for King Lionel looked at her with furrowed brows. "Don't mind him. We've been friends since childhood. I need at least one guard to keep me in line."

They strode through the door into a short hallway. After a few steps, the corridor opened into a round room with elevated rows of seats encircling it. No onlookers were present, but eight individuals sat around a circular table in the center of the room.

Dellwyn's eyes landed on Lord Collingwood, and she felt heat burn through her chest. She had remembered that he was on the council, but encountering him in public for the first time had her hands shaking. How was she supposed to act around him? Did the others know that he frequented the Rudder and that she was his courtesan there? And if he did have Madam Huxley murdered for Dellwyn, how could she meet his eyes? She wished Lord Collingwood would have greeted them outside instead of the king. She needed answers.

King Lionel motioned for Dellwyn and Sybil to seat themselves in two of the empty chairs. He sat in the other, between a man Dellwyn recognized as the bishop and a petite blond woman with piercing blue eyes. Sir Laurel stood sentry by the doors.

"We have Miss Dellwyn Rutt and Miss Sybil Tanner here to be questioned about the alleged murder of Madam Lilliette Huxley," King Lionel began. Dellwyn couldn't recall hearing the madam's first name before. Surely she would have remembered something so lilting and innocent, so unlike the madam. It made Dellwyn's chest hurt to have the madam humanized in that small way.

King Lionel motioned to the small man next to him. "Bishop, would you please swear them in?"

The bishop straightened in his seat, still more than a head shorter than King Lionel. He held a ring-clad hand over his chest. "Please cover your hearts." Dellwyn and Sybil complied. "Do you swear on the grace of the Benevolent Queen, and on your own integrity, to speak truthfully and completely?"

Dellwyn nodded. "I do."

"I do," Sybil repeated, keeping close watch on Dellwyn from the corner of her eyes.

"Thank you." King Lionel rubbed his hands together. "I assume you know the bishop?"

Dellwyn and Sybil nodded.

"Very good." King Lionel motioned to his left. "This is Her Highness Zedara Ollessen, the queen dowager and one of my most trusted friends." He gave Dellwyn a pointed look, indicating that the queen dowager was a friend to her as well. But Dellwyn already knew. Aya had told her about Zedara's role in the mission to get rid of King Archon. "Next to Her Highness is Lord Stanton Collingwood, my uncle and chief adviser. The four of us make up the core of the council."

Lord Collingwood nodded at Dellwyn, but when the others looked toward the next person to be introduced, he gave a small shake of his head. Dellwyn raised an eyebrow. Was that gesture meant to signify that Madam Huxley's death hadn't been by his hand? Or was he merely expressing his frustration that Dellwyn was suspected in the murder? Dellwyn would have liked to express some frustration of her own. Was she the only person in Desertera who didn't speak the language of ominous head gestures?

King Lionel continued his introductions, and Dellwyn was forced to turn to the next council member. "On Lord Collingwood's left is our Sternville representative, Mr. Jack Wellman."

As Dellwyn took in Jack's toothless grin and grimy, dirt-covered clothes, she withheld a sneer. She didn't know Jack well, but she knew his children—a litter of grubby-handed little thieves. And in Dellwyn's experience, the children of Sternville were almost always miniatures of their parents. Even she had ended up in her mother's profession, after all.

"Our Portside representative is Miss Heidi Baker."

Dellwyn turned her attention to Miss Baker, a heavyset woman with round, red cheeks and a stern countenance. She wore a stained apron, and her graying hair was tied back under a plain white scarf, which made her appear even more formidable. Thank goodness Miss Baker sat between Jack and Sybil.

King Lionel motioned to the individual seated on Dellwyn's other side, a thin man with an infectious grin and upturned mustache. He also wore an apron, though his was spotless and crisp. "And to your left, Dellwyn, is our palace representative, Mr. Stefan Chef."

Mr. Chef stuck out his hand for Dellwyn to shake. "Fabulous to meet you, sweethearts."

"Likewise." Dellwyn shot King Lionel a questioning glance, but he merely smiled. Sybil did not say anything.

"Next to Mr. Chef is Mrs. Eveline Farmer, representing Bowtown, of course."

Mrs. Farmer sat straight and stiff, her sun-bleached hair braided and hanging over her shoulder. She kept her hands on top of the table, and Dellwyn noticed the telltale calluses on her fingertips. Dellwyn glanced down at her own fingers and admired their smoothness. At least she had made it out of the Rudder unscathed, physically speaking.

"And between Mrs. Farmer and the bishop, we have our Starboardshire representative, Lord Ulberion Varick."

Dellwyn froze, her gaze slowly slipping up from her hands to meet the dark, beady eyes of Lord Varick. Even obscured by small, round spectacles, they were chilling. He wore an elaborate velvet suit, deep purple in color with gold embroidering, and a matching top hat, which he removed with a gloved hand to give a seated bow to Dellwyn and Sybil. His smile revealed sharp, impeccably white teeth. An ivory cane lay across his lap, its end held in the crook of his elbow. Dellwyn had only ever seen ivory in small pieces of jewelry, and the extravagance of Lord Varick's carved scepter made her loathe him more.

So this was the man who had raised Aya from the Rudder and provided her a chance for vengeance—only to betray her. Dellwyn had so many words for Lord Varick, but she held her tongue. More than anything, she wished she could ask King Lionel how Lord Varick was allowed to be the Starboardshire representative when he lived in the stern of the palace.

King Lionel took a deep breath. "Now that we are all introduced, I will begin with the questioning. And I am obligated at this time to remind you of your oaths."

Dellwyn and Sybil nodded to show that they remembered.

"When was the last time you saw Madam Huxley?"

"Last night." Dellwyn wrinkled her nose. "I guess you all would probably call it early morning. Right before sunrise."

"And you, Sybil?" King Lionel asked.

Sybil swallowed. "Same."

"And where was this?"

"The Rudder," Sybil replied. "After work."

"Dellwyn, I'm told you and Madam Huxley argued." King Lionel glanced toward Lord Collingwood, and Dellwyn wondered if the king knew about her connection to his uncle. "Could you tell us what happened?"

Dellwyn looked around the table. Most of the council regarded her plainly. Their only expressions were of mild interest and tiredness. However, Lord Varick and Jack Wellman watched her intently, with narrowed eyes.

Dellwyn sighed and focused on King Lionel. "It's complicated. To put it simply, I didn't agree with how Madam Huxley had been running the Rudder ever since the adultery law was revoked. I confronted her about it. The farmer, Rykart, was there, too. He and Madam Huxley were arguing because he had been harassing the clients. I made him leave so I could talk to the madam myself. In the end, our argument couldn't be resolved, and I quit."

"You stopped arguing with her?" King Lionel's voice didn't have quite the right inflection. Dellwyn suspected he already knew the truth.

"I quit the Rudder." Dellwyn patted Sybil's hand under the table. "As did Sybil."

Sybil nodded and squeezed Dellwyn's hand.

"What happened then?" King Lionel asked.

"We left." Dellwyn shrugged. "We walked back to our home, went to bed, and didn't wake up until Sir Laurel came to retrieve us."

"Very well." King Lionel leaned back in his chair. "Does anyone else have any questions for Miss Rutt and Miss Tanner?"

Mr. Chef rested his hand on Dellwyn's shoulder. "Do you two have anyone else who can speak to your whereabouts today?"

Dellwyn shook her head. "A few of the other workers saw us leave the Rudder, but unless someone was watching us sleep through the windows, I don't have any other witnesses."

Mr. Chef smiled and squeezed her shoulder before releasing it.

The queen dowager cleared her throat. "Did you recognize the murder weapon?"

"It looked like Rykart's scythe." Dellwyn couldn't explain why, but guilt stirred in her gut. "But I don't know if it belonged to him or not. For all I know, all the farmers have them."

"They don't. Not like that." Mrs. Farmer's gaze didn't leave her hands. "Rykart's is unique."

If Dellwyn's suspicions were right and Rykart were innocent, how would the true murderer have gotten a hold of the scythe? She shot a glance at Lord Collingwood then quickly looked down at her lap.

"And how well do you know Rykart?" The former queen tapped her fingers on the table. "What can you say about his character?"

"I must admit, I don't know him well. But from everything I've seen, he doesn't seem violent. Crazy, absolutely. Unnerving, sure." Dellwyn shuddered, remembering Rykart's mismatched eyes. "But I don't think he's dangerous."

"He saved me once." Sybil scooted forward in her seat. "From a bad man in a mob. Rykart wouldn't kill anyone. He's good… he just has an odd way of showing it."

The queen dowager leaned over and whispered into King Lionel's ear. He nodded. "We'll take your remarks under consideration," he said.

"Meaning no offense, dears"—Miss Baker crossed her arms—"but if Rykart Farmer is innocent, that makes you two our top suspects."

Dellwyn felt Sybil tremble at her side. "We told you. We were at home. Asleep."

Before Miss Baker could retort, Lord Collingwood cut in. "Why don't you tell us *why* you were upset with Madam Huxley? Perhaps that would help us understand your perspective."

Dellwyn's face heated. Lord Collingwood wanted them to pity her because pathetic people never hurt anyone. They didn't have it in them.

"She sold all of my time to a single client and removed all restrictions on his behavior." The women at the table, even the rough Miss Baker, grimaced. "Essentially, she made me his slave."

"And you, Sybil?" Lord Collingwood gave her a reassuring smile.

"Last night, Dellwyn had to leave work for a while." Sybil stared straight at Lord Collingwood, who looked down in shame. Dellwyn couldn't help but feel proud. "And that same client made me… assist him."

"And you dragged this poor girl up here for questioning?"

The queen dowager slammed her fist against the table. "How dare you, Lionel! It could have waited."

Unfazed, King Lionel gently placed his hand over hers. "Your Highness, may I remind you, you're not my stepmother anymore."

The queen dowager narrowed her eyes but held her tongue.

King Lionel turned to Sybil. "How old are you?"

"Fourteen." Sybil fidgeted with her sleeve. "Lord Derringher didn't... not that. But he..." She touched her mouth.

Lord Collingwood rubbed his forehead, and Dellwyn's skin warmed from righteous satisfaction, then from anger at her own pettiness.

King Lionel clenched his jaw. "Do you have any proof?"

"No." Sybil bit her lip. "No one else was there, and Madam Huxley and I were alone when she ordered me to Dellwyn's room."

"I see." King Lionel frowned. "Bishop, when we're done questioning these ladies, please summon Lord Derringher. I'd like to hear his side of the story."

The bishop nodded, and Dellwyn's breath caught. It might not be enough to get Lord Derringher imprisoned, but at least he would receive a firm warning and the knowledge that he couldn't misuse young women as he saw fit. Sybil's eyes watered, and Dellwyn took her hand, relieved that she hadn't lied to her young friend about King Lionel seeking justice, after all.

Before Dellwyn could thank King Lionel, Lord Varick chimed in for the first time. "It certainly makes for a tempting motive, though, does it not?" Lord Varick stroked his chin, the white of his glove only a few shades lighter than his pale skin. "After all, if someone had subjected me to a similar fate, I would be inclined to take revenge."

"Not all of us solve our problems with schemes and executions," Dellwyn spat.

Lord Varick grinned like a parent whose child was

exhibiting her first moment of defiance. King Lionel and the queen dowager exchanged sideways glances.

"Well then," Lord Varick continued, his smile still smug, "can you think of anyone who would elect such methods?"

Dellwyn kept her eyes from wandering to Lord Collingwood, but she couldn't keep her mind from drifting to Alisa and her skillful avoidance of Aya's question. Alisa had been frustrated with Madam Huxley as well, and she had insisted several times that the madam's greed needed to be stopped. But Dellwyn didn't believe she was capable of murder, either. Alisa had always been all talk and little action.

Dellwyn pursed her lips. "I don't think so." Even if Alisa were guilty, Dellwyn wouldn't give the council her name. Not until she had talked to Alisa herself.

"Very well." Lord Varick arched an eyebrow. "And you, Miss Tanner?"

Sybil shook her head. "I know plenty of people who disliked Madam Huxley, but I don't think any of them are murderers."

Lord Varick's lips puckered and twisted, but he didn't say anything further. Dellwyn hoped he stayed silent for the rest of the meeting. She wasn't about to give him the slightest hint of satisfaction, not that she knew what he was after. Probably her and Sybil's guilt because that outcome would hurt Aya the most.

King Lionel broke the silence. "Does anyone else have any questions at this time?"

Dellwyn braced herself for more, but no answer came. She let out a long sigh of relief. She couldn't imagine how a guilty person would sit through a questioning; being perfectly innocent during one was nerve-wracking enough.

"Do you have any other information that may help us, ladies?" King Lionel asked. His hazel eyes bore into the two of them, and Dellwyn couldn't tell whether it was for the rest of the council's benefit, or whether he was trying to discern if they had been fully honest.

"No," Sybil replied, straightening up in preparation to leave.

"I can't think of anything," Dellwyn added.

"Then you are dismissed." King Lionel's face relaxed, and he smiled his charming smile. "But please be aware that you may be called in for further questioning as new evidence arises."

Dellwyn stood, and Sybil followed suit. "We understand. Thank you."

"One more thing." King Lionel held up his hand. "I know neither of you works at the Rudder any longer, but I thought you might be interested to know that we're having a meeting tomorrow at midday to decide what shall become of it. Right in this very room, in fact. Madam Huxley did not specify a successor, and I daresay the community, and the employees, would not be too pleased if the business simply shut down."

Dellwyn's eyebrows rose. "So soon?"

"We realize it would be in better taste to wait until after the funeral." King Lionel looked pointedly around the table. "But given that the guards need more time with the… evidence, we've decided to settle this matter now. We need to place the Rudder in good hands."

The king's gaze returned to Dellwyn, and he gave her a smile. It took all her self-control to withhold one of her own. "Thank you for letting us know."

As Sir Laurel escorted them out of the courtroom, Dellwyn managed to keep her grin at bay. However, she utterly failed at denying the dangerous hope that swelled in her chest.

When Dellwyn and Sybil returned to their hovel, the sun long set below the horizon, they found Augustus waiting for them. He paced outside the front door, a thin trail carved into the dirt by his anxious footsteps.

The moment he saw them, he rushed forward and scooped

them both into a hug. "Oh, thank goodness they let you go. I was beginning to think you'd been arrested."

Dellwyn pulled back and stared up at him. Though less puffy than before and only slightly red, his eyes still shone with sadness. She reached up and touched a hand to his cheek. "We're all right. Let's go inside."

Augustus nodded and followed Dellwyn and Sybil into the hovel. He took a seat at the table, while Sybil rushed over to the water jug to pour them each a cup of water. Feeling useless, Dellwyn sat in the empty chair across from Augustus and intertwined her fingers. "How are you?"

"Sad, scared, angry." Augustus put his head in his hands. "Not to mention wracked with guilt. I'm so sorry, Delly."

"Sorry?" Dellwyn didn't even glance at the cup of water Sybil placed in front of her. Instead, she stared at Augustus's rumpled hair. He seemed a little too torn up about her and Sybil being questioned. "What could you possibly have to be sorry for?"

"I think... well, it's my fault that they targeted you." Augustus picked up his own cup and downed it in one gulp. "I'm the one who told them that you and Madam Huxley had been fighting. It didn't even occur to me... they just asked about the last time I saw her... you know, alive... and I mentioned your argument."

The way Augustus stumbled over his words made Dellwyn frown. Even in crisis, he'd always been a smooth talker. Something was wrong with him, something more than grief. She sighed and sipped her own water. "You didn't do anything wrong, Auggie. You just told the truth. Now, what's really got you so upset?"

Augustus's lips quivered. "How did you know?"

"We've been friends long enough." Dellwyn reached across the table and took his hand. "What's going on? You wouldn't have come here if you didn't want to tell me."

Augustus swallowed. "I'm the one that found her."

Dellwyn sucked in a breath. Poor Augustus—no wonder he was such a mess.

"Oh, that's horrible." Sybil wrapped her arms around Augustus. "Are you okay?"

"No." Augustus returned Sybil's embrace with his free arm. With his other hand, he clenched Dellwyn's palm tighter. "I can't stop seeing her face. It's there every time I blink. She didn't deserve to die like that."

Dellwyn rubbed her thumb against his skin. "No, she didn't. But King Lionel and the council will find out who did this. They'll give her justice."

Augustus gently pushed Sybil away. "Not if they keep wasting their time questioning innocent people." He frowned again. "I can't believe how stupid I was."

"It's fine." Dellwyn released her hold on him then waved her hand to dismiss his concerns. "As you can see, they didn't waste time arresting us. Just asked us a few questions."

"Everyone was very nice." Sybil patted Augustus's shoulder. "And we met Aya's King Lionel. He's going to have Lord Derringher arrested and make him answer for what he did to me."

"That's wonderful." Augustus smiled—a small one, but it was enough to tell them that he was done with their sympathy and ready to change the subject. "And given your blush, I take it the king's as handsome as everyone says?"

Sybil pressed her lips together and nodded.

"I must say, I'm so proud of you." Augustus placed his hand over Sybil's. "You've been very strong through everything that's happened the past couple days."

"I don't have a lot of options." Sybil shrugged. "I can go on with my life, or I can be a crying mess. It's easier to be strong now that I know Lord Derringher will pay—and that I never have to work at the Rudder again."

Dellwyn felt a knot untie itself in her stomach. She was so proud of Sybil, and she wished that she could as easily leave the Rudder behind. But in spite of everything, Dellwyn's heart tugged at the thought. The Rudder was one of the few places where she had ever felt valued, talented, as though she was really worth something. And now that Madam Huxley was gone, maybe she could help it be a place like that for others again. Of course, she would never force Sybil to return. And for the time being, she might be able to support them both on one salary, especially if it was a madam's salary. Sybil could decide what she wanted to do with her life in a few years. She could enjoy being young a while longer.

"Well?" Augustus stared at Dellwyn expectantly. When she met his eyes with a blank look, he shook his head. "I said, what about you, Delly? Will you return to the Rudder now that Madam Huxley is gone?"

Not wanting to reveal too much about her half-formed plan, Dellwyn shrugged. "I'm not sure. I suppose that depends on what becomes of it."

"Ah, yes. That is the question." Augustus leaned in conspiratorially, as if eavesdroppers stood beyond the walls. Instinctively, Dellwyn pictured the farmer lurking outside the window before remembering that he was in custody. "The guards told me there'll be a meeting in the palace courtroom tomorrow to decide who should take ownership of the Rudder."

Dellwyn took another drink of her water. Why would Augustus bring this up? It didn't seem like a happy topic, especially after what he'd revealed. "King Lionel mentioned it. I'm not sure that I'll go."

"Of course you should go." Augustus retook her hand. "You should be first in line."

Dellwyn watched his face, but it remained calm and smooth, not a hint of jest or insincerity in sight. "You really think so?"

"Of course I do." Augustus offered a small smile, and Dellwyn could imagine the wheels turning in his mind. "You've been there since you were younger than Sybil. You're good at your work, and in normal circumstances, you enjoy it. All the other workers respect you. Better than that, they trust you. And in all the time I've known you, I've never seen you harm anyone. Not even a sand beetle. You'd be perfect."

Dellwyn fought the urge to smirk. It was extremely validating to hear someone else voice her own positive opinions of herself aloud. But something still felt off. Dellwyn shrugged. "I figured Alisa would want to be in charge. Or maybe you."

"Me?" Augustus rubbed the back of his neck. "I'm no good with the business part. I can please a man—and a woman, goodness help me—with the best of them, but that doesn't make me fit to take care of the clients' other needs. Let alone the employees."

"Madam Huxley did have a way with people when she wanted to." Dellwyn scoffed but softened her face when Augustus's eyes watered. "For all her other faults, she was a great businesswoman."

Augustus nodded and bit his lip.

Sybil refilled his cup. "Who do you think did it, Auggie?"

Augustus slowly twirled his cup. "It's obvious, isn't it? They found the farmer's scythe in her back."

"I didn't think he had it in him." Dellwyn shook her head. "He always seemed so peaceful. Even in arguments, he rarely raised his voice."

"If not him, then who?" There was a challenge in Augustus's voice, and he gave Dellwyn a pointed look. While the expression was meant to remind Dellwyn of her questioning, Augustus's tone had sounded defensive. Dellwyn shook it off. Everyone she had talked to was defensive at the moment. They had to be.

"I know the guards have Sybil and me pinned as the next most likely suspects. And you're right, the farmer has the clearest motive and owns the murder weapon." Dellwyn frowned. A nagging feeling wriggled in her gut, but she decided not to divulge her own theories. "But I think we'd be short-sighted to rule out other options at this point."

"Maybe, but I still think he did it." Augustus let out a long breath. "I wonder what his Benevolent Queen has to say."

"Oh, don't worry." Dellwyn rolled her eyes. "Innocent or guilty, I'm sure he'll tell everyone exactly what She says at his trial."

"Will we be allowed to go?" Sybil asked. "I mean, aren't nobles usually the only ones who attend murder trials?"

"That's how it used to be," Augustus said. "But I daresay King Lionel will have different rules."

"Even so," Dellwyn added, "I'm sure we'll be called to testify."

From the changing line of Sybil's lips, Dellwyn couldn't tell if she was pleased or troubled by the news. Then again, Sybil probably didn't know either.

Augustus took one last drink from his cup and rose. "I should let you two get some rest. I could use the beauty sleep myself." He chuckled, but the sound fell flat.

"Thank you for checking in on us." Dellwyn stood and walked him to the door. "And if you need anything, let us know. You've been through something terrible, Auggie. We all have. But you never have to be alone."

"Thank you, Delly." Augustus hugged her quickly then waved to Sybil. "Stay safe, ladies."

At his words, Dellwyn's chest tightened. It hadn't occurred to her that she and Sybil would be in any danger. But if her instincts about the farmer were correct, then Madam Huxley's killer was still on the loose. And who was to say he or she wouldn't come for them, or any of the Rudder's other workers, next?

"Yeah." Dellwyn swallowed. "You too."

18

———

The courtroom buzzed the next day. The rows of seats were packed with chattering nobles, gossipy merchants, and whispering courtesans who huddled together in shabbily clad clusters. Part of the crowd had spilled out onto the main floor, creating a ring of bodies around the room. Dellwyn watched the activity from the center of the courtroom along with a half dozen others who had decided they had some right to the Rudder.

The round table had been replaced by a long, rectangular one, and extra chairs had been set out in front of it for the hopeful businesspeople. Dellwyn had situated herself in the middle of the chairs, hoping that she could observe how others made their cases before she was forced to speak in front of the large crowd. King Lionel and his council had not yet arrived, but before that fact could make her too anxious, Dellwyn reminded herself that she had come early.

She glanced to her left where Sybil and Aya sat in the front row. While they were still several feet above the main floor, they were close enough that Dellwyn could make out their expressions, even read their lips if need be. At first, Dellwyn had thought the choice of seating had been for her benefit—until she saw Aya's nervous green eyes glancing to the empty table.

But Dellwyn didn't mind. It could only work to her advantage to have Aya seated within the king's sight.

All at once, the room quieted, and Dellwyn looked up to see the bishop standing next to the table. As he raised his ringed hands, his billowing white sleeves slipped down to his elbows, and silence fell. "His Royal Majesty, King Lionel Willem Monashe, and his esteemed council."

As the crowd, Dellwyn included, rose, she reached her hand up to discreetly rub her ear. No one had needed to be quiet—the bishop's booming voice could have been heard by the entire population of Desertera.

King Lionel and the rest of the council filed in and took their seats. Dellwyn noticed Lord Collingwood staring at her, but she kept her attention fixed on the king to avoid raising any suspicion… and to avoid facing Lord Collingwood's potential guilt in Madam Huxley's death.

When King Lionel noticed Dellwyn among the seated hopefuls, he smiled at her. In response, Dellwyn inclined her head toward the upper seating. As the king's gaze landed on Aya, his beam widened, and he didn't even attempt to hide his wink. Aya bit her lip, and a bright-pink flush spread from her chest to her cheeks. Those seated nearby either cupped their mouths to whisper or rolled their eyes, but neither Aya nor the king broke their gaze.

Dellwyn grinned. She'd never seen the two of them together before, but the devotion in their eyes was unmistakable. They seemed like a good match, and Dellwyn found her chest swelling for Aya, a momentary distraction from the nerves.

After one last, long breath, King Lionel turned back to the assembly. He bowed his head in greeting. "Please be seated."

The crowd sat, but the bishop remained standing. "We are here today to determine who shall take ownership of the institution known colloquially as the Rudder. While the establishment cannot be purchased, as it was the sole property of Madam Huxley, we seek a candidate who can prove financial independence to keep the Rudder neutral and uninfluenced by other commerce. Please declare your initial intended invest-ment in its operations. And of course, an intimate knowledge of its business practices is also preferable."

Dellwyn took a deep breath and fingered the leather purse tied to her belt. The weight of it was comforting. The purse contained a combination of her and Sybil's savings, plus another hundred gold coins from Aya, who swore it was the least she could do after Dellwyn had supported her for the last decade. Looking at the jeweled nobles and well-dressed merchants seated around her, Dellwyn could almost guarantee that it wouldn't be the highest bid. But she hoped that, when combined with her experience and a few of the council members' bias, it would be enough.

A chair squeaked behind her, and the bishop scowled at the latecomer. Despite her intense curiosity, Dellwyn didn't turn around to gawk. After all, it was probably just another name-less noble, and she didn't need to look insecure or unprofes-sional, however accurate those words might be.

The bishop swiped at the end of his sleeves, as if brushing off the interruption. "Now then, I would like to invite the indi-vidual in the first chair to present his offer. Mr. Cobbler, if you please."

Dellwyn wrinkled her nose. What would a cobbler want with the Rudder? The same as everyone else there, she supposed—a practically guaranteed profit and easy access to a good bedding.

The cobbler told his offer—seventy-five gold coins—along with some romanticized story about how the Rudder was the one place where he felt truly happy. During the story, Lord Collingwood tried to catch Dellwyn's gaze several times, but she kept her eyes locked on the cobbler. She knew Lord Collingwood felt the same as the man standing before them all, and she didn't need his distractions.

The next person, a noblewoman, declared she would invest five hundred coins in the Rudder, and Dellwyn wondered how much money it took to prove one's financial stability. And for that matter, what was the necessary ratio of coin to knowledge?

The criteria seemed too vague, too subjective to elicit a fair judgment. She supposed that was why King Lionel had gathered such a diverse council.

When it was Dellwyn's turn, she stood up tall and clasped her hands behind her back so the council couldn't see her clenched knuckles. She spared a glance at Sybil and Aya, who smiled encouragingly. Here it was, her chance to employ herself on her own terms, to make a respectable name for herself in Desertera, and to improve the lives of her coworkers. All she had to do was prove her worth to the king's motley crew.

"My name is Dellwyn Rutt, and until two nights ago, I had been employed at the Rudder for nearly fifteen years." She paused to inhale and recall the next part of the speech she had spent all morning preparing. Instinctively, her eyes finally found their way to Lord Collingwood, and though she felt her stomach twist, she didn't tear them away. "I quit because I did not agree with changes Madam Huxley had made to the business—changes that harmed the quality of life for the workers and elevated prices for the clients. I only have 168 gold coins to my name, but I know how the Rudder works, how it *should* work. There is not a person seated here that is more qualified to take ownership of it than I am."

Lord Collingwood and King Lionel nodded their heads in approval. The bishop tapped his chin. "Thank you, Miss Rutt. You may be seated."

As Dellwyn lowered herself into her seat, her legs shook. She cast another glimpse at her friends and was rewarded discreet thumbs up. Despite the small size of her offering, Dellwyn couldn't help but feel the warmth of hope spread through her chest. True, her investment would less than half as large as some, but no one else knew the Rudder from the inside. In that aspect, she was uniquely qualified.

The next few individuals pronounced their intended commitments—a butcher with two hundred coins, a guard with two hundred fifty, and a count with an impressive seven hundred, who claimed an intimate knowledge of the Rudder because his favorite courtesan had birthed his bastard in Room J twenty years ago. At his announcement, shocked gasps issued throughout the courtroom, but King Lionel remained unfazed. Apparently, the king intended to keep his word that past adulterous actions would go unpunished.

As the bishop motioned for the last candidate to stand and make his case, Dellwyn felt a wave of relief wash over her. Only one more person to go—and still, no one had her experience. With King Lionel and Lord Collingwood on her side, and probably the queen dowager as well, Dellwyn didn't see how she could lose. By the end of the day, the Rudder would be hers.

"Good afternoon, everyone."

At the sound of his voice, Dellwyn's heart pounded. What in Desertera was Augustus doing? He had encouraged *her* to try for ownership of the Rudder. He'd said himself that he didn't have any business sense. And last night, he'd been a complete mess over Madam Huxley's death. Yet there he was, cool and collected, competing for the one thing Dellwyn wanted more than any other.

"I am Augustus Rutt. Like many employees of the Rudder, I was abandoned by my mother at a very young age, for I served as a constant reminder of her regrets."

At this point, Dellwyn turned around to stare at Augustus. His gaze stayed focused on the council members, and his eyes gleamed with tears that threatened to spill over at any moment. It was all Dellwyn could do to keep from scoffing. She had never heard Augustus use his childhood to garner sympathy or get his way. Then again, perhaps there had been no place for it at the Rudder. As he said, his sob story wasn't unique there. Most of the workers carried the surname Rutt.

"When I came of age to work, Madam Huxley took me in. At first, she sheltered, clothed, and fed me. She taught me her craft, and I learned that I do have talent, that I can make a positive difference, however temporary, in the lives of others."

Dellwyn glanced up at her friends. Sybil sat with her arms crossed and her lips pressed into a thin frown. Aya wasn't watching Augustus. Her eyes were fixed on King Lionel, and she narrowed them to show her irritation. King Lionel nodded at Aya, and when he noticed Dellwyn watching them, he gave the tiniest wave of his hand, as if to dismiss Augustus's speech.

Augustus paused and cleared his throat. "As Madam Huxley's closest confidant, I received insights into the business that she *never* revealed to another person. I truly believe that I know the inner workings of the Rudder better than anyone else."

Dellwyn bit her lip. *Oh, of course.* She didn't know if Augustus's claim was true or not, but it didn't really matter. What mattered was whether the council believed him, and most of the members were nodding their heads in approval.

"To demonstrate my commitment to my home," Augustus continued, "I am ready to invest my life's savings. One thousand gold coins."

A chorus of whispers erupted throughout the courtroom, and Dellwyn nearly choked. How had Augustus accumulated that much money? Sure, he was good at what he did, and yes, being the only man working at the Rudder for several years had given him a unique advantage. But *one thousand* gold coins? There was no way he could have saved that much, not after buying his nice house on the Portside border, and definitely not without help.

The bishop stood and raised his arms to quiet the assembly. "Thank you, Mr. Rutt. Now that we have heard from all the candidates, the council shall deliberate. If any questions arise, we will send a guard to retrieve the answers. While we are away, please feel free to visit amongst yourselves."

With King Lionel leading the way, the council members stood and left the courtroom. Once they were out of sight, Dellwyn turned around in her seat and glared at Augustus. He was already looking at her—no doubt he had been waiting for her scorn—and he stuck out his bottom lip in a pout. "Please don't be mad, Delly."

"Don't be mad?" Dellwyn marched back to his seat,

towering over him for once. "How can I not be mad? You're the one who talked me into this."

"Oh, hush." Augustus frowned. "You wanted to be here. I just gave you the final push."

"So why are *you* here?" Dellwyn held up a hand before he could answer. "Not that I should believe anything you say. Last night, you were a sulking mess who knew nothing about the business, and today you're Mr. Level-Headed Businessman, Madam Huxley's closest confidant."

"That's not fair. I was upset last night, and I still am. But I can't show it here." Augustus glanced from side to side. "Besides, I told you that I'm not *good* at the business part, which is true. However, I do *know* how Madam Huxley operated the Rudder. There is a difference."

Dellwyn rolled her eyes. "But of course, you neglected to share the full truth with the council."

"Of course. I'm not going to harm my chances." Augustus leaned in to whisper. "Do you want to know why I wanted you here today?"

Dellwyn huffed. "Obviously."

"I knew I had a pretty good shot of getting the Rudder. However, I wanted to make sure my stiffest competition came from the next most-qualified candidate—one of *us*, not some lord who would use it as his private pleasure palace."

As angry as she was with Augustus, Dellwyn could appreciate his logic. She sighed. "I see your point. I wouldn't want to work for some lusty lady or some greedy merchant. And I don't think any of our coworkers would either."

Augustus raised his eyebrows. "*Our?* Does that mean you'll come back when I'm in charge?"

Dellwyn put a hand on her hip. "You haven't won. But... I would consider it." She smirked. "For the freedom to choose my own clients and a substantial raise."

Augustus stuck out his hand. "Deal."

"Oh, no you don't." Dellwyn took a step back. "You're not in the position to be making any agreements yet."

Augustus's lips curled up at the corners. "But you admit it's inevitable?"

"Sure. I'll admit it." Dellwyn narrowed her eyes. "After you admit to me where you found the coins for your investment."

A flicker of concern flashed across Augustus's face, but otherwise, he remained controlled. He crossed his legs and leaned back in his chair. "As I told the council, it's my life's savings."

"Really?" Dellwyn did the sum in her head one more time for certainty. "So you've managed to buy yourself one of the nicest houses in Sternville, refresh your wardrobe more than once a year, *and* save over three years' worth of wages."

Augustus waved his hand. "Do you think me so self-sufficient? You must know I receive plenty of extra tips and gifts from my most loyal clients, the same as you." His eyes traveled up and down Dellwyn's curves. "It's not like you eat so well on your salary alone."

Dellwyn balled her fists. "Would you like to try that sentence again?"

Before Augustus could fumble through an apology, the chattering around them ceased, and the bishop reentered the room. Dellwyn glowered at Augustus then returned to her seat. As the council filed in, Dellwyn tried to catch King Lionel's eye, but his gaze was fixed firmly on Aya. Dellwyn sighed, wishing he could forget his lovesickness for the two seconds it would take to signal the decision to her.

Dellwyn looked at Aya to see whether her expression betrayed good or bad news, but if she knew anything, she didn't show it. Sybil smiled and gave a small wave. With pursed lips, Dellwyn turned back toward the council. Very well, then. She would wait for the announcement just like everyone else.

Despite the heavy silence in the courtroom, the bishop stood and extended his arms. Dellwyn was beginning to think he liked the pageantry of his position more than anything. "The council has come to a decision." He bowed to King Lionel. "Your Majesty."

King Lionel stood. "I believe it is obvious that two strong

candidates emerged, both with significant experience working at the Rudder and with respectable financial investments. As such, the vote was close, five to four."

Dellwyn's heart sank in her chest. She didn't need to hear another word to know the verdict. King Lionel's apologetic explanations and unwillingness to meet her gaze were enough.

"In the end, the council decided that Mr. Augustus Rutt is most fit to take ownership of the Rudder." King Lionel cleared his throat, finally looking at Dellwyn. "There will be a one-month probationary period, after which time, the council reserves the right to reevaluate its decision."

It was kind of him to let Dellwyn cling to hope in that way, but it didn't matter. If the council had chosen Augustus once, they would do it again. One month wasn't long enough for the Rudder to fall apart under his leadership, assuming it ever would.

Dellwyn sighed and tuned out the rest of King Lionel's speech. The disappointment settled around her like a sand dune. As its sting slowly faded, a new emotion welled up in her gut. Anxiety. Augustus would want to know whether or not she would come back to the Rudder.

A moment ago, when Dellwyn had still held the foolish hope that she would be the Rudder's new madam, joking about returning hadn't bothered her. But going back to her old position didn't seem as attractive. While she cared for Augustus as a friend and believed he felt the same about her and the other workers, she didn't have a guarantee that greed wouldn't eventually corrupt him as it had Madam Huxley. After all, Dellwyn had trusted the madam to do right by her employees for years. And look how that had turned out. She didn't know if she could handle that level of betrayal a second time, especially from a friend.

King Lionel finished his speech, and the crowd began to filter out of the courtroom. Dellwyn sat in her chair, unsure what to do. She didn't want to leave yet—fighting the crowd and looking like a sore loser didn't appeal to her. Nor did she have the heart to speak with Lord Collingwood, who stood conspicuously nearby, conversing with a merchant. And most of all, Dellwyn wasn't ready to congratulate Augustus and face his inevitable gloating. So when King Lionel motioned for her to approach the table, it was a welcome gesture.

Dellwyn walked up to him, her eyes flitting around the courtroom. "Is it okay that we speak in public like this?"

King Lionel raised his eyebrows. His reply began with a laugh, but he matched her whispered tone. "It's fine. I'm simply explaining our judgment to you. Besides, the whole kingdom knows I'm not one to stand on ceremony or avoid my subjects."

"That's certainly true." Dellwyn nodded her head so it would appear as if King Lionel were answering her questions. With their voices low and conversations arising in different clusters throughout the space, she imagined no one could hear them, but that didn't mean others weren't watching.

The king's face grew serious. "I'm sorry I couldn't sway the council for you. Preventing my own bias is exactly what I intended the council to do, but it's still frustrating to not get my way."

Dellwyn chuckled at his boyish pout. "I appreciate you trying. Even if it was more for Aya than me."

King Lionel frowned. "It's not just about Aya. After doing some research into Augustus, I wasn't sure he was the best fit. He seems a bit shallow and more than a bit arrogant. Those aren't good qualities in a leader."

From the hardened look in his eyes, Dellwyn knew the king was talking about his father. She decided to change the subject. "Can I ask how the council voted?"

King Lionel glanced to either side, and Dellwyn followed his gaze. All of the council members had vacated their seats and either joined other conversations or left the courtroom altogether. The queen dowager stood nearby, talking to Aya and Sybil. Lord Varick remained standing at the end of the table, in a conversation with a group of merchants.

"Zedara, my uncle, Mrs. Farmer, and myself voted for you." King Lionel inclined his head toward Lord Varick. "He pretended to be the swing vote, but obviously that was an act. He'd never do anything that helped Aya, Zedara, or me."

Dellwyn leaned in closer, lowering her voice to a true whisper. "Pardon me if this is rude, but how did Lord Varick get on the council? He doesn't live in Starboardshire."

"It surprised me, too." King Lionel rubbed his forehead. "Since Starboardshire consists of nobles, the residents asked if *any* noble could represent them, regardless of whether they lived in the palace or village. Stupidly, I agreed. I should have known Lord Varick would get the nomination then. He's got all the nobles fooled. I mean, first his daughter is executed by King Archon, then his heroic effort to take in a ward turns tragic when she proves herself a prince-seducing upstart."

Dellwyn couldn't help but snort at the thought of Aya as an accomplished seductress.

King Lionel smirked and shook his head. "Seriously, though, you can imagine how he uses that to his advantage. They think he's a saint—a lonely, childless widower—yet still so jubilant and charming. Their inability to see past his act proves the inbreeding makes them more idiotic."

As if Lord Varick could sense himself being discussed, he finished his conversation and walked over to Dellwyn and King Lionel. He bowed to each of them then held out his gloved hand for Dellwyn. Reluctantly, she put her palm in his, and he gave it a firm squeeze. "I wish you all the best, Miss Rutt. I hope you do not view our ruling as a setback, and that you may find opportunity in it."

Dellwyn withdrew her hand. "Thank you, Lord Varick. But I think the opportunity was taken more than given."

Lord Varick narrowed his beady eyes and *tutted*. "You would be surprised what can be found when you only begin looking."

Dellwyn repressed a shiver. Everything about him screamed untrustworthy, manipulating slime. "I'll keep that in mind." Even if she hadn't known his true character, Dellwyn didn't think she ever would have been able to fall for his widower act.

Lord Varick smiled, showing his pointed teeth. "Good day, Miss Rutt. Your Majesty." And with another small bow, he left. The clacking of his walking staff echoed throughout the courtroom.

Once Lord Varick had turned his back, King Lionel grimaced.

Dellwyn allowed the shiver to rack her body before speaking. "Everything about him is unsettling."

"Who is unsettling?" Augustus asked, his shoulder brushing against Dellwyn's as he came to stand beside her. Then, as if he realized his present company, a rare flush overtook Augustus's face, and he bowed. "Forgive me, Your Majesty. It was rude to interrupt."

King Lionel waved his hand. "It's all right."

"I wanted to come over and say thank you for entrusting the Rudder to me." Augustus smiled. Dellwyn wished she could smack the smug expression off of his face. "I assure you it is in good hands."

"I hope so." King Lionel's pleasant countenance had disappeared, and he straightened to stand over Augustus with the full force of his height. It was the first time he acted how Dellwyn expected a king to act, and it made her stomach twist.

She stepped to the side. "I should be going, Your Majesty."

"Very well." King Lionel inclined his head. "Have a good day, Miss Rutt."

Dellwyn curtsied, feeling the distance between their stations for the first time. "And you as well, Your Majesty."

As Dellwyn retreated from the conversation, the sensation of being followed overtook her. Maybe it was the men's eyes gazing after her. Maybe it was her own desire to avoid Augustus and any decision relating to the Rudder. Maybe it was that her only real chance of bettering herself and her life had just been ripped from her by a nobleman that exuded evil. No matter what it was, Dellwyn couldn't shake the feeling that someone was watching her.

Having said their goodbyes to the queen dowager, Aya and Sybil came to meet Dellwyn in the center of the courtroom.

They both frowned at her, and she realized that a thin sheen of sweat had broken out on her brow.

"Are you two ready?" Dellwyn asked. "I need some fresh air."

Sybil nodded.

As they exited, Aya took Dellwyn's arm in hers. "What did Lord Varick want?"

"To gloat." Dellwyn rolled her eyes and painted her voice thick with sarcasm. "And wish me all the best."

"That seems about right." Aya squeezed Dellwyn's arm. "I'm sorry he's targeted you because of me. It kills me to be the reason you lost the Rudder."

"It's not your fault, Aya," Sybil chimed in.

"Sybil's right," Dellwyn said. "You shouldn't blame yourself for Lord Varick's cruelty."

Aya mumbled a halfhearted acquiescence.

As the cooler air from the hallway washed over her, Dellwyn felt her chest loosen and her breath flow freely again. With the courtroom no longer looming, she thought back to Lord Varick's words. Why should she let them get to her? His words held only the power she gave them, and if she wanted, she could use them for good. While Lord Varick may have been faking reassurance, that didn't mean she couldn't choose to find comfort and truth within his message.

Maybe there *was* an opportunity hidden in today's defeat. And maybe, once she started looking for it, it would find her.

19

____

ellwyn had never been to a funeral before. They
happened, of course—she had seen the smoke from
the departed rising over the village, smelled the burning
remains when the wind blew through Sternville—but she had
never actually attended one. Until today.

Having decided that no further evidence could be gathered
from Madam Huxley's body, the council agreed to put her to
rest only two days after her life's work, the Rudder, had been
given away. An impressive crowd had come out to mourn the
madam—or rather, witness the spectacle for themselves.
Dellwyn couldn't remember the last time someone's life had
been taken by anyone other than the executioner, and she
doubted many in the crowd could either.

As the individuals who had been closest to Madam Huxley,
the Rudder workers huddled in the front of the crowd, the one
time they received preferential treatment over the rest of
Desertera. Various merchants and people who'd had business
dealings with Madam Huxley stood in the next row. Toward
the rear of the crowd, Sternville peasants and nobles mixed
together—one group amused by this arrangement, the other
disgusted.

Although Dellwyn was too short, and it was too dark for
her to see far behind herself, she knew that Aya would be

standing somewhere with the other merchants in spite of her former employment. Lord Collingwood and King Lionel would be in one of the last rows, no doubt with a sizable group of guards in case anyone decided to make trouble. Or in case the murderer decided to reveal themselves.

Sybil nudged Dellwyn in the side, and Dellwyn turned to face the front again. Madam Huxley lay on the low pyre. Its frame was constructed out of metal pipes and bars salvaged from the depths of the palace. Around its base and under the madam's body, someone had stuffed dried cactus husks and tumbleweed kindling. Dellwyn wondered how many Sternville residents had lain on this same pyre, and how long it would be until it was her turn to burn.

Before Dellwyn's morbidity could consume her thoughts, the bishop stepped up next to the pyre. He pulled two flat stones from the pockets of his robe, bent down, and smacked them together. The spark seemed twice as bright against the black of the night, and its light bathed Dellwyn and the other workers as the tumbleweeds took flame.

His task completed, the bishop stretched his arms out and bowed—a gesture meant for the Benevolent Queen, not the crowd. Kalinda had told Dellwyn before the funeral began that there wouldn't be any service as Madam Huxley had no family in need of comfort. But Dellwyn still found the bishop's demeanor cold. Blood relatives or not, the madam still had people to mourn her. And besides, after the horrendous way in which she had left the world, didn't Madam Huxley deserve that small show of respect? Dellwyn wished she had the courage to speak on the madam's behalf, but she couldn't find the words and didn't need to draw more attention to herself with the investigation unfinished.

Save for a few whispers from the back, the group stood in silence. Dellwyn watched the flames as they moved up the pyre, inching their way toward Madam Huxley's flesh. When they finally reached her, the smoke darkened, and its hypnotizing swirls thickened as they curled toward the stars.

Dellwyn and Sybil held their handkerchiefs over their

noses. A glance down told Dellwyn that Sybil was crying, but Sybil made no sound, nor did she wipe the tears away. A few muffled sobs and even a wail erupted nearby. Dellwyn looked around to find the source of the outburst. One glimpse of Kalinda's convulsing shoulders gave her the answer. Dellwyn frowned. It seemed a bit dramatic to mourn one's cruel employer so enthusiastically.

Jasmine stood next to Kalinda, her arm wrapped securely around her friend, quiet tears slipping down her own cheeks. Next to them was Augustus, who stared transfixed at the fire. His eyes were red and swollen, as if they had been wrung dry. Dellwyn spied Alisa off to the side of the crowd. Her arms were crossed, and her uncovered nose was wrinkled. With the flames reflected in them, Alisa's unblinking eyes seemed to shine in the night, not a glimpse of sorrow to be found.

Dellwyn watched Alisa for the rest of the burning. A few times, Dellwyn noticed a clear hitch in Alisa's breath, but she couldn't tell if that was from Alisa trying to hold back her emotions or from the stench.

As the flames died down and the smoke began to thin, the bishop lifted his arms to regain the crowd's attention. "May the Benevolent Queen's merciful waters wash over Madam Lilliette Huxley."

"Praise be to Her," the crowd replied.

Neither Dellwyn nor Sybil spoke. Sybil shot Dellwyn a nervous look, and Dellwyn shrugged. How were they supposed to know what to say?

The crowd remained in place for a few moments longer, but once the first brave souls decided to disperse, it only took a matter of minutes for everyone but the Rudder workers to disappear. The workers looked around at each other, as if they did not know what to do owithout the madam's guidance. Dellwyn, too, felt lost, torn between lurking with her former coworkers and returning to her hovel to sleep.

Augustus stepped forward and took a deep breath. "We should head back. Nothing gets people in the mood like staring their mortality in the face." With a forlorn glance at the pyre, he continued. "If you don't want to work tonight, consider yourself excused. As for myself, I don't intend to take any clients."

The workers nodded, a few murmured their thanks, and most turned to walk back to the Rudder or their homes. Dellwyn and Sybil did the same, but before they could break off from the main group, Augustus slipped in between them and put his arms around their shoulders. "Are you two okay?"

"Yes." Sybil's forehead wrinkled. "It doesn't seem real yet."

Augustus sighed. "No, it doesn't."

"I feel bad that I don't feel... something." Dellwyn shook her head. "I'm not sad, I'm not mad or relieved. I'm just... numb."

"Me too." Augustus gave her shoulder a squeeze. "Will I see you back at work soon?"

Dellwyn rolled her eyes and ducked out from under his arm. "Can we not talk about this tonight?"

"Of course." Augustus kissed Sybil's temple. "You ladies have a restful evening, and I'll be in touch."

"Thank you." Dellwyn sighed. "Have a nice night."

"Good night," Sybil added.

With a wave, Augustus turned and headed toward the Rudder. Dellwyn watched him walk away for a moment then groaned. Why did he possibly think tonight would have been an appropriate time to talk business? Maybe Madam Huxley *had* taught him a thing or two. But still, he should have known better. The madam's body was still burning, for goodness sake.

Dellwyn spared a glance back at the pyre, surprised to see that someone still stood before the flames. Even from a distance, the silhouette revealed a woman's slender frame. Dellwyn wondered who might have stayed behind to mourn the madam in private, and as if the Benevolent Queen had heard her question, the fire swelled once more to illuminate the individual. It wasn't much, but a ring of gold shone around the person's head, and Dellwyn had her answer. Yes, she really did need to speak with Alisa.

~

THE NEXT TWO weeks passed in a slow, controlled routine. Dellwyn and Sybil kept daytime hours, rising and sleeping with the sun. In the mornings, one of them would fetch water from the Sternville well, and the other would venture to Portside or Bowtown for the day's meals. They spoke about their plans in lofty terms, staying firmly in the hypothetical and never mentioning Madam Huxley's funeral, nor broaching the subject of money. Not that they needed to—Dellwyn felt all too strongly the increasing weight of the madam's unavenged death and the lightening weight of their coin purse.

After Augustus won the Rudder, Dellwyn had insisted on returning Aya's investment. It had taken some arguing, but eventually, Aya had relented—on the condition that Dellwyn take it back if things got too tight. But Dellwyn wouldn't let her and Sybil's situation grow that strained, no matter what it took.

Dellwyn and Sybil passed their days inside the hovel. No one came to visit—though Augustus did send wildflower bouquets, dinner rolls, and other trinkets to try to win Dellwyn back to the Rudder—and they didn't seek out anyone else's company. As much as Dellwyn wanted to approach Alisa about her suspicions, she couldn't bring herself to reenter the Rudder. Not yet. Not without a plan.

Therefore, Dellwyn and Sybil focused on the hovel, dusting every surface, sweeping the dirt floor until it lay perfectly level, mending clothing, turning whatever clothing was beyond mending into fresh curtains, tablecloths, and dust rags.

As the days dragged on, Dellwyn found herself growing increasingly tired. Staying cooped up indoors was more exhausting than working through the night, and racking her brain for new projects made her mind weary. As much as she adored Sybil, even their conversations had grown tiresome, and Dellwyn struggled to think of new things to say.

Another bouquet arrived from Augustus, and Dellwyn set it in an empty jar on the table. She would have liked to let the flowers soak in water, but she couldn't waste the precious resource on something that was already dead. She sat down and stared at the flowers, her imagination flying her across the desert to the Starboardshire field, where they were likely picked. There they had lived, thrived, been beautiful and desired—until someone's greed had grown too great and they'd plucked them from their home. Now, they sat in her hovel, their petals slowly curling, their stems shriveling and necks drooping. And there they would die. A splash of violet in a wasteland of brown.

Dellwyn stood and crossed to the window. She couldn't see the palace from this side of the hovel, but she could gaze out over Sternville. The streets were quiet. The wellmen were at work, and their wives and children were hidden away from the bright afternoon sun, eating their meager lunches or taking naps. Hovels and tents filled Dellwyn's vision, their flimsy walls creaking or fluttering in the hot wind. Sternville was all she had ever known, and as sad and dirty as it was, it felt like where she belonged.

The Rudder felt the same. Despite everything that had happened with Madam Huxley, and even Lord Derringher, Dellwyn still thought of the Rudder fondly. She missed her coworkers, gathering together in the lobby to hear the news, sharing gossip in the changing room before clients arrived. She missed her clients or, more accurately, the way they treated her —how their eyes drank in her curves, how their lips stretched and curled in reverence of her talents, how they shuddered against her touch. And if Dellwyn were being entirely honest, she missed being surrounded by the precious gifts from her admirers and the soft, colorful fabrics adorning her room.

She glared at the flowers. They seemed to wilt under her stare, and Dellwyn remembered the metal flower from Lord Collingwood, likely still sitting on her nightstand in Room B. It would never wilt. Like so few things, it was eternal.

Sybil came out of her room then, twirling around in one of her old dresses. "Look! I figured out how to let out the side seams, and it fits again."

Dellwyn smiled. In their time off, Sybil had become a

rather accomplished seamstress. She seemed to have a natural talent for pulling clothing apart and piecing it back together in new ways—much like Aya could do with mechanical objects. Dellwyn envied them the blessing of solitude. Their skills could be exercised alone, with only raw materials and time. Dellwyn needed other people to validate her craft, and she found herself craving them more and more as the days passed.

"It's perfect. Well done." Dellwyn's gaze drifted back to the window. "Why don't we take it out and show it off?"

Sybil scrunched her nose. "Where would we go?"

"Oh, I don't know." Dellwyn was already pulling her cloak off its hook. "We could take a stroll around the palace, see what strikes our fancy."

Sybil noticed the flowers on the table, and her face brightened. "Could we walk around the edge of Starboardshire? I love the wildflower fields."

"Sure." Dellwyn tied the strings of her cloak. "If you're not going to wear a cloak, at least take your hat. The sun is brutal today."

Sybil grabbed her wide-brimmed bonnet, and off they went.

The sun hung directly over the palace, its light glinting off the ship's metal railings. As Dellwyn and Sybil walked past the Rudder, Dellwyn attempted to peer through the gap in the propellers. Only blank iron walls and inner blackness greeted her—what else had she expected in the middle of the day?

When they strode past the bathing house, a group of freshly primped noblewomen emerged at the same time. The fragrance of their bath oils danced on the breeze, and Dellwyn breathed in lavender, mint, and spice with a heavy heart. Without her bathing allowance from the Rudder, she didn't know when she would enjoy a warm soak again.

Pushing the thought out of her mind, Dellwyn lifted her chin and smiled. It was a pleasant, though scalding, day, and she and Sybil were out among people. For now, that was all Dellwyn could ask for.

A line of shadow traced the ground, hovering under the

anchor chain that marked the Sternville-Starboardshire border. It swept over Dellwyn's body like a thin cloud, a momentary haven from the sun's unrelenting rays. But the respite didn't last, and as Dellwyn took in the grandeur of Starboardshire, she felt her body flush with a more intense heat.

On this side of the anchor line, the houses were, well, houses. Each was constructed by artisan carpenters with wood and metal salvaged from the innards of the ship. Although the homes stood in neat rows, they were spaced far apart. Skinny blades of grass dotted the dirt between them, which was marked with footprints from where the gardeners had stepped in it after watering. Dellwyn's mouth went dry at the mere thought of all that water spent on aesthetics, when it could have gone to the crop fields in Bowtown that fed both people and animals alike.

As Dellwyn and Sybil walked down the side of the anchor line toward the rear of the village, a bright swath of color emerged in the distance. The wildflower fields had naturally adapted to the arid climate. When Dellwyn was young, she imagined that their roots dug as deep as the wells, tapping into some underground body of water she couldn't see, but that wellmen insisted lurked beneath their feet. But when she learned that the flowers merely survived on the few inches of rain the sky granted each year, she grew to respect them even more.

Nearing the edge of the wildflower fields, Dellwyn and Sybil passed by the last few rows of houses. A single large fence contained the dwellings, their inhabitants, and most importantly, their horses. Within this boundary, each house contained a smaller pen, patches of bare dirt in a veritable pasture, where the horses stayed when not grazing.

Sybil grabbed Dellwyn's arm with one hand and pointed to the nearest pen with the other. "Look at them!"

Dellwyn did, and her eyebrows rose. Two horses stood together—one black with a white ring around one hoof and one brown with a wide white stripe down its face—gnawing on each other's necks.

Before Dellwyn could stop her, Sybil sprinted through a gate in the wider fence and moved toward the smaller pen. Dellwyn cried out for Sybil to stop, but when she didn't, Dellwyn ran after her, hoping no nobles were around to witness their outbursts.

As Sybil approached the fence, the horses broke apart and reared back. Dellwyn could see the muscles under their skin working as they kicked out their front legs. The brown one let out a frightened whinny, and Sybil jerked to a stop a few feet away from the pen.

Dellwyn grabbed Sybil and pulled her back several steps. She had to force her reprimand out through her desperate breaths. "What were you… thinking? They could have… hurt you."

"They were hurting each other!" Sybil shrugged off Dellwyn's grasp and walked back up to the pen. Her hands were steady as she rested them atop the driftwood fence. The horses eyed Sybil from the other side of the pen, motionless except for the contracting of their sides as they panted. "I didn't know horses ate other horses."

A delicate laugh came from the nearby house, and Dellwyn squinted against the sun to see the queen dowager standing outside the back door. "They weren't eating each other." The former queen walked over, not bothering to hold up the skirts of her pristine yellow dress. "They were necking."

Sybil didn't remove herself from the fence. "Necking?"

Dellwyn stepped forward and nudged her away, then they both curtsied for the noblewoman. "Forgive us, Your Highness. We didn't mean to startle them."

The queen dowager laughed again, much heartier this time. "For goodness sake, don't do that. Who do you think I am?"

Dellwyn furrowed her brow. "You were the qu—"

"Don't say it." The noblewoman put her hands on her hips. "That woman is dead, like the rest of them. If you allow me to call you Dellwyn, Miss Rutt, you may call me Zedara."

Dellwyn nodded. "Very well."

"Good." Zedara's dark-blue eyes traveled over Dellwyn's curves, and Dellwyn couldn't decide whether Zedara was sizing her up or drinking her in.

Already back at the fence, Sybil craned her neck to look at the two of them then shrugged. "Zedara, why do the horses do that?"

"Two reasons." She tucked a stray golden curl behind her ear. "First, it's a sign of affection, kind of like kissing. Second, it's the only way they can each get a good scratch back there."

Sybil grinned. "Are your horses friends, then?"

"They're brother and sister, actually." Zedara moved to stand next to Sybil then rested her forearms on the fence. "The black one is Onyx; he's the youngest. And the bay is Jessa."

"Why do you have them?" Dellwyn asked. When Zedara's scrutinizing gaze met hers again, Dellwyn felt her cheeks burn. She hoped that hadn't been too rude. "I mean, you don't eat them. They don't provide wool or other materials. So what is their purpose?"

Zedara took a deep breath, and the thin smile that played on her lips told Dellwyn she had answered that question before. "The horses are a deep part of our legacy. Queen Hildegard chose to save them from the floods because they make for great working animals and loyal companions. The breeds she selected came from the desert parts of the world before, so they were already adapted to this kind of climate. When the ship first moored in Desertera, horses carried explorers far beyond the horizon, looking for other survivors."

Dellwyn tried not to scoff. *That's if any of those old stories are true.* "Fine. But what do they do now?"

"Sometimes, nobles loan them out to farmers to help with the crops, pulling tills or heavy carts." Zedara reached her hand over the fence, and Onyx came over. He nuzzled his nose against her palm then gently pressed his thick lips around Zedara's fingers. "Mostly, they are here out of love. But rest assured, Dellwyn, when they die, we do use what we can. Unfortunately, though, most of the materials don't make it out into the other villages. I think it's because we don't view them as livestock or consider their remains products. Personally, I see it as granting beloved friends a sliver of immortality."

While Dellwyn still thought the horses were a waste of space, she admired Zedara's defense of them. After all, they served a need in people to give and receive affection. And wasn't that, in a way, exactly what Dellwyn did?

"They do seem sweet," Dellwyn admitted. She reached out her hand to Jessa, who had walked over, and ran her fingers along the horse's face, down the thick white stripe of hair to her pink nose. To Dellwyn's surprise, the horse's muzzle felt like velvet.

"So why are you ladies out in the daylight? Shouldn't you be sleeping in for a hard night's work?" Zedara winked.

"We didn't go back to the Rudder." Sybil shivered, despite the heat. "I'm never going back."

"I'm sorry." Zedara's tone was sincere, and Dellwyn remembered her outburst at their questioning. "I shouldn't have assumed that you would just because Augustus is now running the place. What about you, Dellwyn?"

Dellwyn looked at Sybil. They hadn't discussed their employment plans openly yet, and she hoped Sybil wouldn't take her answer as a betrayal. "I'm not sure, but I do miss it, the way it used to be."

Zedara nodded. "Well, if either of you are interested—that is, if it wouldn't be too awkward to work for me—I'm in need of a new lady's maid. Mine left me to get married, and I can't stand any of the stuffy old women my father has tried to force on me. It would be a relief to hire someone whose company I enjoy."

Sybil perked up, her bright face trained on Zedara. "What would the position entail?"

"Oh, simple tasks. I'm nowhere near as demanding as most ladies. My maid helps me dress—I don't know why the dressmaker can't make buttons women can reach—and washes and mends clothing. She keeps my room tidy, though I try to do that myself. Mostly, she runs errands or joins me during my day. Unless, of course, I'm in a council meeting."

Sybil pursed her lips, as if she were seriously considering the job. Dellwyn felt her heartbeat quicken, both with hope for her friend and fear of the distance that would inevitably come between them.

"How much does it pay?" Sybil asked.

Zedara shrugged. "That's up to my father, but I'm certain it would be at least three times what you earned as a maid at the Rudder. Additionally, your meals would be covered, as you'd eat with my mother's maid, my father's valet, and our butler while you were here."

"Would I have to live with you?" Sybil wrinkled her nose at the big house, and Dellwyn let out a chuckle.

"If you wanted board, we could provide it." Zedara glanced at Dellwyn and grinned. "But if you want to stay at your home in Sternville, you are welcome to do so."

Sybil nodded. She reached up and stroked Onyx's mane for a few moments, her eyes distant. With a shake of her head, she came back to reality. "I would like to apply for the position, with one condition."

Zedara raised an eyebrow. "And that is?"

"I'd like to help with the horses." Sybil bit her lip. "Or at least be able to visit with them."

"Done." Zedara extended her hand, and they shook. When Zedara released her, Sybil turned and gave Dellwyn a hug. Dellwyn smiled and squeezed her back.

Pending Lord Ollessen's approval, Sybil was free of the Rudder. She would never have to suffer the lust of another client, never again be subjected to force, never be snubbed in shops. She could live a normal life as maid to a respected family and to a lady who Dellwyn knew would never treat Sybil poorly. It was perfect.

Sybil released Dellwyn and beamed at Zedara. "Thank you so much. This means more than I can say."

"Think nothing of it." Zedara waved her hand. "You're doing me a favor as well. I'd much rather pass my days with you than some grumpy crone."

"What happens next?" Dellwyn asked. Zedara acted like

Sybil's hiring was already confirmed, and that made Dellwyn nervous.

"Sybil will need to have an interview with my father, but it's merely a formality." Zedara rolled her eyes. "He's so desperate to find me a new lady's maid that he'll hire anyone I approve at this point. Could you come back tomorrow around this same time?"

"Of course." Sybil bounced on her heels twice then caught herself and went still. "I'll see you then."

"Fantastic. I'll make the arrangements." Zedara shook both their hands. "It was lovely to see you again, Dellwyn."

Dellwyn smiled. "You too, Zedara. Thank you."

Leaving Zedara to tend to her horses, Dellwyn and Sybil continued on their way to the wildflower fields. As they reached the edge, Sybil leaped forward and lay down in the bed of flowers. Dellwyn bit her tongue, telling herself that the flowers would bounce back after Sybil left and that Sybil deserved a moment to celebrate.

The young girl fanned herself with one hand and waved at Dellwyn with the other. "You should lie down. It's really soft."

Dellwyn grimaced, imagining how smashed the flowers would be under her frame, not to mention the hassle of pulling herself back up off the ground. "I'm fine up here. I like to watch them."

Sybil turned her nose to sniff a pink flower. As she let out the breath, she stated, "You should go back to the Rudder."

"Is that so?" Dellwyn scoffed at Sybil's confident tone. "I don't think it's that simple."

"Yes, it is." Sybil stroked another flower's thin yellow petals. "Augustus wants you back. You miss the people and the adoration. All you have to do is show up at sunset."

Dellwyn crossed her arms. "And what will I be paid? How can I be sure that Augustus won't do exactly what Madam Huxley did?"

Sybil shrugged. "You can't. All you can do is hope that Augustus is a better madam... mister?" She giggled. "Regardless, you know he'll agree to whatever terms you have. I'm sure business, and morale too, are suffering without you."

With a sigh, Dellwyn crouched down as close as she could to Sybil's level without sitting. Her next statement needed to be said face-to-face. "And what about you? The only reason you've handled everything so well is because we've cut ties with the Rudder. Do you really want a daily reminder of what happened there as I come and go from work?"

Sybil propped herself up on her elbows, her face stony. "I think I deserve a little more credit than that. We've talked about the Rudder twice now, and I haven't dissolved into tears —other than at Madam Huxley's funeral, which I think is justi-fied." She lowered her gaze to the flowers, and her voice followed. "I still think about him… and what he did. But I'm okay. I refuse to let what happened ruin my life."

With tears in her own eyes, Dellwyn reached over and wrapped Sybil in a hug.

They stayed there for a long while until Sybil pulled away. "I understand why you want to return. I really do." As she looked up at Dellwyn, she squinted against the sun. "And I want you to be happy. If the Rudder makes you happy, that's where you should be."

"Thank you." Dellwyn gave Sybil another quick hug, then they helped each other to their feet.

The sun hovered just above the Portside railing. Afternoon was slowly fading, and in a few more hours, it would be sunset.

Dellwyn looked from the sun to Sybil and back. "Well, then. I suppose I should start getting ready for work."

And figuring out what in Desertera to say to Alisa.

20

———————

ellwyn waited to leave for the Rudder until the sun had fully set. She hoped that by being late, she could avoid the nightly workers' meeting and speak with Augustus alone before heading to her room. Plus, it would delay her encounter with Alisa for at least a few more hours, if not another night. But as Dellwyn passed under the propellers, she realized her plan had failed. Augustus's voice echoed off the walls, and Dellwyn emerged at the back of the crowd of courtesans.

She lurked behind the gathered group. For a couple of minutes, she remained unnoticed. Then Augustus's gaze stretched to the back of the room. He paused, mid-speech, then broke into a wide grin. "Oh, Delly! I knew you'd return to us!"

The other workers turned around, and looks of surprise, happiness, and disappointment met Dellwyn in equal proportions. To her own shock, their attention didn't make her nervous or embarrassed. Instead, the warmth of confidence, of *rightness*, washed over her.

She put her hand on her hip and smirked. "What can I say, Auggie? Flirting isn't as fun without the coins."

"Ha!" Augustus clapped. "I think the rest of you have

suffered enough of my rambling tonight—you're dismissed. Delly, after you say your hellos, come to my office, and we'll discuss terms."

Dellwyn nodded. She weaved her way through the crowd and returned the greetings, hugs, and pats on the back she received. The last person she met was Alisa, and before Dellwyn's mind could fumble through something to say, Alisa grabbed her and pulled her into a tight embrace.

As they separated, Dellwyn raised her eyebrows.

Alisa frowned. "That was a one-time hug. I hope you enjoyed it."

Dellwyn forced herself to smile. "Thank you. It's good to be back."

Alisa glanced around the lobby. Everyone else seemed to be out of earshot, but she whispered anyway. "I didn't think you'd return."

"For a while, I didn't think I would either. But peasant life doesn't agree with me." After a moment of consideration, Dellwyn added, "And I have some unfinished business to attend to here."

Alisa arched a brow, but she didn't comment. "How's Sybil?"

"She's doing well. Actually, it looks like she'll be a lady's maid as of tomorrow."

Alisa offered one of her rare grins. "That's great."

Dellwyn scanned the lobby. "How is everything here?"

"Much better without Madam Huxley running the place." Alisa rolled her eyes. "As much as I hate to admit it, Augustus is doing things right. He allows us to deny appointments if there's someone we don't want to see; he lets us choose from the walk-in clients; he's raised our pay *and* given us weekly bathing allowances."

Dellwyn felt her eyes widen. "Was Madam Huxley really taking that much of the profit?"

"Of course." Alisa wrinkled her nose. "And since she didn't have an heir or beneficiary, King Lionel let Augustus have all of her savings. Augustus says these new expenses are Madam Huxley paying us back in death."

"Wow." Dellwyn shook her head. "I have to say, I'm proud of him. I was worried he'd get greedy."

Alisa chuckled. "It's only been two weeks. As sweet as Augustus may be now, there's still plenty of time for the business to break him."

Dellwyn smirked. "Oh, how I've missed your optimism."

"It's my best trait." Alisa placed a hand over her heart in mock sincerity. "Anyway, go negotiate your wages. And don't settle for anything less than three times your previous salary."

"Noted." Dellwyn tapped her temple then headed toward Augustus's office. Alisa seemed to be in good spirits. There had been an edge to her voice when she spoke of Madam Huxley, but nothing that wouldn't have been in Dellwyn's, too. Dellwyn would just have to wait until she could talk to Alisa in private to have her questions answered.

As Dellwyn entered Augustus's small office, the oddness of the Rudder's situation finally settled around her. Nothing had changed. Augustus sat behind the exact same desk and in the exact same chair as Madam Huxley had—the furniture bore the bloodstains to prove it. He hadn't added any new decorations, and the obsolete guest book still rested untouched on the side table.

He motioned for Dellwyn to sit. "Tell me what I have to do to convince you to come back, and consider it done."

Dellwyn settled into the chair, her hands clasped in her lap. "A raise, for starters. I'm told the going rate is three times my old pay."

"For you, Delly, quadruple." Augustus snapped his fingers. "What else?"

"I want sole ownership of my client list. I will serve whom I want, when I want, and I will keep all of my tips to myself." Dellwyn watched Augustus's face for hints of discomfort or irritation, but if he felt her demand was unfair, he didn't show it.

"Of course. You may also choose whether you take on any

walk-in clients and have your pick of the group." Augustus waved his hand, as if this were all commonplace. "Anything more?"

Dellwyn bit her lip. A fair wage and control of her schedule were the most important factors to her, but it felt like a defeat if Augustus did not resist at least one of her demands. She wondered how far she could push him before she actually had to negotiate.

"I'd like every fourth day off—*with* pay—to rest my body and attend to personal affairs."

Augustus raised his eyebrows but nodded his agreement.

Dellwyn hid her shock by tapping her chin in thought. *What will make him flinch?* "And I'll take Room A."

"That you can't have." Augustus wagged his finger. "I'm still working right along with you all."

"I see." Dellwyn had to admit she was impressed—and hopeful. If Augustus stayed working in Room A, perhaps he wouldn't grow out of touch with the rest of the courtesans. "Then I'd like to be exempt from all future room reassignments."

"No need." Augustus shrugged. "I intend to offer promotions and demotions whenever I see fit, based on the feedback of clients and coworkers."

"Oh. That's actually a good idea." Dellwyn pursed her lips. There was one more request she could make, and it might very well reveal his limits. "I want Lord Derringher permanently banned from the Rudder."

Augustus's jaw dropped, and Dellwyn smirked. "Dellwyn, I would never make you serve him again, not after Madam Huxley shackled you to him in that way, but I can't ban him for pushing your... sense of adventure."

"Fine." Dellwyn crossed her arms. "Don't ban him because of me. Ban him because of Sybil. She's only fourteen. What he subjected her to was illegal."

Augustus sighed. "Unfortunately, we don't have any proof. It's his word against hers."

"That's horseshit, and you know it." Dellwyn pointed

toward the workers' corridor. "What happened in there *happened*. King Lionel believes it. At our questioning, he agreed to arrest Lord Derringher for the crime. As you say, there's no evidence, so I doubt a conviction will be made. Therefore, I want to be sure he can't return and misuse anyone else."

Augustus shifted in his seat. "Dellwyn, I—"

"If you don't agree, I'm walking out this door." Dellwyn gave him her hardest, most defiant glare and hoped against all hope that he couldn't see her trembling knees. "That's my final condition."

Augustus mulled it over, his eyes flitting back and forth, as if he were calculating the numbers in his head. After a moment, he ran his fingers through his blond hair and let out a loud groan. "Fine."

Dellwyn guffawed. "Really?"

"The profit you bring in should outweigh what he provides as a customer." Augustus frowned. "But you just used up a big favor. You better not forget this anytime soon."

"I won't." Dellwyn beamed, feeling near giddy at her victory. "Thank you, Augustus."

"You can thank me by marching yourself into Room B and getting ready. When I saw you come in, I sent one of the priming girls to alert your regular clients that you had returned —Lord Derringher excluded, thankfully." Augustus let out a low whistle.

Dellwyn raised her eyebrows. "That was rather cocky of you."

"I wasn't about to accept no for an answer." Augustus shook his head. "And I think I'm done taking your shit for the evening. You're dismissed."

If it weren't for the softening wink he added, Dellwyn might have been offended. As it was, the friendliness was there, Augustus had given her a substantial raise and full control over her clientele, and she would never have to cross paths with Lord Derringher again—at least not there. With all those factors on her side, Dellwyn nearly skipped to Room B.

~

THE FIRST KNOCK on Dellwyn's door came right as she finished changing. She opened it to see the bright, smiling face of one of the lesser noblemen. They'd shared a few appointments before Lord Derringher had bought all of her time, and Dellwyn had enjoyed his company. Starting with this noble was a relief in more ways than one. If it hadn't been for his constant grin and wide, desperate eyes, Dellwyn might have felt bad for how much she used him for her own pleasure.

Shortly after her first client left, one of her few merchant clients—a wealthy glassmith—arrived. Then she served another, much higher-ranked, nobleman, who gave her nearly a full week's wages in tip. A guard captain came next, and as he left, Dellwyn flung herself back onto her bed. Muscles she had neglected over the past two weeks ached, and smooth, flat ovals had overtaken her kneecaps.

Another knock sounded at the door, and Dellwyn smiled to herself. Despite the aches, it was gratifying to be back at the Rudder. Each knock was another hungry client, another piece of walking proof that Dellwyn was desired and talented and where she belonged. That was how it was supposed to be.

Dellwyn wrenched open her door, and it took all her self-control to keep her face still. Before her stood Mrs. Eveline Farmer from King Lionel's council. Dellwyn motioned for her to come inside. "I didn't take you for the type." She chuckled. "I don't usually serve women, but I'll give it a try."

"I'm not here for that." Mrs. Farmer looked around Room B, her nose scrunched in disgust.

Dellwyn wondered if Mrs. Farmer's distaste was for the Rudder in general or the distinct smell of human passion that filled the room. She shook her head. "What can I do for you, Mrs. Farmer?"

"I need to speak with you about Madam Huxley's murder." Mrs. Farmer eyed the closed door.

"It's secure." Dellwyn gestured to the fainting couch, and

Mrs. Farmer sat. "Trust me, it's meant to muffle sounds much louder than your voice."

"Of course." Mrs. Farmer pulled her shawl tight around her shoulders. "Rykart is innocent."

The woman didn't mince words, Dellwyn had to give her that.

"I suspect as much." Dellwyn sighed. "But I hope you have more substantial proof than I do."

Mrs. Farmer sent another nervous glance around the room. "The day the madam was murdered, Rykart came back to Bowtown. Apparently, you had demanded he leave the Rudder's premises."

Dellwyn furrowed her brow. "That's right."

"Well, he returned with all of his belongings but one."

Dellwyn's hands balled into fists. "The scythe."

Mrs. Farmer nodded. "He thought it must have slipped out of his belt while he was packing, and perhaps it did. It would have made a perfect weapon for anyone who stumbled upon it. But I don't think it was lost. I think it was stolen from him and used to frame him."

"Unless Rykart was lying. Maybe he only pretended to misplace his scythe to make himself seem innocent." Upon seeing Mrs. Farmer's lips purse, Dellwyn held up her hands. "I'm just thinking like King Lionel and the rest of the council. It is rather convenient."

Mrs. Farmer relaxed. "I understand."

"Why haven't you come forward with this before now?" Dellwyn shuffled in her seat. "Why hasn't Rykart said anything?"

"Rykart hasn't spoken a single word to the council or anyone else. He believes the Benevolent Queen will save him."

Dellwyn rolled her eyes. "And you?"

"I hope our divine goddess does liberate him, but I cannot put all my faith in Her, and I wasn't sure whom I could trust." Mrs. Farmer squeezed her hands together, as if she were praying to Dellwyn. "But I believe I can trust you. You're a good woman, and you know in your heart that Rykart is innocent."

Dellwyn crossed her ankles. "What am I supposed to do with this information?"

"Solve the murder. Free Rykart. Avenge your employer." Mrs. Farmer's tone was matter-of-fact. "No one else seems to be trying."

Dellwyn rubbed her forehead. Her night had been going so well. Why couldn't Mrs. Farmer have wanted to experiment with her sexuality? "You think the scythe was stolen. But when I left the Rudder on the morning of Madam Huxley's murder, Rykart was already packing up his belongings. And I remember seeing the scythe then. How could someone have stolen it between the Rudder and Bowtown? Especially if he walked along the palace, near the guards."

Mrs. Farmer glanced around the room. "You were not the last Rudder worker to see him. He said he talked to some of your coworkers before he left."

"And you think one of them stole his scythe and murdered Madam Huxley?" Dellwyn put her head in her hands.

The last three people at the Rudder that morning, besides the madam, were Alisa, Augustus, and Kalinda. Dellwyn didn't think Kalinda could squash a beetle, let alone stab a human. And Augustus had been Madam Huxley's closest, maybe only, friend—and had discovered the body. He might have been skilled at faking satisfaction, but he wasn't that good of an actor. As for Alisa, Dellwyn had her suspicions, of course, but she still wasn't convinced that Alisa was foolish enough to risk her employment—or her life, for that matter—over her anger at Madam Huxley.

"It couldn't have been any of them." Dellwyn lifted her head. "They're all my friends, and I know them well. I don't think any of them are capable of, or stupid enough for, murder."

Mrs. Farmer stood. "Then it must have been someone else. The fact remains; Rykart is innocent. I will not stop searching for the truth, and I hope you won't either."

Dellwyn rose as well and attempted to match Mrs. Farmer's resolute expression. "I won't." As Dellwyn moved to open the door, a singular thought occurred to her. She let her hand fall from the knob and turned to face Mrs. Farmer. "Why do you care so much about Rykart? Who is he to you?"

Mrs. Farmer's eye twitched. "Is it not enough that he's an innocent member of my village?"

Dellwyn shook her head.

"He's my cousin." Mrs. Farmer sighed, and her shoulders slumped. "He's a good man, always has been, but he's so misguided."

Dellwyn nodded. "I can tell. I'll do my best to help him."

"Thank you." Mrs. Farmer clasped Dellwyn's hand. "Benevolent Queen bless you, Dellwyn Rutt."

Despite how the words burned in her throat, Dellwyn responded in kind. "And you as well."

Even though it was not customary, Dellwyn walked Mrs. Farmer to the lobby and bid her farewell. A few clients stood around, smoking pipes and talking amongst themselves, but Dellwyn did not see any she recognized as one of her own. She wasn't sure how Augustus intended for the workers to differentiate the walk-in clients from the scheduled ones, but Dellwyn decided she didn't want to take on someone new her first night back. After four rounds, she was far too tired to impress.

Besides, the lobby entrance showed the faintest hint of gray light, meaning that the sun would be rising in an hour or two. There was still a chance that one of her old regulars would come to see her, and she would hate for them to be turned away, as they no doubt had been when her time belonged to Lord Derringher.

Dellwyn smiled and curtsied for the clients in the lobby before turning and heading back to Room B. As she reached the workers' corridor, a deep voice hollered after her, and her heart leapt into her throat. She wheeled around to see two guards escorting Lord Derringher from the premises.

When they reached Dellwyn, Lord Derringher stopped and

stared down at her, hurt in his eyes. "Dellwyn, tell them that you want me here. Tell them I can stay."

With all the courage she could muster, Dellwyn held his gaze. "I'm sorry, but I can't do that." She took a deep breath and straightened her spine. "You abused one of our underage workers, and according to the new owner's policy, you can no longer do business here."

"I didn't know she was fourteen!" Lord Derringher's voice twisted into a whine. "She didn't say anything. I wouldn't have touched her if I knew."

For all of her loathing of him, Dellwyn could hear the sincerity in Lord Derringher's plea. But it didn't matter. Even if he never violated a child again, knowingly or not, he would still harm the regular workers with his games. Dellwyn couldn't allow another person to be put through what she had. No one deserved to be bound to a single client or treated like an animal.

Dellwyn held her chin high. "Whether intentional or not, you broke the law. There may not be enough evidence to imprison you, but Mr. Rutt trusts the word of his workers. You have to go."

"How can you be so formal, so cold?" Lord Derringher reached out to touch Dellwyn, but one of the guards blocked his hand. "I thought we shared something. You understand me like no one else."

"And yet you never cared to understand me." Dellwyn pinched the bridge of her nose. "There's nothing else to say. Remove him."

As instructed, the guards each took one of Lord Derringher's arms and ushered him down the corridor. His protests echoed off the metal walls, but as they grew quieter, a weight lifted from Dellwyn's chest. Lord Derringher might protest or find a way to go over Augustus's head, but for now, Dellwyn had won. Sybil remained out of Lord Derringher's reach, and Dellwyn had done everything she could to prevent him from harming her or anyone else at the Rudder in the near future. And with King Lionel on her side, there was a decent chance that Lord Derringher would never enter these halls again.

Soft footsteps approached Dellwyn from behind.

"It's done." Augustus's tone hovered somewhere between a statement and a question.

Dellwyn didn't turn to face him, but a shadow of a smile played on her lips. "Yes. It's done."

21

Although Dellwyn couldn't control what Lord Derringher might do next, for her part, she had meant what she said. She was done with Lord Derringher in thought and action. As she returned to Room B and lay on her bed, her mind drifted to her conversation with Mrs. Farmer.

The woman was convinced that one of the other courtesans was to blame for Madam Huxley's murder, and if Rykart's claim was true, it was entirely possible. It only reaffirmed Dellwyn's belief that she needed to speak with Alisa—at least Mrs. Farmer had provided her with the perfect entrance into the conversation.

Whether for Mrs. Farmer and Rykart, for Madam Huxley, or for her own morbid curiosity, Dellwyn would keep her word and attempt to solve the murder. But for now, she was bound to her room and any clients who might stop by, so she decided to relax.

Reaching over to her bedside table, Dellwyn picked up the mechanical flower from Lord Collingwood. Instead of twisting the base to open the flower, she turned the tiny winder on the base's side until it grew too difficult to move. As she released the winder, the same soft, twinkling melody floated from the flower, but this time, its petals clicked slowly back and forth, as if jostled by a breeze. *No, as if they were dancing.*

The sound comforted Dellwyn, though she couldn't say why. As she closed her eyes, images of Lord Collingwood flashed through her mind. His soft hazel eyes, his crooked, confident smirk, his gentle, caring touch. Lulled by the music, Dellwyn found herself, for only a moment, wondering what her life would have been like if she had been born a noblewoman. Would Lord Collingwood have waited for her to come of age to marry? Would he have divorced his wife for her? Would they have had an affair and risked execution in a less-protected environment? Who was to say? Dellwyn wouldn't have been the same person. She probably would have been more likely to chase after King Lionel than his uncle.

The music ceased, but thoughts of Lord Collingwood remained, intermingled with puzzlings over the murder. Dellwyn tried to shake both topics from her mind, but before she could succeed, another knock came from her door. She called for the visitor to enter, grateful for the distraction and hopeful that the client would be skilled enough to pull her mind away from her troubles.

Her wish was granted, though she didn't realize it until he spoke.

"I've missed you, Dell." Lord Collingwood's eyes bore into hers, and Dellwyn's breath caught in her throat.

She didn't have an excuse. It might have been the stress of the past couple of weeks. It might have been her worry that Madam Huxley's murderer remained at large. It might have been her relief at banishing Lord Derringher or the coincidence unfolding before her. But whatever it was, all the tension Dellwyn had felt upon seeing Lord Collingwood in the courtroom disappeared. She leapt off the bed and pushed him up against the door. His arms wrapped tightly around her, and their lips locked in a desperate exchange.

As Lord Collingwood's fingers gripped her rib cage, Dellwyn let out a sharp breath. She hadn't realized how sore her muscles had become. His eyes met hers and cringed as they took in her wincing face. "We don't have to do this. You should rest."

Dellwyn forced a smile and fiddled with the buttons on his jacket. "Isn't this what you came for?"

Lord Collingwood took her hands in his. "I came for you. Simply speaking with you again is a gift."

Dellwyn felt tears prick her eyes, so she turned her head and led him to the bed. Lord Collingwood lay down and stretched out his arm so Dellwyn could lay her head on his chest. His heart beat slow and strong under her ear, and she smiled to herself. It was as if the tumultuous night in his chambers had never happened. All at once, she was safe again—they were safe again.

"Was that my music box I heard?" Even without seeing his face, Dellwyn could hear the grin in Lord Collingwood's voice.

"It was." Dellwyn searched for something more substantial to say, but the perfect words eluded her. "It's soothing. I like it."

Lord Collingwood rubbed her back. "I'm glad."

"I'm sorry about the way we left things, Stanton." Dellwyn nestled closer to his side to disguise the pleasurable shiver that slipped down her spine as he ran his fingers along her back. "I know you were trying to help me, and I shouldn't have gotten so defensive."

"Think nothing of it, my darling." Lord Collingwood kissed the top of her head. "I'm merely pleased that you're free of Lord Derringher now."

Dellwyn's body froze. "How did you know?"

"I passed him in the stairwell." A different kind of satisfaction painted his voice.

"I'm relieved, too." Dellwyn sighed. Now that the rush of passion had seeped from her, the tension crept back in. She could avoid Alisa for now, but not Lord Collingwood. She swallowed hesitantly. "I have to ask you something, Stanton. And it's not an accusation, but I need you to be honest with me."

Lord Collingwood gently pushed Dellwyn off his chest and propped himself up on his side so they could speak face to face. "Yes?"

"You swore that you would get me out from under Madam Huxley's thumb." Dellwyn took a deep breath. "Did you?"

"No." Lord Collingwood frowned. "I love you, Dellwyn, but I don't think I'm capable of murder, even for you."

Dellwyn's eyes widened. Though she already knew he loved her, Lord Collingwood had never said the words aloud before, and she didn't know how to respond. After a moment of debate, Dellwyn decided on honesty. "I know, and I'm so grateful you do."

Lord Collingwood took her hand in his then kissed her knuckles. "And I'm grateful that you've given me as much of yourself as you can. That's all I can ask."

"Thank you." Dellwyn pushed down the guilt that threatened to spill out of her. It would only hurt him more to hear how much she wished she could love him.

To her relief, he resumed the subject at hand. "I take it you're innocent as well, then?"

"Of course." Dellwyn glanced to the door. "Why? Does someone suspect me?"

Lord Collingwood pursed his lips. "Not here, but on the council. Lord Varick believes you're the most likely candidate, given Madam Huxley's treatment of you and your argument the morning of her death. Luckily, Lionel and Zedara silenced his concerns before the rest of the council could latch onto them… and before I had to reveal my connection to you in your defense."

Dellwyn put her hand on his arm. "You would have risked your reputation? For me?"

His arm slid around her waist, pulling her close enough to kiss. "In a heartbeat."

"That would have been incredibly foolish, Stanton." Dellwyn shook her head, but softened the chastening with a coy smile. "Sweet, but foolish."

Lord Collingwood shrugged off her comment. "May I ask *you* something now?" He waited for her to nod. "What is your relationship to my nephew? He has a fondness for you. I don't think the rest of the council has noticed, but I have."

Dellwyn bit her lip. She had kept her connections to herself, and for good reason, up to this point. However, Lord

Collingwood had proven himself to her more than once, and she knew he deserved an answer. Dellwyn merely hoped he would understand why she hadn't been more forthcoming all along.

"Do you know Aya Cogsmith?"

Lord Collingwood's brow furrowed. "Of course. She's captured the entire kingdom's attention with her involvement with King Archon and my nephew."

"Aya is my dearest friend. We met when she came to work here, and we lived together in Sternville. His Majesty favors me because of my friendship with Aya." Dellwyn paused to take a breath—partly for courage and partly to consider how much Lord Collingwood might know about Aya's part in King Archon's execution. "While Aya was at the palace, she made an enemy of Lord Varick. I believe that's why he attempted to make me appear guilty."

"I see." Lord Collingwood's eyes squinted in thought. "That would explain why Zedara likes you as well. She, Lionel, and Aya have quite a bond now."

Dellwyn breathed a sigh of relief. "You know?"

"Yes. When Lionel informed me that he was in love with his father's last conquest, I was, understandably I think, concerned. But after he explained the full situation, my worries were assuaged." Lord Collingwood's eyes hardened. "I never liked, nor trusted, my brother-in-law—especially not after my sister's death."

"Aya told me everything from the beginning." Dellwyn felt her chest lighten. She and Lord Collingwood had no more secrets—they were both laid bare for the other. "For what it's worth, I haven't told His Majesty that you and I are involved. I don't believe Aya has either, but I don't know."

Lord Collingwood tucked a strand of hair behind her ear. "It doesn't matter whether she has or not."

Dellwyn raised her eyebrows. "Doesn't it?"

"Lionel knows I've been coming here for years. While he doesn't approve, he has never told anyone. I think his secrecy would only increase if he knew he was protecting you as well."

"It must be difficult for him, knowing that you don't love his aunt." Dellwyn looked down at the bed sheet. "And for her, too."

"Lionel and my wife both know that we did not marry for love." Lord Collingwood smirked. "In fact, now that Lionel has lifted the penalty on adultery, she spends fewer evenings at home than I do."

Dellwyn smiled. She hoped Lady Collingwood was happy with whomever she passed her nights. As much as Dellwyn loved her job, being the splinter in a spouse's ring finger had always filled her with guilt.

Lord Collingwood kneaded Dellwyn's shoulders. "How was the rest of your first night back?"

Dellwyn cringed. "We don't have to talk about that."

"I don't mind." Lord Collingwood's fingers worked a knot between her shoulder blades, and Dellwyn groaned. "Why would I be jealous when what we share is far more intimate?"

Dellwyn played with her hair so that she didn't have to meet his eyes. "I had five visitors before you. The first four were standard clients. The fifth, well, that may be worth discussing."

Lord Collingwood's hand rested in place. "Oh?"

"Mrs. Farmer, from the council, came to see me. She swore that Rykart was innocent and that he lost his scythe as he left the Rudder the morning of Madam Huxley's murder."

"That's a good, though convenient, excuse." Lord Collingwood frowned. "And you did say you think he's innocent. But if Rykart isn't the killer, things become much messier."

Dellwyn huffed. "Exactly. And I don't want to believe the murderer is any of Mrs. Farmer's suspects. They're all my friends."

Lord Collingwood caressed Dellwyn's cheek with his thumb. "Have you spoken to them about it?"

She leaned into his touch. "I know I should, but what could I possibly say? How could I accuse them?"

"I don't mean any offense, my darling, but your best friend orchestrated the execution of our land's king for revenge."

Lord Collingwood gave her a pointed stare. "Are you certain that same hatred couldn't have sent someone else you love down a similar path?"

Dellwyn glared at his chest. Lord Collingwood's words were logical, and they only confirmed the nagging suspicion in the back of her mind. She resolved again to speak to Alisa—and Kalinda and Augustus, too—about everything that had happened that morning.

"You may be right." Dellwyn sighed. "But if it is one of my friends, I don't know that I want to know. How could I face them after confirming what they did?"

Lord Collingwood shrugged. "Your relationship with Aya remains unchanged."

"Yes, but King Archon was a murderer. He called for the executions of dozens of innocent people. For all the cruel things Madam Huxley did, she never took a life." Dellwyn bit her lip. "And besides, I'd have to report them to the council. I couldn't let Rykart take the blame for a crime he didn't commit. But how could I turn my friend in, knowing it would bring about their death?"

Lord Collingwood placed his hand on the nape of her neck. "Finding out their guilt may not mean their execution. My nephew would understand if your friend had good reason, or perhaps acted in self-defense. There would penalties, of course, but it would be fine."

"Assuming it was for their own safety, or that of others." Dellwyn shivered. "What if it was just cold blood?"

"Then, friend or no, turning them in would be the right thing to do." Lord Collingwood rubbed her neck. "But this is hearsay. For all we know, Rykart lied about losing his scythe, and he is the true killer."

Dellwyn shook her head. "Maybe. But I've thought about it for too long now. I have to know the truth."

"What are you going to do?" Lord Collingwood's eyes shone with genuine concern, and Dellwyn felt her heart, and something a bit lower, ache.

"At sunrise, I'm going to start asking questions."

Lord Collingwood arched a brow. "And until then?"

Dellwyn smirked and pushed him onto his back. A surprised grin graced his face as she swung her leg over to straddle him. "I'm going to send both our worries into oblivion."

~

FOR THE SECOND time that night, Dellwyn strayed from protocol and walked with her client to the lobby. This time, only a few stragglers remained, either lined up outside Augustus's office to book their next appointments, or visiting with other clients to procrastinate the inevitable return to reality. Dellwyn planted a kiss on Lord Collingwood's cheek then left him to stand in the scheduling line. As much as she would have liked to linger by his side for a few more moments, she needed answers. And she couldn't wait any longer.

Dellwyn walked back down the workers' corridor and stopped at Room C. Before knocking, she leaned her ear against the door to listen for a client. No sound. With a deep breath, she put her fist to the metal. It only took one rap for Alisa to swing open the door.

"Forget something, hon——" Alisa's smooth voice stopped short, and she yanked her robe shut and tied it. "What do you want?"

If Dellwyn's visit had been purely social, she would have made a comment about Alisa's snappy tone. As it was, she let it go. "Can I talk to you? Inside?"

Alisa crossed her arms. "I'd rather not. I'm tired."

"It'll only take a few minutes." Dellwyn leaned in closer. "It's about Madam Huxley."

Alisa's eyes narrowed, but she stepped aside so Dellwyn could enter the room. "I thought we would have stopped talking about her by now."

Dellwyn chuckled. "I don't think that will happen until her murder has been solved."

"What's to solve?" Alisa sat down on her bed. Dellwyn took

the armchair in the corner. "It couldn't be more obvious that it's the farmer. If everyone didn't pity his insanity, he'd already be executed."

Dellwyn allowed her eyes to search Room C for any sign of Alisa's guilt. Alisa's outfits from the night lay strewn about the room, and her coat rack had been overturned in the heat of some moment, but nothing appeared suspicious.

Dellwyn turned her attention back to Alisa. "Whenever the farmer argued with Madam Huxley, you stood up for him, the same as me. Why aren't you now?"

"I only did that to piss her off." Alisa rolled her eyes. "But the evidence speaks for itself. His scythe was lodged in her spine. It doesn't get much clearer than that."

The memory of Madam Huxley's corpse flashed through Dellwyn's mind, and she shuddered. "I had a visitor from Bowtown tonight. She says Rykart's scythe was stolen that morning."

Alisa wrinkled her nose. "Oh, how convenient."

Dellwyn took a breath, bracing herself for the half-truth she was about to tell—and for Alisa's impending fury. "She also said that you were the last one to talk to Rykart before he left the Rudder."

"I suppose that's true." Alisa paused to glare at Dellwyn. "I did say 'good riddance' as I passed him on my way home."

Dellwyn bit her lip. "But you didn't—"

Alisa held up her hand, and her voice dropped to a level Dellwyn had never heard before. "You better think very carefully before you accuse me of something. I'm not an enemy you want to make."

Dellwyn swallowed, her eyes following the movements of Alisa's hands, scanning the folds of her robe for any concealed weapons. It was a warning to be sure, but it fell on Dellwyn's ears like a confession.

"The afternoon of the murder"—Dellwyn sucked in another deep breath—"Aya asked us all if we'd done it. You—"

"I said I was innocent, same as you."

Dellwyn shook her head. "Not in those words. You refused to give a straight answer."

"Does it matter what words I used if the message is the same?" Alisa's fists clenched. "I don't have to defend myself to you or anyone else."

"You don't have to put up that wall with me." Dellwyn looked at the ceiling. It was easier to lie when she didn't stare Alisa in the face. "I know you had good reason to do it. Shit, I wish I'd done it myself. I wouldn't turn you in; I'd thank you."

Alisa scoffed. "If that's what you're after, then you're welcome."

It took every muscle in Dellwyn's jaw for her to hold it in place. Her heartbeat quickened, and her palms slicked with sweat. If Alisa's warning hadn't been a confession, this had to be. For the briefest moment, Dellwyn wondered what it was about her that attracted such vengeful people.

Seeing Alisa's raised eyebrows, Dellwyn swallowed and said, "You killed Madam Huxley." She couldn't decide whether it was a statement or a question, but she figured Alisa's answer would tell them both.

Alisa's lips hardened into a thin line, and she stared at Dellwyn for a long moment. "I watched the life drain from her eyes. Is that enough of an answer for you?"

Dellwyn felt as if the air had been pushed from her lungs. She wiped her hands on her skirt, and dark spots emerged against the fabric. A vision of Madam Huxley's blood-soaked dress overtook her thoughts, and she shuddered. "Yes."

"Good." Alisa stood and wrenched the door open. "You can leave now."

Dellwyn rose, her mind barely registering that she couldn't feel her legs as they carried her to the doorway.

"You've always been one to keep your word, Dellwyn." A snarl played on Alisa's lips. "I'm going to believe that hasn't changed."

"It hasn't." The words tasted bitter on Dellwyn's tongue, and even as she spoke them, she didn't know whether or not they were true.

Without another word, Alisa shut the door behind her. As if in a dream, Dellwyn walked across the hallway and closed the door to Room B. She pressed her back into the cool metal then fumbled for the lock. It clicked, and she let out a long breath.

Even though Rykart's riddle had pointed straight to Alisa, and even though Dellwyn had had her own suspicions about her friend, part of her had still clung to the belief that Alisa was innocent. Alisa had always been temperamental—she could go from calm to furious to apathetic in under a minute—but she had never been violent. At least, as far as Dellwyn knew.

Dellwyn crossed the room and sat down on her bed. Her distracted mind hardly noticed when her fingers found the flower's winder and its soft lullaby drifted into the air. The sound soothed her, and Dellwyn allowed her eyes to close as she rested her head against the wall.

Something from her conversation with Alisa nagged at Dellwyn, but she couldn't quite place it. She thought back through Alisa's answers—her insistence that she needed no defense, her acceptance of Dellwyn's thanks, her confession. All of Dellwyn's unease settled around the end of their interaction. The *way* Alisa had confessed didn't seem right.

The flower's winder clicked to a stop, and the music whined as the gears ground into each other. As if a spell had been lifted, Dellwyn realized what was wrong.

Madam Huxley had been behind her desk when she died. The farmer's scythe had been lodged into her spine. Her eyes had faced the doorway, her mouth open in a scream... or a plea.

If Alisa had watched the life drain from Madam Huxley's eyes, she couldn't have been the one to stab the madam in the back. She would have been standing in the doorway—the target of Madam Huxley's desperate stare. Alisa was an accomplice at worst, and a witness at best.

Dellwyn set the flower down then trudged to her armoire to retrieve her cloak and wrap it around herself. After everything she had learned in the past few hours, new questions vibrated in her weary mind. Her hands shook as she tied her cloak strings. As she left the Rudder, Dellwyn cursed Mrs. Farmer for dragging her deeper into the mystery and hoped that this plan would finally unveil the truth. It would take a lot of begging and a little bit of luck, but Dellwyn knew where she would find her answers.

22

"You've got to be mad." Aya's jaw clenched, and she crossed her arms in a huff. Her telltale red flush rose from her chest to her cheeks, and Dellwyn wondered whether this was too much to ask of Aya.

"Please, Aya. I have to talk to him. It's the only way I'll know for sure that Alisa's confession is true." Dellwyn widened her eyes the way a small child begs her mother. "You know I wouldn't ask if I could do it myself."

Aya sighed. "Alisa isn't an imbecile. Why would she lie about committing murder?"

"I don't know, but I have this feeling… I just can't place it." Dellwyn scanned Aya's cluttered workshop, as if the answer lurked under one of the disassembled machines.

"A feeling?" Aya scoffed. "You want me to grossly abuse Lionel's affections for a feeling?"

Dellwyn spread her hands out on the table, grounding herself for the argument's lowest blow yet. "You know my intuition has always been strong. And besides, it's not like you have any problem throwing around Lionel's love to get what *you* want."

"That's not fair!" Aya slapped her own hands down on the table. "Both times I've done it were to help *you.*"

Dellwyn batted her eyelashes. "What's one more time?"

As she had hoped, Aya relaxed and leaned back in her chair. "Why can't you go through Lord Collingwood? He has an even stronger connection to Lionel than I do."

"Oh, I doubt that." Dellwyn puckered her lips, and Aya narrowed her eyes. "Moreover, to my and Lord Collingwood's knowledge, Lionel doesn't know about our... relationship. Personally, I'd rather keep it that way."

Aya frowned. Dellwyn knew that she had made several fair points, but the firm stare in Aya's eyes told her she hadn't won quite yet. There was one final argument Dellwyn could make. She had been trying to avoid it to spare Aya's feelings, but it seemed she had no choice.

Dellwyn let out a long breath and shook her head. "I can't bear the thought of Rykart sitting in that dungeon if he *is* innocent. I'd hate to see an innocent man executed for another person's wrongs, wouldn't you?"

It was enough. Aya's face paled, and she stared down at her hands. Dellwyn could see the calculation in her eyes, from the steely squint of resistance to the slow blink of relent. She didn't wait for Aya to speak. "Thank you, Aya. I promise I'll make this up to you."

"You better." Aya ran her fingers through her hair. "And I suspect you want to leave right away?"

Dellwyn stood. "Absolutely."

With a groan, Aya rose, grabbed a leather satchel from the corner of the room, and slung it over her shoulder. "We should at least blend in with the other merchants." She pointed to a toolbox sitting against the wall. "Carry that with you."

A few minutes later, the pair waited with a group of merchants and delivery boys outside the port side of the palace. The ship's wall creaked, and the metal slowly clicked back to reveal the interior. As the gangway lowered to the ground, Aya's hands grasped the strap of her satchel, and she shifted her weight from foot to foot. "I hate entering the palace this way."

Dellwyn glanced from the lowering bridge to Aya's agitated shuffling. "This is how you went with your father."

Aya nodded. "I've done it a few times now, but it still unnerves me."

"It's okay." Dellwyn took Aya's hand in hers. "I've got your back this time."

The gangway finished its descent, and the two climbed the steep incline into the ship. As they stepped over the threshold, Dellwyn couldn't help but gasp. Now that she had the luxury of admiring the palace's interior, she marveled at its beauty. Tall iron columns held up the high ceilings. Marble lined the floor, the same as in the stern, but this time Dellwyn noticed the intricate white and gray swirls of the stone. Like in the corridors Dellwyn had explored, portraits decorated the walls, and statues stood sentry at even intervals. Down the hallway, Dellwyn thought she spied a few machine-like relics resting on raised platforms.

A line of maids and butlers waited for the merchants, each one stepping forward as they saw their awaited delivery. Aya walked past them and up to a man who seemed to be directing the traffic.

The man smiled as they approached, his thick mustache wiggling with the gesture. "Good morning, Aya. What brings you to the palace today?"

"What else, Castas? Always more goods to deliver." Aya patted her satchel, then inclined her head toward Dellwyn. "And I figured I'd bring my toolbox along in case anyone needed my skills. Every time I come here, I end up fixing some estate's door hinge, or some lord asks me to tinker on his room's radiator, as if a wrench will magically bring back the steam power."

Castas chuckled, hearty and deep. "Very well. Do you need a guide?"

"I can take it from here, thanks." Aya waved farewell, and they headed toward the center of the ship.

Once they were out of earshot, Dellwyn elbowed Aya in

the side. "Speaking of your skills, your deception has gotten much better."

Aya shrugged. "Oh, Castas is an old friend; he'd believe anything I said. And I didn't lie. I'm delivering you, and it's always good to have tools handy."

"Fair enough." Dellwyn shook her head. "But I'm still impressed."

They walked for a long time, rounding corners and ascending three flights of stairs. The farther they went into the maze of the palace, the less Dellwyn focused on the paintings and the more she focused on Aya's face. Wrinkles had emerged along Aya's forehead, and her lips pursed as her eyes scrutinized each corridor.

As they exited another stairwell, Dellwyn cleared her throat. "Um, Aya, do you know where we're going?"

"Basically." Aya stopped, looked in both directions, then turned left.

Dellwyn raised her eyebrows. "Basically?"

Aya sighed. "To my knowledge, there are only two ways to enter the king's chambers. They're on the seventh level of the ship. We can either walk through the main corridors—where the ballroom and courtroom are, and where many of the nobles live—or we can go down a passageway from near the deck."

Dellwyn huffed. "And of course, you had to choose the way with the most stairs."

"This is how the servants travel the ship. It's the best way to ensure we aren't noticed by too many nobles." Aya rolled her eyes. "Trust me, if you're seen by one, the whole palace knows about it by teatime."

Dellwyn sighed. "Fine."

A wide staircase came into view. At the top stood a set of glass double doors. The bright morning light streamed in through their panes. The red carpet matched Aya's skirt, and its folds seemed to melt into the floor. Aya stopped in front of a large portrait, which depicted an angry queen steering a ship through a torrential rainstorm.

Dellwyn scrunched her nose. "Who is that?"

"Queen Hildegard." Aya slid the portrait to the side, revealing a long, dark tunnel.

Had Dellwyn not visited Lord Collingwood's secret chambers through the same method, she might have been surprised. Instead, she followed Aya inside then reached behind to close the door. As they walked down the passageway, Dellwyn traced the wall with her hand. It felt rough, like wood. "As in the name of the ship?"

"Yes. She was the monarch during the flood." Aya's voice echoed along the corridor, making her sound far away. "Many of the nobles revere her as a savior. They respect her memory more than the legend of the Benevolent Queen."

"*Humph.* At least Queen Hildegard was real." Dellwyn stumbled as her foot caught on something on the floor—a nail head, most likely—and the toolbox clanged between her thigh and the wall. "Even if her actions weren't."

Aya didn't respond, but Dellwyn didn't need her to. She could sense the eye roll through the darkness. They walked the rest of the way in silence until Dellwyn's chest bumped Aya's outstretched arm.

"We're here." Aya's voice shook.

Dellwyn uselessly glanced around in the dark. "What's the matter?"

"I haven't been back here since…" Aya took a deep breath. "And I haven't spoken directly with Lionel since…"

Dellwyn fumbled for Aya's shoulder and squeezed it. "It'll be fine. If you want, I can do all the talking."

"No." Aya's curls swept across Dellwyn's hand as she shook her head. "It's about time we face each other again."

"Why haven't you?" Dellwyn knew Aya was shy, but after all she and the king had shared, it seemed foolish for her to be nervous around him now.

"After everything that happened with King Archon and the trial, I needed a break from Lionel, from the palace." Aya sighed. "That, and I thought I should enjoy being a cogsmith awhile before I become queen."

"Ha!" Dellwyn's outburst sounded twice as loud in the narrow space. "So you admit it."

Aya shook Dellwyn's hand off her shoulder. "Before I *consider* becoming queen," she amended.

Dellwyn smiled, but she felt the heaviness in Aya's tone. As Dellwyn had never been in love, nor had the option to hold such an important position, she didn't know how to comfort Aya. So she simply said what she would want to hear if she were in Aya's place. "It won't make a difference. Whether you're Queen Aya or Miss Aya, you'll still be the best cogsmith in all of Desertera."

Aya scoffed, but there was humor in it. "I'll be the *only* cogsmith in Desertera."

"But you'll still be one." Dellwyn tightened her grip on the toolbox, pleased with what had become their personal joke. "King Lionel would never take that away from you."

"No, he won't."

Light illuminated the tunnel, and Dellwyn shielded her eyes. They emerged into a cylindrical sitting area. Dellwyn turned in a slow circle. "What's with all the round rooms?"

"No clue." Aya closed the tunnel. A bookshelf obscured this end.

Other than said bookshelf, the space was relatively empty. As with the corridors, a few portraits hung on the walls. Scuffs marred the center of the marble floor, where a piece of furniture must have once sat. To the left, a narrow passageway opened, and Dellwyn assumed it led to the main hallways Aya wanted to avoid. To the right, a tall wooden object stood in between two doors.

"It's a grandfather clock," Aya explained. She traced her fingers along a thin crack in the body's glass pane. "Bastard."

Dellwyn ignored the utterance and turned her attention to the two doorways on either side of the clock. "Which one?"

"Left." Aya eyed the other portal. "Two men have told me the right one doesn't go anywhere, but I don't believe them. I suspect they simply lack the key."

"Strange." Dellwyn shrugged and headed to the door on the left. "Do you want to do the honors?"

Aya cringed, but she came over and knocked. Silence. "I hope he's here." Her green eyes shone with worry. "The only thing worse than him being here is him not being here."

Dellwyn chuckled and rapped hard on the door. This time, footsteps answered on the other side, growing louder as they approached. With their sound, the gravity of the situation finally settled upon Dellwyn, and her heart began to race. She had, out of her own selfish quest for answers, disturbed *the king* —Aya's lover—but still. And assuming King Lionel agreed to take her to the dungeon, Dellwyn would shortly be faced with the man who very well could have murdered Madam Huxley. She could learn the horrible truth that her friend had watched it happen or the terrifying reality that the murderer was still free. Or perhaps, the truth was some alarming combination of all three.

The lock on the door clicked, and Dellwyn could hear King Lionel's voice on the other side. "Eldric, I have an hour until—" He swung the door open and fell silent. His eyes darted between Aya and Dellwyn for a surprised moment before he recovered and raised his eyebrows. "This can't be good."

Out of the corner of her eye, Dellwyn saw Aya's body stiffen, so Dellwyn curtsied and said, "We apologize for disturbing you, Your Majesty, but we hope the news *is* good."

Aya didn't curtsy, but Dellwyn's actions seemed to have anchored her. "I'm sorry, Lionel. I didn't mean for us to meet again under these circumstances."

King Lionel frowned. "I don't know if I'll ever get used to you calling me by my given name."

"We'll find out, won't we?" Aya offered a small smile before placing her hand on Dellwyn's arm. "Dellwyn has new evidence relating to Madam Huxley's murder."

"Oh?" King Lionel's tone settled somewhere between disappointment and intrigue, but he turned to Dellwyn, alert. "Have you told anyone else?"

Dellwyn shook her head. "We're the only two that know. We came straight to you."

"Good." King Lionel glanced down toward the narrow corridor and furrowed his brow. "Did anyone see you come here?"

"Just Castas, who was directing the merchants, and a few servants in the interior hallways." Aya motioned toward the bookshelf. "We took the tunnel."

King Lionel's lips twisted. "How did you—right." He closed his eyes, as if to shut out bad memories. "What is your news?"

"One of my coworkers more or less confessed to Madam Huxley's murder." Dellwyn paused to let the information sink in. "But I don't think they're telling the whole truth."

King Lionel crossed his arms and leaned against the door-frame. "Why would this person confess if they're innocent?"

Dellwyn chuckled. "If you knew how stubborn this person was, you'd hardly be surprised. They'd rather be thought a murderer than lower themselves to plead in self-defense."

"I see." King Lionel rubbed his chin. "Do you want me to have them brought in for questioning?"

"Not exactly." Dellwyn swallowed down her nerves and forced herself to hold the king's gaze. "I'd actually like to speak with the farmer. I have reason to believe he has the information I need."

King Lionel shook his head. "The man is mad. I don't think I've heard him say a reliable word since we arrested him."

"He'll talk to me. Sensibly." As Dellwyn spoke the words, she realized she believed them. Despite their differences, Rykart had always listened to her and respected her—even when she hadn't returned the courtesy. She hoped she could repay him now.

King Lionel looked at Aya, and she nodded. "Very well." He reached back into his room and retrieved his top hat from the coat rack next to the door. "To the dungeon."

~

AFTER WINDING their way down to the bottom level of the palace, they stopped in front of an iron door with a wheel on the front. King Lionel knocked, the wheel spun as if on its own, and the door wrenched open. A guard stood on the other side. His bushy hair, eyebrows, and beard left nothing exposed on his face except for his dark, angry eyes.

Dellwyn noticed Aya loop her arm through King Lionel's and nestle closer to his side. With a pang in her gut, Dellwyn realized that Aya would have been imprisoned there, if only for one night, before King Archon's trial. And now Dellwyn had dragged her friend back down to face whatever memories—this guard included, it seemed—haunted her. She would have to make it up to Aya later, or at least try.

"Miss Rutt is here to speak with Rykart Farmer." King Lionel inclined his head toward Dellwyn. "You will allow her a *private* audience with him for as long as she requires." He turned to Dellwyn and leaned in to whisper in her ear. "Aya and I will wait out here. If he tries anything, you yell for us."

Dellwyn nodded. She didn't know whether the king meant the farmer or the guard, but she imagined the order applied to both. With a deep breath, she followed the guard into the dungeon. He slammed the door shut behind them, but he didn't lock it. Then, he pushed past Dellwyn and led her down a narrow hallway.

Doors lined the walls every two feet. Barred windows had been placed near the top of each door, allowing the guard a glimpse inside. The doors all had small openings at the bottom, probably so scraps of food and small cups of water could be slid through. Most of the cells seemed empty, but every now and then, Dellwyn heard shuffling or a whimper as they passed.

The guard stopped in front of a cell and stuck his face close to the barred slot at the top. "You have a visitor, lunatic. I'm gonna open the door. Don't you dare move."

He pulled out a key ring and unlocked the door, only opening it enough for Dellwyn to squeeze herself inside. Once she had, the guard shut and locked the door behind her. "I'll be down the hall. Holler when yer done."

His footsteps retreated, and Dellwyn let out a breath she hadn't realized she'd been holding. She turned to Rykart, who sat cross-legged in the corner. From the smile on his face and the pleasant look in his mismatched eyes, Dellwyn almost forgot that she was visiting him in the dungeon and not outside the Rudder.

But his attitude didn't match his appearance. That same smile betrayed cracked, bloody lips, and his gray eye was swollen and bruised. His clothes hung loosely from his limbs, stains marring the surface. A bucket sat in the corner, its contents close to overflowing, and its stench pervaded the small cell.

"Hello, Rykart." Dellwyn swallowed down the bile that the situation had drawn from her stomach. No matter where she stood, she couldn't position herself more than three feet away from the farmer, and with his potential crime hovering over her, the closeness made her chest hurt.

Rykart's grin widened. "We've been expecting you, Dellwyn."

"We?" Dellwyn rolled her eyes, irritation replacing her fear. "Right. You and the Benevolent Queen."

"She is always watching." Rykart's gaze lifted to the ceiling. "She is always here."

"Yes, I remember." Dellwyn tapped her foot. "Rykart, as much as I would love to talk about Her, I came to ask you a few questions."

Rykart scratched his head, and it occurred to Dellwyn that he wasn't wearing his cap. No tool belt, either. Their absence didn't surprise Dellwyn—she knew the guards would have confiscated Rykart's personal items—but she thought he looked smaller, weaker without them.

"Your cousin, Eveline, came to see me." Dellwyn watched

his face for any sign of recognition, but Rykart showed none. "She said that you think someone stole your scythe."

His eyes stared up at Dellwyn—or perhaps through her—but he nodded.

"Right." Dellwyn huffed. *Would it kill him to reply with words?* "Well, then I talked to Alisa, another courtesan from the Rudder. Do you remember her?"

Again, he nodded.

"Alisa confessed to Madam Huxley's murder, but I don't believe her." Dellwyn crossed her arms. "But I don't think you murdered Madam Huxley, either."

At this, Rykart's face grew solemn, and he hung his head. "I am guilty."

Dellwyn took a step back, only to find herself flat against the cold metal wall of the cell. "Excuse me?"

"I… I fantasized about harming Madam Huxley." Rykart wiped his eyes, and his hands returned to his sides wet. "She killed her to punish me."

"Who killed Madam Huxley?" Dellwyn knelt down to Rykart's level. "Alisa?"

"No. *She* did it. She acted through someone to show me the price of my evil thoughts." Rykart's voice broke. "I… I never meant to anger Her. I never meant for Her to hurt anyone."

"Damn it, Rykart!" Dellwyn banged her palm against the cell, and Rykart flinched. Remembering the way Aya had reacted to the guard, Dellwyn took a calming breath. Who knew what Rykart had been subjected to down there? She didn't want to add to his suffering, but his religious zealotry only increased her frustration. So Rykart didn't kill Madam Huxley—he merely blamed himself, or the Benevolent Queen. Either way, the information answered only one of her questions.

Dellwyn swallowed. "It's not your fault, Rykart. You are the most loyal follower She has. She would not do this to punish you. She probably meant to punish Madam Huxley for aiding in the people's infidelity."

Rykart sniffed and stared up at Dellwyn the way a child looked to a parent for comfort. "That could be true."

"I know it is." Dellwyn crouched down and shuffled closer to him. "The Benevolent Queen wouldn't want you to stay in this cell. You should be out there, spreading Her word."

Rykart pursed his lips. "You're right. She sent you to help me."

"I think She did." Dellwyn withheld a wince. "Now, you told me you're innocent of the murder. That's a good start. But if you didn't kill Madam Huxley, we need to know who did. The Benevolent Queen would want justice for their sins."

"She does." Rykart tilted his head, as if listening to someone whisper in his ear. "I can hear Her cries."

Dellwyn nearly scoffed. *Oh, sure.* Now *his goddess loves him again.* "Good. So, whoever killed Madam Huxley must have had your scythe. Who could have taken it from you?"

Rykart's eyes scanned the cell, and Dellwyn shivered. His eyes, and the mystery of what he could see, still unnerved her. "I don't know."

Dellwyn put her fingers to her temples and rubbed them in firm, slow circles. "What do you mean you don't know?"

"The kind one, with dark hair and eyes—"

"Kalinda?" Dellwyn perked up. This was good. Kalinda was real. Kalinda had been there the morning it happened.

"Yes. She came to speak her nice words." Rykart squinted. "She took me into the village, and we ate at her table. I returned to my camp then went home to the fields."

Dellwyn mulled it over. "Did you speak to anyone else that morning?"

Rykart shook his head. "They spoke to her. The angry blond ones. They came, one after the other, like tidal waves, and washed over me. They tried to take the nice one away. She wouldn't listen to them."

"Right." So Alisa and Augustus had both tried to talk Kalinda out of having breakfast with Rykart, but Kalinda had been determined to do it. Why? Out of sheer kindness? Or because getting Rykart alone gave her the perfect opportunity to steal his scythe? "And your scythe was gone when you got back to Bowtown?"

Rykart nodded.

Dellwyn pursed her lips and tried to think of anything else that would be useful. "Did you take it out of your tool belt at any point?"

"No." He sighed. "I always keep my treasures close."

Then whoever stole the scythe would have had to have taken it off Rykart's hip. And the only person he spoke to, the only one close enough, was Kalinda.

The revelation burned in Dellwyn's stomach, and she tried to think logically about the situation. Like everyone else at the Rudder, Kalinda had probably had a difficult time under Madam Huxley's tyranny. And Kalinda despised conflict—she'd especially hated the feud between Madam Huxley and Rykart. Killing the madam and blaming it on the farmer would have solved both of those problems. And if Alisa had witnessed Kalinda's crime, of course she would have stayed silent. Alisa would never betray one of her own.

But even though Dellwyn could imagine Kalinda's motives, opportunity to acquire the murder weapon, and Alisa's potential involvement, none of it felt right. Kalinda had always been kind, gentle, and frankly, weak-willed. The thought of her killing Madam Huxley was almost comical. Then again, Dellwyn never would have guessed that Aya would have successfully seduced and orchestrated the execution of a king, either. Maybe Lord Collingwood was right; maybe Dellwyn didn't really know her friends.

With a sigh, she reached out and patted Rykart's shoulder. Her palm came back sticky. "Thank you for answering my questions. I think I have enough to set you free."

Fresh tears welled in his eyes. "I can go home?"

"Not right now, but soon." Dellwyn stood, realizing for the first time all morning how incredibly tired her body felt. "I need to find some more answers. I'm not sure how long it will take."

Rykart's dry lips stretched into a smile. "Thank you, Dellwyn Rutt."

Dellwyn replied with a small smile of her own then knocked on the door and called for the guard. As the guard unlocked the cell, Dellwyn paused in the doorway and turned back to Rykart. "That golden device you carried, the one you used to look at the stars. What was it?"

"An astrolabe." Rykart held out his palms as if he could show it to Dellwyn. "The Benevolent Queen gave them to the sailors to help them navigate the great rains."

Dellwyn nodded and left the cell. It was a small start, but for the time being, giving Aya a new project to research was all Dellwyn could offer as recompense.

As Dellwyn and the guard walked back down the hallway, a heaviness settled in her chest. Rykart had been open with her, and as such, Dellwyn could save an innocent man from execution. But she still didn't know whom to put in his place, and she wasn't convinced that either Alisa or Kalinda were guilty. It was all such a mess.

The incessant puzzling made Dellwyn's head throb, and she choked down the yell that threatened to rise in her throat. She couldn't do this anymore. She couldn't keep asking these impossible questions, couldn't keep chasing down answers only to receive riddles and half-truths, couldn't be responsible for the potential imprisonment of her friends.

Dellwyn had kept her promise to Eveline Farmer—Rykart would go free once Dellwyn explained his story to King Lionel. But that wasn't all Dellwyn would tell the king. She would tell him everything—from the details of Alisa's confession to Kalinda's potential motives. It stung Dellwyn to betray her friends' confidences, but she couldn't go on like this any longer. Only King Lionel and his council should act as the upholders of justice. Dellwyn had no right to play the courtesan's avenger.

The dungeon door groaned open, and Dellwyn stepped out into the corridor with King Lionel and Aya. They still stood next to one another, Aya's arm looped through his. As their inquisitive gazes met hers, Dellwyn's mouth went dry. Where should she even begin? And how could she possibly describe what she felt? She took a deep breath and started with the least important piece of information, resolving to tackle the rest in a moment. "He calls it an astrolabe."

23

———

*O*nce they had returned to the main level of the palace, Dellwyn parted ways with Aya and King Lionel, electing to leave through the rear of the ship. After she had told them about her conversations with Rykart and Alisa, King Lionel had ordered his guards to retrieve both Kalinda and Alisa for questioning. Guilt gnawed at Dellwyn for bringing suspicion upon her friends and letting go of the investigation, but her shoulders also lightened with relief. At this point, she figured the last responsibility she held in the matter was to stop by the Rudder and let Augustus know what had happened so he could cancel both women's appointments for the evening. Then, she would be done with Madam Huxley's murder for good.

Following Aya's instructions, Dellwyn passed the ballroom and reached the end of the main corridor. Before her stood a hideous, tall statue, carved in smooth stone. The plaque at the figure's feet told Dellwyn that it depicted Queen Hildegard, and Dellwyn rolled her eyes. The nobles really did worship the dead queen like a goddess. At least they believed in someone who had once been real, even if their stories had morphed her into legend.

With a shake of her head, Dellwyn turned left toward the stern and hurried to the staircase without taking the time to observe any more of what the nobles considered art. She had been at the palace longer than she'd intended, and it had to be past lunch. Augustus would need a few hours' notice to cancel the appointments without complication—it was the least Dellwyn could do after everything she had messed up for the Rudder today.

As Dellwyn reached the stairwell, she kept up her quick pace, racing to the bottom level and emerging breathless into the workers' corridor of the Rudder. With the lightest steps she could manage, Dellwyn walked down the hallway. Being at the Rudder in the daytime always made her uneasy. It was hollow —no people bustling about or murmuring behind the doors— just blank walls leading to small rooms, filled only in these moments by secrets and memories.

As she stepped into the lobby, Dellwyn crossed the space and turned left toward the new workers' corridor and Augustus's office. At the opening to this hallway, voices made her take pause. They filtered out of the office. The door was ajar, and candlelight spilled into the barren corridor.

Dellwyn recognized Augustus's voice, but she could not identify the other man. A smile crossed her lips at the thought that maybe Augustus had a lover. If so, she didn't want to intrude, but she had to. Her news involved two of his employees, one or both of whom could be imprisoned, or worse, over the next few days. Augustus needed to know. And as much as the thought of betraying her friends still knotted Dellwyn's stomach, the damage was done. All that was left was to play the messenger.

As Dellwyn inched forward, taking a few more cautious steps, she strained to hear Augustus's conversation. The closer she got to the office, the more clearly the voices came to her, and Dellwyn realized Augustus was not receiving a social visit. The man's voice was soft and slick but laced with a controlled anger. A customer, then. A well-educated one. A furious one.

Dellwyn stalled. Lord Derringher. What if he had returned to argue his case again? Augustus would never give in to the lord's demands—not when it meant losing Dellwyn as a courtesan—but what if Lord Derringher's anger turned violent? After all, if he was so rough in lovemaking, what was Lord Derringher capable of in his fury?

All at once, the man's voice broke into a yell. "How could you let this happen?"

It wasn't Lord Derringher—the voice wasn't deep enough. Dellwyn let out her breath and cocked her ear toward the door. Then who could it be? Watching her feet to avoid tripping, she sidestepped closer to the doorway. Now only an arm's length away, Dellwyn could hear the conversation plainly. She still didn't recognize the man's voice, but as his and Augustus's words unfolded before her, her heart hammered even harder against her rib cage.

"What do you mean, you didn't let anything happen?" The man released a noise akin to a growl. "Just hours ago, the cogsmith came to the palace, accompanied by a woman matching Dellwyn's description."

Dellwyn clamped her hand over her mouth to avoid gasping. How did the man know about her and Aya's movements? And why did he care?

"My guard followed them through the corridors, up to the ship's deck, then lost them." The man's voice fell quiet again, but his agitation remained. "When he found them again, they were returning from the dungeon with the king. They'd been to see the farmer."

"So?" Augustus's voice sounded equally irritated. "Dellwyn's always felt sorry for him. She probably wanted to ask why he killed Madam Huxley."

"And I wonder what his answer would be." The man's tone dripped with sarcasm. "He must have told her something valuable. Both Alisa and Kalinda have been summoned to the palace for questioning."

Augustus scoffed. "Kalinda doesn't know anything."

Dellwyn's knees wobbled, and her hand began to shake against her lips. No, it couldn't be. They had been so close. Madam Huxley had trusted Augustus above all others.

"But Alisa does—your carelessness made sure of that. Do

you think her loyalty will withstand another round of interrogation? Especially now that they will know for certain she was involved."

"Of course it will." Dellwyn could imagine the indignant scowl on Augustus's face. "She would never betray her own kind. And if she considers it, you can hand her another heavy bag of coins."

So Dellwyn had been right. Alisa had witnessed Madam Huxley's murder by accident then stayed quiet for loyalty… and money. Only, it hadn't been Rykart or Kalinda on the other end of the scythe. Dellwyn couldn't even think it—and she wouldn't, not without definitive proof. Augustus had *found* the body, for goodness sake. Maybe he was another witness, or perhaps he had been part of some scheme that had gone wrong. It didn't all have to be blood and cruelty, right?

"That might be difficult, considering how much it cost me to get you control of the Rudder."

Dellwyn nearly cried out. She knew it. Augustus never could have afforded the Rudder on his own. He had a benefactor, and this man was it—the true owner of the Rudder. But why did a nobleman need to purchase the Rudder through Augustus? Why couldn't he have bought it outright, without the pretense?

"And it will be well worth it." Augustus let out a heavy sigh. "You just have to give me more time."

"Don't you see?" A bang issued, as if the man had hit the desk with his fist, and Dellwyn jumped. "We don't have time. They have Alisa. They have the farmer. It's only a matter of days before the trail leads back to you and you lead them to me."

"I would never betray you." Augustus's voice cracked, and Dellwyn could hear the tears in it.

"Is that what you told your last employer? Was that before or after you stabbed her in the back?"

Dellwyn didn't need to hear any more. She shuffled down the corridor and into the lobby. A few shouts followed her, then footsteps echoed in the otherwise silent hallway. There wasn't time to dash for the exit, so Dellwyn darted down the workers' corridor and into Room B. She feared shutting the door completely in case the man heard it click into place. Instead, she pushed it as far shut as she could and hoped he wouldn't notice, or think anything of, the fact that it wasn't latched.

Crouched down behind the door, Dellwyn held her breath as the footsteps drew nearer then passed by her room. A shiver wracked her body, and she clamped both hands over her mouth. She listened to the sound of their retreat, and she felt as if an eternity passed in the darkness. Metal groaned as the door to the palace's interior opened then slammed shut.

Dellwyn released her held breath and lowered her hands to clutch the collar of her dress. The footsteps hadn't been alone. Between each one, Dellwyn had heard a deafening clack. She only knew one nobleman who walked with a staff, and he had every reason to hide his investment in the Rudder.

Alone, in the silence of Room B, Dellwyn allowed herself to finally whisper the truth. "Augustus murdered Madam Huxley. Lord Varick helped him do it. And Alisa knew all along."

24

———

Instead of running straight back to King Lionel or Aya, Dellwyn sneaked out of the Rudder and scurried to her hovel. With the door shut firmly behind her, she walked on shaky legs to the table and collapsed into a chair. She rested her head in her hands and took big, loud gulps of hot air, hoping the action would clear her mind.

After a few moments, the roar of pumping blood in her head quieted, and the truth slid through Dellwyn's veins like cold well water. *Augustus killed Madam Huxley.* She whispered the words over and over until they finally began to sink in.

Dellwyn pounded her palm on the table. "Damn it!" How could Augustus have done that to Madam Huxley and everyone at the Rudder? How could he sit in that chair—the same chair in which Madam Huxley had died—night after night?

Dellwyn scowled. *With Lord Varick's money, that's how. At least he's one person I'll enjoy turning in to the king.*

The thought made her frown deepen. That was what she should do. She should compose herself, march directly to King Lionel's chambers and recount the conversation she had overheard. But would her word be enough? If Lord Varick held half as much influence as the king had said, why would the unbiased council members, or the public for that matter, believe Dellwyn over a nobleman? And if Dellwyn had to stand trial next to Augustus, he could easily argue that she was simply jealous he had won the Rudder. No, her word, even supported by King Lionel, wasn't a guarantee.

And despite her better judgment, the remnants of her friendship with Augustus tugged at her sympathy. After all, Dellwyn's rush of nerves left the whole encounter hazy in her memory, and she couldn't remember Augustus admitting to the crime outright. No, he hadn't. Lord Varick had been the one to imply that Augustus had stabbed Madam Huxley in the back. It could have been the literal truth or, knowing Lord Varick's aptitude for twisting words, it could have been a metaphor, perhaps even a threat to pin the crime on Augustus. If Dellwyn was going to act as investigator one last time, she needed better evidence and an absolute confession.

Before she could begin forming a plan, the door to the hovel opened. Sybil and Zedara entered, each carrying a small trunk.

Sybil beamed. "Oh, good! You're home." She took a closer look at Dellwyn then set her trunk against the wall and grabbed Dellwyn's hand. "What's wrong?"

Dellwyn sighed and squeezed back. "It's a long story."

Zedara placed her trunk next to Sybil's and came to stand next to them. "We have time."

Dellwyn glanced over her shoulder at the trunks. "What's in there?"

"My new maid uniforms." Sybil squared her shoulders. From Dellwyn's seated position, Sybil actually appeared formidable. "Don't change the subject."

Dellwyn blew out a long breath. Where to begin? Sybil adored Augustus; she would be devastated. Dellwyn searched Sybil's concerned eyes, and the look in them made her pause long enough to realize how badly her own heart ached. She had trusted Augustus. Madam Huxley had trusted Augustus. And he had betrayed them both. Frustrated and embarrassed, Dellwyn returned her head to her hands and allowed herself to cry as Sybil and Zedara patted her on the back and made soft shushing noises.

After a moment, Zedara knelt beside Dellwyn and gently pulled her hands away from her face. "If you don't want to talk about it, that's fine. But is there anything we can do to help?"

Dellwyn took in Zedara's kind expression—from her bright eyes to her small, comforting smile. A few weeks ago, Zedara had existed only in stories from Aya's time in the palace. Now, there she was, crouched on the dirt floor of Dellwyn's hovel, making an offer of friendship. In that moment, it occurred to Dellwyn that maybe friendship wasn't about who she'd known the longest, who she worked with, or who shared her social class. Maybe it was about who helped her in a crisis, who was forthright despite their pride, and who treated her like the person she was trying to be, not necessarily the person she was.

"Are we friends, Zedara?"

The noblewoman didn't even blink. "Yes. We may not know each other well, but you are Aya's dearest friend, and I owe Aya my life." Zedara paused, the corners of her mouth tugging up into a wider smile. "And I hope, in time, we may become friends in our own right. Why do you ask?"

"I need a favor." Dellwyn swallowed. "And I wouldn't... I couldn't... ask it of anyone who isn't my friend."

Zedara's brows knitted together. "Ask away."

Dellwyn looked up at Sybil and nodded to reassure her that everything would be all right. The young girl replied in kind. Satisfied, Dellwyn turned her face back to Zedara. The longer the plan brewed in her mind, the more confident she became. She leaned back in her chair and folded her arms over her lap. "Can I borrow some money?"

AUGUSTUS'S COUNTENANCE showed only mild curiosity as Dellwyn entered his office that evening. Ever the polite host, he gestured to the chair in front of his desk. Dellwyn sat, clasping her hands to hold herself together. Before saying anything,

Augustus moved to shut the office door, and Dellwyn cursed under her breath.

When Augustus returned to his bloodstained chair, Dellwyn took in his features. Dark circles hung under his eyes, and his hair lay greasy and unkempt. If it had been anyone else before her, Dellwyn would have sworn that she saw wrinkles etched into his forehead.

Augustus rubbed his temples with his thumb and middle finger. "What can I do for you, Dellwyn?"

She bit her lip, and her gaze traveled to the red stain on Augustus's desk. "I'm afraid I have some bad news. Kalinda and Alisa have been called into the palace for questioning."

Even though Augustus already knew, he feigned surprise and banged his fist on his desk. Dellwyn winced. "For fuck's sake. Why can't that blasted king see the farmer is to blame?"

This time, it was Dellwyn's turn to feign ignorance for Augustus's benefit. She shrugged. "I guess His Majesty sees what he wants to see."

Augustus sighed. "Is that all you needed to tell me?"

Dellwyn's heart beat faster. "Actually, it's not. I had a strange visitor last night, and it reminded me of one you told me about a while back."

"Oh?" Augustus leaned back in his chair, but Dellwyn saw hints of fear in the twitch of his lips.

"The man who came to visit me, he didn't want our regular services. Instead, he wanted to talk."

Augustus shrugged. "Sometimes companionship is more intimate than anything else. You know that."

"Yes, but he was different, Auggie." Dellwyn fished in her cloak, grabbed Zedara's leather coin purse, then tossed it on the desk. It landed with a heavy clunk. "And he gave me more than a bottle of wine for my time."

Augustus stiffened, staring at the bag as if Dellwyn had thrown a venomous snake on the desk. "What's going on, Delly?"

"Lord Varick thinks he might have backed the wrong whore." Dellwyn heard the door creak, so she tapped the desk as if emphasizing her point. Augustus's eyes didn't leave the bag of coins. "He's asked that I buy you out."

"I… I don't believe you." Augustus lifted his chin in the air. "In fact, I don't know what you're talking about."

"Really? You're going to play stupid now?" Dellwyn reached forward, untied the bag, and dumped the coins out onto the desk. With a melodious clinking, they cascaded over the bloodstain. "This is only part of it, of course. But you know Lord Varick. He loves his theatrics."

Augustus frowned and picked up one of the coins. "No, Lord Varick wouldn't do this to me."

"Oh, sure." Dellwyn laughed. "So I suppose this is my life savings, then? And I guess I magically divined the details of your deal with Lord Varick?"

Augustus huffed. "Well, *you* wouldn't do this to me."

"Are you shitting me?" Dellwyn guffawed. "I wanted the Rudder. I *deserved* it. And you stole it out from under me by taking money from some scummy nobleman. Now that I know the *real* rules, I'm happy to reenter the game and take what's mine."

Augustus sneered at Dellwyn, but he didn't reply. Instead, he turned his attention back to the coin in his hand, twirling it to and fro in front of his face, as if inspecting it for any imperfections.

"It's all real, Auggie." Dellwyn rolled her eyes. "Look, here's how this is going to go. You will resign as owner of the Rudder, and you can take whatever coin of Lord Varick's you have left as compensation back to Room B. And me and my purse here will take your seat and Room A."

"No!" Augustus stood, slapped both hands down on the desk, and leaned over Dellwyn. She jumped at the noise but forced herself to remain calm. "Lord Varick and I had a deal. I did my part. Now he has to honor his."

Dellwyn's knees quivered under Augustus's cold stare, and she gripped them with her hands to hold them still. "Lord Varick is a businessman, and you are no more than an asset he owns. If he wants to remove you from power, he can." Dellwyn raised her lip in a snarl. "You should have thought of this before you took his money."

"I earned that money. I did what he asked," Augustus growled. He grabbed the ties of Dellwyn's cloak and pulled her face up to his. "You think I wanted to do it? I loved her more than I've ever loved anyone in this damn desert. But something had to be done."

"You're really sticking by the love argument?" Dellwyn placed her hand over Augustus's, partially to intimidate him and partially to alleviate the tightness around her neck. "How can you say you loved her? You killed her then took the only thing in the world *she* loved."

"She loved *me*." Tears formed in Augustus's eyes. "She would have wanted me to run this place if she couldn't."

In spite of her fear, Dellwyn forced herself to chuckle. "Yes, because Madam Huxley was always so forgiving."

"Don't say her name!" Augustus shook Dellwyn once then let her go. He ran both hands through his hair and let out a long breath. His change from furious to calm was immediate, unsettling—and proof to Dellwyn that he had grown accustomed to acting normal when he most certainly was not. "I'm sorry, Delly. I know you wanted the Rudder, but it's mine. I don't care what new deal you and Lord Varick have made."

"You always have to do things the hard way, don't you?" Dellwyn shook her head. "Give it up, Augustus. You've lost. Short of killing me too, there's nothing you can do to keep a hold of the Rudder. You murdered Madam Huxley for nothing."

"Shut up!" Augustus lunged over the desk and grabbed Dellwyn. Before she could scream, his hands latched around her throat. She tried to pry them off, but she wasn't strong enough. His grip tightened, and her chest screamed for oxygen, her lungs writhing uselessly beneath her rib cage.

As she stared into Augustus's wild eyes, fury rose up in Dellwyn. With a growl that came out like a squeak, she reeled her hand back and punched Augustus square in the nose. He released her, stumbling back over the desk and clutching his face. Red streaks dripped from his nostrils.

Dellwyn wheezed through her victorious grin. "Stop lying to me, Augustus. Why can't you just say it? Why can't you admit what you've done?"

Augustus stepped backward around the desk, retreating toward his chair. Dellwyn followed, matching him step for step. His eyes were still fierce, but they also carried a trace of fear. Dellwyn intended to use every bit of it to her advantage.

"Say it, Auggie." She kept her eyes locked with his, but she saw his hand sliding under the lip of the desk. "Come on. Tell me you killed her. Be a man for once."

He lunged at her again, but this time, Dellwyn was ready. She grabbed Augustus's arm in midair, the knife hovering only inches above her eye. Dellwyn gritted her teeth to keep from crying out. Unlike Rykart's scythe, the knife was long and wide, nearly the size of her forearm—the kind the butcher used to hack apart carcasses.

Augustus reached toward her with his other hand, but Dellwyn managed to catch his arm at the elbow. Helped by her rage, Dellwyn twisted Augustus's wrist until the knife pointed at the ground between their feet.

"Is this how it went?" Dellwyn spoke through clenched teeth, and her arms began to tremble against the force of his. But she couldn't give up now. She had come too far, and she could feel the confession bubbling up in his throat, the same way she could sense the words "I love you" before they spilled from her young clients' lips.

"Almost." A vein bulged in Augustus's neck as he strained to turn the knife back toward Dellwyn. "You both gave me no choice. You both drove me to this." He paused to lick the blood that had dribbled near his mouth. "And like the first time, this will break my heart."

The knife slowly pivoted back to face Dellwyn. She shrieked, and her heart rate accelerated until she thought the poor organ would burst. As she glanced between Augustus and the knife, every muscle in her body screamed to let go. *No, just a little longer.*

"Say it, Augustus. Admit that you killed Madam Huxley." Dellwyn lifted her foot and kicked him in the groin with all the force she could muster.

Augustus hollered and doubled over. As he fell, he grabbed Dellwyn around the waist. They landed in a heap on the desk. Before Dellwyn could push herself up, Augustus pinned her against the wood in the same place where he had stabbed Madam Huxley. Dellwyn looked up at him with wide, fearful eyes. Augustus panted over her with the knife held above his head. *This can't be the end. Say it, damn it.*

"I killed Madam Huxley." Augustus's body trembled from his hands to his lips, but his voice held steady. "I stole the farmer's scythe while Kalinda distracted him, and I buried it in the madam's spine. Can you die in peace now?"

A group of Rudder workers burst into the room. Dellwyn grinned, a flood of triumph and elation soothing her quivering limbs. It was over. She had gotten Augustus to confess. She was safe.

"Drop the knife!" one of the new men commanded.

Augustus's face paled, and Dellwyn tried to push herself up. Out of the corner of her eye, she could see the workers circling the desk. Sybil, as instructed, lingered in the back of the group.

"Drop it!" said the same gruff voice.

Augustus started to lower his arm, but halfway down, something in his eyes changed. Dellwyn lurched her body to the right, but she wasn't quick enough. The knife sank into her torso. Her flesh ripped open, and hot blood gushed from her side. A crack followed as the knife's point bit into a rib.

The edges of Dellwyn's vision blurred, and the world seemed to melt together before her eyes. Two of the workers had grabbed Augustus, attempting to pull him away from her. As Augustus struggled against Dellwyn's accomplices, he dropped the knife, and it fell to the desk with a clatter.

Without thinking, Dellwyn reached for the knife. A shot of

pain seared her side, and the wound tore open further. Her fingers latched around the warm handle, and her arm jabbed as if on its own. Augustus cried out, the sound immediately drowned by a dull roaring, not unlike the wind during a sandstorm.

Then everything went black.

25

———————

ellwyn felt as if she'd been buried in sand. A heavy weight held down her eyelids, and a warm, soft object wrapped around her body. As she struggled to open her eyes, the world filtered in, one hazy image at a time. Black dots sifted through her field of sight like grains of sand slipping down a hill.

"Well, it's about time." The voice sounded familiar and happy.

A strange scent wafted under Dellwyn's nose, and a cool, wet sensation dabbed at her forehead, awakening the final bit of her senses. With a groan, Dellwyn opened her eyes and found herself in a finely decorated room. A beautifully woven wool blanket covered her body. Beyond that, she saw intricately carved bedposts, and past them stood ornate wooden furniture. Pink light streamed in through the windows, and Dellwyn winced against it.

"Close the curtains." The voice now hovered near Dellwyn's side. She turned her head and squinted. It took her a minute to recognize the blond woman before her.

Zedara held a jar of perfume in one hand and a wet cloth in the other. "Good morning."

Dellwyn furrowed her brow. Morning? How could it be

morning already? It had just been night—she had been talking to Augustus…

Zedara put the items on the bedside table then patted Dellwyn's shoulder. "Don't fret. You're fine—everything is fine. I sent the maid to fetch the others and prepare you something soft to eat."

Dellwyn nodded, but she didn't fully understand Zedara's meaning. Was there reason to worry, for things *not* to be fine? Whom did the maid go to get, and why was Zedara so specific about the food? Better still, where in Desertera was Dellwyn?

A shock of copper hair appeared in the doorway, and Sybil bolted over to Dellwyn. Without hesitation, Sybil reached down and wrapped Dellwyn in a hug. "I'm so glad you're all right."

Sybil's squeeze sent a sharp pain through Dellwyn's side, and she cried out, only to feel more daggers slice at her throat. That was all it took for the horrors of the night to come racing back to her—coercing a confession from Augustus, wrestling for the knife, its blade piercing her flesh…

Sybil jumped back and lifted the blanket. "I'm sorry! I'm sorry!" Dellwyn shivered against the cold of the morning, which only hurt her side more. Sybil's fingers traced over Dellwyn's wound, and Dellwyn realized the tight sensation around her middle was a bandage. "It's not bleeding. The doctor said the knife didn't go deep enough to do any major damage. Your ribs stopped it."

Zedara reappeared in the doorway, followed by Aya and Lord Collingwood. Dellwyn startled at seeing the nobleman in this place. Her face must have revealed her shock, for Lord Collingwood closed the distance between them and took her hand. "Oh, Dell. I'm so relieved to see you awake. How are you feeling?"

Dellwyn glanced at her friends, all of whom did not even blink at Lord Collingwood kneeling by her bedside. Dellwyn offered a small smile. "Pretty damn sore, but fine." She winced again and swallowed. "What are you doing here, Stanton?"

Lord Collingwood stared at her with wide, hurt eyes. "When I arrived for my appointment, one of the workers told me what happened. Sybil was kind enough to leave a message for me." He grinned at Sybil, and Dellwyn's chest swelled with fondness for him and pride for Sybil. "I couldn't stay away, knowing you were injured. I had to be near you. Do you want me to leave?"

"No." Dellwyn squeezed his hand. "I'm grateful you're here—that you're all here."

The group exchanged relieved looks. Aya came over and sat at the foot of the bed, next to where Lord Collingwood knelt. "Do you remember what happened?"

Dellwyn nodded, trying to use as few words as possible. "Did I stab him?"

Zedara beamed. "You certainly did."

"Right in the thigh," Sybil mimed stabbing her own leg. "Augustus could barely stand, so he was easy to detain until the guards arrived. When they did, they had to carry him to the dungeon."

Dellwyn cocked an eyebrow. "Are you okay?" Sybil seemed to be handling the situation much better than Dellwyn would have expected—certainly much better than when Dellwyn had first told her of Augustus's betrayal.

"I'm fine." Sybil straightened. "If there's one thing I've learned since working at the Rudder, it's that you can't dwell on bad things. You just have to learn what you can from them and move on."

Dellwyn smiled—they all seemed to be doing a lot of that this morning. Sybil had matured so much over the past few weeks, and seeing her this composed sent a wave of calm over Dellwyn. For a moment, she forgot about the pain in her side and was simply thankful for her friends and even more grateful to be alive.

"Lionel sends his regards." Aya patted Dellwyn's leg. "He came with the doctor, but he couldn't stay. The whole of Desertera has been chaotic for the past two days, and he's had to handle it."

Dellwyn used her free hand to massage her throat. "I slept for two days?"

Aya nodded while Sybil grabbed a cup from the bedside table and held it to Dellwyn's lips. Even the tiniest sips of water sent Dellwyn's throat blazing, but after she stopped drinking, she felt refreshed enough to speak more. "Lord Varick?"

Zedara rolled her eyes. "Under house arrest until the trial."

Dellwyn frowned. "When—"

"This evening," Lord Collingwood cut in, his forehead wrinkled in concern. If lifting her arms weren't so painful, Dellwyn would have cupped his cheek and smoothed out his worry lines. "With the Rudder's workers overhearing Augustus's confession, there are enough credible witnesses to move forward immediately. Lionel was only waiting for you to wake. We've already sent word to him."

Dellwyn nodded and turned to Zedara. "Thank you for your help."

"Of course." Zedara waved her hand. "I was happy to assist. I'm just glad my part in this mission was less dangerous than my last."

"Such a meddler." Aya clicked her tongue. "You're going to get a reputation."

Dellwyn chuckled but stopped when a pain wracked her ribs, followed by several sharp tugging sensations. A quick touch of the bandage told her the stitches remained intact.

"Well, maybe if you gossipy women would stop scheming, I could stay out of trouble." Zedara shook her head and turned back to Dellwyn. "Seriously, though. What are friends for?"

A dark cloud passed over Dellwyn's mood, and she frowned. *For getting each other killed, it seems.* Before she could recover and form an appropriately cheery response, one of Zedara's servants peeked his head around the doorframe. "Excuse me, Your Highness. You have more visitors."

Zedara shot the group a curious look, only to be met with shrugs. "Send them in."

Through the doorway emerged a trio Dellwyn never thought she would have seen together—except, perhaps, at a trial. Kalinda's dark eyes widened upon seeing Dellwyn, and Dellwyn grimaced at the thought of how she must look. Rykart bowed—to whom, Dellwyn wasn't sure. Alisa stood behind them with her arms crossed and her face as stoic as ever. Dellwyn hoped Alisa wasn't there to cause trouble, because she didn't have the voice to defend herself.

Kalinda spoke first. "Hello." She took a tentative step toward Dellwyn. "How's your side?"

"Only marginally worse than my throat." Dellwyn offered Kalinda a small smile. "I'm surprised you all came to see me."

"Of course we did." Rykart moved to stand at the end of the bed. Dellwyn noticed recognition flit across Aya's face. "You uncovered the truth, saved us. And you were right—the Benevolent Queen did not mean to punish anyone but Madam Huxley and the other propagators of sin."

"Is that how you all feel?" Dellwyn bit her lip as nerves rippled through her body. "More or less, anyway?"

"Yes." Kalinda stood next to Rykart and patted Dellwyn's feet. "His Majesty explained everything. I know you were trying to do the right thing by having me called in for questioning. I would have done the same in your position."

Dellwyn swallowed. "And you, Alisa?"

Alisa stepped forward, her arms still crossed protectively in front of her. "Well, as Augustus so blatantly blabbed, I'm actually guilty, so I'd rather you not have given the king my name." She let out a heavy sigh. "I thought I could trust you, Dellwyn. You promised you wouldn't say anything."

Zedara scoffed, but Alisa had the good sense—or the good practice of being polite to nobles—to ignore it.

As Dellwyn considered her apology, her stomach trembled. At least the others would interpret the shaking as pain and not nervous guilt. "I know. I shouldn't have made that promise, and I'm sorry for breaking your trust, Alisa." She took a deep breath. "But I couldn't let Rykart be executed for a crime he didn't commit, and you were the best proof of his innocence I had at that point."

"Well, it's the last time I'll tell you any secrets." Alisa's lips twisted up into a smirk. "But as you can see, I'm not in that deep of sand over it all. So we're fine."

"What's going to happen to you?" Sybil asked, her brow knitted in concern.

"I have to testify at Augustus's trial." As Alisa spoke, her hands tightened into fists then relaxed. "But King Lionel has assured me that I won't face any time in the dungeon."

"The king shouldn't make promises either." Lord Collingwood raised an eyebrow at Alisa. "Not unless you can overcome your pride enough to admit that fear was the dominant motivator for keeping quiet. In my humble estimation, protecting your person is less damnable than feeding your material greed."

Alisa moved her hands to her hips. "Says the man who's never wanted for anything in his life."

Lord Collingwood added a patronizing grin to his raised brow, and Alisa lowered her fierce gaze to the floor. Through gritted teeth, she said, "Of course I was scared. How do you think *my* conversation with Augustus went?" She pointed at Dellwyn. "See what he's capable of? Like I was going to let *that* happen to me." With her face flushed, Alisa turned to Rykart. "I'm sorry, Farmer, but if it's your life or mine, I'm choosing mine every time."

Rykart nodded. "The Benevolent Queen gave us each a strong sense of self-preservation. It would please Her that you do not lightly throw away Her gifts."

"Praise be to Her," Kalinda added.

An awkward silence fell over the group. Before it could become too painful, the maid appeared, holding a tray of food. The smell of it sent Dellwyn's mouth watering, and she noticed another pain in her stomach—hunger.

Zedara cleared her throat. "I think we should let Dellwyn eat in peace and get some more rest. Anyone who wants to is welcome to join me in the dining room for breakfast." She motioned to the bedside table. "If you need anything, Dellwyn, ring the bell and someone will come attend to you."

"Thank you," Dellwyn replied. Lord Collingwood helped

her sit up, while Sybil propped pillows behind her back. Her side burned at the effort, but she situated herself without complaint. The maid set the tray over Dellwyn's lap.

Lord Collingwood kissed the crown of head. "If not before, I'll see you this evening."

Dellwyn perked up. "Will the doctor let me go?"

"She has to. You're a key witness."

Dellwyn tapped her side and winced. "I don't know if I can walk."

"Zedara and I have taken care of that." Aya's smile held too much amusement for Dellwyn's comfort, but Dellwyn was too tired to question her. "Don't worry about the trial. Just eat and get as much rest as you can."

One by one, the group said their goodbyes and left Dellwyn alone with her food and her thoughts. She stared down at the meal before her. A bowl of soft, gray oatmeal steamed in the center, with little blue balls tucked into the mash. Dellwyn realized they must be some kind of fruit, and she cautiously lifted one to her mouth. It popped when she bit it, the juice tangy, but sweet. Aya was right. Fruit was delicious.

As she ate, Dellwyn's thoughts kept wandering back to Augustus. Even though he had tried to kill her—and even though he *had* killed Madam Huxley—Dellwyn couldn't help but feel sorry for him. Whether to the extent Augustus claimed or not, Dellwyn had no doubt that Lord Varick had planted the seed of murder in his mind. The kind, playful man Dellwyn had known never would have resorted to violence to gain control of the Rudder. He would have bedded Madam Huxley, as Dellwyn had once suspected, or perhaps he would have exposed the madam's questionable business practices and swayed public opinion against her instead.

But no matter how much Lord Varick coerced or threatened, he wasn't fully to blame. In the end, Augustus had decided to pick up the scythe. The guilt was his to bear. And whether the council sent Augustus to his execution or let him walk free, the fact remained: Dellwyn had lost a friend. She would bear the scar of his betrayal on her side for the rest of her life—until the day she burned on the pyre and her ashes intermingled with the sand.

A tear slipped down her cheek, and her stomach cramped. She rang the bell, and the maid came to take away the tray, its contents only half-eaten. Dellwyn didn't know what the trial would hold, nor did she know how she would handle any of its possible outcomes. All she knew was that she wanted to slide back beneath the covers and slip into unconsciousness, where none of this could touch her, for as long as she could. And that was exactly what she did.

26

"Absolutely not." Dellwyn stared up at Onyx's back, wincing as her fearful swallow constricted her purple throat. Only the support of Sybil and Zedara's servant kept Dellwyn from wobbling where she stood. "I couldn't get up there even if I hadn't been stabbed."

Zedara smirked. "And what if he comes to you?" With a firm hand on Onyx's shoulder and a gentle clicking of her tongue, Zedara signaled for the horse to lie down. He did. "Good boy. All right, Dellwyn. Your turn."

"I don't think so." Dellwyn shook her head, and the silk scarf Zedara had loaned her agitated her neck. "I can barely walk."

"Exactly. Riding to the palace will be much easier." Zedara ran her fingers through Onyx's dark hair. "You simply sit atop and hang on to his mane. Onyx and I will do the rest."

Before Dellwyn could protest again, Sybil and the servant led her forward. Zedara helped Dellwyn swing one leg over Onyx's back, while the servant made sure she didn't fall. With gritted teeth, Dellwyn lowered herself onto the horse.

Zedara took Dellwyn's hands and showed her how to grab Onyx's mane. "You'll be fine. If you can, squeeze with your legs while he stands. It'll help you balance."

"Am I supposed to ride like this?" Dellwyn glanced down to

her spread legs and her ruffled skirt, which sat bunched above her knees.

"No." Zedara chuckled. "But you're not strong enough to sit like a proper lady. You'd probably slide right off."

Dellwyn wasn't convinced that she wouldn't fall off anyway, but she offered a brave grin. "Well, good thing I've never been a proper lady then."

"Indeed." Zedara winked and turned to Onyx. Dellwyn clenched her eyes shut and held on as tightly as she could despite the sharp protesting in her side. As he moved beneath her, Dellwyn shrieked, and she heard the other women chuckle. Then, Onyx went still.

"You can open your eyes now," Sybil said.

Dellwyn did, and she breathed a sigh of relief. The top of Sybil's head was level with her thigh, and Dellwyn realized she wasn't as high up as she had expected.

"Ready?" Zedara asked.

Dellwyn nodded, and Zedara stepped forward, reins in hand. Onyx followed without prodding, and Dellwyn's body bobbed back and forth with the motion. She gasped and released one hand to touch her side.

"Riding uses more muscles than people think, especially in your torso." Zedara didn't look back. "But trust me, this will still be less strenuous for you than walking."

Dellwyn chose not to argue, and the group made their way through Starboardshire in silence. When they arrived at the palace, Zedara commanded Onyx to lie down again. This time, Dellwyn kept her eyes open, but she still let out a squeak as the motion jarred her forward and back. Once Onyx lay still, Sybil helped Dellwyn to the gangway. After giving Onyx a treat and a pat on the neck, Zedara joined them, and the servant led Onyx away.

A moment later, Aya emerged from the palace, pushing a wheelchair. She beamed at them. "Right on time! How was your ride, Dellwyn?"

Dellwyn shrugged. "I don't know if I'd do it again, but it wasn't as bad as I thought."

"Well, this one will be much easier." Aya stopped and turned the wheelchair around so that it faced the top of the gangway. Unlike other wheelchairs Dellwyn had seen, Aya's contained a large mechanical component on the back—a mess of tubes, tanks, and levers. Dellwyn pursed her lips. The contraption didn't look much safer than the horse, but she allowed herself to be plopped in the seat.

"My latest machine." Aya leaned over Dellwyn's shoulder. "It's not powerful enough to go on the sand—it would get stuck —but it should do well on the palace's floors."

Dellwyn inspected the chair, as if it might bite her. "I've seen people use these before. You push it like a cart, right?"

"You can. The seated person can also use their hands to propel the wheels forward." Aya's hand shook with excitement as she pointed to the arm of the chair. "Or you can use that stick to steer and let the machine wheel itself."

With that, Aya's hand disappeared, and Dellwyn felt her tugging one of the levers in a series of short, fast pulls. The chair rumbled and trembled beneath Dellwyn, and she held her breath until it moaned to life. Under Aya's direction, Dellwyn pushed the stick forward, and the machine chugged up the gangway. Though the chair rolled smoothly, it creaked and groaned with every inch. As a guard peered down the gangway to stare, Dellwyn blushed and looked back at her friends. A trail of steam puffed out from a fat pipe, veiling their encouraging smiles in a thin cloud.

When Dellwyn reached the top of the gangway, the guard averted his gaze. Her friends came to stand next to her, and they moved in a row through the corridors. The entire way to the courtroom, Aya rambled about the mechanics of the machine and how she had spent weeks working on it, relieved that she had completed it right before Dellwyn happened to need it. At any other time, Dellwyn would have listened with interest—or at least politely feigned interest. But as more and more nobles fell in line behind them, and more and more whispers reached Dellwyn's ears, she fidgeted in her seat. She wondered which they enjoyed gawking at more—the ancient contraption or the mangled whore seated in it.

When they reached the courtroom, a heaviness settled around Dellwyn. Her friends said a quick goodbye, and she steered the chair toward one of the tables in the room's center. As the chair came to a stop, Dellwyn pulled the side lever as Aya had instructed, and the machine gurgled into silence. Without the noise from the chair, Dellwyn could hear even more of the nobles' comments, but she held her face still. The only thing more embarrassing than being a spectacle would be to acknowledge that she was one.

To Dellwyn's left rested another table with three chairs behind it. In front of her, on a raised platform, five thrones stood in a line. Dellwyn assumed those were for the council, but if that were the case, there should be nine seats.

Before she could puzzle about it further, four members of the council filed in from a doorway on the other side of the courtroom, and the crowd fell silent. Each stood before one of the thrones, leaving the center one empty. Dellwyn repeated their names in her head, in case she needed to address them during the trial—Mr. Jack Wellman, Miss Heidi Baker, Bishop, and Mr. Stefan Chef.

Next came King Lionel. He held his cog-embroidered top hat in his hands, his fingers nervously tapping against the brim as he stood before his throne. His hazel eyes looked glassy, almost sad, but his jaw was firmly clenched. Dellwyn didn't know what to think of the king's agitation—only that it made her side ache even more. She waited with held breath for him to speak.

Finally, King Lionel cleared his throat, the sound seeming guttural in the quiet courtroom. He fixed his gaze on one point in the crowd, and Dellwyn didn't need to look to know that was where Aya sat. "Mr. Augustus Rutt is dead."

The gasp that escaped Dellwyn's lips clawed at her throat on the way out. She grabbed her neck, failing to soothe either her pain or her shock. A dull murmur vibrated around her, and she knew the nobles must be whispering and exclaiming, but they sounded leagues away.

How could this have happened? It couldn't—it couldn't have been her fault, could it? Was it his wound? Would he have died so quickly from an infection? Tears rolled down Dellwyn's cheeks, and her entire body trembled. *Please say I didn't kill him.*

"He was found in his cell in the dungeon this afternoon. It appears Mr. Rutt chose to take his own life." King Lionel's face hardened further, a faint shade of red tainting his pale complexion. "It is still unclear how the guards did not find the instrument he used during their search of his person, but rest assured, there will be a *full* investigation."

Dellwyn wiped at her eyes with the ends of Zedara's scarf. It was one thing to lose Augustus to betrayal, and it would have been another to see him slain by the executioner's ax. But to know that Augustus had been so tormented by his actions that he had killed himself—Dellwyn could hardly bear the thought. A small part of her wondered whether he had done it as a redemptive act—his own form of justice for himself and the world. Another part wondered whether he had felt too scared or ashamed to face the people of Desertera at his trial. And a tiny rumbling deep in her gut told her that Augustus never would have taken his own life—under any circumstances. He would have remained hopeful to the end.

"That being said, we shall proceed with what remains of the trial. You all may sit." While the crowd did as instructed, King Lionel placed his top hat on his head and straightened his back—all at once, he appeared the calm, controlled monarch. "Please bring in the accused."

The doors behind Dellwyn opened, and a pair of guards escorted Alisa and Lord Varick into the courtroom. They took their places behind the table to Dellwyn's left. From Alisa's red-rimmed eyes and Lord Varick's hung head, Dellwyn knew they had been told about Augustus.

King Lionel motioned to his fellow council members. "As you can see, only five of the council members will preside over today's trial. Lord Varick is dismissed for obvious reasons. Likewise, Her Highness the queen dowager, Lord Stanton Collingwood, and Mrs. Eveline Farmer have all been excused for their personal attachments to the case."

Dellwyn frowned. That couldn't be good—three guaranteed votes for Lord Varick's guilt had been swept away. Hopefully, the other council members would be smart enough to see the truth in his web of excuses and cleverly spun phrases.

King Lionel turned to face his fellow council members. "Bishop, please deliver the oath to our participants."

The bishop stood and placed a ringed hand on his chest, as he had during Dellwyn and Sybil's questioning. "Please cover your hearts."

Dellwyn, Alisa, and Lord Varick obeyed.

"Do you swear on the grace of the Benevolent Queen, and on your own integrity, to speak truthfully and completely?"

"I do," they replied in unison.

With a small bow, the bishop returned to his seat, and King Lionel stepped forward once again. "Miss Alisa Rutt." Alisa shuddered at King Lionel's voice. "You have been accused of accepting a bribe to withhold information about the murder of Madam Lilliette Huxley. How do you plead?"

Alisa swallowed. "Guilty, Your Majesty."

"You may be seated." King Lionel turned to Lord Varick, and Dellwyn noticed the king's knuckles had gone white from balling his fists. "Lord Ulberion Varick, you have been accused of unlawful investment in the Rudder, issuing a bribe to Miss Alisa Rutt, and accessory to the murder of Madam Lilliette Huxley. How do you plead to these charges?"

Lord Varick made a show of flicking a tear from his cheek. "Innocent to all, Your Majesty."

At the hushed chorus of approval filtering through the room, Dellwyn rolled her eyes. King Lionel had been right—Lord Varick had the noble population wrapped around his walking stick. And that dramatic show of upset, what had that been about? Of all the people in the courtroom, he had the least right to mourn Augustus—even if he was pretending. But why was he pretending... unless he needed to look even *more* innocent… Dellwyn's heart skipped a beat. *He couldn't have.*

"Please be seated, Lord Varick." King Lionel turned to Dellwyn. "Miss Dellwyn Rutt."

Dellwyn pulled herself from her thoughts and attempted to stand, but King Lionel motioned for her to stay in the wheelchair. Grateful, she nodded to the king and dabbed at her side to ensure she hadn't split open her wound.

King Lionel continued. "You levy these accusations against Miss Rutt and Lord Varick. Please state your case, beginning with the allegation of bribery."

Dellwyn took a deep breath and folded her hands in her lap. She didn't know how much truth she could tell without getting her friends in trouble, so she skipped over their involvement. "When I heard the news about Madam Huxley's murder, I couldn't believe that Mr. Farmer was guilty. From my limited interactions with him, he had always seemed peaceful… a bit eccentric, but peaceful. Therefore, I went to Alisa, who also knew Mr. Farmer, and asked whether she knew anything about the murder. During this conversation, she implied that she had witnessed the murder. I did not learn the truth of this implication, or that she had been bribed to stay quiet, until a later time."

Miss Baker waved her hand to claim Dellwyn's attention. "What exactly did Miss Rutt say to make you suspect her?"

Dellwyn grimaced. "She said, 'I watched the life drain from Madam Huxley's eyes.'"

Miss Baker's face paled. "And you didn't suspect her of the murder with that language?"

"At first, sure." Dellwyn shrugged. "But Alisa maintained her innocence, and as I thought about it, I realized that the murderer would have had to stab Madam Huxley from behind. How could Alisa see the madam's face unless she was standing in front of her?"

Mr. Wellman grunted. "And you didn't come forward then?"

Dellwyn frowned. King Lionel must have skirted over her

initial involvement, probably so the council wouldn't learn of their trip to the dungeon. "I didn't have any real evidence. How could I make an accusation like that without solid proof?"

The council members nodded.

King Lionel gestured to Alisa. "Will you confirm that Miss Rutt is telling the truth?"

"Yes." Alisa gritted her teeth. "That's what I said, and her suspicions were correct."

King Lionel nodded. "And how did you receive the bribe?"

Alisa looked at the floor. "Lord Varick's guard brought it to me after Madam Huxley's funeral."

"Can we bring in this guard, please?" King Lionel waved toward the doors, and they opened to produce the guard.

Dellwyn gasped. It was the same man she had met in the hallway on the night she went to visit Lord Collingwood—the night before Madam Huxley's murder. She would have recognized his crooked, yellow smile and kind eyes anywhere. *He must have been delivering Lord Varick's orders to Augustus.*

The guard stood between the two tables, his gaze shifting from Lord Varick to the king. The bishop swore him in. Once the oath was finished, King Lionel squared his shoulders. "You know why you are here, correct?"

The guard bowed. "Yes, Yer Majesty."

"Good. Did you deliver a package of any sort to Miss Alisa Rutt"—King Lionel pointed to Alisa for clarification—"on behalf of Lord Varick?"

The guard shook his head. "I'm sorry, Yer Majesty, but I most certainly did not. I ain't never seen that woman befur."

King Lionel pursed his lips. "You realize that lying in the royal court is punishable by a year in the dungeon, yes?"

"I do." The guard looked at Lord Varick then cast his eyes to the floor. "But I can't say that I delivered anythin' to that woman, Yer Majesty."

Dellwyn frowned. His defense was strangely worded. There must be a catch—maybe the guard only dropped the money off at an agreed-upon location or gave it to a third party to deliver to Alisa. Knowing Lord Varick, the message was a lie, but its phrasing was true.

King Lionel sighed. "That will be all. Thank you."

The guard bowed again and turned around. As he walked away, Dellwyn saw him wipe sweat from his brow. Innocent people didn't get that nervous.

"Lord Varick, both you and your guard maintain your innocence." King Lionel's jaw tightened again. "So I must ask, if you did not bribe Miss Alisa, why is she accusing you? Why would she accuse *herself* of accepting a bribe and withholding information?"

Lord Varick looked at Alisa for a long moment then sighed. "I don't know, Your Majesty. The only possible reason I can conceive is that Miss Rutt is the true accomplice to Mr. Rutt, and that her confession of accepting bribery is but clever misdirection."

Dellwyn clenched her fists. *Of course he has it all worked out.*

"That's horseshit!" Alisa spat. "You know it, Your Majesty. He's ordered his guard to lie and is twisting the truth. This is why I didn't come forward sooner—because Lord Varick is a liar." Alisa stood and pointed at Dellwyn. "And I didn't want Augustus to do *that* to me!"

King Lionel closed his eyes and pinched the bridge of his nose. Dellwyn knew he saw the truth in Alisa's words, but also that, with the current evidence, he was powerless to deliver anything but an innocent verdict to Lord Varick.

"Lord Varick, do you have any proof of your theory?"

Lord Varick's tone dripped sly charm. "No, Your Majesty. It is simply the only answer my mind could formulate."

"Right." King Lionel lowered his hand, a noticeable sag in his shoulders. "Allow me to confer with the council."

The five presiding members huddled together in a circle. Dellwyn heard each voice murmur a word in turn before returning to their respective seats. She cursed under her breath. The deliberation was too short.

Once each individual had sat, King Lionel turned back to the crowd. "Given the lack of evidence against Lord

Varick, the council unanimously agrees that he be cleared of the crime of bribery." A ripple of applause broke through the crowd, and Lord Varick nodded and mouthed "thank you" to his supporters. Without waiting for the noise to die down, King Lionel continued. "Miss Alisa Rutt, the only evidence of your accepting a bribe is your word. We shall take that at face value and demand financial restitution, to be paid to the council's fund and used for public works projects."

Alisa smoothed down her hair. "Thank you, Your Majesty, council."

King Lionel turned back to Dellwyn. "Now then, to the matter of Lord Varick's unlawful investment in the Rudder and his role in Madam Lilliette Huxley's murder. Miss Dellwyn Rutt, please make your case."

Dellwyn's mouth suddenly felt dry, and she licked her lips. If Lord Varick had squirmed his way out of the bribery charge, he could do it again. She had to remember everything perfectly and use the most damning language she could muster.

With a deep breath, she began. "Three afternoons ago, I went to the Rudder while it was closed to tell Aug—Mr. Rutt— that two of his employees were being taken in for questioning and would not be at work. Mr. Rutt had a visitor in his office, so I waited outside for my turn to speak with him."

Dellwyn paused to swallow, hoping that the council and the audience could understand her weak, scratchy voice. "I tried not to eavesdrop, but they were speaking too loudly to ignore. I discerned that the visitor was Lord Varick. During their argument, Lord Varick pointedly reminded Mr. Rutt that he was indebted to him for supplying the money to secure the Rudder. Lord Varick also threatened to expose Mr. Rutt as Madam Huxley's murderer."

King Lionel inclined his head. "Do you have any witnesses to confirm your statement?"

"Yes." Dellwyn had to resist the urge to grin. "That night, I went back to the Rudder to question Augustus about the conversation. His confession was overheard by several workers at the Rudder."

A hint of a smirk played at King Lionel's lips. "Bring in the witnesses."

Sybil, Jasmine, and four of the newer workers that Dellwyn didn't know by name filed into the courtroom and lined up in front of the king. He smiled cordially in greeting. "Do you all know why you are here?"

The workers nodded in unison.

"Good. Bishop, please conduct the oath." After the vows were taken, King Lionel resumed his questioning. "Starting with Miss Sybil Tanner and moving to my left, please answer the following question honestly." King Lionel paused for emphasis. "Did you overhear Mr. Augustus Rutt confess to accepting money to invest in the Rudder from Lord Varick?"

"Yes." Sybil's head bobbed in confirmation. And to Dellwyn's relief, the rest of the workers said the same.

"Thank you." King Lionel didn't smile, but his forehead smoothed. "And did you overhear Mr. Augustus Rutt confess to murdering Madam Lilliette Huxley?"

Again, a line of affirmation. Dellwyn allowed herself to smirk.

King Lionel rubbed his hands together. "And was it your impression that Mr. Rutt murdered Madam Huxley as a result of receiving the investment from Lord Varick? In other words, did Mr. Rutt and Lord Varick plan to murder Madam Huxley to allow themselves to take over the Rudder?"

Sybil, Jasmine, and one of the new workers replied that this was their impression. The three other workers replied that they weren't sure. Dellwyn's chest deflated some. Had Augustus not been clear enough for them? Or had Lord Varick's coins already slipped into their pockets? Either way, Dellwyn still clung to hope. Half wasn't terrible—surely, the other council members would pass the workers' uncertainty off as dumbness. They would be prejudiced—even Jack Wellman—right? At all other times they were.

"Thank you. You may go." King Lionel waited for the

workers to leave then motioned to Lord Varick. "Would you like to speak in self-defense, Lord Varick?"

"Please." Lord Varick stood and took a long, deep breath. "I must admit; I did give Mr. Rutt a sizable amount of money…"

Dellwyn raised an eyebrow. There was the half-truth, but what would be the twist?

"I'm ashamed." Lord Varick hung his head. "I was lonely, and I went to the Rudder for comfort. Augustus served that purpose, and I was so grateful that I gave him a large tip, including both money and wine." Lord Varick's voice cracked. "How was I supposed to know Augustus would use my gift to obtain the Rudder?"

The pieces snapped together in Dellwyn's mind. *Of course!* Before she could stop herself, she blurted out, "That's not all of it!"

Startled, King Lionel turned to Dellwyn. "Do you have something to add, Miss Rutt?"

"Yes. I know that Lord Varick did visit Augustus at the Rudder, but it wasn't about *comfort*. It was about their plan to take the Rudder from Madam Huxley." Dellwyn saw doubt in the king's eyes and held up her hands. "I went to Augustus's house one morning after work. He shared the wine with me and told me about this mysterious, generous client. When I left his house, I caught a man spying on us. It had to be Lord Varick's guard, checking to make sure Augustus didn't reveal their scheme."

Lord Varick *tutted*. "You poor girl, you misunderstand. I did send my guard after Augustus, only to see how he lived. I…" Lord Varick made a show of closing his eyes to hold back false tears. "I was so taken with him—he was so charming. I wanted to see how he lived, if I could help improve his station."

King Lionel asked for the guard to be brought back in, and of course, the guard corroborated Lord Varick's statement. Dellwyn cursed, not quite under her breath, and clutched at her skirts. How much was Lord Varick paying that guard, and where did she sign up for such a wage?

When the guard left, Mr. Stefan Chef raised his hand to speak. His curled mustache twitched as he spoke. "Lord Varick, if you cared so strongly for Augustus, I'm inclined to think that you *did* help him secure the Rudder—out of affection, if not for your own gain."

Lord Varick tapped his chin, as if he were seriously considering Mr. Chef's statement. "I can see how you could reach that conclusion, Mr. Chef, but that is not the case. Though unfortunately, I have no proof. It is my and my noble guard's word against the claims of our dear, departed Mr. Rutt—who was obviously very troubled and guilt-ridden—and his former employees. You may choose to believe whom you wish."

To Dellwyn's relief, the other members of the council frowned or shifted in their seats. It seemed that Stefan's question had echoed some of their own doubts, and the case might yet turn in Dellwyn's favor.

Lord Varick must have noticed the same because he placed his hand on his chest and spoke with more ardor than Dellwyn thought possible for such a heartless man. "I truly regret that Augustus used my gift for his own gain. However, that is exactly what it was—a gift. I never instructed him on how to spend the money, nor did I imply that he should take control of the Rudder by any means.

"As such, I think it is obvious that I had no motive for or interest in Madam Huxley's death. I stood to gain nothing— the benefit lay solely with Augustus. And as you have rightly determined, I did not bribe Alisa to stay quiet about the murder—I did not even know Augustus was to blame until his arrest was announced."

Lord Varick paused and fixed his beady eyes directly on King Lionel. A thin smile spread across the lord's face. The crowd would take it as self-admonishing, but Dellwyn knew the real target. "I am but a foolish man who fell for the charms of a whore."

King Lionel's hands returned to fists, but otherwise, he kept his composure. He turned his back to Lord Varick and addressed the council members. "Does anyone else have any questions for Lord Varick or Miss Rutt?"

The bishop scooted forward in his seat. "Miss Dellwyn, Lord Varick is right. With the evidence as it stands, it is essentially your word against his."

Dellwyn swallowed and nodded.

"Lord Varick asks us to believe that he acted out of care for Mr. Rutt and was ignorant of Mr. Rutt's criminal intentions. You ask us to believe that Lord Varick orchestrated the takeover of the Rudder and Madam Huxley's death alongside Mr. Rutt." The bishop clasped his ringed hands together. "Why should the council trust the word of a courtesan over the word of a nobleman?"

It took all of Dellwyn's strength to stay calm, then not to grimace as her clenched stomach screamed in protest. But instead of erupting into an outburst as Alisa had, Dellwyn channeled all her emotion into her voice. "Because it's the truth. Because Augustus confessed when he thought he had nothing to lose." She lifted her hand to her throat. "And less than two days after his words threatened Lord Varick, Augustus was found dead."

THE COUNCIL DELIBERATED FOR HOURS. During that time, no one was allowed to leave the courtroom without the escort of a guard, and no new individuals were allowed to enter. The guard restricted everyone to their seats except for Alisa, who they allowed to join the larger crowd. That all suited Dellwyn fine. As much as she loved her friends and appreciated their sympathetic glances from their elevated seats, she couldn't stand the idea of answering their concerned questions and putting on a fake smile. No, she wasn't okay. And she didn't have to be, either. Not today.

So she sat in her steam-powered chair, leaving the courtroom only once under the demand of her bladder. She barely even noticed the nobles' continued scrutiny—it was difficult to see their gazes through the tears she fought back. Poor Augustus. He had crawled in bed, whether literally or metaphorically, with a snake. And Lord Varick had clearly learned from his mistake with Aya. This time, he didn't let his prisoner make it all the way to the courtroom.

Finally, the door beyond the thrones opened, and the council members filed into the courtroom and took their seats. They looked about as bad as Dellwyn felt—collars unbuttoned, cheeks red and splotchy, foreheads marred with wrinkles. It had not been an easy, nor unanimous, decision, then.

King Lionel remained standing and gestured for Lord Varick to do the same. Dellwyn couldn't read the king's face. More than anything, he looked tired. His voice confirmed as much, as it was soft and creaky when he spoke. "Lord Varick, given the sparse evidence in this case, the council does not feel that there is adequate proof—or adequate doubt—of your guilt. We could not agree whether we would be sending an innocent man to the dungeon or setting a guilty man free."

Lord Varick bowed his head. "I understand, Your Majesty."

"We did, however, reach a compromise." King Lionel sighed, and Dellwyn's heart dropped. It might not be as clean this time, but Lord Varick had gotten away again. "You shall be placed under house arrest for one year with only supervised visitation allowed. During that time, the council will continue to investigate the circumstances of Madam Huxley's murder and Mr. Rutt's death. If evidence of your guilt in either arises, you shall be formally sentenced. If not, you shall go free with our apologies."

"A fair agreement, Your Majesty. I want justice for them as much as anyone in this courtroom." Lord Varick clasped his hands together, and Dellwyn turned her head away. Immediately, she wished she hadn't. Before her, Dellwyn watched the crowd harden against King Lionel. The eyes of Lord Varick's allies and enemies alike narrowed into slits as they observed the king—both sides dissatisfied that their desired verdict had not been reached.

"Very well." King Lionel motioned to the guards. "Please escort Lord Varick to his estate."

The same guards who had brought Lord Varick into the courtroom each took one of his arms and ushered him out. As Dellwyn watched him walk away, a heavy pit buried itself in her stomach. She knew, as Lord Varick and her friends also did, that no evidence would arise. All the council had done was send him to wait and plot in his estate—while making themselves appear indecisive and weak.

"Miss Rutt." King Lionel's voice startled her out of her thoughts.

She swallowed. "Yes, Your Majesty?"

"There is still the matter of your fate to discuss." His face betrayed no emotion, and Dellwyn's hands shook. If the council did not fully believe Lord Varick, that meant they didn't fully believe her, either. She didn't know if she could stand being locked up in her hovel for a year—especially when she had no family wealth to rely on.

King Lionel and the rest of the courtroom must have noticed Dellwyn's distress. But if he did, he didn't let on. He retained the calm, reserved facade of a monarch and motioned toward the door behind the thrones. "Please, come with me."

27

———

The bishop held Augustus's funeral a week later. Given that Augustus had no living family, or at least none that would claim him, Dellwyn took it upon herself to organize the event. She stood next to Sybil before the funeral pyre, and as the bishop lit the kindling, Dellwyn let her tears fall unrestrained.

The flames licked at Augustus's wrapped body, and Dellwyn lifted Zedara's scarf to her nose. While the bruises on Dellwyn's neck had almost healed, a faint tinge of green and yellow still blotched her dark skin. Zedara had told her to keep the scarf as long as she needed, and Dellwyn thought that might be a few more days.

One inch at a time, the flames encircled and overtook Augustus. Dellwyn observed what remained of her former friend with a mixture of anger and grief. Augustus had brought his fate upon himself. No matter what the council had determined as truth, Augustus had accepted Lord Varick's generous *gift*, and he had murdered Madam Huxley to create an opportunity for himself. He had let Lord Varick control his actions, manipulated Alisa's fear and greed, and attempted to murder Dellwyn to hold onto his power.

Dellwyn thought back to several weeks before—it felt like

years now—when King Lionel had first announced the repeal of the adultery law. She had been talking to Augustus and had remarked on how he made the courtesans sound like the unsung saviors of Desertera. What had he said? *You're damn right we are.*

By all accounts, Dellwyn was a savior. King Lionel had told her as much after the trial when he had thanked her for not giving up on the case and for having the courage to solve Madam Huxley's murder by herself. But Dellwyn didn't feel like a hero. As she stood with Sybil, rubbing her back and whispering reassurances, Dellwyn did not feel brave or clever or noble. She felt like someone with an immunity—the one person in the plague who didn't get sick, the one left standing after the illness had eaten away the bodies and spirits of those around her.

As the smoke and sparks from the pyre floated up into the night sky, Dellwyn tilted her head to look for the Benevolent Queen in the stars, only to be met by a blanket of gray clouds. Where did Rykart see Her? How did She appear to him? If She did exist and control everything, why had She spared Dellwyn? And why had She chosen Dellwyn for the task ahead?

Dellwyn couldn't fathom the answers—but just in case Rykart was right about the universe, she sent out a little thank you. Though guilt still burned in her gut, she was thankful to be alive and grateful to be starting her new life that night.

The fire began to die down, and the bishop stepped in front of the pyre, arms stretched toward the sky. "May the Benevolent Queen's merciful waters wash over Augustus Rutt."

"Praise be to Her," the crowd replied—Dellwyn and Sybil included.

With the ceremony complete, the people dispersed. It had been a small group, the bulk of Desertera having already forgotten about Augustus now that the scandal had been settled. The bishop shook Dellwyn's hand and praised her for seeing to Augustus's departure from this world. She shared tearful hugs with Aya and Zedara and thanked them for coming. King Lionel kissed her cheek and wished her luck that evening. Lord Collingwood placed a kiss on her head and promised to see her in a few hours.

As the five of them walked away, Mrs. Eveline Farmer and Rykart approached Dellwyn and Sybil. Mrs. Farmer embraced Dellwyn and thanked her, yet again, for helping set Rykart free.

Rykart did not touch Dellwyn, but he bowed to her. "Thank you for doing Her work. She will find a way to repay you, I know it."

Dellwyn offered a small smile. "It was the right thing to do."

"Still, I appreciate you, Dellwyn Rutt." Rykart gazed up at the sky. "And so does She."

He held out his hand in front of Dellwyn, and it seemed as if time slowed before her eyes. A single drop of rain fell from the sky and landed in Rykart's palm. Dellwyn gasped and extended her own arm. Sure enough, a fat raindrop plopped onto her skin. They came faster then, one after another, and Dellwyn saw the people of Sternville emerge from their hovels, holding out bowls, jugs and even their mouths. Sybil giggled and twirled with her own tongue outstretched.

The shower only lasted a few minutes, and it wasn't enough to soak through Dellwyn's dress, but she opened her arms, closed her eyes, and turned her face to the sky, savoring each cool dribble as it kissed her skin. Maybe it was a sign from the Benevolent Queen. Maybe it was merely coincidental timing. But whatever it was, Dellwyn knew to be grateful for every drop that fell.

"The Benevolent Queen approves." Rykart watched Dellwyn in her reverie, his mismatched eyes boring into and through her. "You must do your work now. It will be good. Better. *Your* heart is pure."

Dellwyn smiled at Rykart, feeling refreshed, cleansed. "Thank you." The moment lingered between them, quiet and still, then passed as quickly as it came. Dellwyn hooked her thumb over her shoulder. "I should be getting back." She turned to walk toward Sternville, and someone grabbed her arm.

Sybil's eyes shone with curiosity. "Can I come with you? I want to see it."

Dellwyn bit her lip. "Are you sure? I don't expect you to."

"I'm sure." Sybil looped her arm through Dellwyn's. "Really."

The pair strolled arm-in-arm to the Rudder. When they arrived, they walked through the lobby and veered right. At the doorway, Sybil stopped short, and Dellwyn sat down at her new, unstained desk.

A grin spread across Dellwyn's face. "I thought the office could use some color." She motioned to the ornate rug that lay before her desk, then to the old, stretched-out bedsheets she had hung on the walls as curtains. "I want the workers to feel comfortable here, safe."

"They will." Sybil smiled, and her eyes flitted between the two front corners of Dellwyn's desk. On one sat her flower from Lord Collingwood, and on the opposite side rested a tin vase, holding her final, dried bouquet from Augustus. "Rykart is right, you know. You're the owner the Rudder has always needed."

Dellwyn ran her hands along the desk. "I hope so. I've wanted this for so long—dreamed of being more for longer. I hope I don't let them all down."

"You won't." Sybil tucked a lock of hair behind her ear. "You're smarter than Augustus and kinder than Madam Huxley. You'll do great."

Dellwyn laughed and rapped her knuckles against the desk. "Well, I'll do the best I can, but if I get greedy, they know how to solve the problem."

"Not funny." Sybil stepped into the room and perched herself on the edge of Dellwyn's desk. "So, what's your first order of business?" As Sybil turned to face Dellwyn, the knee she'd propped on the desk collided with the mechanical flower and sent it crashing to the floor. Sybil shrieked. "Oh, I'm so sorry!"

"It's fine. You didn't mean to." Dellwyn stood and walked around the desk. "I'm sure Aya can—"

The sight on the rug sent Dellwyn to her knees. Her still-wounded side ached in protest, and her hands shook as they touched the unhinged petals. The base of the music box had broken off from the flower itself, exposing its inner workings. She couldn't believe it.

"What?" Sybil sank to the floor in front of Dellwyn and picked up the base, holding it between the two of them.

Though it was no longer sore, Dellwyn's throat had gone dry, and she had to swallow before she could speak. "I can't... there was one in the palace the whole time."

"What?" Sybil's breathing quickened, and she shoved the base toward Dellwyn as if it would hurt her.

"Do you see that?" Dellwyn pointed to the piece in the center, counting off its tiny appendages with her finger. Nine.

Sybil sighed. "What are you looking at?"

Dellwyn tore her eyes away from the piece to meet Sybil's perplexed ones. "This *has* to mean something." Between this and the rain, she was starting to think Rykart might have been onto something... whether given by a divine figure or brought about by sheer human will, this was a sign that they were all in the right place at the right time. The world didn't give gifts like this to the undeserving. She pushed the base back toward Sybil. "Go. Take it to Aya."

Sybil clutched the base in her hands. "Why? What is it?"

The gold glinted in the candlelight, and Dellwyn felt tears prick her eyes. She put her hands on Sybil's shoulders and squeezed. "It's a vortric cog."

Sybil frowned at the mess of gears. "A what?"

"Take it to Aya." Dellwyn stood and ushered Sybil to her feet. "She'll explain."

Sybil nodded. She walked toward the door then stopped halfway. With one eyebrow raised, she turned back to Dellwyn. "What are you going to do?"

On the inside, a warm sensation spread through Dellwyn's chest, and her heart swelled with unabashed pride. On the outside, Dellwyn shrugged, and her lips curled into a satisfied grin. "What I'm meant to do. Lead the unsung saviors of Desertera—as Madam Dellwyn Rutt."

THANKS FOR READING!

Ready for the next adventure? Join King Lionel in *The Tyrant's Heir (Desertera #3)*.

Want to know what happened to Aya between books? **Get a FREE short story** when you join Kate's Reader List: http://www.katemcolby.com/newsletter

If you enjoyed *The Courtesan's Avenger*, please leave a review on websites of your choice.

ACKNOWLEDGMENTS

I want to express my sincerest gratitude to my friends, family, and the friendly Internet strangers who read *The Cogsmith's Daughter* and anxiously awaited the sequel. Your kind words, encouragement, and consistent (loving) badgering were the fuel that powered me when I felt too frustrated or tired to write. I promise the third book won't take a year to produce.

A few people who deserve special thanks: my husband Daniel, who puts up with my best and worst writing days; my mom, who always requests a special edition so she can read my work first; my "bro" Jonas, who keeps me accountable; and my Word Count Slayer cabin mates, who have been some of my biggest supporters.

Once again, thank you to the wonderful editing team at Red Adept Editing. Every time I work with you, I become a better writer. And thank you to the design team at DamonZa-.com for another stunning cover. It's perfect.

And to you, reader, I give my deepest gratitude of all. Every purchase, review, and social media share brings me one step closer to my dream of full-time authorship. Thank you for joining me on this journey.

ABOUT THE AUTHOR

Kate M. Colby writes paranormal fantasy novels that feature female anti-heroes, dark magic, seductive monsters, and spooky locales. She has also written a steampunk dystopian series and dabbles in creative nonfiction and poetry.

Kate is pursuing a Master of Liberal Arts in Creative Writing and Literature from Harvard Extension School. She has won local awards for her short fiction, and her first novel, *The Cogsmith's Daughter*, has been taught in college courses.

When not writing or studying, Kate enjoys traveling, wine tasting, playing video games, and giving amateur tarot readings. She lives in the United States with her husband and their feline familiars.

You can learn more about Kate and her books on her website: www.KateMColby.com.

facebook.com/authorKateMColby

instagram.com/katemcolby

goodreads.com/KateMColby